Praise for

Romeo, Romeo

by Robin Kaye

Kaye's debut is a delightfully fun, witty romance,
making her a writer to watch.
—*Booklist*

Kaye's portrayal of modern romance
against the background of an old-fashioned,
gossipy extended family rings true, and Nick's
efforts to wow Rosalie with fabulous home
cooking are endlessly entertaining.
—*Publishers Weekly*

The main characters in this all-around
feel-good read have so much personality
they almost jump off the page.
—*The Romantic Times, 4/5 Stars*

Overall this was a snappy, funny, vivid,
and romantic story. I had a wonderful time reading it,
and can't wait for Robin Kaye's next release.
—*All About Romance*

Romeo, Romeo is a rollicking romance
that's sure to please even the most discerning
reader. Robin Kaye's flair for giving the
mundane a dramatic twist brings every
character—even the dog!—off the pages.
—*Romance Reader at Heart*

If you're looking for a sweet, light, straight-up
contemporary romance, I'd highly recommend this
one. This is one novel I'll reread again and again.
—*The Book Binge*

Kaye's writing is a refreshing change from the
typical contemporary romance… I highly
recommend this read to all romance lovers.
—*I Just Finished Reviews*

The sparks between the hero and heroine light up the
pages and create a believable motivation for them to
work through the conflicts that get thrown their way.
—*Alpha Hero Reviews*

Wonderful, Laugh-Out-Loud Humor, a sexy
and precious love story with twists and turns until
the very end. Do Not Miss This Treasure!!
—*Single Titles*

Kaye's writing is just about perfect for this kind of story, as she balances… romance, sex, and family, all of which come together with ease. The result is the totally irresistible *Romeo, Romeo*.
—*A Book Blogger's Diary*

The author has crafted this story line so well it's easy to relate to the players and fun to read. I adore her writing style and found this a great book from first page to last.
—*The Romance Studio*

Debut author Robin Kaye strikes gold in *Romeo, Romeo*—and deserves to have her name added to your favourite new author list.
—*Book Loons*

The author does a wonderful job of drawing large Italian families and two passionate people who fall in love… I found *Romeo, Romeo* to be a quick, entertaining, and easy read.
—*RomanceNovel.tv*

Robin Kaye's *Romeo, Romeo* is sensational! I loved everything about this novel. The story, characters, and writing are all five star material.
—*Crave More Romance*

Delightfully funny and wonderfully romantic, I stayed up all night to read this book!
—*Night Owl Romance*

Too Hot to Handle

ROBIN KAYE

SOURCEBOOKS CASABLANCA™
AN IMPRINT OF SOURCEBOOKS, INC.®
NAPERVILLE, ILLINOIS

Friends are my favorite characters to write. They're the people who tell it like it is, hold your feet to the fire, love you, laugh and cry with you, and share your joys and sorrow as well as their own.

Friends are a huge part of my life, and I've been blessed with the best friends a woman could have, so here's to you.

Gregory Olsen, Cary Dominguez, Charlie Dodge, Ken and Dianne Tyson, Millie Gemando, Leslie Hourdas, Jennifer Griffith, Cheryl McKissick, Becky Hazel, Rhonda Plumber, Deb Barger, Debbie Styne, Jennifer Shark, Kevin Dibley, Ana DaSilva, Dalia Schulman, Amy Green-Phillips, Robin Linear, Jeannde Hersom, and April Line.

Chapter 1

GHOSTS DON'T HAVE SEX, DO THEY? ANNABELLE Ronaldi wasn't 100 percent sure of the answer. Floating between sleep and wakefulness after a night of way too much champagne, she figured she'd either had mind-blowing sex with the ghost of her dead boyfriend, Chip, or his double. She crossed her fingers for the latter.

She'd only slept with two men, so the chances she'd increased that number by 50 percent beat the hell out of the odds of her waking with a ghost—especially when she thought about it in a semisober state. A state she hadn't been in the night before.

She had to admit her relationship with Chip would have been a lot better if he'd been half as good in bed alive as his ghost was last night—if, in fact, it was Chip's ghost sleeping beside her. Which brought her back to her initial question regarding the ability of ghosts to have sex—really, really good sex.

Annabelle opened her eyes and screamed. Loud.

The guy asleep next to her awoke and sat straight up as she jumped out of bed. "My God, you're real." Yep, definitely real, and very much alive.

He stared at her with such heat she was surprised she wasn't incinerated. Which, under the circumstances, would be preferable to standing there like an idiot. An idiot wearing nothing but a blue garter. She ripped the sheet off the bed, leaving him naked, only he didn't look

like an idiot. On the contrary, he looked… big and um…
happy to see her. Very happy.

Annabelle was speechless.

"Belle… " He scooted toward her. She backed away
until she hit the dresser with a thunk. Belle? Chip never
called her Belle. If she hadn't almost totally dismissed
the whole ghost question as a possibility, being called
Belle would have cinched it.

"Hey, take it easy. I'm not gonna hurt you."

"Who are you?"

"I'm Mike… Mike Flynn, your brother-in-law's best
friend; we met at the wedding. You look like you've
seen a ghost."

"No kidding." He didn't seem like the ax murderer
type, not that she knew what that type looked like, but
she was pretty sure it required an ax, and he didn't have
one or anywhere to hide one either. She found herself
staring at… him. Probably not the polite thing to do.
Annabelle took a deep breath and moved the direction of
her stare past his washboard abs and nice chest, straight
to the eyes of Chip's double. He looked almost exactly
like Chip, a.k.a. Christopher Edmond Van Dyke Larsen,
except for the eye color, a slight bump on his nose, and
the size of a certain appendage.

"Hi… um."

"Mike. Mike Flynn."

"I knew that." You'd think she'd offered to sell him
the Brooklyn Bridge, and he wasn't buying. "I've never
done this before—"

"This, meaning brought home a nice guy, had mind-
boggling, earth-shattering, world-rocking sex?" He
winked at her. "Yeah, if it makes you feel any better,

I don't make a habit of it either—especially the part where the beautiful woman can't remember my name. Aside from that, I can't think of a more pleasurable morning."

Annabelle's wish to disappear wasn't happening, so she had no choice other than to deal with… whatever this was.

"Anyone ever tell you you're beautiful when you're embarrassed? Well, you're pretty much beautiful all the time."

She shifted her weight from foot to foot. "So, we really did… um… you know?"

"Oh yeah. Several times."

Maybe her mind was playing tricks on her. Maybe he didn't look and sound like Chip. Maybe she'd had a mental breakdown. Lord knew, with everything she'd been through recently, taking a vacation from reality wouldn't be that big of a stretch.

Pictures of the two of them stumbling through her new apartment undressing each other flitted through her mind like a grainy sex video. She winced again as she remembered the sound of ripping fabric and her bubbling laughter when she'd realized her little black dress had suddenly become a lot smaller. If her memory was correct, she was surprised her dress hadn't spontaneously combusted from the heat they'd generated.

"You want me to give you some time? I'll take Dave for a walk."

"How do you know Rosalie's dog?"

"I'm Nick's best friend, remember? I've known Dave since Nick and Rosalie got together."

"Oh, right."

"I'll take Dave out, pick up some breakfast, and then we can talk, and you know, do the first date thing."

"The first date thing?"

"Yeah, you tell me your middle name. I'll tell you mine. We can do a fast run-through of our families, occupations, and the normal stuff. Then, us sleeping together won't seem so premature."

"It won't?"

"Well, like I said, I don't make a habit of ravishing women within hours of meeting them. In fact, it's never happened before. I figure exchanging the first date info is worth a try. What do you say?"

"Okay." She squeezed her eyes shut and thought he'd leave—at least temporarily. Then he moved closer and cupped her face in his hands. Before it registered in her addled mind, he pressed soft kisses on her eyelids, then her lips. She opened her eyes, and he smiled at her as if she were the most adorable creature on earth. The man obviously needed to get out more.

Mike brushed one more kiss on her shoulder, which seemed to be hardwired to her nipples. Her breath caught in her throat, and Mike gave her a very satisfied smile before he searched for his clothes.

She had never seen that satisfied a smile on any man she'd shared a bed with. Though, it's not like she'd slept with many men. There was Chip, then… ugh… Johnny, and now… um… Mike. Right, Mike.

Dave, the dog she was watching until her sister came back from her honeymoon, strolled into the bedroom with a pair of jockey shorts in his mouth. She'd hazard a guess they were Mike's. She winced. "Sorry about that."

Mike pulled on his gray pinstripe suit pants and zipped them. "Hey, have you seen my shirt?"

"It's in the living room."

"Ah, so now you remember. Sure helps the ole bruised and battered ego."

Before she could think of anything to say, the phone rang. Annabelle peeked at the clock. Since it was still early, it must be Becca. "I'm sorry—"

Mike held up his hand. "No, it's fine. Go ahead and take your time. Dave and I will be back."

Mike turned and left the bedroom, closing the door behind him.

She threw herself on the bed, pulled the sheet over her, and reached for the phone. "Hello?"

"So, you did survive the wedding. See, you were worried for nothing."

"Becca? You don't by any chance have a cousin in New York, do you?" She heard Mike whistle for the dog, the jangle of the choke collar striking dog tags, then the front door closing.

"A cousin?"

"Yeah, a male cousin, about thirty, blond hair, gray eyes, totally hot. A cousin who looks a lot like Chip. Exactly like Chip, except his lips are a bit fuller, his nose looks like he's broken it more than once, and well, he has bigger... feet."

"Bigger feet? Annabelle, are you all right?"

She felt like screaming, "No, I'm not all right." How could someone wake up wondering if they'd had sex with a ghost and be even remotely all right? But Becca would drop everything, jump on the first train out of Philadelphia, and run straight to Brooklyn if she thought

Annabelle needed her. As much as she loved Becca, she wasn't sure she could handle everything that calling Becca into this situation would entail.

"I'm fine. I just met this guy yesterday. His name is Mike Flynn, and he has an amazing resemblance to Chip. He must be related to you somehow."

"Annabelle, my brother's been gone two years. Don't you think it's time you let go?"

"Geez, Bec. I just said that I met a guy who looks like Chip. I'm not hanging on to Chip's memory. Hell, I've moved on. Up until a few weeks ago, I was engaged."

"To the scum-of-the-earth mortician."

"Johnny wasn't that bad."

"Johnny was caught with his pants down, the makeup lady's skirt up, doing the nasty right next to a corpse—"

"Yeah, Mrs. Nunzio." Annabelle crossed herself. "God rest her soul."

"Face it. That pretty much screams scum-of-the-earth behavior."

"Fine, if you want to get technical about it. But Johnny had nothing to do with Chip."

"Johnny had everything to do with Chip. Everything you've done since Chip's diagnosis has been a direct result of Chip. Including planning to marry the scum-of-the-earth mortician."

"Look, sweetie, as enlightening as this conversation is, I don't have time to talk right now. I have to get dressed. Was there something you needed?"

"I just wanted to make sure you're okay. It must suck going to your own wedding as a guest and not the bride."

"I'm fine."

"Liar. You're way too shallow to be fine. No matter how much you love your sister, and I know you do, the fact she hijacked your wedding day has to chap your ass. It would rankle an angel, and we both know you're no angel. I know you didn't take this lying down."

"Actually, I did." To prove her point, Annabelle sat up and kicked the sheet off her naked body. Naked except for the scratchy blue garter she wore high on her thigh. "Oh God." She'd forgotten about that.

"Okay, that's it. I'm on the next train to New York. You're scaring me."

"No. I'm fine, really. I… um… I just noticed the time, and well, I have to… meet someone for breakfast, um, brunch, and I'm not dressed. I promise to call you back later. I swear. I'm fine. Really."

"Okay, but I know something's up. I'll talk to you later this afternoon. If I don't hear from you, I'll be there in the morning banging down your door."

"I promise I'll call. Bye." She hung up the phone and groaned. Her head ached, her teeth were fuzzy, and she was pretty sure someone had spiked her champagne with battery acid. She pulled on her robe and stumbled into the bathroom.

Mike was right about one thing—her memory was coming back. She'd been at her sister Rosalie's wedding reception. The wedding reception Annabelle had planned, the wedding reception she'd dreamed of since she got her first Wedding Day Barbie, the wedding reception that would have been hers if she hadn't broken her engagement to Johnny. Watching her sister living her dream wedding mortified her enough, but then she'd seen Chip's double talking to her new brother-in-law, Nick.

He had the same broad shoulders and dirty blond hair that was long enough to curl up over his collar. And the similarities didn't stop there. No. He had the same posture, the way he stood with his feet spread and hands on his hips as he laughed. It had made the hair on her arms stand up and had her fighting the urge to cross herself.

Chip's double had turned and stared directly into her eyes. Annabelle remembered grabbing the chair beside her as her head spun, gray narrowing her vision. She'd dropped her glass. She'd heard it break. She'd heard the buzz of three hundred people conversing, but it had all seemed so far away. Still, she'd been unable to take her eyes off the man walking toward her.

He'd been rushing, yet moved in slow motion. His warm hand grabbed her elbow. "Sit down before you fall down."

"Chip?" she'd mumbled.

"I'm Mike. Are you okay?" He pushed her into the chair and crouched in front of her as he held her wrist and glanced at his watch.

"Fine." She'd pushed away from his grasp and rubbed her arms, trying to dispel the chill.

His eyes were different from Chip's; they were gray and assessing. Chip had one brown eye and one half brown and half green, lit with a constant sense of wonder. It must have been magical to see the world through Chip's eyes. He only saw beauty. He left everyone else to deal with reality.

"You don't look so good."

"Thanks, that's what every girl wants to hear."

"I mean you don't look well. I'm a doctor. Have you eaten today? Are you taking any medication?"

"Look, Doc, I'm not sick. I thought I saw a ghost, that's all. I was wrong, obviously, since you are definitely not a ghost."

"Huh?"

"You look a lot like someone I used to know." Annabelle rose, and Mike followed suit. "It was nice meeting you—"

"Mike."

"Right." She'd walked blindly to the other side of the room, wishing she could leave. Only the fear of her mother's wrath had kept her from going any farther than the deserted terrace overlooking Park Avenue.

Later, she'd been too drunk to remember to drop the bouquet after she'd caught it. Mike caught the garter. And before she could duck out, she'd been forced into a chair in the middle of the dance floor while, to a chorus of wolf whistles and clapping, Mike very slowly slid the garter and his hands beneath her dress and high onto her thigh. The higher his hands went, the darker his eyes became. She was still trapped by his gaze as he helped her out of the chair and into his arms for the obligatory dance. The next thing she knew, they'd been in a cab on their way back to Brooklyn.

Annabelle wished her mind were like an Etch A Sketch, and she could give her head a good shake and start with a clean slate.

Mike left Annabelle's apartment with Dave ambling beside him. He walked right to the nearest light post and banged his head against it. Hard.

"Fuck." He opened his eyes and saw an old lady, a lace shawl covering her head and rosary beads hanging from one hand. The scowl she shot him had him ducking his head in shame. "I'm sorry," he said as she passed.

She muttered something in Italian. Shit, he was batting a thousand this morning.

"Great show, Mikey. Now tell me what the hell you're doing with my dog, outside my sister-in-law's apartment, at the crack of fuckin' dawn."

"Nick? What are you doing here? You just got married less than twenty-four hours ago."

Mike tried unsuccessfully to keep the dog from jumping on Nick.

Nick handed Mike a couple of the bags he held so he could pet Dave. The expression on Nick's face made Mike thankful that Nick wasn't the violent type. "No, don't tell me." He studied Mike, seeing all the signs of the morning after that it was. "You didn't sleep with my sister-in-law, did you?

"Do you really want to know the answer to that question?"

"What, you've gone through all my old girlfriends, and you're starting on family now?"

"It's not my fault your old girlfriends ran to me for solace. With my work hours, it's almost impossible to sleep, much less meet women. It's been five or six years since I had the time or opportunity to meet a woman without the letters MD or RN after her name."

Mike had had bed buddies, and even a couple relationships that went beyond sex, not far beyond, but there were a few he'd felt an emotional connection to.

Nothing had prepared him for Annabelle Ronaldi. She was almost too hot to handle. When he touched her, the charge he'd felt was only slightly weaker than the one he'd gotten the day he'd been playing in the wet basement and come close to dying of electrocution. "Annabelle's different."

"Yeah, she's my fuckin' sister-in-law. You couldn't find another chick to sleep with?" Nick raised his arms and slapped them against his thighs, obviously forgetting that he carried several bags from the deli and bakery down the street. "From the look on your dopey face, I guess the answer to that question is no. And I'm thinking now is not a good time to stop by the apartment and pick up that bag Rosalie left."

Mike couldn't hold back a smile. "You're right both times."

"I'm gonna pretend I didn't see you."

"Isn't Rosalie going to wonder why you didn't stop?"

"I'll tell her to buy a new one. Besides, you know how much Lee loves chocolate. She's gonna take one look at these chocolate-covered doughnuts, and she'll forgive me for forgetting to look for her bag. I'll tell her I couldn't stand to be away from her. After all, it's the truth."

Nick took his bags back.

Mike knew exactly how Nick felt. Well, almost. The gods had smiled on him last night, because the first time his eyes met Annabelle's, she seemed to have the same reaction to him. Annabelle was the type of woman who made him glad he wore loose-fitting pants, not only because she was beautiful and sexy, but because she'd stared at him as if she couldn't believe her eyes. From that moment on, her eyes never left him. He might as well have been the only man in the room.

Mike wasn't going to let her get away. He just needed to make sure she'd never forget him again.

Annabelle tossed on a pair of yoga pants and a workout top and stepped out of the bedroom as Mike and Dave returned.

Mike had folded the remains of her dress, her panties, and her stockings, and laid them neatly on the couch. His suit jacket hung over the back of a chair with a tie rolled and stuffed into the breast pocket. He had on the wrinkled shirt that was missing a button or two, his suit pants, and black dress shoes. Even wearing clothes that had spent the night on the floor, she'd be hard-pressed to find a better-looking man.

Her only question now was what to do with him.

"Hi." Mike placed two bags on the table and handed her a cup of coffee. "I didn't know how you like your coffee…"

Annabelle removed the cover and took a gulp of the steaming liquid, trying to think of what to say.

"Ah, damn." Mike pulled a cell phone off his belt and read the screen. "I'm sorry. I have to go. I know we need to talk, but this is an emergency." He removed the tie from his suit pocket, flipped the collar of his shirt up, and tied a perfect half Windsor without looking in the mirror.

She used to have to tie Chip's ties for him on the rare occasion she got him to wear one. She'd always wondered if he was pulling her leg. A kid who'd spent his life in prep school should have known how to tie a tie in his sleep. Maybe that was why he'd refused to wear one as an adult.

Mike cinched the knot up to his throat and didn't even make a face. Chip always looked as if he were being garroted. How weird was this? Here she was watching Mike get ready for work. Well, he hadn't specifically said he was going to work, but if her fuzzy memory was accurate, he'd said he was a doctor, and doctors had to take care of emergencies. She shuddered as the memories of times she'd taken Chip to the hospital spilled over the dam she'd built in her mind to hold them back. She remembered all the times she'd waited for the doctor to give her more bad news.

Watching her with concern, Mike tugged her into his arms. "Hey. What's this about?" He tipped her head up and stared into her eyes. She opened her mouth to tell him it was nothing, but before she could press the words out, he cut her off with a kiss. A coffee-, cream-, and sugar-flavored kiss that packed so much heat it stole her breath.

He didn't taste like Chip, he didn't smell like Chip, and even with their uncanny resemblance, he didn't feel like Chip. When in remission, Chip had been hard and strong. He'd been a marble statue, beautiful to admire, but uncomfortable to lean against. She'd found out the hard way that when you leaned on a statue, he either wobbled until he dropped you or took you down with him, shattering when he hit, and leaving you lying bruised and bleeding on a pile of rubble. Alone.

Mike was comfortable, firm but not chiseled, strong and solid, and he held her. She didn't have to lean. He drew her to him, pulling her weight against his body and steadying her. For a second, she rested in his arms, her eyes closed as she savored what was a false sense of security.

"As much as I'd like to stay and find out what's going on in that busy mind of yours, I really do have to run. I hope it won't take long." Annabelle opened her mouth to ask if he was coming back, but he kissed the thought away, turned, and walked out.

Dave sat on his bed with Mike's jockey shorts hanging from his mouth and whined. The dog might weigh a good one hundred and fifty pounds and look like a cross between Cujo and the Black Stallion, but he was nothing more than a puppy in the body of an ox. She sat on the couch and stared at the door. Dave sauntered over and rested his enormous St. Bernardish head on her lap. The jockeys seemed to staunch the flow of slobber, thank God. Dave's deep brown eyes stared into hers, and he let out a plaintive whine.

Annabelle absently rubbed his big head. She wasn't sure what she felt, but she felt something. Too much. Was it better to spend life in a vacuum or to be shot through a veritable galaxy of feelings, unable to identify them? The vacuum of emotion she usually swam in was a lot more comfortable.

Annabelle struggled to move a crate of canvases from the storage area in the basement of the apartment. Before Rosalie had gotten engaged to Nick and rented her apartment to Annabelle, Rosalie had offered Annabelle storage space when she'd moved back from Philadelphia. It had been two years since Chip's death—past time to go through her things. Johnny wouldn't have understood her hanging portraits and nudes all over the house, especially since most of the paintings were of Chip. She'd keep a few of the small portraits for herself, offer the others to Becca, and destroy the nudes. Well, all but one. She couldn't part with the first. No, no matter what, even if it stayed wrapped in paper in the back of her closet until the day she died. She'd never be able to part with that.

"Annabelle!" Wayne yelled when he saw her sliding the crate up the basement steps to the first floor. "What are you doing? Henry, come out here and help me." Wayne, Rosalie's—no, make that her—neighbor, slid beside her and picked up the crate. "Why didn't you give us a holler? We're right upstairs, and we're always here to lend a helping hand. We're so thrilled you've taken over your sister's apartment. You call us if you need help moving anything. Anything at all. I can't tell you how Henry and I have been dreading the thought of losing touch with our Rosalie. Now, with you here… Well, we're just so thrilled to have you. You have to come to dinner so we can get to know you. Was that handsome gentleman I saw leaving this morning your boyfriend? Girl, you have almost as good taste in men as your sister. Isn't he just too cute? I mean really, if I were ten years younger, and if he wasn't straight, I swear he'd give Henry a run for his money."

Wayne finally took a breath. Annabelle stared at him blankly. "Um… What was the question?"

Wayne put his arm around her. "Dinner, then boyfriend."

"Oh, yes, well, I'd like to have dinner with you and Henry. Rosalie has told me so much about you both." She flipped her hair and pasted on her best smile.

"Rosalie gave me your number in case I can't get home to feed Dave. I hope that's okay."

"Nice try, gorgeous, but that only works on straight men. Now dish. Tell me about Mr. Big, Blond, and Beautiful."

"That's Dr. Big, Blond, and Beautiful to you." Annabelle followed him into her apartment and directed him to the small room that was labeled a den but looked more like a walk-in closet with a window. "You can put the crate up against that wall."

Wayne positioned the crate and then followed her to the kitchen. He watched as she rooted around the junk drawer.

"Whatcha looking for while you're avoiding talking about Dr. Good Love?"

"A hammer so I can pry the crate open. You're not going to let this go, are you?"

"No." Wayne went to the door. "Henry, bring a pry bar and a hammer when you come down, will you, sweetie?" he hollered up the stairs.

Wayne sashayed back, not even waiting for Henry's response. Rosalie had spoken a lot about her neighbors, and Annabelle had always wondered if she'd exaggerated. So far, she had to admit, Rosalie was dead-on. Knowing all the stories, and seeing firsthand proof, she wondered how Wayne managed to wrap Henry around his little finger.

He came up beside her and bumped her with his hip. "You won't be sorry you've confided in me. Just ask your sister. If it weren't for Henry and me, Rosalie and Nick would still be pretending the other didn't exist. Just think of us as your Fairy Godfathers."

That was it. Annabelle couldn't keep a straight face no matter how hard she tried. By the time Henry joined them, she and Wayne were laughing so hard, she was having a difficult time catching her breath. She wrapped her arms around her aching sides and tried to breathe. God, it had been so long since she'd laughed.

Henry saw the two of them and scoffed. "Wayne, look at her." Henry handed Wayne the tools, took his crisply ironed handkerchief out of his pocket, and dried the tears from Annabelle's face. Henry was tall. She didn't often look up to men, but she had to tip her head back to stare into his eyes. Kind eyes. Wayne had good taste. Henry was very hot if you went for the metrosexual type. Not to mention the gay type.

"What'd I miss?"

"Wayne was just teasing me." Annabelle wasn't used to people touching her, and Wayne and Henry were definitely touchy-feely people. She stepped back and noticed Wayne was gone.

The sound of hammering filled the apartment and then the squeaking of nails being pulled from wood. She ran to the den, but before she could stop him, Wayne had the crate open. There it stood for all the room to see—a thirty-six-by-sixty oil of a very naked Chip. Oh God. She hadn't imagined it. Mike looked exactly like Chip.

"Well, lookie here." Wayne put his hands on his hips and let out a wolf whistle while he examined the painting. "My, my, my, it seems you know Dr. Big, Blond, and Beautiful better than I thought."

He didn't take his eyes off the nude, shaking his head and tsking. "If this painting is accurate, we have to rethink the big part of the good doctor's moniker. Such a shame. No matter what *Cosmo* says, we both know it ain't just how a man uses it that counts."

Annabelle sputtered and pointed to the painting. "B…
but, that's not Mike."

Chapter 2

AFTER HENRY AND WAYNE LEFT, ANNABELLE WENT back to bed and tried to get her bearings. She needed to go through the few things she'd been able to bring from Philadelphia and somehow turn Rosalie's apartment into her own.

Rosalie and Nick had leased the apartment to her furnished, which was nice. They didn't need Rosalie's furniture. Nick's castle of a brownstone held the stamp of a professional decorator. One who Rosalie said had dated Nick and decorated it to her taste—stuffy, showy, and uncomfortably fake—nothing like Nick. There wasn't one room in the entire brownstone she'd call relaxing. Even the bathrooms looked as if you could break them, which was one reason Dave stayed with her until Nick and Rosalie redecorated and doggy-proofed their love nest.

The phone rang, and she contemplated not answering it. No one had her new number other than her parents, Rosalie and Nick, and Becca. She didn't think Rosalie would call today, and she'd already spoken to Becca. That only left her mother. Shit.

"Hello, Mama."

"Annabelle. Why aren't you here for dinner?"

Dinner... damn, she'd forgotten all about Sunday dinner. She peeked at the clock. It was a quarter to one. "Um, I'm sorry. I, um..."

"Oh, you have a date with that nice doctor friend of Nick's, don't you? It was so cute the way he tackled that young man about to catch the garter. I saw him watching you all night, not that you did anything to encourage him. But then your aunt Rose said he took you home."

"Yeah, he did. He's… nice."

"Don't forget single and a doctor. You know—"

"Yeah, Ma, I'm not getting any younger. I know the drill."

"After the disaster you've made of your life by canceling your wedding, you better make the most of Nick's circle of friends. There were several very nice, successful men at the wedding. Speaking of the wedding, you should be thankful it wasn't a total loss. It was wonderful how Rosalie saved the day by marrying Nick quickly. They had a beautiful wedding."

"Yeah, thanks to me."

"What did you have to do with it?"

"Gee, I don't know, Ma. Other than planning every detail of that entire affair—I spent a year of my life working on that wedding."

"Thank goodness Rosalie had the time and money to change it to suit her and Nick's needs."

"They didn't change a damn thing other than the invitations and the head count. Hell, they even used my seating chart for our side of the family."

"No wonder you can't find a nice man to marry. Listen to the language coming out of that mouth of yours. You better go to confession. Besides, we all know you're not capable of organizing anything more complex than your closet. Stop trying to take the credit away from Rosalie."

"Look, Ma, I'm tired, and I'm not up for dinner. I'm sorry I didn't call before, but I'm just going to take a nap."

"Okay, get some beauty sleep. You need it. Remember to look your best—"

"Yeah, I know. I'm not getting any younger. Bye, Ma."

"I can do it. I can do it, damn it!" Tom Mullany wheezed, the crackle in his lungs loud enough to be heard down the hall.

Mike held up his hands in surrender.

"You!" Mr. Mullany pointed his arthritic finger at the poor nurse trying to hold the wheelchair. "Put the break on and get the hell away. I don't need you looking at my bare, bony ass hanging out of this damn hospital gown."

A cross between Walter Matthau and Oscar the Grouch, Tom Mullany was one of Mike's most challenging patients on a good day. This was not a good day—not for Tom at least. The poor old guy was scared. He'd never smoked a day in his life, but after spending his whole career in the bond room of a Wall Street giant where everyone else smoked, Tom Mullany suffered from chronic COPD and emphysema. He'd had a bout with pneumonia, and now, a relapse. Since his wife's death last winter, Tom had never been more alone or more sick.

Mike stood close by, allowing Tom the dignity of getting into bed by himself, but not too far away in case the old man teetered. Moving around would be difficult since he had both IV and oxygen tubing tethering him.

Waving away the nurse, Mike figured he might as well play nurse and orderly. After all, it wasn't as if he had anything better to do than help the old guy protect his pride.

After Tom managed to get into bed under his own steam, Mike put the side rails up on one side, replaced the pulse oximeter, positioning it on his pointer finger, and checked his blood oxygen level—82 percent. Still low, but since he'd been moving around, not surprising.

"I still don't see why you won't let me go home." Tom ripped the oxygen tubing off his face and held it in the trembling hand he pointed at Mike. "I'd be better off there where I can get some rest. Here they poke and prod me all the damn day and night."

Mike took the tubing from Tom and draped it back over his ears, to position it under his nose. "If I did that, I wouldn't have you to keep me company."

Tom's hand went back up to the tubing, and Mike shot him a hard look. "I can replace your tubing with a face mask and a big orderly if that's what it takes to keep you breathing."

Ignoring the old man's grumbling, Mike went to the window and opened the blinds so Tom could look out onto the courtyard below.

"So I'm suffering because you don't have anything better to do than sit here torturing an old fart like me?" Mr. Mullany laughed, wheezed, and coughed. "You need to get a life, boy."

"I'm working on it." Mike sat back on the chair beside the bed, stretched his legs out in front of him, and crossed them at the ankles.

Tom pressed the button to raise the head of his bed and stared at Mike over the plastic tubing. He was an ornery old cuss. He licked his dry lips and smiled. "I hope to hell your door don't swing both ways because I for one ain't interested. But it would give me an excuse to get a new doctor and see if I could get myself out of this place."

"No such luck. I was talking about a woman. It looks as if you're stuck here until I release you."

Tom stared at Mike. "You know you're missing two buttons on your shirt, Doc."

Mike smoothed down his tie, which he'd thought covered the evidence of last night's extracurricular activities.

"That new girlfriend of yours try to rip your shirt off?" Before Mike could deny it, Tom continued. "Why the hell are you here if you could be with that hellcat of yours?"

"Because I got a page that you were being brought into the ER, and believe it or not, I wanted to make sure you were okay."

Some color came back to Tom's face. Mike checked the monitor, Tom's O2 levels were up to 85 percent, and he looked more relaxed with little or no retraction. The IV steroids and breathing treatments were doing their jobs.

"You've got yourself a girlfriend then?"

"I hope so."

"A woman ripping the buttons off your shirt is a pretty good sign—at least it was in my day. I hope to hell things haven't changed that much."

"We'll see." Mike didn't feel comfortable talking about his private life with patients—not that he'd had much of one to talk about, but since the death of Tom's wife, he and Mike had gotten pretty close.

"Where did you meet this girl—you did say she's a girl, right?"

Mike rolled his eyes. "I met her at a wedding. Her sister married my best friend." He saw no reason to tell him that the wedding took place just yesterday.

"Well, I hope you like her. You know, I met my wife at a wedding some fifty-odd years ago. When you pick up a girl at a wedding, chances are she's wishing she were the one wearing white. Don't be surprised if she gets ideas about more than just ripping the shirt off your back."

Mike pretended to look over his chart and made a few notes.

"Heat like that is pretty hard to find. You don't just leave a woman who ripped off your shirt the night before. Do you have another date with her?"

"Tom, come on, I'm your doctor."

"Doctor, schmoctor." He waved his hand again, dismissing Mike's attempt to keep his love life out of it. "You're young enough to be my son... make that grandson. And let me tell you, boy, I've had more sex in my lifetime than you will ever hope to have."

"Mr. Mullany—"

"You just got up and left?"

"No. I went out, brought back coffee and breakfast, and then I got the page—"

"Did you at least kiss her good-bye and make another date?"

Great, he was getting a sex talk from an octogenarian. "I'm not stupid. I kissed her good-bye and kept a spare set of keys."

"Well, at least you've got a little bit of a brain. Seeing as how you're my doctor, I'm glad for that much. Still, you shouldn't leave her wondering if she's going to see you again. Send her flowers, call, and ask her out to dinner. That is, if you want to see her again."

Mike checked his watch. He definitely wanted to see Annabelle again, but no matter what Tom said, it had been fifty-five years since the man's last date. Things had changed. "I have a few minutes before I go. Are you comfortable? Can I get you anything?"

"You got a new pair of lungs lying around?"

Mike shook his head, but he did have a few other things in his bag of tricks. What Tom needed couldn't be found in a hospital—not yet, anyway.

"I'm going to give these orders to the nurses, and I'll be back to say good-bye before I leave."

Tom waved him away. The old guy was tired—not that he'd ever say so.

Mike went to the nurses' station and dialed the emergency contact number he'd found in Mr. Mullany's file. Tom wasn't the only one who could give advice. While he waited for an answer, he tossed an empty coffee cup in the garbage, collected the pens lying on the desk, and put them neatly into the pencil holder where they belonged.

"Hello, is Kathryn Evans available, please? This is Dr. Michael Flynn."

"This is Katy Evans."

"Ms. Evans, I treat your grandfather, Tom Mullany."

"Oh my God, what happened? Is he okay?"

Mike leaned against the counter and crossed his legs. "He's going to be fine. He's in the hospital—"

"Oh no. What hospital? Why hasn't someone called me? What's wrong—"

"Calm down. He's going to be fine. He's had a relapse of pneumonia—"

"A relapse? Grandpa never even told me he was sick!"

Mike chuckled. "Yeah, I figured as much. That's why I called. I've been sitting with him for a while now. He wasn't happy when I admitted him, but his blood oxygen levels were low, and he needs to be monitored. He's also lost a lot of weight, and I don't think he's eating right. I was hoping you could see to it that he starts eating better, and if he knew you were coming to visit, he'd have something to look forward to. He's been a little depressed since your grandmother passed away."

"I'm sorry, Doctor. He's canceled visits with me three times now. He never said he was ill. He usually just left messages on my voice mail. I think he's kept me playing phone tag on purpose. He hates when people fuss."

"Yeah, I got that message loud and clear."

"I'll be right over—"

"No rush. He's pretty tired. He should sleep for a couple of hours. Maybe you can come about lunchtime and see if you could force him to eat—or better yet, bring him some real food."

"I will. I'm sorry you had to take time out to call me. Once he gets better, I'm going to kill him for scaring the life out of me."

"Ah, I can see the apple doesn't fall far from the tree."

She laughed. "So I've heard. Thank you so much for letting me know."

"It's my pleasure. I'm sure I'll see you around the hospital. Your grandfather's quite a character. I really enjoy seeing him."

Mike got off the phone and smiled. Poor Tom was going to get an ear full when Katy visited him later. If there's one thing Mike had learned treating geriatric patients it was that they recovered much more quickly when they were around people they loved, whether they wanted to be or not. After talking to Katy Evans, Mike had no doubt that the old man would have more company than he knew what to do with. Maybe he'd stop giving Mike advice on his love life—or lack thereof.

Mike had walked around the hospital all day with a dopey grin plastered on his face and Annabelle's keys in his pocket. He smiled, jangling them. She might be mad about him not returning her keys, but at least he'd have an excuse to see her again. He'd have to return them, apologize for the "mistake," and make it up to her. He couldn't wait to see her and hear her voice, but he didn't want to look as if he was too anxious.

Just about ready to head home, Mike hung his lab coat in his locker and picked up all the coffee cups lying around the doctors' lounge. He trashed the paper cups, washed out the sink, and wiped down the counters. Checking to make sure he was alone, he tackled the refrigerator.

Everyone teased him, but if he didn't go through it once a week and toss everything that looked like a lab experiment, no one else would. Heck, when he'd started working at the hospital, it took at least three boxes of baking soda to remove the smell of rotten broccoli. He definitely did not want to go through that ever again.

He had his head stuffed into the refrigerator, giving a carton of Chinese food of questionable age the sniff test when he heard humming.

He pulled his head from the refrigerator only to be accosted by three nurses who started singing the Mr. Clean jingle in three-part harmony.

"Very funny." He removed the box of rotten Chinese, made a two-pointer into the trash, and then did the only other thing he could think of—he pushed his shirt-sleeves up a little higher and flexed his biceps. At least the nurses were laughing with him, not at him. Gus giggled. Which, coming from a six-feet, two-hundred-fifty-pound black man who sounded like a cross between Mike Tyson and Joan Rivers, made Mike a little uncomfortable. But not nearly as much as the way Gus looked at him—as if Mike were a tub of Ben & Jerry's that Gus would like to eat with a spoon.

Gus struck a pose and ran his hand over his shiny shaved head. "So, do you do houses on the side, Dr. Clean? 'Cause you can come over to my place anytime. I've seen what you can do in a supply closet." He fanned himself. "The two of us together could make magic with my place." Gus waggled his eyebrows and blew him a kiss.

Mike rolled his shirt-sleeves back down. "Sorry, Gus. Just because I organize the supply closet doesn't mean I'm *in* the closet."

"Ah, such a shame, all the good ones are straight. Still, a man can dream."

Tami, the little nurse who worked with Gus a lot, poured herself a coffee and looked at him over the rim of her cup. "I thought you had a thing for George Clooney."

Gus sighed and leaned on the counter. "Na, just doctors in general." He smiled at Mike. "Y'all look so cute in those white coats and scrubs." He clicked his tongue and winked.

Mike patted the big guy on the back. "Sorry to disappoint you bud, but I'm a one-woman man." Woman being the operative word. Mike donned his suit jacket, folded his tie, put it in his pocket, and went to say goodbye to Mr. Mullany.

Heading home, Mike's commute seemed to fly, maybe because he'd been thinking about Annabelle. He unlocked the door to his apartment, switched on the light, and kicked the door shut behind him. Since the Russians took over Coney Island, the area had gotten much safer, as long as you didn't piss them off. The cost for the relative safety was spending your life smelling of borscht and sauerkraut. Considering the hours he kept, Mike saw it as an even trade. Still, he could never bring Annabelle there. Just the thought of her climbing the steps to his fourth-floor walk-up and down the dingy, dimly lit hallway had him contemplating moving to a nicer place. Lord knew, anywhere would be an improvement. Not that it bothered him. Hell, the only things he did there were clean, sleep, and change clothes. He kept his place very clean—he was a bit of a neat freak, though he'd die before he admitted it to anyone. Ninety percent of the time he spent in the apartment he was asleep, so the institutional green paint job and olive green carpet circa 1970 didn't matter to him. It had everything he needed. A kitchenette on one wall, an ugly brown and tan plaid couch and a coffee table he'd picked up at the Salvation Army took up the wall opposite the windows where his dresser sat and served as a TV stand. The other wall held his bed, a small closet, and the door to the bathroom. In the middle of the room, he'd thrown another Salvation Army find—a Formica table and chairs that were probably older than he was. The place was depressing but temporary—for the last five years.

Mike couldn't stop thinking about Annabelle and the way she'd stared at him the first time they met. Immediately intrigued, the instant connection shocked him with its strength. She felt it too. Annabelle's shock had her pulse racing so fast she'd almost passed out. He'd felt attraction before, but this thing with Annabelle went far beyond sex—although he wanted that too—badly. Nevertheless, there was something else. Something that made him want to break down the walls he'd seen so clearly. He wanted to find out what was behind the air of mystery she wore like a cloak. He wanted to know what she hid and what caused the pain and mistrust that shadowed her eyes. She had an acerbic wit that came out of a deceivingly angelic mouth—a mouth that was anything but angelic when it was anywhere on his body.

For the first time in his life, Mike wanted to protect and care for someone other than his mother. Damn, talk about bad timing.

He thought of the hundreds of thousands of dollars he owed in student loans and tried to calculate how many decades it would take him to afford a real home, no less a girl like Annabelle. Once he finished working off his buy-in at the practice, and they took him on as an official partner—if they took him on—things might get better. The way things had gone in the last few weeks, Mike wondered if that was ever going to happen. He was even beginning to wonder if he wanted that to happen. But right now, he'd just assume everything would work out as planned. After a few quick mental calculations, it still seemed like forever.

He stripped as he walked through his place toward the bathroom. He couldn't very well show up in the suit she'd ripped off him the night before. Mike turned on the shower and waited for the hot water to work its way through the noisy pipes. What he needed was a plan. If things went the way he hoped they would with Annabelle, his five-year plan might change drastically. He just hoped hers would change too.

Annabelle stretched out under her cool cotton sheet. Even with the blinds blocking out the worst of the afternoon sun and the air conditioner going double-time, she was still too hot. She'd slept, but her dreams kept her from resting. She awoke itchy, frustrated, and undeniably horny, which, after her escapades last night and early this morning, was nothing short of amazing.

Sex had never been her thing. She never saw what the fuss was all about. Really, what was so great about having a guy grab you, breathe on you, and rub his sweaty, hairy body all over you? And that's before the act itself—which was either utterly boring or uncomfortable.

What's with men thinking every woman turns into elastic girl when they hit the mattress, floor, kitchen table, or any surface when their panties are removed, or worse, nudged aside? She didn't have much experience, but she and Becca decided men had a penchant for twisting a girl into a pretzel and expecting her to enjoy her legs wrapped around her head.

Oh baby, do it to me. Yeah, right.

Then, to add insult to injury, literally, a man felt as if he had to bend a girl around like a Gumby doll and wouldn't leave her alone until he'd come and she'd faked three orgasms, giving him the ego stroke necessary to break his arm while he patted himself on the back for being the world's greatest lover.

Even with Chip, sex had been... not fun, although not nearly as disgusting as it had been with Johnny. Mike had, for the first time in her life, made the whole sex thing enjoyable—an understatement to the nth degree. Annabelle couldn't help wondering if it was Mike who made the difference, or if it was because she was completely blitzed and possibly temporarily insane.

Unfortunately, the only way to find out would be to have a repeat performance sans alcohol to see if lightning did indeed strike twice. The problem was, if it did, she could see herself becoming a total nymphomaniac—something that until today, she could never wrap her head around. And if it didn't, she'd live her life incredibly disappointed.

The phone rang, and she stretched across the bed. Taking a deep breath, she inhaled Mike's scent on her pillow.

"Hello?"

"Annabelle? Did I wake you? It's Mike Flynn."

She smiled, an unusual occurrence. "Hi, Mike, um... no. I'm in bed kind of lazing after a nap. How are you?"

"Good." He paused. "I forgot to return your keys this morning, and I was wondering—"

"Do you want to have dinner? I could probably find something to throw together. That is, if you're free."

"That sounds great. I can bring takeout, or if you want, we can go out for dinner so you don't have to cook."

Annabelle rolled over, picturing Mike as he stood naked with his back to her that morning. Did he know what a great ass he had? He already had a little bit of a tan, which was unusual considering it was only mid-May.

"I don't mind cooking if you don't mind eating Italian. Unfortunately, that's about the only kind of food I've learned to make."

"Italian's my favorite. How 'bout I pick up some wine?"

"Good, um, when can you be here? I mean, what time do you want to come over?" Oh God, she hoped she didn't sound too desperate.

"Maybe we can do an early dinner and catch a movie or something."

He sounded uncertain and really cute. "Sure, early dinner and then… whatever. Sounds good."

Annabelle hastily calculated how long it would take her to change and cook one of the three meals she could manage. Okay, so Suzie Homemaker she wasn't. She hoped that by the time she'd used up her three-meal repertoire, the guy wouldn't care that she wasn't a Betty Crocker clone.

"It'll only take me a couple of hours. I don't know about you, but I skipped lunch, and I'm going to be famished. What do you think of… let's say four?

"Great. See you then."

❖❖❖

The table was set, Jamie Cullum was on the iPod, the curtains were drawn, and the lights were low. Annabelle had the antipasto she'd picked up at the deli arranged on a platter chilling in the refrigerator with the Caesar salad. She'd emptied the ingredients out of the bag, and this time, thank God, she remembered to fish out the crouton bag before squeezing the dressing from the packet. The last time she'd made the mistake of serving it with the croutons still in the bag. The garlic bread was heating in the oven—yes, she admitted she was a wine stain on the lace tablecloth of her heritage because she purchased premade frozen garlic bread. She crossed herself and apologized to her dead grandmother, whom Annabelle was sure was rolling over in her grave… continuously. By buying frozen garlic bread, and, in more than one instance, purchasing canned sauce, she'd broken the twelfth commandment. *Thou shalt cook from scratch everything served at your table, be it dining, breakfast, or picnic*. Let's face it. Annabelle had broken all of the commandments above number ten and several below it. She was doomed to spend a long time in purgatory. At least she'd be among friends.

Annabelle held the phone between her chin and shoulder as she tried to get the tissue paperlike peels off the smelly garlic cloves. Of course, the leaking juice made the peels stick as much to her hands as they did to the garlic.

Becca never answered her phone without checking the caller ID, and no one could blame her. Becca avoided her mother at all cost, especially since Bitsy Larsen had found her new mission in life. Annabelle's mother was bad, but compared to Becca's, she was a regular Carol Brady with a Roman nose and a Brooklyn accent.

Bitsy, a true high-society matron, had terminal lockjaw. Her name and lineage were emblazoned on the pages of the *Social Register* knighting her as a founding member of the United Sisterhood of Main Line Society's Sphincter Police. She belonged to the Junior League, the Philadelphia Garden Club, and was a member-since-birth of the Merion Cricket Club. With all the time spent dishing with other society matrons of her ilk, planning fundraisers, and going to lunches at the club—not to mention her escapades with the tennis pro—it's a wonder she had a spare minute to bother Becca. But since Chip's death, finding Becca a suitable "match" and passing on the family torch had become an obsession. As altruistic as Bitsy Larsen tried to make that sound, it was anything but. Too bad for Bitsy, Becca stopped trying to please Mommy Dearest after she forced Becca to have a debutante ball.

"Hi Annabelle. You sure took your sweet time getting back to me. I've been waiting all day. Now tell me all about the wedding. Was it perfect?"

"All except for the bride, which wasn't me. Though, the groom was a definite improvement over the one in the originally scheduled program. If Nick Romeo wasn't married... ah well, you know."

"You'd look, but not touch. Annabelle, you've never picked a man up in your life. Heck, if Chip hadn't crashed at our place, you'd still be a virgin, or worse, you'd have lost it to Icky Johnny. Face it, except for Chip, you've only dated losers. As for improving on Johnny the mortician, that's not exactly hard to do.

The Unabomber would be an improvement, and I hear he's single."

"Thanks for the 4-1-1, but I'm not interested." Annabelle drained the liquid from a can of artichoke hearts and threw them in the food processor along with the garlic. She planned to pulse the food processor whenever Becca got on her nerves. Maybe Becca would get a clue.

"Tell me about this guy you met."

Annabelle took the parsley, basil, a lemon, and Parmesan cheese out of the grocery bag and wadded it up. "His name is Mike Flynn, and he's a doctor. He bought me breakfast, but then he was called to the hospital before we ate. He seems nice, and he's really good-looking—"

"I know. He looks like Chip but with bigger feet, whatever the hell that means. Oh my God! Annabelle, you don't mean... you do. You didn't sleep with him, did you? You did! You slept with him."

"I... well... I had too much to drink. And I caught the bouquet, and he caught the garter, and we danced—"

"Sounds to me like you did a hell of a lot more than that, if you know his shoe size."

"When I woke up this morning, he was in bed with me." She grated lemon peel, trying to avoid the white stuff just below it. The last time she'd fixed this meal she'd forgotten that the white stuff was bitter—big mistake. She held the grater over the food processor bowl and slid her finger down the back to remove the lemon peel.

"Go on."

Annabelle turned on the heat under a sauté pan and

tossed a handful of pine nuts in to toast. "Go on? What do you want from me?" She shook the pan, careful not to burn the nuts like she did the last time.

"Specifics."

"What ever happened to privacy?" Annabelle chopped the lemon in half, squeezed it over the artichokes, and then fished out the seeds. The last time she'd made this she'd forgotten to remove the seeds and choked on one. The choking incident and the smell of burnt pine nuts made for a less-than-impressive dinner.

"Oh come on. There's nothing I don't know about you, and I still love you. If you can't tell me, who can you tell?"

"Fine, we had sex—" Annabelle waved a hand over the toasting nuts and caught their scent. She switched off the heat before she burnt them and dumped them into the food processor with a hunk of cheese and a handful of parsley and basil. "A lot of sex. And from what I remember, he's quite talented."

"It's about time. Now that you've entered the realm of the sexually satisfied, aren't you glad you didn't marry the scum-of-the-earth mortician?"

"What if it's a fluke? What if it's because I had too much to drink, or maybe I dreamed the whole thing?"

"Or maybe you found a god in bed? Stranger things have happened."

"Not to me."

"Yeah, sweetie, I know. But it's not as if you've been with a ton of guys. Two is not a large enough popula-tion from which to form an educated hypothesis. And, as much as I loved my brother, he was spoiled and kinda selfish, so he probably wasn't the most considerate lover. I know he wasn't a considerate boyfriend. And then there was Johnny. Need I say more?"

"No."

"So, when are you going to see this sex god again?"

"This afternoon. He's coming over for an early dinner." She turned on the food processor and hoped it wasn't the only thing she'd be able to turn on. She pulsed it a few times. As the machine whirled, she drizzled olive oil into the bowl, finishing off the artichoke heart pesto.

A quick glance at the clock told her that Mike would be there in ten minutes.

"Ah." Becca broke the silence. "So are you going to seduce him and see if he's as good when you're sober as when you're drunk?"

"Becca, I'm no seductress. I don't know how to do that."

"Honey, girls who look like you don't have to do anything but show up and look welcoming. I'm sure he'll take care of the rest."

"You think?"

Chapter 3

MIKE SPENT THE TWENTY-FIVE MINUTE TRIP FROM Coney Island to Park Slope lecturing himself about proper first date behavior. He'd purposely emptied his wallet of condoms so he wouldn't be tempted to attack Annabelle again. However, all the good intentions in the world hadn't stopped him from mentally ticking off every pharmacy between his place and Annabelle's during the ride.

It would have been a lot easier if she'd agreed to go out to dinner. Even without condoms, Mike wasn't sure how much control he'd have in the same room where he'd all but ripped off her clothes less than twenty-four hours before. Shit, he'd been half hard all day. As it was, a picture of her sleeping beside him wearing nothing but a sexy blue garter was permanently burned in his memory. He'd carry that vision to his grave.

Mike didn't know what Annabelle was making for dinner, so he stopped at Nick's cousin's restaurant, DiNicola's, to pick up wine.

"Hey, Vinny, you here?" Mike strolled through the double swinging doors into the restaurant's kitchen and was assaulted with the scent of garlic and onions sautéing in olive oil—one of his all-time favorite smells. Mike might be Irish by birth, but his taste buds never got the message. He'd grown up working at DiNicola's and eating as much Italian food as possible.

Vinny, wearing his usual chef's garb of a splattered white jacket and black-and-white checked pants, took his attention from the stove. "Of course, I'm here. The question is, why are you?"

Vinny poured two huge cans of tomato puree into the stockpot along with about a gallon of wine before pouring himself a glass and turning the bottle toward Mike. "You want?"

"No thanks. I came to pick some up. I've got a date."

Vinny's unibrow rose. "Who you going out with? I thought that blonde doctor chick dumped you for the head of cardiology?" A knowing smile crossed his face. "Oh you got a date with Nick's new sister-in-law, what's-her-face. I saw you leave with her last night. How'd you manage that? Nick didn't date her before he dated Rosalie, did he? That would be real awkward at family get-togethers, if you know what I mean."

Mike leaned back against the stainless steel counter and crossed his arms. "I am capable of getting a date Nick hasn't already dumped, you know. I asked Annabelle out myself. I don't need him to get me a date." Actually Mike had called her, and she'd asked him out, but he wasn't about to tell Vinny that. "I don't know what she's cooking, so I thought I'd grab a couple bottles of wine. Do you mind?"

"What the fuck do I look like, a feak'n liquor store?" He nodded toward the wine cellar. "You gonna get it? Or do I have to?"

Mike walked past him and smiled. "Thanks, Vin, I owe ya."

"Yeah, yeah, yeah. I'll put it on your tab. You got money for flowers? That Annabelle, she's a classy chick. I've got some scratch if you need it." He reached into his pocket and took out a thick billfold.

"Thanks, but I'm good." Mike went into the wine cellar and grabbed a bottle of red and a bottle of white. He returned and bagged the wine at the carryout station.

Vinny came out of the walk-in refrigerator carrying a tub of sausage. "Grab the meatballs, will ya, Mikey?"

Mike retrieved the tub of meatballs and set it on the stainless steel counter.

Vinny took his cleaver and cut the sausage into separate links. "You wanna eat before you go in case she don't cook too good? Or are you going there for more than food? I saw you leave with her last night. Did you get lucky, Mikey? Did you get some of that?"

Mike was used to being razzed by Vinny, and it'd never bothered him before. Today he had to fight off the urge to tell him to mind his own business. Mike usually gave Vinny shit about vicariously enjoying the fact he and Nick had a sex life—something that most married men envied. But even though Vinny and Mona had been married since before the earth cooled, Mike still caught Vinny copping a feel as Mona walked past in the kitchen. Hell, he even caught them getting busy in the wine cellar one day before his shift. Something he wished he could erase from his memory bank.

When Mike didn't answer, Vinny smiled. "Oh man. What's with those Ronaldi women? They got wine-flavored nipples?"

Annabelle had something all right—something that had Mike counting the minutes until he'd see her again. He checked his watch.

Vinny laughed. "Go, go. I know that look. I saw it often enough on Nick when he started seeing Rosalie. Have a good time, Mikey. And bring her in soon so Mona can get a better look at her." Vinny reached over and grabbed Mike's arm before he finished nodding his agreement. "I got some rubbers in my desk if you need 'em."

Mike tried not to laugh. Vinny had been preaching safe sex to him and Nick since before they could shave. Some things never changed. He was tempted to throw all his good intentions out the window and take a handful, but he stood strong. "No thanks." He held up the wine. "This is all I need for the night. I'm gonna see if I can make this last for more than a few weeks."

"You like her, eh?"

Mike nodded.

"So you're what? Not interested in sex all of a sudden?"

Mike laughed. "Oh no, I'm plenty interested, but I want her to know that's not the only thing I'm interested in."

"Hold on there, Dr. Mikey. You using that reverse psychological shit? You what? Pretend you're interested in what she's saying instead of just gettin' laid, and then when she realizes you don't wanna have sex, that's all she'll want? That actually work for you?"

"Vinny, I am interested in what she has to say. We didn't talk very much last night—"

"Too busy gettin' laid, eh?"

Mike didn't even dignify that with an answer, but his guilty conscience gave him more than a moment of discomfort for exactly that reason, and because he hadn't realized she was more than just tipsy. She must have been in order to have slept with him and not remembered who the hell he was. So, okay. Tonight he'd make it up to her. He'd be the perfect gentleman.

"Thanks for the wine, Vinny. Give my love to Mona."

"Yeah, yeah, yeah. Get outa here. I got work to do."

Mike stopped at Carmine's flower shop to buy Annabelle roses. Not red roses. He didn't want to scare her off. He picked out yellow roses with coral tips. He wasn't sure what significance yellow roses had, so he asked the clerk, who instead of answering, stared at him as if he'd asked if he could have fries with that. He could call his mother. She'd know, but then she'd also know he was buying roses for a woman, and she'd give him the third degree until he promised to bring Annabelle over for supper. He was better off taking his chances.

Mike took a deep breath, climbed the brownstone steps, and buzzed her apartment. Two men, one of whom held Dave's leash, opened the security doors. Dave ran out. Mike braced himself moments before the mutt jumped on him and placed both paws on his chest.

"Hi," the smaller guy said, struggling to pull Dave down. "Sorry about that."

Mike put the roses under his arm so he could pet the dog. "Hey, buddy. How you doing?"

"You must be Mike. I'm Wayne and this is Henry." Wayne pointed to the taller man beside him.

Mike nodded and shook Henry's outstretched hand. "Hi." The other guy, Wayne, was staring at Mike's crotch. He looked down to make sure his fly wasn't flying at half-mast, or worse, open. Nope, everything was covered. Henry must have noticed Wayne's stare,

since he elbowed Wayne hard enough to knock the wind
out of him.

Since Wayne was now unable to speak, Henry took
over. "We live upstairs and are good friends of Rosalie
and Annabelle."

"Mike Flynn. Nice to meet you."

Henry grabbed Wayne's arm and pulled him out the door.
"We were just going for a walk in the park and borrowed
Dave for the evening. Have a nice time tonight."

"Thanks." Mike turned toward Annabelle's door just
as she opened it.

Wow, she looked almost as good dressed as she did
naked. She answered the door barefoot. Her toenails
were painted coral, and a thin gold chain encircled her
delicate ankle. He followed what seemed like a mile
of leg, past two perfect knees to tanned, toned thighs
worthy of a standing ovation. His eye hit the hem of
a coral v-neck T-shirt dress that Mike was sure didn't
scream sex until she put it on. She'd pulled her riot of
black curls up in a twist held with ebony chopsticks. A
few unruly curls escaped to frame her face.

Annabelle didn't wear makeup, well, none that he
could see anyway. Her tanned olive skin glowed. When
she bit and then licked her full bottom lip, every thought
Mike had about keeping his hands and the rest of his
body parts to himself evaporated.

She wrung her hands and then bit her lip again. Her
bright blue eyes met his. Instead of doing what he should
have done, like give her the roses and say hello, he
tossed them on the table, placed the wine beside them,
and kissed her until they were both breathing heavy and
the chopsticks hit the floor.

His hands skimmed over her ass, which seemed to be bare of anything except his hands and, of course, the dress. He was about to pull her dress up to see if he was right when reality smacked him in the head. He hadn't even said a word to her.

Things were going according to plan seduction-wise, and Annabelle was thrilled to be getting tingles in all the right places, too. Maybe she hadn't imagined the orgasms. Maybe the sex wasn't too good to be true. She was just giving herself up to the possibility that Mike was indeed a sex god when he pushed her away and stepped back.

Damn, she'd been congratulating herself on her apparent seductive prowess and for planning a dinner that could sit for however long and be thrown together in ten minutes.

Guys got hungry after sex, and if she was lucky, Mike would be very hungry. Later. Much later.

"I'm so sorry."

She did a double take. "What? What are you sorry about? Coming over?"

"No. God no." He scrubbed his hand over his face, picked up the hairpins, and handed them to her before he stuffed his hands in his pockets.

Some seductress she'd turned out to be. Maybe she hadn't done enough to him. But gosh, once he started kissing her and running his hands down her body, any rational thought about what her hands should be doing took a backseat.

"I upset you. I'm sorry I took advantage of you last night. I didn't mean to. Honestly."

Annabelle raised her head. "Hold on. If someone was taken advantage of last night, it was you. Not me. No one takes advantage of me. Ever." At least not ever again.

He had the audacity to smile. "You make a habit of taking advantage of poor, unsuspecting men?"

No fair. One smile and all that good, righteous indignation disappeared without a trace. "No, I wouldn't call it a habit… yet. But I have to admit, it's growing on me."

His smile was crooked in a really sexy way. It reminded her of someone. Not Chip. Chip's smile had been perfect, almost fake-looking. She used to tease him about being a poster boy for toothpaste commercials. She couldn't figure out who it reminded her of, but at the moment, she had more important things on her mind—like how to get her seduction back on track.

Annabelle thought back to all the movies she'd watched. Most of the characters didn't have any trouble getting men in bed. Hell, sometimes they just asked for it. She didn't have the nerve. Of all times for Becca to be wrong. She said all Annabelle would have to do was look welcoming. Ha!

She didn't know how she could look any more welcoming without answering the door naked. Though the way his eyes were looking at anything but her, even that wouldn't have worked.

The door swung open, hitting her in the back. Rich, her big brother and new resident pain-in-the-ass, walked in like he owned the place. All six feet three inches of him seemed to fill the room. His short-cropped brown hair stood up on top as if it were styled, although he never had to run a brush through it. A girl could hate her brother for his perfect hair and long, thick black eyelashes. Especially as blue as his eyes were. Right now, they held a Dennis the Menace quality.

Rich was still angry that she had gotten Rosalie's apartment before he could snatch it up. Lucky for her, Rich had kept his plans to leave his position as a professor at Dartmouth for a professorship at Columbia a secret, or she would have lost the apartment to him for sure. Her parents would have insisted Rosalie turn the place over to him. After all, Rich, the eldest child and only son of Paul and Maria Ronaldi, held a special place in their hearts. If her parents had anything to do with it, Rich would become the only living saint. Even Rosalie couldn't compete with Rich, the anointed one.

"Thanks for letting yourself in, Rich. What are you doing here, and where did you get my keys?"

"I'm just checking up on you. I was worried when you didn't show up for Sunday dinner. And as for the keys, I've had them since I stayed here with Rosalie over Christmas break. So, are you sick, or are you pouting because it wasn't you walking down the aisle yesterday?"

Just when Annabelle thought things couldn't get any worse, Mike stepped out from behind the open door.

"Hi, Rich." Mike shook his hand. "Nice to see you again. I'm afraid it's my fault Annabelle didn't go to dinner. I've been keeping her busy." He put his arm around her and drew her close.

Rich puffed up like the big blowhard he was. "Busy doing what?"

Could a person die of embarrassment? The only thing more annoying than Rich's saintly status was his position as the world's most irritating and overprotective big brother. Annabelle stepped between the two men, and with both hands on Rich's chest, pushed him toward the door. Hard. He didn't move.

"I've been fixing dinner, not that it's any of your business."

Rich raised an eyebrow but didn't question her response, thank God. All she needed was Rich to start telling disaster stories about her kitchen exploits. Taking off his leather jacket, he winked to let her know he had something to hold over her head.

"Good, I'm starved. You know I can't eat dinner at one o'clock. That's about the time I get around to eating breakfast when I'm not teaching. What are we eating?"

"You? Nothing, since you're not invited. What's wrong? Does your girlfriend think your once-happy long-distance relationship has become too close for comfort now that you're only a subway ride away?" She turned to Mike. "Rich didn't bother telling anyone, including Gina, his girlfriend, about his plan to leave New Hampshire and move back to Brooklyn."

Rich gave Mike a hard look. "So, what are you doing having dinner with my little sister?"

Annabelle growled and wished she had a handy two-by-four to clobber her overbearing brother. "Richard Antonio Ronaldi, who do you think you are? I invited Mike. Besides, who I have over to my own home is no concern of yours."

Mike, with his arm still around her, slid his hand from her shoulder to her wrist, then back, sending sparks flying through her system. Damn Rich.

"No, it's all right." Mike let her go and moved away. "I just got here. See, I haven't even had a chance to give Annabelle her flowers." He picked up the roses he'd thrown on the table before he kissed her and handed them to her. "These are for you. Thanks for inviting me."

She accepted the roses and threw Rich's jacket on the couch. Mike smiled at her, and if she read that smile correctly, it said, *let's placate the jerk, and maybe he'll go away,* but it also held a look of relief. She was usually good at reading people, but Mike's mixed messages were confusing.

Annabelle held the roses to her chest and took a good long sniff, trying not to swoon. No one had ever bought her roses before—not even for an anniversary. Chip said he was allergic to flowers, but Becca said he was allergic to spending money on anyone but himself. Annabelle hadn't minded that he was frugal—but she really appreciated that Mike wasn't. She wanted to savor the moment and bury her face in the beautiful blossoms, but with Rich there, it would be embarrassing.

"Thanks. I'll put these in water. Mike, why don't you bring the wine into the kitchen?"

"Okay. Great."

Mike was both relieved and frustrated by Rich's presence. On one hand, it would certainly help him keep his hands to himself, but then it looked as if Annabelle had her own agenda, and hands-off was not part of it. He had a feeling that her agenda would be a whole lot more enjoyable than his. And if she wasn't worried about things moving too fast, he could learn to live with it.

Yeah, no problem there.

It looked as if she'd gone to a lot of trouble. The apartment was definitely staged for romance—the lights were low, the table set for two. Sultry jazz played in the background, and the scent of garlic swirled in the air. Everything was perfect for dinner and... dessert, except for Annabelle's brother in the living room. He'd put a real damper on the dessert part of the evening.

Mike followed her into the kitchen, trying not to notice how the skirt of her dress hugged her extraordinary ass without even a hint of a panty line—she either went without, or she wore a thong. The fact he'd stopped himself before he could find out did nothing to keep his blood pressure from shooting into the danger zone. He tried to ignore the way her calf muscles tensed with every step and how sexy that ankle bracelet was. He was so busy ignoring things that he walked into her when she stopped to open a drawer. His arms went around her to keep from knocking her down. The way she stood with her back against his front, her scent engulfing him like a riptide over a drowning man, made him wonder if he'd survive. The odds weren't in his favor.

Stepping away, Mike placed the wine on the bar separating the small kitchen from the dining area. Annabelle turned, stomped her bare foot, and tipped her head back to meet his eyes. "I want to kill him. I'm so sorry."

Mike took both her hands in his and was about to kiss the pout off her lips when Rich went to the bar, ostensibly to check out the wine. Mike had seen guard dogs less conspicuous.

He rolled his eyes and coaxed a smile out of her. "If this isn't a good time, I understand. Do you want some time alone with your brother?"

"No, it's okay. It wouldn't do any good to leave me alone with him now. It takes time to plan the perfect murder. Besides, he can't stay forever."

Mike wasn't too sure about that.

Rich came around the bar and helped himself to a plate and silverware. He made room for himself at the table between the plates Annabelle had set. He gave Mike a sly smile. "What did you make, Annabelle?"

"Antipasto, pasta with artichoke pesto, garlic bread, and a Caesar salad."

"Ah, I knew dropping by was a good idea. You better put that water on to boil. You *do* know you have to boil the water... right?"

Annabelle shot Rich a look that would annihilate mere mortals. The jerk hooked his thumbs into his jeans pockets, rocked back on his heels, and smiled. "I'm starved."

She put the pot of water on the stove to boil and turned to Mike. "Do you want to open the wine?" She glared at her brother. "I could use some." After finding a corkscrew, she handed it to Mike.

"Red or white? The white's not chilled yet."

She pulled the salad from the refrigerator and passed it to Rich without a word. "Why don't you open the red, and I'll put the other bottle in the freezer."

"Sounds like a plan."

On the way back to the kitchen after placing the cheese on the table, she smacked Rich upside his head. He only smiled.

Mike poured the wine and brought two glasses into the kitchen. Ignoring Rich, he handed Annabelle a glass and raised his. "To you." He touched his glass to hers and then sipped the Cabernet while he held her gaze.

Rich held up his glass. "Salute."

Annabelle groaned and took a drink. The color of her face turned a similar shade of red as the wine. God, she was sweet.

When they sat down to dinner, Annabelle took the middle seat, for which Mike would be eternally grateful.

The tension rolling off Rich was palpable. Mike felt as if he was fifteen again being given the touch-her-and-I'll-kill-you look by his date's father.

"So, Mike. It is Mike, right?"

Mike nodded. Rich grunted and then shot an accusing look at Annabelle. She smiled back serenely, but her eyes told a different story. Mike suspected they were playing footsie under the table—the kind that left bruises.

Rich served himself antipasto and passed it to Mike, who offered it to Annabelle first.

"No, go ahead, Mike. Guests first."

So far, Annabelle was up by two points. Mike sat back to enjoy the show. As an only child, he'd always wanted a sibling to count on, drive crazy, and embarrass. He suspected it wasn't always fun, but never boring either.

Mike piled the antipasto on his plate and took a bite.

Rich wiped his mouth on his napkin. "Mike, do you work?"

Mike swallowed a forkful. "Yes."

"What do you do?"

Annabelle glared at her brother. "He's a doctor."

"I'm a pulmonologist," Mike added.

Annabelle and Rich both stared at him—Annabelle with a look of confusion and Rich as if he'd discovered a dirty secret. Rich winked at her. "That's a lung doctor."

She stabbed an olive as if it had a picture of Rich's face on it. "I know what it means."

"Where did you go to school?"

"Undergrad at NYU, medical school, Columbia. I did my residency and fellowship at Presbyterian."

"Ever married?"

"No, you?"

Rich shook his head. "Any children?"

"No, you?"

Rich never stopped eating. "Nope."

Annabelle wiped her mouth. "Richie, would you please stop with the interrogation? All you're missing is a bare light bulb, handcuffs, and water board. Enough."

He nodded. "Sure, I'll be happy to change the subject." Rich scooped up a bowl of pasta, grated cheese over the top, and pasted on a smile of innocence, which had Mike's spidey sense buzzing like an air-raid siren.

"So, Annabelle. How's Ben?"

She shot another visual dagger at Rich before commenting. "Ben Walsh is my boss."

"Annabelle is a sales girl at his art gallery."

"No, I manage the gallery. I do sales, but I also discover artists, display their work, plan showings, and manage the sales force."

Rich caught Mike's eye before continuing. "Annabelle was engaged until a few weeks ago."

Well, that was news. Mike studied her. She seemed more embarrassed than heartsick at the mention of it. What do you say to that? I'm sorry? But Mike was anything but sorry. Better to keep his mouth shut.

Rich continued on his self-appointed mission. "Ben and Annabelle are close."

Annabelle choked on the wine she sipped. She coughed, her eyes watering. Mike and Rich both came out of their chairs, racing to see who could give her the Heimlich maneuver first. She held up her hands to ward off both of them. "I'm fine."

Rich didn't seem the least bit guilty for embarrassing her. "Yeah, well, I heard Ben came running back to town as soon as he heard you were single again."

"He had the trip scheduled. I can assure you, his visit has nothing to do with me. Ben is a lot of things, but he's not the white knight type. Not that I need one. A white knight, that is."

Rich nodded. "A-huh. Sure."

She ignored Rich and touched Mike's hand. "Ben is my boss and my friend. That's all."

Rich's silence spoke volumes.

Annabelle shifted in her seat. "Mike. What do your parents do?"

"My mother is a court reporter."

She smiled. "Wow. That must be interesting. My mom's a housewife. She never worked outside the house."

Rich continued. "Your mom and dad still together?"

Mike wiped his mouth on his napkin. "No, they're not."

"What's your dad do?"

"He's a doctor. A cardiologist. I've never met him."

"Aren't you curious about him?"

Mike shrugged. "Not really. I know everything I need to know about him. He was doing his residency when he and my mum were dating. They'd talked about getting married. He'd gone home for Easter when she found out she was pregnant. She was waiting for him to come back to tell him in person. You can imagine her shock when she saw the announcement of his engagement to someone else in the society pages. Her parents didn't handle it well. She went back to Ireland to stay with her aunt and had me. We didn't come back to the States until I was two. He doesn't even know I exist, and that's just fine with me."

Rich wiped his mouth on his napkin. "Yeah, I see your point. So, are you a Met or Yankee fan?"

"Mets."

"Islanders or Rangers?"

"Rangers, Giants, and Knicks."

Rich nodded, the mood shifted, and Annabelle visibly relaxed. She seemed happy with him. He wasn't sure who he was trying to impress more, Rich or Annabelle.

Mike knew enough about big brothers not to take the lack of trust and blatant skepticism personally, and it was cute the way Annabelle reacted to Rich. More bluster than bite, she did her share of eye rolling and shooting Rich dirty looks, but in the end, she seemed to appreciate he cared enough to make a pain in the ass of himself. Mike respected him for that, too, because of how protective he was of his own mother. He suspected worrying about a little sister would be worse, especially since Mum never dated.

After dinner and dessert, it became abundantly clear that Rich did not intend to leave before Mike did.

Annabelle stood, and Mike followed and began stacking dishes.

"Let me clear the table."

Annabelle couldn't believe it. "No, that's okay. I'll take care of it." Usually when men helped, all they helped with was making more work. Cleaning the kitchen was bad enough without any "help."

"I insist. Just grab the wine, and let me clean up. It's the least I can do after you cooked."

Annabelle shrugged. She didn't want to be rude. She took the wineglass, sat at the breakfast bar, and figured it'd be five minutes before she would be forced to take over.

She was wrong. Mike definitely knew his way around a kitchen. And Rich, the pig that he was, instead of leaving them alone, took up the rest of the space pretending to help. He all but forced her out of the room.

Mike sent her a wink and ordered Rich around like the incompetent helper he was. Unfortunately, Rich never got that. Mike threw a dish towel over his shoulder, rolled up the sleeves of his blue oxford shirt, and got down to some serious cleaning.

She really wished that Rich would leave. He quickly lost his feigned interest, and after five minutes, he disappeared from the kitchen, parked himself in front of the TV, and turned on a game. When he kicked off his shoes and asked for a beer, it became obvious he wasn't going anywhere.

Annabelle brought the salad bowl in from the dining room and took a towel out of the drawer to start drying.

Mike stopped what he was doing, turned off the water, and took the towel out of her hands. "No you don't. Why don't you just refill your wine and keep me company?"

"Oh, um… okay." Annabelle never realized what a turn-on it was to watch a man work in the kitchen. Maybe because she'd never seen one. Well, except for the chefs on TV. Emeril never did it for her, but Mike was a different story.

"Would you hand me those glasses?

Annabelle blinked and pulled herself out of her musings. "Sure."

She passed them to him one by one as he washed them, taking care not to clink them around in the dish drain like most guys would. He methodically washed the dishes. He took his time and was thorough. Drying them well before replacing them in the cupboard.

"Mum and I always shared kitchen chores, cooking and cleaning up, but most of the time I'd do it. She always worked so hard."

"That's nice. In my house, Richie was the prince, and Papa was the king. Neither of them lifted a finger. Rosalie and I were expected to learn to be good homemakers. Neither of us ever met Mama's high expectations."

Mike laughed as he put his back into scrubbing the pasta pot. His shirt pulled taut across his back. He had really nice hands, and when he bent to put the pot away, she got to see his great butt again in a pair of faded 501s. She was tempted to give it a pat. Every now and then, he'd stop what he was doing, dry his hands, and turn his attention to her as if he could read her mind. When he wiped down the stove, the pendant light hanging there shone in his blond hair and showed off the contours of his muscled forearms. Annabelle showed Mike where the few things she'd used went. Every brush of his hand sent tingles shooting through her. The way he

stood behind her and placed the wineglasses high in the
cabinet above—his body flush against hers—seemed
like a strange kind of foreplay. She'd never realized
bumping into someone in the kitchen could be such a
turn-on. By the time the last pot was dried and put away,
she was practically panting.

He folded the towels and hung them on the door-pull
of the refrigerator. "All done."

When he turned, Annabelle made sure she was right
in the way. "Thanks for helping."

Mike swallowed, his arms came around her waist
and pulled her close, right before he dipped his head to
kiss her.

The man kissed like a dream. He wasn't one of
those come-at-you-with-his-tongue-sticking-out
kissers, or the kind that thinks he's got to grind his
mouth into yours in order to show he's enjoying
himself. No, Mike was the perfect combination of soft
but firm, hot but controlled, and oh man, he knew how
to take his time. He kissed her as if he had all night,
teasing her lips with his until she couldn't stand it and
grabbed him. The man knew how to follow her lead
too, which earned him a full-frontal kiss. Yes, things
were humming right along. Unfortunately, by the
time they'd forgotten Rich, he was in the refrigerator
getting another beer. Annabelle was so frustrated she
wanted to scream, and Mike could do nothing but
stand behind her.

Annabelle walked Mike to the door. "Thanks for coming.
I'm sorry for… Well, you know."

He waved good-bye to Rich and kissed her on the cheek. "Thanks for dinner. I'll give you a call in a couple days."

Annabelle was sure of two things. First, she'd never hear from Mike again. Second, Rich would never bother her on another date, since as soon as Mike was out of hearing range, she planned to kill Rich. Slowly and painfully.

She turned, only to find Rich had donned his jacket and had a hand on the doorknob. "Oh no you don't. You're not going anywhere until after I've murdered you!"

"Come on. What did you expect me to do? Ma was going on and on about you having a date with a doctor. How did I know he wasn't one of the assholes she always threw at you and Rosalie? I couldn't take the chance you'd end up with a brainier version of Johnny DePalma."

She didn't even try to defend Johnny. He was an asshole. "Rich, just because you're my big brother—"

"Look, I promise not to bother you again unless you start seeing someone else. Mike seems like a good guy. If I'd known he was Nick's friend, I would have left you alone. But hey, he didn't seem to mind the fact I horned in on your date."

"Yeah, but I did. I minded a lot. I'll be lucky if I ever hear from him again, thanks to you."

Rich wrapped his arms around her and pulled her in for a bear hug. "Don't worry, princess, he'll call. The poor guy couldn't keep his eyes off you. He's got it bad." He kissed her on both cheeks and then gave her a noogie before turning and walking out the door.

She changed into jogging gear. She definitely needed to let off some steam and sexual frustration.

❖ ❖ ❖

Since he had nothing better to do and needed a distraction, Mike walked to his mother's apartment. If he went home, he'd sit there thinking about Annabelle and all the things he wanted to do with her and to her.

The kiss he'd planted on her even before he said hello gave him pause, especially since he'd spent the whole trip over there lecturing himself. He was a doctor. He was known for his control and stability. That was before he met Annabelle Ronaldi. He saw his reflection in the glass door of his mother's building and wondered what had changed.

He took the stairs to the third floor and let himself into his mother's apartment without knocking, as if he'd never moved out. "Mum, I'm home." He was brilliant. He wanted to keep from thinking about Annabelle, and he'd succeeded. There was absolutely no way he would think X-rated thoughts about anyone—even Annabelle—in the presence of his mother.

Colleen Flynn stepped out of the kitchen drying her hands. "Michael, what a nice surprise. Tell me, have you eaten your dinner yet?"

He gave her his obligatory hug and kiss and waited until she rubbed the lipstick off his cheek. "Yeah, I did. I was on my way home. I haven't seen you in a while and thought I'd stop by."

"You've got a night off, have you?"

"Two. I scheduled it so I could go to Nick's wedding last night and wouldn't have to be on call early this morning. I ended up at the hospital anyway."

"When was the last time you had two days off in a row without going into the hospital or the office at all?"

He shrugged. He couldn't remember.

She put the kettle on for tea and took a crumb cake out of the refrigerator. "Well, I'm glad you're here for whatever reason. Not that you need a reason to come home. You know that, don't you?"

Mike took the teacups and plates out of the cupboard. "I know, Mum."

He put the crumb cake on top of the plates, and before taking the pile off the counter, he reached for a crumb and earned a hand slap.

"Michael Christopher Flynn, you know better than that. Now go set everything on the table while I make the tea."

Mike sat at the table and watched his mother fix tea like he had a million times before. She glanced at him and smiled before measuring the tea leaves for the pot.

"You do look tired. Have you been working around the clock again, or didn't you get any sleep after Nick's wedding?"

"Both. You know how it is. I have to put in a lot of hours until I make partner, then things will slow down."

"I've watched you push yourself since you were a boy. Pushing to get good grades, a scholarship, into medical school, the right residency, the right fellowship, and now partnership. When will you stop pushing and start living?"

"I'll get some sleep tonight. I don't have to be back in the hospital until early rounds tomorrow."

She walked to the table and set the teapot on the hot plate.

Mike stood while she sat and then watched her pour the tea, fixing his the same way she had since he was a child.

"Ah, you were always a good boy, my Michael. I'm glad you'll sleep tonight, but I'm more concerned with your life. Don't you want more in your life than work?"

He drank his tea and almost choked on it as he remembered the way Annabelle looked sleeping in nothing but a garter. Yeah, he wanted more than work. A whole lot more. "I want more. I just don't know if it's the right time."

"It's never going to be the right time." She took a bite of cake, sipped her tea, and placed her cup gingerly on the saucer. "You can't plan when to have a life. You need to have a life and plan when to work. I was hoping you'd meet someone who would take your mind off work for a while. None of the women you've dated so far ever touched your heart."

"I did meet someone at the wedding. Nick's new sister-in-law."

"Really? So does this girl have a name?"

"Annabelle Ronaldi. I had dinner with her tonight." Mike dug into his coffee cake and washed it down with his tea. The cups were small, two good gulps and his was empty. He stared into his cup and watched as the tea leaves settled to the bottom.

"It didn't go well?"

"No. It was fine. Why?"

"It's early yet. If it went so well, why are you here?

"Her brother came by, and three was a crowd."

"So, are you seeing her again?" She wiped the crumbs off the table with the side of her hand, caught them, and tossed them back on her plate.

Pictures of Annabelle in that sexy little dress she wore flashed like a slideshow through his mind. "I sure hope so."

"Well, you best do something more than hope." She picked up her teacup and took the last sip before stacking the plates and adding his cup to the pile. "Maybe you should call her and make a date before it gets much later."

"I don't want to look too anxious."

She laughed. "You don't have enough time to look too anxious. Call her and make another date. Oh, and it would help if you actually showed up for the date you make."

Mike stood and carried the teapot into the kitchen and felt as if he got the bum's rush. She gave him a kiss. "You go now, call that girl of yours, and then get some sleep." She practically pushed him to the door and outside her apartment.

He stuck his hands in his pocket and thought about what she'd said. Maybe Mum did know best.

Annabelle took a five-mile run around the park until she was thoroughly exhausted. As she pulled her keys from the hidden pocket of her shorts, the streetlights flickered on. She was thankful the days were getting longer.

In the shower, she replayed her quasi-date with Mike for the hundredth time. She couldn't help but wonder what would have happened if Rich hadn't shown up and ruined everything. Though, to be honest, it hadn't looked as if Mike was interested in a repeat of the previous night minus the wedding, the champagne, and her drunkenness. Sheesh, she was a complete washout as a woman.

She wrapped her hair in a towel, smoothed lotion on her legs and arms, and tried to get her mind on anything other than Mike Flynn. She'd heard that wearing sexy lingerie made women feel better about themselves and their sexuality. She didn't hold out much hope, but gave it a try. Anything would be better than feeling like a washout, so she slipped into a sexy, new red baby-doll nightie and matching lace itty-bitty boy shorts.

She couldn't remember if she'd drawn the curtains, so she pulled on her short silk batik robe and enjoyed the tingle caused by the cool silk sliding over her sensitized skin. She'd probably stayed under the shower massage too long since she was daydreaming about Mike and the little she remembered about making love with him. Not that they made love. They had sex. It sure didn't resemble what she and Chip had done together, which in her mind, wasn't a bad thing. But her emotions weren't involved. Not that they couldn't be in the future, but really, for right now anyway, she just wanted the sex. A totally new thing for her.

Deciding to take her mind out of the gutter, she left her bedroom and poured herself a glass of wine before she curled up on the couch. She surfed through three hundred channels without finding one thing to watch.

Frustrated, she stomped to the den to check her email. She clicked on the email with "proofs" in the subject line. Great, since she'd planned the wedding and signed all the contracts, the photographer had her email address and sent her the link and password to the site where she could download the proofs. Annabelle forwarded the link to Nick and Rosalie, and since she had nothing better to do, she downloaded the pictures. There was a great picture of Nick and Mike. They could have been a couple of models with Nick in his tux and Mike in a beautiful suit. He had the air of a man who was just as comfortable in a suit as he was out of it. And from what she knew of him, it was true enough. There was a picture of him kneeling in front of her, sliding the garter up her thigh. The look in his eyes was the same he'd given her when he'd kissed her that afternoon. A picture of the two of them on the dance floor. They fit together so perfectly. And another of them dancing together with her looking up at him, laughing.

She closed down the website and stared blankly at her computer's desktop. She couldn't remember ever dancing with Chip. Annabelle lost herself in memories, something she had avoided the last two years. The screen saver of all the photos she'd stored on her computer ran like a slideshow of her life. She watched and wondered what would have been. A photo of Becca taken at the beach filled the screen. She was tall, thin, with long legs and a body most people have to spend a lifetime at the gym to achieve. Not Becca; she was active but never really worked out. It should be illegal to look that way without even trying. Annabelle shook her head. Becca's short platinum blonde hair was perfectly wind whipped. If Annabelle hadn't taken the picture herself, she'd have sworn a photographer had set up a fan to give Becca the perfect look. Becca's almost white hair along with the gorgeous tan she'd acquired in the two days they'd spent on the beach only highlighted her deep green eyes. She flashed her crooked smile, and Annabelle remembered them laughing at the antics of one of the Bethany Beach lifeguards who had been trying to catch Becca's attention.

A picture of Becca and Chip taken before his cancer had returned appeared on the screen, and that's when it hit her.

Mike's smile seemed familiar because she'd seen the very same smile a thousand times.

Mike's smile matched Becca's.

Oh, shit.

Chapter 4

ANNABELLE SHOOK THE IMAGE OF MIKE'S SMILE OUT OF her head and told herself Mike could not be related to Becca. Chip's death had been hard on Becca—probably more so because of the twin thing. Becca felt lost and alone with her psychotic mother and her father, who since his divorce, was more distant than ever. Mike had said his father was a doctor, a cardiologist no less. Talk about an eerie coincidence. Dr. Larsen was a cardiologist, too. Still, was it fair to get Becca's hopes up when the chance of any relation was so minuscule? No. Stuff like that only happened in soap operas or really bad TV movies. Annabelle had never heard of one person discovering a long lost brother, cousin, or even second cousin twice removed. Unfortunately, that annoying little voice in her head—the one she was sure was implanted by Sister John Claire—wouldn't let it go.

Just the thought of Sister John Claire made a shiver run though Annabelle's body, and not in a good way. After thirteen years under the tutelage of nuns, she'd learned a healthy—or unhealthy, depending on how you looked at it—respect for them, bordering on fear. Unfortunately, though she got away from the school, she'd never been able to get away from Sister John Claire's voice. The same voice that kept nudging her to tell Becca everything.

Annabelle grabbed the phone from the sofa table and dialed. "Becca, it's me."

"Gee, I didn't expect to hear from you until tomorrow. How was it?"

"How was what?"

"Oh, that bad, huh?"

"What the hell are you talking about?"

"Sex with Mike. What else would I be talking about? Last week on *As Annabelle's World Turns*…" Becca lowered her voice to sound like a TV announcer. "… Annabelle was going to seduce hot, hot, hot Dr. Mike Flynn and see if he's as good in bed when she's sober as he was when she was drunk."

"That didn't work out. Richie dropped by and joined us for dinner."

"Your brother? Why would he drop by?"

"He knew I had a date, thanks to Mama, and he decided I needed protection. Then, after Mike gave him a free ride in helping with the dishes, Richie planted himself on my couch, took control of the remote, and I couldn't get him to leave without the aid of an incendiary device."

"Poor you. All horny and no one to—"

"Becca!"

"What? You're not horny? Have you given BOB a trial run? Did you have fun? I mean, I know it's not like the real thing, but in a pinch—"

"No." Annabelle could swear she blushed right down to her toes, which was nothing compared to the way she'd blushed when she'd opened Becca's Christmas present. Thank God they'd been alone. Who gives their best friend a battery-operated boyfriend—Becca's way of saying vibrator—for a Christmas present? Annabelle was certain she'd have died of embarrassment if anyone else had seen it. And BOB was so huge. She didn't think the real things were that big—well, until she saw Mike's, and that's only if she'd remembered correctly. She almost hoped it had been the champagne talking, but she'd never heard that alcohol messed with a person's vision. Their reflexes—sure. Their judgment— obviously. But their vision? She doubted it.

"Don't tell me you actually believe that you'll go blind if you have a self-induced orgasm?"

"Bec, I don't need that."

"Honey, everyone needs that."

"You know what I mean. It's like tickling yourself— it doesn't work."

Earlier, for about three seconds, she'd considered trying out her Christmas present but hadn't been able to get up the nerve. She'd never been that good at pretending. No way would she ever be able to think of Mike while holding a pearl-filled fluorescent purple vibrator in the shape of—well, what they're usually in the shape of. What the pearls were for, she had no idea, but she couldn't help thinking they'd be better off on a necklace than in a mechanical version of a silicone penis. Becca had even put the batteries in it after Annabelle had opened her "gift." Four batteries. What it did with all that amperage she couldn't imagine. Did it dance around and sing karaoke? She'd been tempted to rev it up just to see what the dang thing did and probably would have if the slightest chance existed of getting rid of the itchy feeling she'd been unable to ignore since she'd awoken with Mike.

"Has anyone ever told you that you're repressed?"

"Other than you? No. Can we please change the subject?"

"Sure. No more talk of vibrators. Check. So, how do you plan to get laid?"

All Annabelle could do was groan.

Becca smiled as she hung up the phone. Annabelle was just too predictable. Becca stretched out on the window seat and pulled a throw over her legs. The only reason she had the air-conditioning running was to make the humidity bearable. After Mommy Dearest had threatened to have Annabelle evicted from the apartment she'd shared with Chip, Becca helped pack the apartment, and Annabelle had given her all of Chip's sweatshirts. Becca rubbed the soft fleece on her rolled-up sleeve and cursed her brother. As much as she loved Chip, she hated the way he had taken advantage of Annabelle. He'd used her in his battle against their parents. He hadn't protected her from them before he got sick, and he hadn't arranged to protect her from them after his death.

Chip had loved Annabelle as much as he knew how. But it hadn't been enough, and at the time, Annabelle had such a low self-esteem, she didn't think she deserved more.

Becca let out a frustrated breath and kicked the throw off her legs. In the two years since Chip's death, she'd worried that the Annabelle she knew and loved was lost forever. Annabelle was like a living, breathing zombie. She couldn't deal with the pain, so she buried it. She walked through her life numb and so detached, she allowed her mother to run her life and railroad her into an engagement to the pig, Johnny.

The best thing that ever happened to Annabelle was catching Johnny boinking the help. But it wasn't until this morning when Becca spoke to Annabelle that she knew something had changed. Whoever Mike Flynn was, he'd been the only one to reach Annabelle. It sounded as if she could very well have met her own Prince Charming. One night with Mike, and she seemed to have stopped sleepwalking though life.

Thank God.

Less than two hours after Mike had said good-bye to Annabelle, he was outside her apartment, ringing the intercom.

"Yes?"

Good, she was home. Now what? "Annabelle, it's Mike. Do you have a minute?"

"Mike? Um... sure."

The door buzzed, and he opened it. He wasn't sure what he was thinking, showing up unannounced, except that he needed to see her... alone. Mum had been right. It was time to start living.

Mike heard the locks disengage as he stepped up to her door. She met him wearing a short silk robe. Her hand held the top closed, and the tie at her waist was so tight, it looked as if it might cut off her circulation. He could well imagine what the robe covered. Her hair hung in damp ringlets down her back, and she smelled like orange and vanilla mixed. His own personal dreamsicle.

She stepped aside to let him in and continued to back away until she hit the chair. She was nervous, if the white knuckles of her hand holding the top of her robe together meant anything. "Is something wrong?"

"No. Nothing's wrong."

Still holding her robe in a death grip with one hand, she pushed her hair back with the other. "Do you want some wine? There's plenty left over from dinner. I just poured myself a glass."

She stared at his mouth, but not in a way that made him think she wanted to kiss him—more curious than sexual. He smiled, and her eyes widened. "What, do I have something in my teeth? You're looking at me funny."

"Oh, sorry. No. I didn't expect to see you. I actually wondered if I'd ever see you again after that dinner, or should I say, the Italian inquisition. I'm sorry about Rich. He can be such a pain."

"I didn't mind. I know if I had a sister, I'd check out all the guys she dated and threaten them too."

Annabelle blanched, just like the first time he'd seen her. He took her cold hand in his. "Are you okay?"

"Yes." She shook her head, her body language belying her words, and then shook it again. He waited for her to tell him what was bothering her. She said nothing, just bit her lip, and stared with those fathomless blue eyes. Whatever the problem was, Mike wanted to solve it, or at least alleviate the burden. Barring that, he thought he'd take her mind off whatever it was. He bent his head and kissed her, tasting the rich Cabernet she drank, the unease surrounding her, and then he tasted surrender. What started out as an innocent comforting kiss missed the mark entirely. He didn't know when he'd lost control. It started out fine as a couple of soft whisper kisses, a touch of the lips, the tentative swipe of his tongue for a taste, but once she opened for him, everything went haywire. In the space of two heartbeats, his arms enveloped her, her sexy little silk-robed body molded to his, and her scent engulfed him. His hands traveled down to her perfect ass clad in clingy lace, and when she wrapped one of her mile-long legs around his, pulling his thigh between hers, he was lost.

Annabelle could happily spend years kissing Mike. She loved the way he teased her lips before asking permission to enter. When he entered, he was not in a race to examine her tonsils. As his tongue touched hers, she didn't know quite what happened.

Afraid that he'd stop, she did the only thing she could think of: she jumped him. Literally. Luckily, his hand was already on her ass, so when she jumped up and wrapped her legs around him, both his hands cupped her butt and held her tight against him. She couldn't help but wiggle. The hard ridge of his erection rubbed against her. His jeans and her panties together caused enough friction to send tremors strong enough to be picked up on a seismograph.

Mike was on the move, and she was happy he went no farther than the couch because she really wanted to wiggle some more. When he sat, she wiggled around a whole lot while she unhooked her legs from around his waist and brought them to either side of his, their clothes the only things separating them from doing what Annabelle had been dreaming of all day. She took a deep breath and uttered the only word that could improve the situation. "Condoms?"

"Sure, where are they?" Mike pulled her closer and lifted his hips, increasing the pressure against her and in her.

"How do I know? You're the guy."

"I left mine at home. You don't have any here?"

"Why would I have condoms? I never wanted to have sex before, and it's not like I wear them."

"You don't like sex?"

Why had she opened her big mouth? Oh, shit. How was she going to get out of this one? Should she tell him that she'd often been referred to as an ice queen or, her personal favorite, a prick tease? Should she tell him the word "frigid" had been mentioned more than once when she and Johnny had been fighting? Even Chip had been known to mumble that particular F-word under his breath.

She'd been mortified since she'd thought she'd done okay faking it. She'd never turned him down when he wanted to make love—she just never initiated it. Sex was never good between them, and it was all her fault. She couldn't help she wasn't easy to arouse. That's just the way she was, or so she'd thought until she'd awoken with Mike. It was as if being with him had flipped a switch, and all of a sudden, she spent 90 percent of her time thinking about having sex with Mike. The other 10 percent thinking about taking BOB out for a test drive because she was so desperate.

Mike took a deep breath and blew it out. Annabelle winced. He was pissed, and she couldn't blame him. She sure threw water on scorching coals with that stupid comment. Why was it she had no filter around him?

"I'm sorry. Don't be mad…"

Mike smiled, a pained smile, but still a smile. He had an amazing crooked smile.

"Belle, I'm not mad, honey, but I think we need to talk about this—"

She arched her back and pressed her hot body against his. He was still hard. "Can't we talk later?" She couldn't tell if the strangled sound he made was a yes, but she chose to take it that way. "Please?"

Something wet and cold pressed against her butt. She glanced over her shoulder and cringed when Dave's nose nudged her again.

"No, Dave!"

Dave jumped on the couch and sat next to them, his head as high as Mike's, and his doggy breath washed over them. Talk about three being a crowd.

Mike held her and stood. She clung to his neck, and once he cleared the couch, she wrapped her legs around his waist. Mike's walk toward the bedroom was the most pleasurable trip she'd ever taken. The friction made her catch her breath and arch her back. She never knew anything could feel that good. When they got into the bedroom, Mike kicked the door shut, but instead of heading toward the bed, he turned into the bathroom.

"What are you doing?"

He set her on the cold marble countertop and stayed between her legs as he opened the medicine cabinet. "Looking for condoms. I'm hoping Nick left some here from before he and Rosalie moved out."

"You really don't have any?"

He moved things around, searching from bottom to

top. "Do you honestly think I'd be searching the bathroom if I had condoms in my wallet?" He took out her birth control pills. "Are these yours?"

"Yeah." Note to self: now would be a good time to start taking them again.

"So you didn't practice safe sex?"

"With Johnny? Hell yeah, I did."

"But you were engaged to him."

"And I caught the jerk cheating on me."

Mike stopped what he was doing and turned the force of his attention to her. He placed one hand on her shoulder and slid it to the back of her neck and into her hair, tipping her head back. She couldn't avoid those eyes burning into hers. Mike's other hand wrapped around her waist and tugged her closer against him. "The man is a fool."

Annabelle swallowed hard. "It's for the best. Things were never good between us. He said I was frigid."

Mike laughed. "You're joking, right?"

"No, I'm not."

"You're serious?"

"It's not the kind of thing I'd brag about. I mean, it's not like I've had too much experience, but with my only two relationships, well, I never... things were nothing like this."

"Why would you want to marry a man you didn't want sexually?"

"At the risk of giving you a big head or coming off sounding, I don't know, stupid, fake, or like a total brownnoser... I never knew it could be like this. It's unnatural wanting you like I do."

She'd have had to be blind to miss the look of

disbelief that crossed his face. She felt like smacking him. So, she did.

Mike rubbed his arm. "Hey, I didn't say anything."

"You didn't have to. Look, no one is as shocked as I am at the way I respond to you. All this time, I thought there was something wrong with me. Even with my first boyfriend, I never liked it… I mean, I did it when I had to, but it's not like I enjoyed it. I thought all the sex in romance novels was fictional. Who knew?"

Annabelle, frigid? That wasn't a description Mike would ever use. Hot, beautiful, an active participant, sexy as hell. Yeah, like right now. He felt her heat, he smelled her excitement, and the way she stared at him with a pulsing hunger—her eyes dilated, her lips wet and swollen, her face flushed—was enough to have him breathing heavy. Frigid? Never with him.

She'd sure enjoyed it when they'd made love the first time—correction, the first three times. She'd been a little tipsy… okay, maybe she'd been drunk, but that hadn't diminished her amazing reaction to him. And, right now, she was doing a damn good impression of someone who liked sex a whole lot.

"You're the least frigid woman I've ever been with."

Well, he must have said the right thing, because she not only gave him a heart-melting smile, she started unbuttoning his shirt. An improvement over the other night when she'd pulled some of the buttons off, but it didn't excite him in the same way. He'd never had a woman rip his shirt off before, but then he'd never ripped a woman's dress off, either. Maybe she wasn't the only one who took things to a new, heretofore unexplored level.

The word "condom" repeated in Mike's head like a mantra while he ignored the way Annabelle's hands roamed over his chest. He sucked a lungful of air in when her fingers tripped over his ribs, and that same air shot out when they hit his stomach.

When she fumbled with his belt, he searched the drawers. There had to be a condom somewhere. He'd never made love without one. Ever. But looking at Annabelle licking her lips made him want to do anything but run to a drugstore. The woman had more creams and body butters than he'd ever known existed, but no condoms. When she tugged the elastic of his jockeys, he needed to take the search elsewhere. He kissed her, picked her up, hoping his jeans wouldn't slip down while he carried her to bed, and prayed there were condoms in the bedside table.

A man was actually carrying her to bed, and Annabelle wasn't dreading it. Wow, that was a shocker. She didn't know what to do. She'd always avoided this very situation, and when she'd been unsuccessful, spent all her time wishing it were over. This time, with Mike, she never wanted it to end—another new experience for her.

Mike laid her on the bed and followed her down. His belt buckle jabbed into her, so she scooted back and pushed his pants down while he was busy untying her robe. His eyes glazed over when he got a load of her little lace baby-doll nightie. Thank you, Victoria's Secret! She checked to make sure everything was still in the right places and saw why he stared. The deep V halter was doing its job on the cleavage front, and the rest, what little there was of it, was clingy, stretchy, and altogether naughty. Apparently Mike was a fan of naughty.

With jerky movements, Mike turned, grabbed the knob on the bedside table drawer, and pulled so hard the drawer and everything in it fell to the ground. As if in slow motion, BOB—the fluorescent purple, pearl-embedded, silicone penis—bounced once and landed on Mike's foot.

He burst out laughing, and Annabelle prayed she'd disappear. Unfortunately, her prayers were rarely answered. She covered her face, the heat radiating off it burning her hands.

"Oh thank God. Or in this case, thank Nick."

Annabelle peeked between her fingers and saw Mike holding an accordion-folded string of condom packets in one hand and BOB in his other. He thrust BOB toward her. "Friend of yours?"

"No."

Mike looked like the guy on *Dirty Jobs* when he found out he had to stick his hand in a septic tank or something equally gross. She half expected him to drop it. Annabelle hugged herself but couldn't look at him. Unfortunately, the only other thing to look at was BOB.

"I mean, yes, it's mine—" He smiled.

"Oh, good. I thought it was… never mind. I really don't want to go there."

"It was a gift. I never… I just didn't know what to do with it."

Mike gave her one of his you-gotta-be-kidding looks,

complete with raised eyebrow and cocky smirk. "You need instructions?"

"No. I meant I didn't know where to put it."

There it was again, the same smirk. She wanted to hit him again, only harder. Then she realized what she'd said and groaned before throwing herself down on the bed, rolling over, and burying her face in the pillows. Maybe he'd leave, and she could die of embarrassment in peace.

Instead of leaving, though, he sat beside her and gently pushed her hair off her back. "Belle, there's nothing to be embarrassed about." Mike ran his hand down from her neck, over her butt, to the back of her knees, and then slowly made the trip back up. Annabelle didn't know how to get out of the present situation, short of locking herself in the bathroom. She hadn't pulled that particular disappearing act since the day she'd come home with her first boyfriend and found that her cat, Saucy, had gotten into her new tampons and thought they made perfect cat toys. Plastic-wrapped tampons lined the living room. She'd been mortified then. Now was worse.

"Belle, look at me. Come on." He rolled her over like a rag doll. Not that she resisted, but she certainly didn't help. The pillow she held over her face began to smother her. Good thing Mike pried her hands off it and pushed it aside. When she opened her eyes, his were drinking her in. From what she could glean by the look on his face and the slashes of color on his cheekbones, Mike wasn't turned off by the fact she had a BOB—just the opposite.

She pushed herself onto her elbows, and Mike swallowed hard. His Adam's apple bobbed. He threw BOB down, freeing his hands, toed off his shoes, and quickly disposed of his socks. Annabelle tugged the shirt off his shoulders, and when he stood to step out of his pants, she started on his jockeys. He quickly took over, and before she could move to the center of the bed, he crawled over her with a look in his eyes she'd never seen on any other man. It could only be described as predatory. He was so big, and not only in the tall and broad sense of the word. He was big. So big and so hard, she wasn't sure he would fit. Sure, in the back of her mind she knew they'd already had sex, but she didn't remember much about it except the feeling of exquisite fullness, and of course, the memory of bliss she was pretty sure was caused by an orgasm, something she'd never before experienced.

Mike lay on his side next to her and pulled her toward him so they faced each other. He ran his hands through her hair, cupping the back of her head and drawing her toward him.

"Kiss me."

That she could do. And she did. She wasn't used to kissing men. Being kissed by them, sure, but kissing them—not so much. Was she supposed to close her eyes first? She decided no. She wanted to see as much of him as possible, so she kept her eyes wide open and touched her lips to his. He rolled her over on top of him. His hands drew her legs up to straddle him, his breath catching when his cock came into contact with her very damp panties. The way it pressed against her had her moaning, and when she moved, he moaned too. Mike grabbed her hips and raised his off the bed just as their tongues collided and something hot and heavy settled down low in her abdomen. She moved against him, sucking his tongue and feeling unleashed. Her chest pressed against his, her fingernails scratched his scalp, and all she could think of was the feeling of fullness she remembered. She wanted that now, and he hadn't even gotten her nightie off. His hand ran beneath her panties, over her butt, and continued down. When he drove his finger deep inside her, she heard a mewing and realized the sound had come from her. She opened her eyes to find him watching her.

"It's okay, just let go."

Let go? What did that mean? Then he raised his hips and inserted another finger. The friction increased when she moved. Annabelle ground against him, and then she swore she saw stars. She was on fire and melting at the same time. Every muscle in her body tensed, and then wave after wave of pleasure rolled through her, each more intense than the last. She could do nothing but hold on while he continued to move beneath her and within her. She couldn't think, she couldn't breathe, and when she screamed, she didn't even have it in her to be embarrassed.

Annabelle collapsed on Mike. The sound of his heartbeat thundering beneath her ear kept time with hers. She couldn't remember ever feeling so relaxed, her limbs were like jelly. In the back of her mind, she knew she should do something—move, say thank you, something—but she was incapable. When she finally came back to reality, she took stock. Mike hypnotically moved his fingers over her back, tracing the edge of her nightie where skin met lace. She lifted her heavy head and saw the smile on his face. She couldn't help but smile too.

"Welcome back."

"Thanks." Annabelle scooted up, stretched out like a cat in a patch of sun, and kissed him. She took her time exploring his lips, the sharpness of his teeth, the way his breathing changed when she challenged him for control, the feel of his heart hammering against her hand, and the way the muscles of his shoulders bunched when she held on.

Mike rolled them over and broke the kiss. He brushed the hair from her face and pushed himself onto his forearms. "You are so beautiful."

He kissed her neck and worked his way down the column of her throat. Oh, man, what he could do with his mouth. He continued kissing his way down her body, following the deep V of her nightie, and then took a detour to her nipples. She almost rolled her eyes. She couldn't stand the way Chip and Johnny had played with her nipples as if they were knobs on the radio and they couldn't find the right station or squeezed her breasts so hard it hurt. She'd started to mentally file her nails when Mike shocked the hell out of her. He drew her nipple into his mouth—lace and all. The heat of his mouth, the wetness of the lace, and the friction of his tongue mixed together. The combination had her moaning. She held his head to her chest and wasn't sure if she ever wanted it to end. It felt great, but then so would a lot of other things. Not that she wanted to rush him, but she wasn't sure how much more she could take. She had never thought so before, but maybe there could be too much of a good thing.

Mike moved on to the other side, the air from the overhead fan chilling the wet lace. He slid his fingernail lightly over the distended nipple, and she almost jumped out of her skin. Her breathing became ragged. Her hips rose with every pull of his mouth on her breast, and something hard and hot pressed against her panties— panties that should have disappeared a while ago.

She wanted to feel skin against skin. She wanted to feel Mike inside her. She wanted it now. Unfortunately, patience was not her strong suit. She reached under the pillow where she'd seen him put the condoms and tapped him on the shoulder with the sharp, crimped edge of the package.

He stopped what he was doing when she waved the string of condom packs in front of his face.

"What do you want me to do with those?"

"Gee, I don't know. I thought you could make those cute balloon animals. What do you think I want you to do with them?"

Mike smiled one of those smiles he must have perfected when he did his pediatrics rotation. "There's plenty of time later for balloon animals or whatever else you'd like to do with them. I'm just getting started here."

"Huh?"

Mike began pulling her panties off. Yeah, that was more like it. She ripped one of the condoms off and tossed the others in the direction of the bedside table. She tried to figure out where to rip it open when Mike shoved a pillow beneath her butt. Okay. She wasn't sure why, but who was she to question, since really, she was getting her own way, and she did love getting her own way. She ripped the condom packet open with her teeth when Mike lowered his head. Before she could even wonder why, she sucked in a lungful of air and almost inhaled a piece of the condom packet. She tried to pull away, but he held her hips firmly to him as his mouth did amazing things to her nether regions. Oh God. His head was between her legs, and his mouth was hot and wet, and then he started sucking. Annabelle grabbed a handful of hair. She didn't know whether to push him away or pull him closer.

Closer won out.

The condom slipped through her fingers, forgotten, when she found it necessary to hold on to the antique iron headboard. Delirious, Annabelle wasn't in control of her actions, reactions, or vocalizations.

For what seemed to be hours, he held her just this side of complete and utter satisfaction, and nothing, no amount of begging, moving, urging, or demanding, seemed to sway him. He had her teetering on a precipice. The border between pleasure and pain, hell and ecstasy, and when he finally pushed her over the edge, he rose over her as she came, screaming his name. He entered her in one thrust, and the fullness she remembered sent her into another level of pleasure she was sure would kill her. Panicked, she opened her eyes and connected with Mike. His body moved within hers, and his mouth took hers in a mind-searing kiss. She tasted herself on his lips, she tasted the heat they generated, she tasted the controlled passion Mike held in check, and she wanted it all. She wrapped her legs around his waist, her heels urging him on harder, faster, and when she nipped his shoulder, he gave her everything.

Mike had dreamed of making love to Annabelle since the second he'd finished making love to her the last time. He'd thought of all the ways he wanted her. He'd planned to have her going for an hour, to make her come a half-dozen times before he took his turn, but he'd never expected her to be soooo... active. Then, when she bit him, he lost it. He went at her like a rutting boar, and nothing he could do would stop it. The more he lost his hold, the more she responded, and when he finally stopped trying to hold back, she took off like a rocket and joined him. He'd never come so hard, so long, or so intensely. He collapsed and prayed he didn't crush her. He'd move as soon as he could. He needed to dispose of the condom and check if she was okay. The aftershocks of her orgasm were still zinging between their bodies, sending waves of excitement through him, and making his blood pound in what could only be explained as a miracle. He had never thought of himself as a one-shot wonder, but it hadn't even been five minutes, and he was hard again.

Mike held still, trying to get his mind on anything but the woman he was currently lying on, as her eyes opened and widened. A slow smile spread across her face, giving her the look of someone relaxed, slightly drowsy, and infinitely pleased with herself. That's when she giggled, and her giggling sent all sorts of shock waves shooting through him, and from the looks of it, through her too.

"Time-out." He would have held his hands to form a T, but he needed them to push himself off her. He rolled off the bed and wobbled to the bathroom to dispose of the condom. When he returned, he slid into bed and pulled her back to his front, spooning her.

"You okay?"

Annabelle scooted closer and sighed. "Mmmm, yeah, you?"

She sounded as if she was half asleep. Mike checked the clock and wished work could wait. "I should go. I have early rounds tomorrow."

"Stay."

One word and he was sunk. How could he say no to that? "As long as I can."

He held Annabelle, and in a few moments, he could tell from her breathing that she slept. He slipped out of bed and searched the floor for his pants. He checked his cell and pager, turned them both on, and then tossed them on the other bedside table. He picked up their clothes, folded her little nightgown, hung his clothes on the chair along with Annabelle's robe, and opened the bedroom door when he heard Dave sniffing around on the other side. Mike crawled back in bed beside Annabelle and curled up with her. Just as he was falling asleep, the bed behind him dipped and rocked as the big dog stretched out beside him. Mike slid closer to Annabelle and slept.

Chapter 5

MIKE ROLLED OVER IN THE DOCTOR'S LOUNGE AND almost fell off the Naugahyde couch he'd crashed on less than two hours before. Rubbing his tired eyes, he stretched. It had been five long days since that night he'd left Annabelle's bed when he was called to the hospital. She'd been half asleep, blinded by the light when he'd needed to find his socks, and all he could do was apologize and give her a peck good-bye before running out.

His shift ended in an hour, and he didn't have patients to see until after noon. He pulled his cell phone off his belt and dialed Annabelle. He'd be too tired by the time dinner rolled around, but lunch would be good. It would also be safe.

"Hello?"

Shit, he'd woken her up again. Great way to score points. "I'm sorry I called so early."

"Mike?"

"Yeah. I just got up myself. I caught a couple hours of shut-eye here at the hospital, and I thought I'd call before it got crazy again."

"Rough night?"

"Yeah. About as rough as they get." He thought about the patient he'd lost, and that feeling of failure, sadness, and pain crushed him again. Unfortunately, knowing he'd done everything possible didn't make him feel any better.

There was silence on the other side of the phone. "Annabelle?"

"Yes. I'm here. I'm sorry you had a bad night."

"Thanks. Um, I was thinking. I don't have to go to the office until two. Are you free for lunch?"

He sensed a hesitation, but then he heard a deep breath, almost as if she were about to jump off a cliff.

"Yes, lunch would be nice."

"Great, I'll pick you up at noon. What's the name of the gallery?"

"The Benjamin Walsh Gallery, but it's okay, I'll meet you."

"No, I don't mind. Besides, I'd love to see where you work."

Mike heard a page to ICU at the same time his beeper went off.

"I'm sorry, Annabelle. I have to run. I'm being paged." He grabbed his stethoscope. "Bye." He disconnected the call as he ran out the door.

Annabelle got off the subway and walked the half block to the Benjamin Walsh Gallery. She looked forward to getting back to work since taking a week off after the wedding. She took the time off since she had canceled her honeymoon and hadn't had a vacation in over a year.

No matter how depressed she felt, her mood always lifted when she walked through those plate-glass doors and took in the sheer brilliance of the kaleidoscope of color that surrounded her. She studied the collection and admired the talent that produced such thought-provoking, insightful, and arresting works. Whether they emoted pain or happiness, the beauty acted as a catharsis.

"Ah, there's my Annabelle. Right on time as usual."

Annabelle jumped at the sound of her boss's voice. "You're still here!" She ran up to Ben and gave him a big hug, holding him a little longer than necessary. God, it was good to have him back. She thought since she canceled her wedding, Ben would have already left.

"I had planned to stay while you were on your honeymoon, and no, don't put a frown on your beautiful face. You'll start looking like your aunt Rose." Ben lifted her chin with his pointer finger. "This isn't the only business I have on the right coast."

"As opposed to the wrong coast… or is it the left coast?"

"Contrary to popular belief, there is life west of the Hudson River. Besides, you know I can't stay away from you for long."

Annabelle smiled. "Tell me, do the women out west actually buy your bullshit?"

"Is that any way to talk to your boss?"

She thought about it for a nanosecond and nodded. "Yes, it works for me. Now answer the question."

"I'll have you know, women find me irresistible no matter what state, country, or even hemisphere I'm in."

"Sure, you're a regular legend in your own mind. And I don't suppose your irresistibility would have anything to do with the yachts, planes, and other toys you play with, would it, Ben?"

He put his hand over his heart and gave her his patented pained look. "Ah, you wound me."

Ben was the best-looking man she'd seen in, well, forever. He stood tall and lean. The kind of lean only world-class triathletes achieved—with a sense of style only the well-moneyed could pull off. He had a dry wit that the richest, most famous, and most beautiful people sought.

"I thought you'd be off to Italy with that Russian model to sail the Mediterranean."

"That's not until July. And as for the Russian, she might be losing her shine." He wrapped his arm around her and drew her farther into her gallery. The gallery was his, but Annabelle had made it one of the top galleries on the West Side. It was her vision. Her assistants handled the bookwork. Lord knew she was no good with numbers or correspondence. But Annabelle did what she did best—she displayed the art, schmoozed the clientele and artists, and kept the place looking like a million bucks. When she discovered artists she thought would fit in the Walsh Gallery family, she contacted Ben and sold him on their work. She succeeded more often than not.

"Come with me, little girl. I have a surprise for you."

"Aw Ben, you're not going to try pulling that trick again, are you? I used to paint nudes. Nothing on your body would surprise me." She put her hand in front of her mouth to cover an exaggerated yawn.

He crossed his arms, his feet shoulder-width apart. If it weren't for the sparkle in his stunning blue eyes, she'd wonder if she'd gone too far with her teasing. But no, he was enjoying himself.

"I've heard all about those nudes you used to paint, but I've yet to see one."

She shrugged. "They're in storage."

He cocked his head. "For two years? Maybe now that you have your own place, I'll get to see them. I've always wondered what kind of artist you were before you packed away your brushes."

"I'm not an artist."

"That's not what your professors at the Art Institute said. A couple of them asked if I wanted your work for the gallery."

"You never said you checked my references."

"I check everyone's references. You don't think I'd allow just anyone to run my gallery, do you?"

"Look, Ben, I'm good at what I do. I love my job. That other part of my life—it's over. I'm not an artist. Not anymore."

"One doesn't stop being an artist. Either you are, or you're not."

"Then I'm not. Can we drop it? I have work to do."

"I guess you don't want your present then?"

"What's the present for? No, don't tell me. Let me guess. It started out as a wedding gift, but now it's a disengagement present."

He shrugged and rolled up his sleeves.

"Okay, fine. Where's my disengagement present? Will it match my disengagement ring?"

Ben took her hand and pulled her into the elevator that led to his apartment above the gallery. When the elevator stopped, he dragged her along behind him, not to his apartment, but to the space where they'd always stored the seasonal items like Christmas and Hanukkah decorations. He opened the door and turned, blocking her view. "Now close your eyes."

"I don't trust you. What are you up to?"

"Fine, be difficult. I can handle it. I'm bigger than you." He spun her around, put both hands over her eyes, and then walked her into the room. "Are you ready?"

Annabelle pried his hands from her eyes and blinked a few times. She couldn't believe it. Incredible. He'd turned the old storage room into a fully stocked art studio. She'd have given her firstborn to have a space like this available to her when she was painting. She stood before the easel where a large naked canvas silently screamed for paint and touched the brushes neatly arranged on the taboret to its right. Boxes of oil paints, pastels, watercolors, and acrylics filled the low bookshelves beneath the large windows that lined the north wall. She looked at the once-leaky skylights, noting that they'd been replaced. She was stunned speechless.

"All the lighting is full spectrum, so you can paint whenever you want. If it gets too late, you can always crash at my place. You have the keys and know where everything is. I'm hardly ever in town."

"You did this for me? Why?"

He looked like a cat that had brought a dead mouse to the door—he wondered why she wasn't jumping for joy. "Do you like it?"

"I told you. I don't paint anymore. You've wasted your money." Maybe she could rent it out to a struggling artist. Then she saw the disappointment on his face. Christ. She gentled her tone. "Why did you do this?"

"You're my best friend…"

"Ha, I'm the only woman you know under the age of thirty-five you haven't seen naked. And since we discussed the difference between friends and bed buddies, I know I'm your only female friend."

"You're an artist. It shows in everything you do—how you dress, how you look at life, how you choose and display the art in my gallery. I don't pretend to know what happened that made you give up your passion, but it's my job, as someone who would give his left arm to have half the talent I see in you, to make you realize you're wasting a precious, God-given gift. It's a sin. And it's time you stop hiding from whatever it was that made you walk away from the one thing I know you love."

Annabelle crossed her arms. "I didn't walk away. I'm here, surrounded by art, and I'm doing what I should be doing—helping other artists achieve their dreams. I discover beauty. I'm happy with that."

"You can't tell me that discovering beauty beats creating it."

"I don't want to talk about it."

"Fine." He threw up his hands. "Do what you want. But this is your new office. I'll have the rest of your things moved today. I've already had the place wired for the computer network and phone systems. You're going to do all your work surrounded by blank canvases and art supplies. Maybe you'll come to your senses and do something for yourself. You don't have to show anyone. Maybe by painting again, that part of you that you said died will come back to life. It's worth a try. Because you're not living the life you should."

"No." She stomped her foot. "I'm not living the life you think I should. Welcome to the club. My family doesn't think I'm living the life I should either."

"Hold on now. I won't be put in the same club with those people who thought you should marry that bottom dweller. That's an insult."

"Fine, you're not as bad, but our friendship doesn't give you the right to order me around. I know you have the best intentions, but Ben, I can't."

"You won't know until you try. That's all I'm asking of you. Just try." He checked his watch, threw his keys up in the air, and neatly caught them before slipping them in his pants pocket. "I have someplace to be, and you"—he turned her around, and with his hands on her shoulders, walked her out the door to the elevator—"have work to do. The keys to this room are on your desk. You'd better get them before the movers come. I'll be back in an hour."

Annabelle turned and pouted. "You're not serious about moving my office, are you? I can't be that far from the sales floor."

"I am serious. This area has more space for you to look at artist's portfolios, slides, or what have you, and it has so much more planning space. Look at all the dry erase boards I put up in here for you."

Annabelle chewed on her thumbnail. She didn't like the idea of being so far away, but her old office would still be where it was, and there was nothing saying she couldn't use it too. "Fine."

"I hope you know I wasn't asking your permission. Contrary to popular belief, this is still my art gallery, and I am still your boss."

She walked into the elevator, turned to face Ben, pushed the Down button, and rolled her eyes. "Yeah, yeah, yeah... whatever."

The door closed on Ben's too-good-looking face. God it felt good to get the last word.

Mike rounded the corner and saw the Benjamin Walsh Gallery up ahead. Talk about spendy real estate. He checked his watch. He was a little early, so he slowed his pace and turned his face to the sun. He wished he could sneak off to Nick's beach house for a while with Annabelle. Recharge his batteries and spend some uninterrupted time getting to know her. No beepers. No phones. No brothers. No clothes… other than a bathing suit, and where Nick's place was, even that was optional—at least on the deck. The last time he'd had two days off in a row, he'd borrowed one of Nick's cars, drove out to the house on Westhampton Beach, and did nothing but sleep on the sand for forty-eight hours straight before showering and running back to the hospital. Too bad he hadn't known Annabelle then. He would have done a whole lot more than sleep.

A picture of her lying on the sand popped into his head.

Annabelle was beautiful, intelligent, sexy, fun—and in the arms of another man.

Mike stared into the Benjamin Walsh Gallery and watched a man who looked like the Marlboro Man. No, he was more like the Sundance type. The man reeked of money, even though he looked as if he'd be at home in the saddle, on the range, or having sex in the great outdoors—and not the *Brokeback Mountain* variety either. The man even wore cowboy boots and literally carried Annabelle.

Mike's first instinct was to walk away. He was mad as hell, and if he didn't know better, he'd say he was jealous. Not that he had any right to be, but the thought that some guy had his hands on Annabelle had him seething. Maybe in the five days they'd been apart, she'd moved on to greener pastures with ol' Quigley minus the mustache.

Oops, too late. She spotted him, and the guilt written all over her face didn't bode well. He hoped there was a reasonable explanation. Not that she owed him one, but shit, when a man goes to meet a lunch date, was it too much to expect that he be the only guy picking her up, literally and figuratively?

Tex finally put her down but still held her close to his side and looked smug. Mike had never felt the need to wipe a smirk off the face of a competitor with his fist, but he did now.

No way could he avoid this meeting without looking as if he was running away, so he took a deep breath and opened the door to the gallery.

"Mike, hi." Annabelle smacked the man next to her. "Ben, would you let me go already?"

Ben, as in Benjamin Walsh Gallery? Not that it mattered.

The man chuckled. "Annabelle, darlin', I'd let you go, but I don't think you can stand on your own."

Annabelle hopped on her right foot toward Mike, which, he had to admit was one of the most interesting shows he'd seen since the one where she wore nothing but a blue garter.

"It's not what it looks like."

Ben laughed again. "It's exactly what it looks like.

You missed a step on the ladder. You fell. I caught you. Now, are you all right?"

"Annabelle." Mike shoved his shoulder under her left arm, taking her weight. He tried to find a place for her to sit. Ben was paying very close attention to Annabelle, and Mike didn't like it one bit. He wanted to get her away from Ben—as far away as possible. "Where's there someplace for her to lie down?"

She blew her hair away from her face. "I can speak, you know. I'll be fine in just a minute."

"You need to lie down so I can check you out."

Ben nodded and tossed his keys to Mike. "There's a couch in her new office upstairs, and there's ice in my apartment, which is upstairs as well. The elevator's in back. Help yourself."

When she went to hop away, Mike grabbed her up in his arms and carried her. She didn't seem any happier to be carried by him than she was when Ben had her.

Annabelle felt like a hot potato the way she was passed from one man to the other. "Would you please let me down?" She tried to push away from Mike.

"Be still. You might have broken something."

"Look, Doc, I'm gonna break something all right if you don't put me down right this minute."

"That's not what you said the other night."

She let out a frustrated breath. Sure, he'd carried her the other night, but just a few yards. This was different. Every step he took shot pain through her ankle. It was all she could do not to cry.

Ben followed and pressed the elevator button for

them. She shot him her best death-ray glare, wishing she had supernatural powers. The doors swooshed open, and without a word, Mike carried her in and turned. Ben, the jerk, instead of melting like the Wicked Warlock of the West that he was, had the nerve to press the button for the second floor and give Mike the nod. She really wished she had the CliffsNotes to *Alpha-Male Communication for Dummies*. She growled.

"You know, you're really cute when you're mad. That's good because it's probably better for you to concentrate on anger than pain. You're going to have one hell of a bruise."

She cursed under her breath. The whole side of her leg had begun to turn colors and was beginning to match the tie-dyed dress she wore—yellow with splashes of crimson, purple, and green. When she saw the plain silk dress and pictured how great it would look after she painted or tie-dyed it, she had no idea she'd end up making an entirely new fashion statement. Her ankle, which had taken the brunt of the damage, was already swelling. It was her own fault. She had no business climbing a ladder in high heels and a tight dress. Okay, scratch that, it was Ben's fault for coming to hold the ladder when she suspected he only wanted to look up her dress. She was so busy making sure he didn't get an eyeful, she hadn't paid much attention to her footing, or lack thereof.

The thin silk did nothing to protect her from the heat of Mike's body and hands. The square neckline when viewed at a normal level wasn't at all revealing. She suspected it changed when viewed from Mike's position; he was able to see right down the front. The dress was short, not indecently short, but with him holding her, she just hoped half her ass wasn't hanging out. The elevator doors swooshed open, and she directed Mike to her new and hated office. He unlocked it without putting her down and, ever so carefully, got her through the doorway and onto the leather couch. He sat beside her, removed her shoe, and did a great impression of an orthopedist.

"I thought you were a lung doctor. What are you doing?"

"Trying to see if you've broken anything. I specialize in lungs, but I did study the whole body, you know. I even did a rotation in orthopedics during my internship, and believe me, I've spent enough time in the ER to know when an ankle needs an X ray."

Annabelle crossed her arms and tried not to flinch every time he touched her. He dangled Ben's keys in front of her face.

"Any idea which one is the key to his apartment?"

"Why?"

"You need an ice pack and a trip to the hospital. I'll get the ice, and then we'll go to the hospital for a picture of that ankle. I don't think it's broken. It's probably a bad sprain, and I'm concerned about possible torn ligaments and tendons. I don't want to take any chances."

"No."

"No? What do you mean, no?"

"I don't do hospitals."

"Annabelle, you can't be serious."

"Oh yeah, I am."

Mike studied her for a long moment. It seemed as

if he was about to argue, then simply shook his head, pulled his cell phone from his belt, and made a call. The whole time, his other hand never left her foot.

"Hi, this is Dr. Mike Flynn. Is Dr. Doyle available?" There was a pause. "Thanks, I'll call his cell. Yes, I have the number."

He gave her an assessing look and made another call. "Dick, it's Mike Flynn. Good, you? A huh. Well, that's why I'm calling. Is it okay if I borrow your X-ray machine for a few shots? Yes, I think it's a sprained ankle, but I want to be sure. The patient has an aversion to hospitals." Mike checked the time. "About ten minutes. Where are you? Oh. Great. We'll see you there. Thanks."

Mike disconnected the call. "I assume you're okay with an urgent care center?"

Mike knew Annabelle was anything but okay with urgent care centers. She had her arms crossed, her lithe body lying so rigid, he'd seen corpses in rigor mortis that were more flexible. It didn't help that the look on her face told him they wouldn't be playing doctor any time soon. If ever again.

Of all the luck. Most women prayed for a doctor to date. He wasn't sure why, because these days, with malpractice insurance costs and student loans, being a doctor didn't have nearly the cachet or cash it once had. He figured he wouldn't be in the black until sometime in the next century. Leave it to him to find the only woman who'd figured that out.

Either that or she was afraid of doctors and hospitals,

which again, didn't bode well. Mike wondered if it ran in the family. Her sister, Rosalie, hated anything having to do with doctors and hospitals. Rosalie was one of his favorite patients, but that didn't keep her from cursing him in four languages while he examined her. So far, other than the whole fear of doctors and hospitals thing, he hadn't seen much resemblance between the two sisters, except for maybe the curly black hair and the shape of their faces.

Annabelle was guarded, which intrigued him. Mike had always had a love of puzzles, and Annabelle was the human equivalent. Rosalie was an in-your-face kind of person. Subtle she was not—which made her perfect for Nick.

"Hello. Earth to Mike. Are you going to stare at my ankle all day, or are you going to get me some ice?"

Well, okay, maybe Annabelle had some of the in-your-face trait too. He couldn't help but smile. "You've got beautiful legs, and I've got a real nice view here."

She pushed down the short skirt of her dress and scowled. "I thought you said I needed ice."

"You do. I'll get it and be right back."

Mike leaned forward and kissed her, just a quick one. It had been a long time since he'd kissed her last Sunday night, or was it Monday morning? He hadn't counted on her wrapping her arms around his neck and kissing him back. Neither had he counted on her practically pulling him down on top of her, nor the way they fit so well together on the soft leather couch. He'd forgotten how great she smelled, how great she tasted, and how great she felt.

Sunday night had seemed like a dream. Never before

had he clicked with someone so immediately. Usually in a relationship, even ones as short as his, there was a learning period. It took time to find out what a woman wanted in bed—her likes and dislikes. With Annabelle, it wasn't that way. It was as if they had some kind of mental communication. He knew what she wanted, and oh man, right now what she wanted wouldn't be very good for her ankle, or for Mike's relationship with Dickey Doyle, who had cut his lunch short to meet them. Christ, never before had Mike's sense of responsibility been so difficult to heed, and the woman currently wrapped around him knew it.

A light bulb flickered in his mind, which surprised him, considering he wasn't thinking of much other than Annabelle, her body, the sexy sounds she made when he kissed her neck, and how very nice it was that the straps of her dress slid down enough to reveal the top of her lacy bra. Damn it, of all times for his brain to be firing on all cylinders. He pulled away and focused on her eyes, which were dark and unfocused. Double damn.

"You want to get out of having your ankle x-rayed."

Annabelle pulled her elbows behind her, pushing her chest toward him and causing his dick to jump. Damn, damn, damn. Sometimes it sucked being him.

"I can't believe you think I'd make out with you just to get out of an X ray."

Mike pushed the strand of hair that had fallen over her left eye behind her ear. He had no problem imagining how much she'd gotten away with as a kid with her innocent look and petulant tone. "I'm not insinuating it's the only reason you kissed me, just an added benefit."

He couldn't fight the smile pulling at his lips. Her eyes no longer met his. She suddenly found her lap very interesting. She was cute when she was totally busted.

"You're wrong. Kissing you had absolutely nothing to do with my ankle."

Mike laughed. "Do you have any idea what a terrible liar you are?"

Annabelle slumped back on the sofa and crossed her arms. "Yes. You're not the first to mention it—"

"But it doesn't usually matter, does it? All you have to do is pout those beautiful lips, and guys let you get away with it. Don't they?"

She seemed hopeful when she grabbed his tie and pulled him back down to her. "Yeah."

He was sure this would kill him, but he took his Hippocratic Oath seriously. It was the first, do no harm part he couldn't get around. The other parts were easier to ignore, since Annabelle wasn't his patient, and never would be. He couldn't have his girlfriend as his patient, now could he? But he couldn't convince himself that her ankle wouldn't be any worse for wear if they made love. No, unfortunately even in his highly aroused state, that wouldn't fly.

"Too bad it's not working now. Believe me, no one is more sorry about that than I am. Matter of fact, I'm not so sure it won't kill me. Now, you need to let me go so I can get an ice pack or two."

"Why would we need two? I only hurt one ankle."

Mike stood and pointed at his crotch.

"Oh." Then Annabelle smiled, way too pleased with herself in Mike's estimation. "Sorry about that."

He couldn't help but laugh. "You really are a pathetic liar."

She shrugged. "I know. But it wouldn't be kind of me to admit that it's nice to know I'm not the only one who's horny and in pain."

Mike turned toward the door. "I've been horny and in pain since the moment I met you." He couldn't see it, but he knew she had a diabolical smile on her face. Yeah, misery loves company.

Annabelle lay in bed, her ankle propped up on a pillow, an ice bag covering it, and with strict instructions to keep it elevated. Didn't Mike understand her life was on her feet? She couldn't stand to stay in bed, and she wasn't much for TV. She'd been tucked in for all of a half hour, and she was already going nuts. So, okay, she was always a tiny bit hyper. That's why she ran on top of running around the gallery all day. Chip used to say the only time she stayed still was when she was in front of her canvases.

There were times when she painted that whole days passed like the blink of an eye. She'd get engrossed in a painting, and she'd forget to eat. Thankfully, Becca and Chip kept her water bottle filled so at least she stayed hydrated. She'd have her music on, and she'd get in a zone, not unlike when she ran. Now she couldn't run—not for at least six weeks. Annabelle wasn't sure what she'd do.

She sprained her ankle. Well, okay, it was more than just the average sprain. She looked at the sheet Dr. Dolittle had given her to try to remember the tendons she tore, the superior and interior peroneals. Who named these things anyway? She was still amazed it wasn't broken because of the amount of pain she'd felt when she'd injured it. Mike had wanted her to go to a specialist and get an MRI, but when push came to shove, he reluctantly agreed to let her hobble around with her foot in a really ugly bootlike thing and crutches. For a guy who made a big show of claiming not to be her doctor, he'd have a hard time proving it. He was the one who insisted on positioning her foot for the X rays, he was the one who read the X rays, and he was the one always telling her what to do. Yup, Mike did a great impression of someone who was her doctor.

Dr. Dolittle just stood aside and smiled. He seemed nice enough, and he was obviously smart—he stayed out of Mike's way. All he did was write a prescription for painkillers and fail to sufficiently stifle his laugh every time Annabelle argued. Which was the whole time she was in that blasted place. It would have been a whole lot easier to win the argument if Dr. Dolittle would have left the room. She couldn't take Mike's mind off her foot with Dickey Dolittle watching.

Then before she knew it, Mike had her foot in a boot and the two of them, along with a pair of crutches, stuffed in a cab on the way to Brooklyn. When they got to her place, he insisted on carrying her in, bothering Wayne and Henry and enlisting their help to take care of her until he returned after office hours.

Annabelle picked up the phone and dialed Becca's number.

"Annabelle? What's wrong? Why aren't you at work? Are you playing hooky with Dr. Feelgood?"

"No."

"Okay. Are you so horny you can't work?"

"I fell off a ladder, sprained my ankle, and tore a few tendons."

When Annabelle told Becca the story, you'd have thought she was a regular at the Laugh Factory. Okay, it was funny. Especially the way Mike had looked when he saw Ben carrying her. She'd been afraid he'd behave like all the other guys she knew. They'd get jealous and go off half-cocked. He got jealous all right, which she had to admit felt pretty good. But he was man enough to assess the situation and listen to reason before reacting. That made her like him even more than she already did.

"Okay, so all we know about him for sure is that he's not a hothead. He's patient—especially considering what your brother did to your seduction plans. He's helpful in the kitchen—which is a good thing since you've already cooked one of the three meals you know how to make without poisoning someone."

"I didn't poison you. Maybe it was an allergic reaction."

"Annabelle—let's not go there, okay?"

"Fine, but I'm not that bad in the kitchen."

"Back to Dr. Flynn—he must have some kind of power over you to get your butt into a hospital."

"He didn't. He took me to an urgent care center instead. He was okay with me refusing to go to a hospital."

"Well, you'd better figure out how to get over your irrational fear of hospitals. You know the hospital had nothing to do with Chip's death, right?"

"Becca. Please. I don't want to talk about that."

"Too bad, tootsie pop. You'd better figure out how to deal with Chip's death, and you'd better do it sooner rather than later. You're going to screw up this relationship because you haven't buried Chip, and you know I don't mean that literally. Besides, you're dating a doctor. You can't be afraid of hospitals when you're dating a guy who practically lives in one."

"We're not dating…"

"Reality check here. You invited him for dinner, and he came over and brought wine and flowers. He didn't so much as say boo when your seduction dinner got interrupted by your not-so-darling brother—"

"Yeah, but—"

"Then he came back later that night because he just had to see you and then picked you up, carried you to the bedroom, and rocked your world."

"Bec—"

"Hold on, I'm not finished. You gotta admit he scored major points when he didn't wig out about BOB, the bouncing vibrator incident."

"Ah, you had to remind me of that?"

"Yes, and after all that, he asked you out to lunch. A lunch that he gave up to drag you to a doctor. Then he carried you home and got the Fairy Godfathers to watch over you. Sounds like you're dating to me."

"I didn't want to date. I wanted to have sex."

"The two usually go hand in hand. Sorry, Annabelle. It looks like you've got yourself a boyfriend."

"Bad day, Dr. Flynn?"

Mike looked up from the workstation where he'd been dictating notes into patients' charts and saw Millie, his favorite nurse. She was a no-nonsense nurse—there were no histrionics, no temper tantrums, she was kind to the patients, and she always went the extra mile for him, his patients, and from what he could see, everyone else. She also made the absolute best peanut butter cookies Mike had ever tasted. Millie began making them especially for him after she caught him eating more than his share of the cookies she'd brought in for the office. She said he reminded her of her son who was about his age. According to Millie, they were both too skinny.

"Yeah, my girlfriend sprained her ankle and tore the interior and superior peroneal tendons, which made our lunch date… interesting."

"How many lunches have you eaten in the ER?"

"Too many, but she wouldn't go to the ER. I had to take her to an urgent care center. I think she's afraid of hospitals." He couldn't help but wonder if by forcing her to seek medical care, he'd put the last nail in the coffin that was their relationship. He sure hoped not. Lately, she was the only thing in his life that seemed to be going well.

Millie laughed. "Sounds like a match made in heaven."

He shrugged. "Don't rub it in." The office was deserted. "Did Dr. Meyer leave? I didn't see him dictate his notes."

"His last patient was at four, and you know him, he can't wait to get out of here. I jotted some notes in the files with the patients I saw. I'm not sure if his other nurse did the same."

Mike bit his tongue to keep from cursing. He hated working with Dr. Meyer. The old man was a malpractice suit waiting to happen. Dr. Meyer's age wasn't what he had a problem with. What was unacceptable was the fact that the man was a bumbling fool.

Mike suspected she shared his opinion. Millie had

already brought more than one of Dr. Meyer's mistakes to his attention. Luckily, she'd done it before following his orders. Sure, a few of them could be explained away by claiming different treatment methods—methods that didn't take into account the advances made in the medical profession over the last twenty years. Medicine had come a long way since the Dark Ages. Unfortunately, Dr. Meyer missed most of it.

Millie took off her stethoscope. "How did your talk with the partners about Dr. Meyer go?"

"You know about that?"

Millie nodded. "Are you kidding? Tabitha had her stethoscope to the door and took shorthand at the same time. But she didn't feel it necessary to share the information."

"It didn't go well. The partners circled their wagons as soon as I mentioned him. They made it abundantly clear I'm still an outsider."

Millie put her stethoscope in her locker. "You might be an outsider, but you're the bravest one here. No one else had the guts to say anything. All the other doctors are checking up on him, but when it comes down to it, someone's going to miss something, and a patient is going to suffer because of it."

"Yeah, I'm going to have to do something, and it might just get my ass fired. I'm not a partner, and the way it's looking, I never will be."

"That's not fair. You've put in so much time, and I don't know how much they're paying you, but I've been working here for eight years and know enough about them to know it can't be much."

He was buying his way into the practice with what

they called an investment in the six-figure range and less than 50 percent salary for five years. Two of which he'd already served. He would not make partner until he'd put in his five years at slave wages. And, even after his investment of time and cash, all the partners would have to vote him into the partnership. Right now, that was starting to look like a long shot. Even if Dr. Meyer retired and the problem went away, a few of the partners still wouldn't be happy giving Mike a seat at the grown-ups' table.

"No, it's not. And I figure when it comes down to it, I'm not interested in partnering up with a doctor I wouldn't trust to care for my patients, or any doctor who would put his patients in the hands of a doctor like Meyer. Since I have no say about what goes on in the practice and won't until they make me a partner, I'm nothing but a peon. A peon who's causing problems."

Millie got her pocketbook out and put on a sweater. "As much as I hate to admit it, you might be better off somewhere else, Dr. Flynn."

"Yeah, I agree. I wish I knew how to do what's right without flushing my entire career down the toilet. I can live with the fact I've lost a ton of money, but I'm not sure I can live with a death on my conscience because I protected my career."

Mike threw on his suit jacket and grabbed his messenger bag as he followed Millie, who turned off all the lights as they left. They locked up the office and walked to the subway.

He should go home and get some sleep, but he'd never get to sleep unless he made sure Annabelle was all right. The rational part of his brain told him she was fine. After all, it was only a bad sprain and a few torn tendons he knew would heal if she followed instructions to stay off it. It was nothing life threatening. But the other part of him had really hated leaving her alone that afternoon. It didn't help he'd been tempted to call her a hundred times since he walked out of her bedroom. Sure, he'd told her she could page him if she needed him. But Annabelle had made it clear she didn't need anyone. Especially him.

Chapter 6

ON THE WAY TO ANNABELLE'S, MIKE STOPPED AT AN art supply store and bought a sketch pad and a package of artists' pencils that the store clerk had recommended.

All her art supplies must be in her office since he hadn't seen any at her apartment. Heck, he never even knew she was an artist, though it made sense. She had an avant-garde style, the way she dressed, the shoes she wore, and her jewelry looked handcrafted. Even the way she decorated the apartment. He could tell Rosalie and Nick were no longer the residents.

Carrying his purchases, he made his way to the cash register thinking about his bank balance. Artist's supplies were expensive, but he couldn't leave her with nothing to do.

When Mike got off the train, he bought a box of condoms at the corner market. He wasn't planning to make love to Annabelle; after all, she'd just sprained her ankle. But all the times they'd made love hadn't been planned either. The supply of condoms he'd found in the bedside table drawer had to be waning. He checked out the produce and hoped she had something at her place to cook. He'd missed lunch, and his stomach wasn't too happy about it.

Mike let himself into her apartment, and Dave met him at the door. "Hi, big guy."

Dave jumped on him as if to give him a man-hug or to slobber on his shoulder—both of which Dave accomplished. The dog went right to his bed and picked up the jockeys he'd stolen the first night Mike had slept there. He considered trying to get them away from Dave again, but he didn't want to waste time playing tug-of-war with the dog when he could be spending it with Annabelle.

He looked around the apartment, and color seemed to be everywhere—a bright, handwoven blanket draped on the sofa, the brightly colored silk robe, and several unsigned oil paintings, all different colors, styles, and sizes, leaning against the wall, waiting to be hung. He made a mental note to find a hammer and picture hangers and hang the paintings. The carpet needed vacuuming, too, and the pictures on the floor would make that difficult. With Annabelle's ankle, he certainly didn't want her vacuuming. Besides, he'd always enjoyed cleaning, and he'd heard about the vacuum cleaner Nick had left and wanted to check it out for himself.

He tapped on the doorframe. "Can I come in?" Annabelle lay in bed wearing a pink tank top and matching boxers with her ice-bag–covered ankle propped up on a pillow. The tension of the bad day Mike carried melted on her smile.

"Oh, Mike. Thank God, it's you. As much as I love the Fairy Godfathers, I don't think I can take any more futzing."

He made his way to the bed. Had she posed intention-ally to look like a Victoria's Secret model, or did she always look ready for a photo shoot whenever she wore little pajamas or nightgowns? So far, he'd seen cute and sexy—they both drove him crazy.

"They've been great. But Wayne hovers, wringing his hands and suggesting shopping trips, and Henry is always trying to ply me with sweets. I don't eat sweets."

"You don't?" Mike lifted the ice bag off her ankle. It was almost as colorful as the paintings he'd seen at the gallery. The swelling wasn't too bad and didn't seem to be getting any worse.

"No, I'll eat the occasional cookie, but not cakes, doughnuts, or pastries. Not my thing, and I didn't want to be rude…"

"So you ate them." Mike replaced the ice bag and sat beside her. His hand had a mind of its own. He touched the bare skin of her shoulder and followed it down until it rested comfortably on her waist.

She nodded and took his other hand in hers. "Now I feel a little sick. I guess that's why I don't eat sweets."

"Did you eat lunch?"

"No, did you?"

"Annabelle." He squeezed her hand before letting go. "We're talking about you here, besides you're taking pain pills on an empty stomach, which could be why you're nauseous."

She rolled her eyes. "Look, I'm trying to change the subject."

"And I'm changing it back. You need something to eat that's not loaded with sugar and fat."

"Fine. I'll call for Chinese. They deliver."

"No, you won't. I'll throw together some minestra. They had some great produce at the corner market."

"Minestra as in soup?"

Mike rolled his eyes. "Of course soup. I worked my way through school at DiNicola's. I've eaten more minestra than most people in Italy. It was one of the first things Vinny taught me to cook."

"You cook?"

"Just about anything on Vinny's menu in the last ten years. Then there are the recipes I made up."

"That explains why you're so good in the kitchen."

He leaned over so they were nose to nose. "I'm good just about everywhere." The way her blue eyes widened and then darkened before he'd even reached her mouth made him wish for the thousandth time that she hadn't fallen off the damn ladder. He gave her a peck and rose from the bed. The frown that flashed across her face sent his ego on a joy ride.

He was about to leave for the market when he realized he'd forgotten to give her the sketch pad and pencils. "I picked up a few things to keep you occupied."

"You didn't have to do that."

No, he didn't, but it was worth the cost of admission to watch her bounce around on the bed like an excited kid on Christmas morning.

"It's just a sketch pad and some pencils. I didn't think you'd brought any of your art supplies home with you. I had the sales girl sharpen the pencils just in case you didn't have a sharpener here, either. If you want me to run over to the gallery and get anything else, let me know."

"That's so sweet."

But she didn't look happy, and she made no move to investigate the contents of the bag. As a matter of fact, she eyed it as if she expected a snake to slither out.

"Well, I'll run to the market and pick up whatever I need. Do you want anything special?"

"No thanks. Um… look, let me give you some money—"

Mike shook his head. "I've got it covered."

She started to protest, but he cut her off with a look. It didn't stop her from mumbling a curse in Italian.

Twenty minutes later Mike returned from the market with three bags of groceries and peeked in on Annabelle. She was sound asleep with the sketch pad still in its wrapper and the pencils still in their box beside her on the bed.

Dave jumped onto the bed and nudged the book out of the way before he laid his head on her lap.

Annabelle awoke to hammering and the scent of garlic, onions, and tomato; for a second she thought she was back at her parents' home in her old bedroom. Her stomach growled.

By the time she put on the stabilization boot, got her crutches, and hobbled to the hallway, Mike was dishing out soup thick with pasta and sprinkling what looked like homemade croutons and Parmesan cheese over the top of each bowl.

"There's Sleeping Beauty. I was about to wake you."

Well, Sleeping Beauty didn't feel so beautiful. Hungover and groggy was more like it. She moved slowly through her apartment's obstacle course to the bar separating the kitchen from the dining area. Adding Dave to the mix made it twice as challenging. She leaned the crutches against the bar before sliding onto the barstool. Her kitchen was sparkling, the toaster had been put away, and the breakfast dishes she'd left in the sink that morning were on the dish drain drying. Mike had hung all the paintings she'd placed around the apartment, which explained the hammering, and the entire place looked as if it had been cleaned and vacuumed. Mike must have done that, too. She didn't know whether to be pleased or offended, so she settled on pleased. She was no Suzie Homemaker and never would be if she had any say about it.

"You cleaned?"

Mike put a bowl of soup down and began garnishing the second. "I just hung the paintings and gave the place a quick vacuum. I know you're not in any shape to, and the dog hair builds up so fast. I hope you don't mind."

"Mind? Why would I mind? Thanks for all your help. Whatever you cooked smells amazing."

"There's chicken in the oven, and I threw together a salad."

"Wow. How long have I been asleep?"

Mike set the soup bowls on the table and pulled her chair out. "I went to the market an hour and a half ago, and when I checked on you after I returned, you were zonked."

"Yeah, I took a pain pill. After that, I couldn't keep my eyes open."

She scooted off the barstool and tried to grab the crutches, which slid along the bar and crashed to the floor. Hopping on one foot toward the crutches, she bent to retrieve them when Mike's hand wrapped around her arm and stopped her.

"Whoa, I'll get those. The last thing we need is you falling again."

She blew her hair out of her eyes. "Hey, I'm not a complete klutz you know. I only fell off the ladder because I wasn't wearing the right shoes, and I was trying to keep Ben from looking up my dress."

Mike's grip on her arm tightened. "Ben looked up your dress?"

She was tempted to roll her eyes. "I don't know. But he held the ladder, and I didn't want to give him the opportunity."

"Oh, okay."

She did roll her eyes then. "So glad you approve. Now I can sleep nights." She couldn't believe that came out of her mouth—it had to be the drugs. "I'm sorry. I shouldn't have said that. It was rude."

Mike placed the crutches against the wall and wrapped his arm around her waist. Serving as her human crutch, he helped her into the chair.

"No, you're right. I was out of line. Believe me, I don't know where that came from. I'm not the jealous type. At least I don't think I am."

"Hmm. I'm not the snarky type. At least I don't think I am. But then I'm not the klutzy or invalid type, either. I hope it's not you who brings those out in me."

"Yeah, that makes two of us." Mike brought water to the table. "No wine for you." He poured water into pretty goblets she hadn't noticed before.

Rosalie left everything in her kitchen for Annabelle because Nick had everything anyone could possibly want in a kitchen and then some. The kitchen was one room Annabelle wasn't interested in. It was a necessary evil. She only made coffee and the occasional bagel. Well, she didn't actually make the bagel. She sliced it, and sometimes toasted it. That's pretty much as far as it went unless she was forced to cook one of her three meals. Mike seemed to really get off on cooking, so maybe he wouldn't mind that she didn't.

Annabelle took a sip of the soup, and the flavors exploded in her mouth. Wow, that guy Vinny did one hell of a job teaching Mike to cook. She would never have known he wasn't a full-blooded Italian by the taste of his soup. He made a better minestra than her own mother. Mama might be a complete pain, but she was a fabulous cook. This explained why Annabelle and Rosalie never learned. The complete pain part kept them out of the kitchen. And since there was always good food on the table, they never bothered to do anything but reheat. She was killer with a microwave.

"Wow, this is amazing."

"Thanks."

"I have a confession. I only know how to cook three meals, and I usually screw those up." Why was she telling him this? Note to self: lay off the painkillers.

"Really? You did a great job the other night."

"I got lucky. I don't mean I got lucky—I got lucky. I mean I did... well, after you came back..." Oh man, that's not what she meant to say. Mike's eyes were laughing, but thankfully, he was gentlemanly enough not to laugh out loud. "... I was talking about cooking, and what I meant to say was that maybe it turned out okay because I made all the mistakes I possibly could last time I tried to cook. We're talking disaster. Kinda like now, only when it came to food, not when it came to babbling like a complete idiot. I don't know what's wrong with me. I'm usually not like this."

"I'm glad you think you got lucky. I think I got lucky too. I like you, Belle, especially when you let your guard down. Maybe it's the painkillers, but I choose to think you feel comfortable with me."

Stunned, she searched for words. Mike held up one finger just as she was about to speak. He probably saved her the embarrassment of putting her foot in her mouth again.

"I'm going to get the chicken. Hold that thought. I'll be right back."

Mike set out two plates with chicken in a lemon sauce with artichokes and capers, a side of broccoli, artichoke risotto, and a beautiful cucumber, tomato, and olive salad. Annabelle sat and stared. He wasn't kidding about knowing how to prepare everything on the DiNicola's menu. And the way he plated the food made her feel like she was sitting in one of the finest Italian restaurants.

"I can't believe you know how to cook like this, and that you did all this, vacuumed, and hung my paintings in a little over an hour."

"The risotto is instant—I usually make it from scratch, but you needed to eat. As for the rest, I learned to chop things quickly, and really, the prep work is the most time-consuming. I vacuumed and hung the paintings while I was waiting for everything to cook, and as for the cooking… it's really not difficult."

"Oh come on, it's an art. One I don't think I'll ever master." She didn't mention she had no interest in even trying. She tasted a bite of the chicken and closed her eyes. Oh, God, that was good. Amazing. When she opened her eyes, Mike stared at her the same way he had right before they made love. Her breath caught. She didn't know if it was from fear, excitement, or a weird combination of both. But whatever it was, she'd never experienced it before. She wasn't sure she liked it, but didn't know why. She'd think about it later when her head didn't feel as fuzzy.

Mike sipped his water. "There are all different kinds of art. What's your specialty?"

Annabelle bit into the broccoli sautéed in garlic and olive oil. "Hmm?"

"Your art, what medium do you prefer?"

"I don't."

"But your office—it's a beautiful art studio."

She shook her head. "I used to paint, but I don't anymore. Ben thinks that by forcing me to work in a studio he'll make it impossible not to paint. He doesn't understand."

"Understand what?"

She threw her hands up in the air. "It's gone. It's not like I wanted it to go, and now I don't know how to get it back."

"What's gone?"

"Whatever it was that made me a painter. Don't you think I've stood in front of a canvas and tried to do something? Anything? It's like when I lost Chip, I lost that part of me, too. I don't think it's ever coming back. And that's okay."

"It is?"

"I'm fine without it. I'm still in the art world. I deal with artists. I like what I do."

"And Chip was or is…?"

"Was. He died." She didn't remember mentioning Chip's name, but she must have, because how could he have known? She never talked about Chip except to Becca. She wanted to stuff more than food into her mouth—anything to keep her from talking without thinking. It had to be the drugs. She sent up a prayer that Mike took the hint and dropped it.

"I'm sorry."

"Me too." She stared at her plate like she'd never seen it before. When she finally stopped moving her food around, her eyes were shuttered. She might as well have put a big do-not-disturb sign on her forehead. She put her fork down and pushed her plate away, half the meal uneaten.

"I'm sorry. The food is great, but I'm just not very hungry."

Funny, neither was he. "It's fine. You've had a hard day." He stood and took the plates back to the kitchen. Chip, he'd heard that name before. She'd said something at the wedding but he couldn't recall what. He did recall staring at her cleavage… great. That Y chromosome was a real bugger sometimes. Who was Chip? And who exactly was Chip to her?

As she pushed her chair out, Mike rushed over to help her.

"Do you want to go back to bed, or would you rather sit on the couch?"

"I want to help with the dishes."

"Don't be silly. You're injured."

"I know that. Geez, I could do something. I can't just sit. I'll go crazy. I don't know how I'm going to live like this. I have to run or at least walk. I don't do still."

"Shhh. It's going to be okay." He wrapped his arm around her and held her close.

"How do you know? You can go home, go to work, you can run in the park…"

Mike didn't need a degree in psychology to diagnose

this minimeltdown as more to do with that guy Chip than her ankle. He grabbed a napkin off the table and dried her tears.

"Great! Now I'm a blubbering, babbling fool."

She obviously wasn't up to talking about Chip, so he had no choice but to handle the stated problem first.

"It's okay. You'll be able to walk a little bit tomorrow if you use your crutches and don't overdo it."

"I'm crying, and I don't cry. Ever."

"It's okay."

"I can't even help with the dishes."

Mike turned and lifted her face to his. "I don't see the problem. You have the perfect excuse. Sometime when I'm off my game, you can do the dishes."

"I'd probably poison you first. I'm a terrible cook. I poisoned Becca, and I didn't even mean to."

Becca? Another person who meant a lot to her. He'd have to ask Nick and Rosalie about both Chip and Becca.

"We'll get takeout."

"Okay, then I'll do the dishes."

"Deal. Now couch or bed?"

She didn't seem to like the choices. Tough. When he started to help, she pushed him away.

"I can do it myself."

God she looked cute when she acted like a two-year-old. He kept his mouth shut because he figured she'd hit him with her crutch if he said a word. He held his hands up in surrender and began clearing a path between her and the couch. He moved the handmade basket woven with purple, turquoise, and fuchsia reeds, the size of one of Vinny's huge stockpots. It was filled with balls of yarn and a knitting project, more colorful than the basket, with huge needles the circumference of broomsticks. Just as he was almost finished, she changed gears and went toward the bedroom. Rushing ahead of her, he cleared that, too. He didn't say anything when her crutch hit the doorjamb. She headed for the bathroom, stopped, turned, and caught him behind her. The scowl she wore didn't look at all happy.

"Are you gonna watch?"

"No, do you want me to get the door?"

"I can do it."

"Fine."

She managed to hold both crutches under one arm and then slammed the door in his face. Mike was about to go back to the kitchen and start cleaning when he heard a crash and a scream. He was through the door before he even knew what he was doing.

Both crutches were on the floor and Annabelle hopped on her good foot, cursing in Italian again. "What happened? Are you okay?"

"I'm fine. I got mad, and without thinking I stomped my foot. It's a bad habit. It hurt. Then I dropped those ugly things, and I haven't even gone to the bathroom."

"Do you need me to help you?"

Wrong thing to say. She speared him with a glare that would turn lesser men into eunuchs.

"Do I need help to go to the bathroom? No! I've been doing that on my own since I was three. Thankyouverymuch."

Mike bent to gather her crutches. Damn, she'd scared the shit out of him. His adrenaline pumped, and his hands shook. He hadn't felt like this since the first time he saw an autopsy.

When he handed the crutches to Annabelle, she was staring.

"You didn't poison us, did you?"

She took the crutches from him and stared some more.

"No, why? Do you feel sick?"

"No, it's you. Look at you." She pointed to the mirror. "You're white as Wonder Bread."

Mike stuck his hands in his pockets. "I'm fine." He backed out of the bathroom and closed the door before leaning against the wall to wait. His heart beat so fast, he could hardly hear over the sound of blood rushing though his ears. Christ. He swallowed hard. He was getting in deep, and he was making the trip alone.

The toilet flushed and then water ran in the sink. The squeak of crutches being positioned and then the jiggle of the doorknob announced her eminent reappearance.

Shit, he'd better leave.

Annabelle hobbled out of the bathroom and to the bed relieved to see that Mike had left her alone. She needed to get her head together, and she didn't know what was wrong with her, if it was the pain, the pills, or just Mike that made her feel too much. She scooted up on the bed and rested her screaming ankle on the pillows. She put the ice bag that Mike had left for her back on and hissed out a breath when the cold hit her injured ankle. Damn that hurt.

The sketch pad he'd brought her slid into her hip, and she picked it up and broke the seal. She ran her hand across the textured sheet, enjoying the feel of it against her skin. It had been so long. She pulled a pencil out of the box and checked the point. He must have had someone sharpen them for him at the art store.

He really was sweet. The scent of the newly sharpened pencil brought her back to the mornings she would awaken before Chip and lie in bed sketching him as he slept. The memories were so vivid with the scent of the pencils, feel of the paper beneath her fingers, and the softness of the pillows behind her back. She shuddered, flipped the sketch pad cover over, stashed the pencil back in the box, and pushed them as far away from her as she could.

Mike had dashed out of the room and into the kitchen where he made himself look busy while he mulled over his options. He couldn't force Annabelle to talk to him, and when it came right down to it, they hadn't spent enough time together to exchange life stories. But it hadn't escaped him that she skillfully avoided the subject. There was none of the usual "I'll show you mine if you show me yours," which meant she was either not interested, or she was hiding something. Both possibilities threw up red flags.

Since he was seriously sleep deprived, and Annabelle was on pain meds, now wasn't the time for meaningful discussions, especially since she didn't have any more tolerance for narcotics than she did alcohol.

He could do one of two things. Retreat, or he could go blindly into dangerous territory, if he wasn't already up to his neck in it. The prudent thing to do would be to leave and deal with this matter another time.

He spooned the leftover soup into containers, refrigerated half, and froze the rest. The chicken he packed into individual servings. She could get a couple more meals out of it.

After wiping the counters, sweeping the floor, and scrubbing the sink, Mike realized he'd run out of reasons to avoid Annabelle. He went back to the bedroom, half hoping she was asleep. She wasn't.

"Kitchen's all clean."

"Is there anything you're not good at?"

He sat beside her on the bed and smiled. "I take the fifth." Her eyes were still shuttered, and Mike felt like a drowning victim going down for the second time. He kept telling himself that they hadn't known each other long enough or spent enough time together to form a strong bond, except for sexually. That bond was there since the first time he had set eyes on her.

Annabelle rested her hand on his thigh, and she began tracing the inner seam of his suit pants. That's all it took. The way the spaghetti strap of her tank top slipped off one shoulder and the come-do-me-baby look didn't help. Mike swallowed hard and put his hand on hers, stopping her.

"What?" Annabelle slid her hand from beneath his and reached for the button band of his shirt.

"It's getting late, and I need to go."

"You're leaving?"

"Yes, it's probably for the best."

Annabelle moved closer. She licked her lips and ran her hand down the front of his shirt to his fly. It wasn't difficult to guess he wanted her. It was as clear as the bulge in his pants.

"You can stay."

"Thanks, but I can't."

"But why? I need you."

Chapter 7

WHAT ANNABELLE NEEDED AND WHAT SHE WANTED were two different things. Not that Mike was complaining about the sex. Lord knew the two of them were almost too hot to handle. Together, they generated enough heat to melt the polar ice cap. He wanted her to need him. He wanted to become an integral part of her happiness as she'd become part of his.

"Belle. Don't say things you don't mean."

That stopped her. Or it could have been his tone. Sure, he was at the end of his rope, and damn, this definitely cost him, but he refused to fall all over a girl who was just using him for sex. Even if it was great sex. For the first time in his life, great sex wasn't enough.

Annabelle reached for the sheet at the foot of the bed and covered her skimpy tank and boxers. When he reached over to touch her, she shied away.

Great. He was really smooth. "Belle, I've got work in the morning, and I have to get some sleep. I was up most of last night on call."

"Sure, whatever."

"What's that mean?"

"I might not be the mental giant you are, but even I know there's more to this than you being tired. Why else would you leave?"

"Maybe because every time I get a glimpse of who you are, you shut me out. And although the sex is great, it's not enough. I like you. A lot. If you're looking for a bed buddy, I'm setting myself up, and frankly, I don't think I can handle one more failure right now."

Fabulous, she stared at him as if he were a loon. She probably had a point. What was it about her that made him crazy? What made him want to brand her as his and keep her all to himself? What made him want to introduce her to his mother? He closed his eyes and cringed. He sounded desperate, even to himself. God, how embarrassing. "Look, I'm sorry. I have to go. I'll make sure Wayne and Henry will be able to help you out until you're better. Be sure to check in with Dr. Doyle. His number is on the instruction sheet by your meds."

"What do you mean when you say you can't handle another failure?"

Shit, he really didn't want to go into this now—maybe not ever. "Things at work aren't going well. It's a long story."

"And you think I'm just using you for sex?"

"Aren't you?"

She put three fingers over his lips, effectively shutting him up and stopping him from saying too much. As if he hadn't already. Her fingers trembled, and he found his hand wrapping around her wrist. He kissed the center of her palm, closed her fingers over the kiss, and stood to leave.

"Mike, wait."

He stopped. Probably because he was a fool. Definitely because he was a fool. She had him so wrapped it was embarrassing.

Annabelle scooted closer. "You know, I've never felt this way before. I've never wanted anyone like I want you."

"Yeah." Why did that only depress him? Any other guy would be jumping for joy. He turned and walked toward the door.

"Wait."

Mike stopped and took a deep breath. He didn't turn. He really didn't want to see her looking beautiful and injured and confused, maybe even a little hurt. He stretched it with the hurt part, but hey, he deserved a little latitude after what he'd been through.

Arms came around him from behind, her breast pressed against his back. She held tight.

"I want you, Mike. But that doesn't mean I don't like you. I do, you know. I like you a lot. I just want you a whole lot, too."

He turned and lost himself in her eyes. Her admission had cost her, almost as much as walking away had cost him.

She seemed uncertain. "Is that okay? Is that enough for now?"

Relief washed through him, and every muscle in his entire body seemed to relax. He wrapped his arms around her, and when she looked at him, those eyes of hers nearly knocked him to his knees. He wasn't sure he'd have been able to leave before. Now, with her looking at him like that, there's no way in hell he could leave, not if she wanted him to stay.

"I'll stay if that's what you want. It's up to you."

Annabelle pulled his head down for a kiss and then pulled away, her hands still in his hair. "You'll tell me all about what's going on with your job?"

Mike nodded.

"It's a long story, huh?" She kissed him again. Her fingernails running across his scalp made his hair, among other things, stand up. "You might as well get comfortable." She reached for the button band of his shirt. "We have all night."

Annabelle unbuttoned his shirt, ran her hands down his chest, and when she slid them over his flat nipples, he tensed. She loved the way his body reacted to her every move. She kissed his nipple, his heart beating like a jackhammer beneath her lips, and as her hands slipped under his shirt at the shoulders, his muscles bunched under her fingers. She swept the shirt off and pushed him down on the bed, kneeling beside him as she worked the loosened buckle of his belt and flipped the top button of his pants open.

She kissed him, teased him, and listened to the change in his breathing as she slid the zipper of his fly down, reached into his jockeys, and wrapped her hand around his erection. The lamp on the bedside table created shadows, highlighting the washboard of his tensed stomach muscles—ridges she traced with her tongue.

Mike raised his hips, pushed his pants and jockeys down, kicking off his shoes, socks, and pants. His legs spread, and he seemed to be holding his breath. Their eyes met as his hand wrapped around hers, squeezing harder than she thought she should, and moved it up and down, pumping from its base to its head. A drop of semen glistened in the light; her tongue traced the ridge around the head.

Mike's hand moved hers faster and faster. When she gently slipped her other hand around his testicles, she opened her lips around him and every muscle in his body seemed to strain as she went down on him, testing to see how much of him she could take.

His balls tightened in her hand as she advanced and retreated, sucking the sensitive head before sliding her lips back toward the base, until its head hit the back of her throat. The taste of him, the smell of him, and the sounds of his strangled cries drove her higher than she'd ever been, higher than she knew she could be considering he wasn't even touching her.

She squeezed harder and followed her lips with her fist up and down his shaft. His hand made a fist in her hair as a groan ripped through him, egging her on, making her want to control him, just as he'd controlled her.

She sucked harder, tasting him. She heard him begging and tightened her grip around his erection, taking him deeper than she thought she could, and when she raked her nails lightly over his balls, he pulled her away just as he came. She'd never seen anything like it, spurting out over and over again, the power of it running through her hand and shooting over his chest and stomach.

Mike was spent. It was all he could do to breathe, his limbs felt like lead, and he threw his arm over his eyes to wipe the sweat off his forehead, but once he got it there, he ran out of energy. That was the most amazing, intense... He jumped when he felt something cool hit the fevered skin of his stomach. Annabelle sponged him down with a cool washcloth. Christ, he hadn't realized she'd even gotten out of bed. Okay, so he took the selfish bastard prize for the day, and he'd make it up to her just as soon as he could move.

"I didn't hurt you, did I?"

God, was she kidding? He cleared his throat and

put some real effort into rolling onto his side to face her. She looked... concerned. "No, you didn't hurt me, incapacitate me, yeah, but in a good way."

"Oh. Okay. You had me worried there for a minute."

"Baby, you can't wring a guy out like that and expect him to be coherent anytime soon."

"I'm sorry."

Mike pushed himself to a sitting position, and his stomach muscles felt as if he'd just done two hundred inclined crunches. He wrapped his arm around her waist, dragged her close, and kissed her swollen lips, tasting himself on her tongue. Damn, she was so hot; he couldn't believe it, but he was getting hard again.

In between kisses he laid her down, pulled her tight little tank top over her head, and stripped the boxers she wore off her too. His hand roamed over her breasts, and his mouth joined in. His tongue played with her nipples, rolling one between his teeth and the other between his fingers.

Mike slid his hand down her body to the triangle of curls. She was hot and wet, and when he touched her, she moaned and pressed into his hand. He slid two fingers deep inside her as his thumb caressed the tight, hard nub. Mike reached blindly into the bedside table drawer for the box of condoms he'd tossed in there earlier, but his hand landed on something else.

"Mike, please... more."

"You want more?"

"Yes." Annabelle was trembling. He took BOB out of the drawer and looked it over while she rammed against his hand. It was big and purple, and it had a clit-tickler and a couple of buttons on the side of the battery pack.

"Close your eyes, and I'll give you what you want."

As soon as her eyes were closed, he pulled his fingers out and slid BOB in. Her eyes shot open as the vibrator filled her. As soon as he slid it home, he hit both buttons, and she bucked against it. She pulled her leg up and planted her uninjured foot on the mattress, and the second the tickler hit her clit she went wild. He'd never seen anything so erotic. Her back arched and she screamed for more, and he gave it to her. She took his hand in hers and set a rhythm, and when he didn't follow her exact instructions, she pushed his hand away and pleased herself.

He'd never been so turned on. He watched her take herself over the edge and come holding the vibrator deep within her while the tickler vibrated on her nub. Mike grabbed a condom and rolled it on. "Belle, it's my turn." Mike rolled her over onto her stomach, lifted her onto her hands and knees, and tossed BOB aside. He knelt between her legs and slid himself in from behind. She tightened around him, and as he slowly pulled out, Annabelle tilted her ass up and took him deeper than he'd ever gone. She begged him to go faster, harder, and he was happy to oblige. Her orgasm began to take hold. He reached for the vibrator, held it to her clit, and she shattered like glass. The vibration ran through her to his dick. He drove hard, her orgasm gaining strength, gripping him, milking him, drawing him deeper. The combination of vibration and Annabelle's orgasm had him coming so hard he saw stars. Annabelle collapsed onto her stomach, and he not so lightly followed her down. He lay there, still deep inside her, aftershocks shooting through them and the vibrator beside them vibrating away. He turned it off, rolled them over to their sides, and held her until they were both breathing normally. Once he thought he could stand, he slid out of bed and removed the condom. She was asleep by the time he came back to bed. She rolled over, used his shoulder as a pillow, and threw her leg over him without ever waking up. Mike kissed her forehead and fell asleep with her in his arms and a smile on his face.

The next morning, after Mike went home, showered, and changed, he checked the messages on his cell phone. There were three from Nick. He locked his apartment, nodded to Mrs. Kravtsov on his way out, and hit the speed dial.

"It's about time you called me back. What's going on with you and my fruitcake of a sister-in-law?"

"Hi, Nick. Aren't you supposed to be bugging your new wife? You've been married all of, what? A week?"

"Nine days and"—there was a pause—"fourteen hours of wedded bliss... for the most part. However, I wouldn't recommend redecorating on the honeymoon."

"You haven't taken a honeymoon."

"We've got to get the Premier Motors deal put to bed and the house Dave-proofed, and then we're off to tour Italy. I've got a meeting scheduled with the Alfa Romeo people. They're giving us a car for two weeks."

"Only you would conduct business on your honeymoon."

"What can I say? I married the perfect woman."

"Is Rosalie there with you?"

"Of course, where else would she be?"

"Do me a favor. Ask her who Chip and Becca are."

"What kind of name is Chip?"

"I don't know. Would you just ask her?"

"Okay, hold on."

Mike crossed the street at the light and waited for Nick.

"She said Becca used to be Annabelle's roommate a few years ago. Lee says Annabelle never brought her home and was kind of closemouthed about her time away. But then, it wasn't as if Lee and Annabelle were ever really close. Hold on… Lee said she thought Becca may have a brother. She doesn't remember his name, but it could have been Chip. Why the questions?"

"Annabelle's never talked to Rosalie about some dead guy named Chip?"

"Chip's dead?"

"Yeah, that's why she doesn't paint anymore."

"Lee doesn't know anything about any dead guy. You never said what was going on with you and Annabelle. Vinny hasn't stopped talking about you two."

"Vinny has a big mouth."

"Yeah, but only because he's concerned. You haven't been by the restaurant, and Mona said you even skipped out on your weekly dinner with your mother.

"I swear you and Vinny are like a bunch of old ladies. Why don't you find someone else's life to screw with? I've got my hands full without your help."

"You need something?"

"Only a new job, a few hundred K, oh, and possibly a good lawyer."

"What's this got to do with Annabelle?"

"Nothing. Right now, our relationship is the only

thing going well in my life, so lay off, okay? We're just figuring things out, and we don't need anyone getting in the middle of it."

"Mikey, what's the problem?"

"Nothing you can help me with. One of the partners at work is a malpractice suit waiting to happen, and when I voiced my concern, the partners' reactions were less than encouraging. If I go to the New York State Board for Professional Conduct and complain, I'll be blackballed, not to mention I'll be kissing my job, my investment, and my sweat equity good-bye."

"You have to rat him out? Couldn't you threaten to rat him out in exchange for your initial cash investment back?"

"Nick, I caught the errors. I changed the orders. It's in the files. When he eventually screws up—and he will—I'd be left holding the bag by virtue of keeping my mouth shut. Besides, I wouldn't be able to live with myself. I can't let him continue to practice this way."

"What if you threaten to turn in not only him, but the rest of the partners as well? That way they'll pay up, you'll cover your ass and assuage your conscience, and they're on their own."

Mike had to admit that didn't sound like a bad idea. "That might work."

"If you need a good attorney, I'm sure my firm has someone who can handle it."

"Nick—"

"Hey, you know it's there if you need it. If you don't, good. So stop with the Mr. Independent crap—you're wasting precious time. Have you started looking for another position?"

"I don't know what I'm going to do. After this experience, I'm not sure a practice is where I want to be. I did due diligence. I checked out the practice, and look where it got me. Plus, I'm definitely not going to be Dr. Popularity if word gets out, and I doubt I'll leave with a good recommendation."

"You're doing the right thing. How can they hold that against you?"

"Very easily. The more I think about this, the more ominous the situation looks. I might get a job at the hospital. They're always looking for critical care doctors."

"You might want to do that before you threaten to rat out the partner. Just a suggestion."

"Yeah, thanks for that."

"Hey, what's a best friend for?"

"How about letting me use the house in the Hamptons over Memorial Day… oh, and loan me a car to get there?"

"Are you planning to go with Annabelle?"

"What do you have against her, anyway?"

"I don't know. One minute she's engaged to a fuckin' mortician and the next she's going hot and heavy with my best friend, the doctor. It makes me wonder if she's trading up. Ya know? Her mother's a piece of work, and she's been trying to marry both Rosalie and Annabelle off since they turned eighteen."

"You married Rosalie."

"Yeah, but she never wanted to get married. It's different. She only married me because she can't live without me. Not because her mother wants her to be married or because I have money. She married me because she loves me. I'm irresistible."

"And I'm not?"

"How the fuck do I know? All I know is if you had any idea how much her mother pushes them to marry well, you'd watch your back and practice safe sex."

"That's enough. Christ. You don't know a thing about Annabelle. You need to back off. What makes you think she'd be more willing to listen to her mother than Rosalie was?"

"She was engaged to an asshole. Why would she plan to marry an asshole if she wasn't getting pushed around by her mama?"

"I don't know. But what I do know is that there's a hell of a lot more to Annabelle Ronaldi than meets the eye, and I'm enjoying uncovering the hidden pieces."

"I'm sure you are. But shit, Mike, you couldn't uncover some other chick's hidden pieces? You had to choose my sister-in-law? If this ends badly, it could be really awkward."

"And if it doesn't, it could be great. I like her. A lot. And no matter what you say, I'm not backing off. So you might as well get with the program. Now, are you going to let me use the house or not?"

"You gonna take Dave up there?"

"Yeah, I guess, if Annabelle agrees to go, we'll take Dave."

"Christ. Now we have to Dave-proof the beach house, too."

"Annabelle and I can do it when we get there."

"Yeah, right. Why do I have the feeling you're going to be too busy exploring each other's hidden pieces?"

"I don't know… maybe because you're no dummy."

"Fine. I'll send my assistant and her son for the weekend. They can Dave-proof the beach house."

"Thanks, Nick."

"Yeah, well. Just, you know, be careful. I don't trust Annabelle."

"Nick."

"I'm sorry, man. But like you said, I don't know her. I just have a bad feeling about this."

"I'm a big boy. I can take care of myself."

"Yeah, right. But if this comes back and bites you in the ass, don't say I didn't warn you."

"Okay. I stand warned. Now let's drop it. I'm getting on the subway anyway."

"Let me know what happens with the partners, and I'll make sure Lois has all the information in case you need to get a lawyer. Just ask her, and she'll take care of everything."

"Not necessary, but thanks."

"She'll get you the keys to the beach house when you pick up the Dave car."

"Dave has a car?"

"Yeah, I drive the Mustang when I have him with me. No need to get Dave hair all over the others. Besides, he likes the vibration of the engine."

"Has anyone ever told you you're crazy?"

"Yeah, my wife lets me know on a daily basis."

"Later, Nick."

Mike ended the call and went to work with a smile on his face. His career might be in jeopardy, but at least he had a great weekend coming up if Annabelle could get away.

Annabelle was not in a good mood. She awoke alone with her ankle throbbing and nothing but a note on

Mike's pillow saying he had fed and taken Dave out and had to run home to change for work. At least he signed it with XXX. She was pretty sure that meant kisses.

The buzzer for the security door rang, and she slipped out of bed. Hobbling across the apartment to the door, she pressed the intercom button. "Yes?"

"Annabelle, it's me, Becca. Open the door."

"Becca?" Annabelle pressed the security door release and began unlocking the door. A curse and then a thump sounded as she backed up to pull the apartment door open. There stood Becca... with luggage.

"What are you doing here?"

Becca kicked her bag in, blew her blonde hair out of her eyes, and hugged Annabelle. "I know you're thrilled to see me, no matter what you say." She stepped back and examined Annabelle from foot to head. "You look like you're in pain. Satisfied, but in pain. I'm here to take care of you. Now go lie down while I have a look around."

Annabelle's head spun. Oh God. "But, Becca—"

Becca shooed her into the bedroom and plumped the pillows as she waited. Annabelle followed like an obedient puppy, and when she got close enough, handed over her crutches and sat on the edge of the bed. Becca motioned for her to lie down, so she did. There was no talking to Becca when she was on a Florence Nightingale kick.

"How's the patient? Obviously, Dr. Flynn hasn't let you out of his sight long enough to call your best friend."

Annabelle resigned herself to Becca's questioning, all the while wondering how to prepare her for seeing Mike. "Oh, sorry, Bec. I've been on these painkillers, and they make me all fuzzy, but yeah, he came over after work, fixed me the most amazing meal, and stayed over. Except for the fight we had and the fact I had just hurt my ankle, it was a really nice night."

"You fought?" Becca kicked off her shoes and curled up on the end of the bed, careful to avoid Annabelle's Ace-bandaged ankle and foot. She wrapped her arms around her legs and rested her chin on her knee.

"We had a misunderstanding… well, several misunderstandings. I was a little wigged out about not being able to get around. Not only that, but I swear those painkillers had me acting like a lunatic. I even mentioned Chip. I never talk about Chip."

Becca grabbed a pillow and placed it between her and the old metal bed's footboard. She nudged Annabelle with her foot. "You need to. Maybe the painkillers didn't make you crazy. Maybe they made you less repressed."

Annabelle covered her face with her hands, remembering everything she and Mike had done right here in this very bed. God. "Yeah, well, repressed is not how I'd describe myself last night. I've never been so uninhibited in my life."

"Although I'm happy you're finally getting laid and enjoying it, there's more than one way to be repressed. You've made it a full-time occupation. I swear you need a shrink." Becca ran her fingers through her almost platinum blonde hair, letting it fall back into place. She had the perfect style—a blunt A-line cut shorter in the back, longer at the jaw, with choppy bangs.

Annabelle would kill to have hair like Becca's. Becca was one of those perfect women with perfect hair, perfect skin, perfect height and weight, and a great personality. She was so nice that a girl couldn't even hate her. Well, not much anyway. "Italians don't go to shrinks—we go to confession."

"I can see that's working really well for you. You need to deal with Chip's death. Does your family even know about him?"

"What am I supposed to say? I lived in sin with a man for two years until he died, and then I came home? That'll go over well. My mother would probably just move into St. Joseph's. She's got her own pew there as it is."

"Chip just stayed with us for several months, so it wasn't like you were 'living together, living together.' It was more like he just crashed at our place. You weren't really living in sin technically until I moved out.

"When you *were* living together, I understood why you hid it. But since his death, they'd never know unless you told them. And what about me? Don't you think it's weird that we've been best friends for four years, and I've yet to meet your family?"

Annabelle groaned. "Why would you want to meet them? You know what a nightmare they can be."

"Because I love you, you ninny. You met my family."

"I could have lived a long and happy life without ever setting eyes on that mother of yours, and your dad is just as bad, in a quieter, more ominous way. Besides, why do you need to meet them? I talk about them all the time. It's like you know them."

Becca slid off the bed and walked around the bedroom picking things up and putting them back down. "It's not the same, and you know it."

"Do you want to talk about this again, or do you want to hear about last night?"

Becca glanced over her shoulder at Annabelle and waggled her eyebrows.

"Mike thought I was using him for sex. Do you believe it?"

Becca turned, leaned against the dresser, and crossed her legs. "You are."

"Yeah, but I like him, too."

"Oh, and you're so good at expressing your feelings that he knew that?"

Annabelle flopped back on the pillows. "Fine, I'm repressed. I admit it, okay? I'm working on it. I told him I liked him. A lot."

"That's nice. So now I guess it's official. You have a boyfriend. I told you so."

"Yeah, you usually do."

Becca picked up the framed picture of the two of them together. "Maybe you'll start taking my advice. It's not going to kill you to talk about Chip. You have a lot of baggage there." She turned her attention from the frame to Annabelle. "Mike doesn't seem to mind that you're nutty and repressed. He probably thinks it's quirky. Some guys get off on that."

"Becca? So, after you, you know… How long before you can do it again?"

Becca resumed her place at the foot of the bed, but this time she lay on her side across the bed. She pulled the pillow under her head. "Just taking a stab in the dark here, but are we talking about intercourse?"

"Yeah. The night of the dinner… it was over, and we were lying there… together if you know what I mean. Then a minute later, I could have sworn he was ready to go again. And I thought, 'Wow—okay!' But he got up and went to the bathroom."

"I assume you're using protection."

"Yes."

"Well, if you're using condoms, you're not supposed to do it more than once without changing them."

"Oh. But when he came back to bed, nothing happened."

"Did you let him know you wanted to make love again?"

Annabelle sighed, "No."

"You know, the man is a doctor, not the Amazing Kreskin."

"When he came back and didn't do anything, I went to sleep."

"Live and learn. At least you're having sex. I am going through the world's longest drought. I've worn out two vibrators since the last time I saw a real model. Maybe Mike has a brother."

"No. He's an only child."

"Bummer. I can't wait to meet him, though. Is he coming over tonight, or are you going to bring him down for a weekend? Maybe we can meet at the beach house. Since the divorce, Mother and Father don't use it much—no need to hide their lovers anymore."

"Remember when I met Mike, I said he looked a lot like Chip?"

"Yeah."

"Well, I wasn't kidding. I'd swear you guys were related. He looks like Chip's twin."

"Oh, come on, you must be exaggerating."

"I'm not. I even got one of my paintings out because I thought I was on the Insanity Express rounding the bend to Psychosis City. I don't want you to freak if you meet him."

"If?"

"I don't know when I'll see him again, and it's not as if you're moving in. I'm going to work, so you're going to take the train back tomorrow, right?"

"Okay, I'll go, as long as you promise to bring him down soon."

"Mike works a lot, and I'm not going anywhere for a while. He said I had to wear this ugly air cast or stabilization boot and hobble around with crutches for a few weeks. I'm not hitting the beach until I'm good as new."

"Too bad Neimans or Bloomies don't have a medical supply store. They'd design a boot with some style or at least color."

Annabelle rolled over and saw Mike had left a thermal cup full of coffee, a glass of water, and her painkillers by the bed. She took a sip of hot coffee and had to admit Mike staying over did come with several perks, the least of which was coffee—and to a caffeine junkie like her, that was saying a lot.

She took the prescription painkillers. "Maybe I can decorate it."

Becca laughed out loud. "That I'd like to see."

Becca cleaned Annabelle's apartment, not that it needed much. Either Annabelle had turned over a new leaf, or she had a cleaning service come in. But since there wasn't anything else to do, she busied herself by straightening an already-clean place. She was worried about Annabelle, and cleaning was a perfect stress reliever, even if it was hell on the nails, which is why

Annabelle always avoided it at all cost. Becca didn't mind cleaning, and she couldn't believe it, but she felt a twinge of jealousy knowing Annabelle didn't really need her anymore. Maybe Mike did more than just cook. Hmm... interesting. She got out the Comet, scrubbed the already-spotless kitchen sink, and then looked at her nightmare of a manicure. It wasn't as if she kept her nails up anyway. Long nails and clay didn't mix. She thought of her latest sculpture and wished she didn't have to leave it. Her appointment with the gallery owner was in two weeks, and she wanted to get pictures of the new piece to add to her portfolio.

Annabelle had already expressed interest in her work, but in Becca's book that was cheating. Annabelle loved her work because Annabelle loved her, which is why she refused. When she finally made the big time, she wanted to know she'd made it on her own. When she rubbed her mother's nose in her success, she'd do it without ever having to wonder if she'd made it up the ladder by her own steam or because of someone else's.

Becca sprayed Windex on the bathroom mirror. She studied her reflection between the bubbles and smiled, happy with herself for the first time in her life. She liked the person she'd become. She'd come into her own in the two years since Chip's death. She'd taken the time to look at her life and turn it into something to be proud of. Therapy and time had helped. She no longer worried about Chip. He was in a better place. She no longer played the referee between her brother and her parents, or between her mother and her father. She took care of herself, and for now, that was enough. Sure, she missed having a relationship. And she missed the sex that went along with a relationship. A lot. But, she didn't miss the bad relationships, and since every guy she'd dated thus far had been Mr. Wrong, she had no problem not looking for Mr. Right. At least right now.

Now, she only worried about Annabelle. The girl didn't have great taste in men. First, there was Chip. Although Becca loved her brother, he hadn't been the most attentive boyfriend. Before he got sick, she reamed him for being an ass. Granted, considering the relationship their parents had, his behavior wasn't surprising, but that didn't mean Annabelle didn't deserve better. At least Chip had been willing to marry Annabelle, though she'd refused. The last thing Annabelle wanted was to prove their parents right. They'd said she was only interested in his money, and she wanted none of it.

When Annabelle had called to say she was engaged to Johnny, Becca had been hopeful. Unfortunately, Johnny made Chip look like Prince Charming. That's why she'd wasted no time jumping on a train to New York to check out Annabelle's new main squeeze. At least this guy sounded like he knew his way around a woman's body. Not surprising; after all, he was a doctor. He should know something. He also brought flowers, cooked, and from the look of Annabelle's apartment, cleaned too. Always a good sign. She'd sampled his soup and had to admit she was impressed. The man could definitely become a chef if the whole doctor thing didn't work out.

Becca checked on Annabelle—still passed out on painkillers. She was a true lightweight. Becca started tackling the study and straightened the computer table. Annabelle had tossed all her papers in a heap on the table, and Becca went through them just like the old days when they shared a place. She tossed out junk mail, stacked the bills, and it saddened her that she didn't find sketches on every spare piece of paper. She noticed a sketch pad, but when she thumbed through it, she found every page blank. She set the box of pencils on top of the sketch pad and accidentally moved the mouse.

Annabelle's computer came out of sleep mode and a slideshow began. Becca watched the pictures and smiled when she saw a picture of Chip and Annabelle. It wasn't one she'd seen before. Amazingly, he wore a dark suit and danced with Annabelle. Their bodies pressed together intimately, and the look on his face...

Becca clicked on the picture and it bled into the next. Shit. She pulled up iPhoto and opened the library, searching through every picture until she found the gorgeous man who looked like Chip but wasn't. Becca couldn't believe her eyes. She printed the close-up of his face, and the picture of him standing beside his friend, the groom. If it weren't for the color of his eyes, the break in his nose, and the mouth, he'd be Chip. Amazing. They say everyone has a double, but she'd never seen anything as close as this without major plastic surgery.

Annabelle hadn't been kidding when she said Mike looked like Chip. They had to be related somehow. Dr. Mike Flynn. Wow. Now Becca not only worried that he treated Annabelle well, but worried that the only reason Annabelle dated the poor guy was the amazing resemblance to her lost love. It didn't take Einstein to spot trouble ahead.

She stared at the pictures until it hurt. Mike looked so much like her brother. The brother she remembered before the cancer came back. She rubbed her eyes and refused to cry any more tears over the past. She took the two pictures and stuck them in her backpack; she needed to do some climbing on the family tree and see where this limb fit. She'd have to do something she'd been avoiding—she'd have to go and see her father.

Chapter 8

ANNABELLE LAY ON THE COUCH IN HER NEW OFFICE, generally hating life. The stabilization boot was as ugly as sin. After ten minutes on her feet, her ankle throbbed. Relegated to lying on the couch donning an ice bag, she looked through submissions from hopeful artists, while Ben the Beneficent hung paintings and displayed sculptures in all the wrong places. No matter how explicit the directions she gave, the diagrams she drew of the floor plan with the exact location of each piece detailed, when she left Ben to follow them, the placement always turned out wrong. It was maddening.

Her phone beeped twice to let her know it was an out-of-office call. Thank God. She really didn't think she had the patience to talk to Ben about their newest Jackson Pollock wannabe. "Annabelle Ronaldi. Can I help you?"

"Do you know how hard it was to get you on the phone? And why are you resting?"

"Hi, Ma. I, um… had a little accident and sprained my ankle and tore a tendon. I can't walk around on it much, but it's fine."

"You hurt yourself, and this is how I hear about it?"

"What should I have done? Taken an ad out in the *Post*? It's not a big deal."

"You always were so clumsy. You'd come home with scrapes and bruises daily. I swear you're lucky you don't have any bad scars. You don't, do you?"

"No, Ma, my body is pretty much scar free. I wasn't clumsy. I was active. There's a difference. I'm at work, and my foot hurts. Did you want something?"

"We need to talk about Mother's Day."

"Okay. Fine. Talk."

"What? I'm the mother. You're supposed to make the plans, and I'm supposed to be treated like a queen for at least one day out of the year. My own children—"

"Okay, okay. Maybe Richie and I can get reservations somewhere."

"But Rosalie always makes plans—"

"Yeah, but Rosalie is going to be on her honeymoon. I doubt she's planning to fly back from Italy to spend Mother's Day with you."

"I don't know. Nick is an only child. How could he leave his poor mother alone on such an important day?"

Annabelle closed her mouth and forced herself to think. She already had half a pain pill in her, and she knew her filter was severely affected by them. The last thing she wanted to do was say what she really thought—that Mother's Day was conceived to establish a holiday when buying cards and presents were necessary, thus giving the mother yet another thing to hold over the child's head. As if the 102 hours of labor wasn't enough.

"I'm sure Mrs. Romeo has other family to celebrate Mother's Day with. So, how's Papa? Isn't it his job to do Mother's Day?"

There was silence on the other side of the phone. Oh, so it was one of those times. Great. Nothing like a nice family dinner when the only thing too thick to cut was the tension. "I'll call him and make sure he doesn't have the whole day already planned. Maybe we could go out to dinner and then to the Botanical Gardens. I'll bet you haven't been there in a long time."

Probably not since she'd chaperoned Annabelle's last class trip for ninth-grade biology. Sheesh, she loved it there, but God forbid she should go and enjoy herself. Annabelle wondered if her mother made herself miserable for some deep-seated psychological reason or was it strictly to guilt her children. Never a conversation went by without her bringing up the fact that she'd sacrificed her life for them. Then she'd make the sign of the cross and beat her breast while praying to the Virgin Mother.

"I hear you saw the doctor."

"Yes, we had dinner together. He's very nice."

"So?"

"So what? We ate dinner."

"Are you going to see him again? Has he asked?"

"Yeah. But he's working insane hours, so we're keeping it light."

"Light? What does that mean, light? Nonsense. You know, you're not getting any younger. You need to be understanding of his time and make yourself available to him. But whatever you do, don't complain. He gets enough of that at work, I'm sure."

"Yes, Mama."

"Good. So, when are you going to see him again?"

"I don't know. I'm sure I'll hear from him eventually." She couldn't keep the smile off her face when she felt that little tingle, the one that ran right through her every time she thought of Mike.

Ben popped his head into the office, and Annabelle waved to him. "Mama, I've got to run. My boss is here." She rolled her eyes. "Yes, the good-looking one. Okay, bye."

She disconnected the call and immediately saw her message light blink. Great. She pushed herself up, and the ice bag slipped off her ankle. "Thanks for saving me."

"From falling off the ladder or from the conversation with your mother?"

"Both. But it would have been nice if you'd done a little better job on the ladder debacle. Next time, see if you could catch me before part of me hits the ground."

"I'll do my best."

Ben stared at the shoji screens she'd bought to hide all the art supplies. "When I set this studio up for you, I wanted you to be surrounded by the art supplies. This," he said as he pointed to the screens, "defeats the purpose. Don't you think?"

"Yes. That was the point."

"God, you're stubborn."

Annabelle shrugged. "You're just mad because I one-upped you."

"No, I'm mad because it's bothered you to look at all the supplies, so much so that you took drastic steps to hide them instead of doing what you should do. Would it kill you to just try?"

Maybe, it almost had the last time she tried to paint. "Is there something you need?"

"Other than a gallery manager without an attitude? No. I'm going to grab some lunch and thought you might want me to pick something up for you since you're laid up."

"Um... thanks, but I think Mike is coming by for lunch." She checked her watch. "He should be here any minute."

He tossed his keys in the air and caught them before slipping them back into his pocket.

"I'll keep you company until he gets here."

He sat on the end of the couch, lifted her feet onto his lap, and ran his finger over her instep, which sent her into peals of laughter. She was so ticklish it wasn't funny... really. She'd just die of embarrassment if she peed herself or something equally heinous.

Once Ben got started, the twelve-year-old boy in him took over, and he moved up to her stomach, which had her curling into a ball on her side and Ben practically lying on top of her, trying to pry her arms away from her middle while she tried kicking him with her good foot. Wrestling with Ben didn't feel any different from wrestling with Richie, because she'd never looked at her boss in that guy and girl way.

The first time she met him, she wasn't sure if he was straight, and she figured if she had to ask herself the question, she wasn't interested. He was too... pretty. Maybe not pretty—no, he was too perfect. The man always looked as if he'd just walked off the set of *Queer Eye for the Straight Guy*. Except that he wasn't gay. Well, she was pretty sure he wasn't. She'd seen all sorts of women on his arm and leaving his apartment in the morning long after the gallery opened.

She was screaming and laughing and crying all at the same time when Mike closed the door behind him. After she succeeded in pushing the big hulk of a man off her, she saw Mike's face and cringed. He turned a reddish purple. She smoothed down her skirt, which had ridden dangerously high, while she scooted back into a sitting position. Ben, the schmuck, sat there grinning like a fool. She gave him another kick, and he stood, handed her the ice bag, dusted off his slacks, and winked at her.

"Well, I'll just be going." He tossed his keys in the air, caught them, and nodded to Mike. "She's all yours."

He must like living dangerously, because she was sure she saw steam come out of Mike's ears.

Mike set the food he'd brought on the desk and watched Ben saunter out. That's the only way it could be described. Like the man wasn't in danger of being permanently maimed.

Annabelle was bright red, pulling her skirt down, straightening her blouse, and then popping off the couch, the ice bag flying off with her. She bopped around on one foot without the aid of crutches or air cast and wrung her hands together.

"Mike. Um…"

So, he wasn't the only one at a loss for words. At least she remembered his name. He was afraid to open his mouth, because he wouldn't be able to take back whatever popped out of it, and right now, it would be nothing productive. He reached into the bag and pulled out a sandwich, determined it was Annabelle's, and passed it to her along with a Diet Coke and a napkin.

"Thanks. Um… wanna sit on the couch?"

He raised an eyebrow. Shaking his head, he sat on a chair beside her desk, straightened up the piles of papers, photos, plans, and paraphernalia to make room for his food, and unwrapped his corned beef on rye with swiss and coleslaw. Mike had been starving before he walked in on Annabelle being felt up by Ben. He took a bite, even though the last thing his stomach seemed to want right now was food.

"Mike… I'm sorry. Ben and I usually don't carry on that way. Really, he's never tickled me before… and I doubt he'll ever do it again."

Not if he wants to live. Mike chewed and took a sip of his drink. Eventually, he'd have to say something, and, according to her, it was innocent fun—at least on her part. Ben's intent was another story. Mike had never gotten into a pissing match over a woman—he'd never found one worth fighting about—but when he'd seen Ben holding Annabelle a few days earlier, he'd wanted to rip the man's head off and shove it down his throat. The fantasies that played in his mind today made that seem tame.

"Annabelle, I'm not sure what to say here. I guess we should talk about expectations."

"Expectations?"

"Yes, as in what you and I expect from whatever it is we have together."

She stared at him while playing with the paper wrapper of her sandwich.

Okay, this wasn't going well. "I guess we need to talk about what you want… what we want from…" She was going to make him say it, wasn't she? The dreaded "R" word. "… this relationship." There. It was out, and she wasn't running away. Not that she could, considering the shape her ankle was in, but even without her ankle keeping her still, he hadn't expected her to run. He hadn't expected to have this conversation either. Unfortunately, it seemed to be necessary for his peace of mind.

Their relationship didn't run on the typical relationship course—at least not typical of any he'd known. You were supposed to ask a girl out. Sleep with her after the third date, if you're lucky and still interested. Make tentative plans together and feel each other out. Maybe beat around a bush or two, and then wait until she brings up the "R" word—all the while keeping your eye out for something or someone better.

Not-pick up a girl at a wedding. Have mind-bending sex. Fall all over yourself scheming to get a date with her. Think about her every spare minute of the day. Sleep with her as often as humanly possible. And enjoy every minute spent with her even when you're fighting. No, this wasn't a typical relationship.

She still looked worried. Her embarrassment had taken a backseat to something else. Great, one look from her and he felt like an ogre. What the hell was she expecting him to do? "Do you think we should talk about this?"

Annabelle nodded but kept her mouth shut. She was being real helpful here. Nothing like making him fly solo.

"It's kind of hard to have a conversation when I'm the only one talking."

She peeled the plastic label off the soda bottle. "I don't know what you want me to say."

"Why do I feel as if you're waiting for me to punish you? I understand that I walked in on something that looked bad. I gathered it was innocent on your part. I'm not so sure about Ben's. But what he wants doesn't really matter, does it? It's only what you want that matters."

"Whoa. Ben and I are friends. There's never been anything else between us."

"Okay."

"Okay, what?"

"Okay, nothing. I just said okay. I don't doubt you believe there is nothing between you and Ben."

"Ben knows there's nothing between me and him, too."

"Are you sure about that?"

"Of course I'm sure. I've worked with him for a year and a half now, and he's never even hinted there was something more than a purely platonic friendship between us."

"Did he know I was coming by for lunch?"

There, that got her thinking. Yeah, he sure as hell knew. Now she was getting mad... hopefully at Ben.

"You think he planned this? For you to show up and—"

"Think he was on top of you doing something other than... tickling you? Hell yeah, I do. That way I'd draw the wrong conclusion, I'd come off like a jealous asshole, we'd fight, and you'd dump me. Because, let's face it, there's nothing attractive about a jealous boyfriend, is there?"

"No. But there is something definitely attractive about a smart one. I'm not so sure you're right about Ben's motives. After all, he's never looked at me twice—"

"I find that impossible to believe. Maybe you're the one who never looked twice. Besides, when was the last time you were single?"

"Other than the last month or so, um…"

"Not since you met Ben. Right?" Annabelle crossed her arms under her breasts, which did amazing things for her already-spectacular cleavage.

"Right. So, all this…" She made a turning motion with her hand. "This was so that you'd catch us. This was just to make you jealous?"

"I'd bet my next weekend off on it."

"You have a weekend off?"

Mike couldn't hold back his smile. He sat beside Annabelle and pulled her onto his lap. "Yeah, I have Memorial Day weekend off." He didn't mention that he'd practically had to sell his soul… and his body to get a four-day weekend. "I thought maybe if you can get off too, we could spend some time together in the Hamptons."

"The Hamptons? As in, where the rich and famous like to play and pay?"

"Yeah. Nick has a place on Westhampton Beach, and since Rosalie married him, she does too."

"My sister owns a house in the Hamptons? She doesn't even like the beach. Do you think she knows?"

Mike shrugged. "Does it matter? The less time they use it, the more time there will be for you and me. Nick said it's ours if we want it. As long as we take Dave with us. Just think, you, me, the sun, and surf for four days. Can you get the time off?"

"I've had time off scheduled for almost a year. My plans changed, obviously, but I still have the time saved up. It shouldn't be a problem. That's one of the reasons why Ben's in town."

Mike found it interesting that he'd show up even after he knew Annabelle wasn't taking her honeymoon, but decided to keep the thought to himself. "So we're good then?"

She wrapped her arms around his neck and kissed him. "Yeah, we're real good."

Mike couldn't disagree.

"He asked me to go away with him over Memorial Day weekend." Annabelle ran her pencil across the blotter on her desk, picturing Mike when he was steaming mad at her. He was pretty cute when he was jealous. She moved the pencil, enjoying the sound of carbon against paper. It was relaxing somehow, even if it was just scribbling.

She heard Becca's sigh. She knew that sigh, even when heard over the clanking of the Acela Express and the high-pitched hum of a passing train. The sigh was the beginning of one of Becca's Little Miss Optimistic rants.

"Oh, this relationship is moving right along. Wow, a weekend together, that's serious stuff."

"No, it's not. It's uninterrupted sex, that's all."

"If it were just uninterrupted sex, why leave Brooklyn?"

Good point. She had no idea why they were leaving Brooklyn.

"He wants to do something nice and romantic. You really should expect more. I know Chip took you away for the weekend sometimes."

"Yeah, but that was only when he had beach volley-ball tournaments."

"Oh, right. I'll bet Mike is taking you somewhere to impress you, someplace romantic."

"The Hamptons."

"Wow, sometimes I amaze myself. I'm just too good. But why aren't you happier about this?"

"I was when I thought it was uninterrupted sex. Now you're attaching all sorts of meaning to it, and well, I'm not ready for—"

"A loving relationship?"

"Whoa! No one said anything about love."

"No one has to. This is like a trial weekend. To see how you'd get along if you moved in together—"

"No, it's not. It's a long weekend, three nights and four days of sun, surf, and sex."

"Oh honey, don't you know how this works? An overnighter insinuates he's ready to spend quality time but doesn't want to commit. A weekend means he's on the fence but likes you enough to contemplate a commitment. And a long weekend means he's over the moon but thinks it's too soon to ask you to move in with him, or he's not sure if you feel the same. Though in this case, I bet it's both."

Annabelle tossed her pencil aside and stood to pace the floor of her new office. Back and forth from her desk to the window. Her boot made a weird sound as it thunked over the polished wood surface. "Where do you get this stuff? It's all those stupid magazines you read, isn't it?"

"Calm down, girl. You need some time to come to grips with this. I just hope he doesn't spook you."

"Mike is not the one spooking me. You are. Now, why don't we stop talking about my... um—"

"Love life?"

"Sex life. Yeah, so how's your sex life?"

"Yours is so much more interesting. My love life and sex life are nonexistent. I am, however, considering adopting."

"A child?"

"No, I thought I'd start with a cat and work my way up from there."

"Sounds like a plan. Maybe then you can meet a cute veterinarian."

"One can only hope."

"Yeah, well, I'll see if Dr. Mike knows any vets. The doctor he dragged me to wasn't your type."

"Somehow that's not a surprise, since I don't think I have a type. We're heading into Philadelphia, so I better get off the phone."

"Okay, thanks for cleaning the apartment. I'm sorry I slept all afternoon."

"Not that there was much to clean. Promise you'll come visit me soon and bring Mike. I can't wait to meet him."

"Okay, I promise. Love you Bec."

"Take care, and I love you, too, sweetie. Bye."

Annabelle hung up the phone and tried to imagine Becca meeting Mike. She'd have to show her a picture of him before she introduced them. She'd have to prepare Becca for the shock. Lord knows it would have been nice if someone had prepared her, but then who could have? No one she knew in New York knew Chip even existed. And damn if that didn't make her feel guilty too. Thank you, Sister John Claire.

Becca turned onto the drive leading to the club. A mile-long driveway over rolling green hills led to a Tudor-style mansion turned country club. Bitsy got custody of the Cricket Club in the divorce, so Daddy had to find himself a new place to play.

She pulled up to the front entrance. A uniformed attendant stood ready to open her car door before she'd even shifted into neutral and raised the parking brake. She disengaged the door locks. The door swung open, and a strong hand helped her out of the low-slung car. Becca took the hand, and when the attendant's eyes lit up, she wished he were looking at her rather than her car. Pity. He was obviously new to the job. Becca's car was nice, but nothing compared to some that frequented the club. She took the receipt and put a tip in his breast pocket, patting it down just for kicks. That earned her a crooked smile as she walked toward the front door. It was a sad day when a girl had to tip a man to get more attention than her car. Maybe she should sell the damn thing and get a beater. Then she'd never be allowed on the club grounds. Hmm, not such a bad idea at that.

She tossed her Dolce and Gabbana purse over her shoulder, pushed her Pucci sunglasses to the top of her head, and smoothed the Tracy Reese strapless dress over her hips. She dressed to impress by necessity. All she really wanted to do was go back home to her loft apartment in South Philly and hang out in her cutoff Levi's and a T-shirt. Unfortunately, she didn't want her comfort as badly as she wanted information. The only way to get the facts was to give her father what he wanted—a well-behaved, well-bred, well-dressed daughter.

Becca let her eyes adjust to the dark, formal foyer and began the search for her dad. She walked by the club room and checked the bar. He wasn't there. Great. She took a deep breath, pasted on a smile, and pretended she was on stage, which wasn't much of a stretch. She stopped at the formal dining room's entrance, and before she could even scan it, the uniformed maître d' bowed slightly. "Ms. Larsen, so nice to see you again." He tucked a menu under his arm and raised his nose. "Please follow me. Your father is expecting you."

Well, no kidding. He walked like a general over-looking his troops, leaving her to follow in his wake. The people she passed took notice and didn't seem to find anything offensive about her attire. Score one for

Becca. At least she wouldn't be getting the old why-can't-you-dress-to-your-station lecture or the why-must-you-always-embarrass-me lecture. Though, the times she'd received both, she'd thoroughly enjoyed doing whatever it was she did to deserve them. Ah, the life of a reluctant debutante.

Christopher Edmond Larsen stood and gave her a regal nod and a quick kiss on the cheek before pulling her chair out for her. She sat, and the maître d' placed a napkin on her lap, then handed her an opened menu as a busboy rushed over to deliver a water glass.

She smiled her thanks and waited for her father to start the volley, which was the only way to gauge his mood, because Daddy was the king of cool.

"This was an unexpected surprise."

He obviously wondered if she was there to ask for money. He should know better, since she was the twin who'd never stooped so low and couldn't be bought— much to his consternation.

Becca took a sip of water and set it back on the table. "It's been a while. How you're doing?"

An eyebrow rose, and his lips quirked before he shut down the smile. Hmm… some real trust issues. Either that or a sure sign that a little paranoia goes a long way. He should know she was never in Mommy Dearest's camp—or his for that matter. When it came to her parents, she was Switzerland. Not that it mattered now. The divorce had been final for a year and a half.

"I'm fine, same as usual. Between my practice and my position on the hospital board, I've been busy."

"That's nice." Becca would have given her fortune for a dinner roll or a time-out to place an order. She looked over the menu and tried to figure out what would be kindest to her stomach. The tension roiled the little she'd eaten in the two days since she'd seen the photo.

"Are you going to tell me what this is about, Rebecca, or are we going to spend our meal with pleasantries?"

"It's hardly pleasant, Daddy. You haven't even asked how I am."

"Fine. How are you?"

"I'm doing well. My work is getting noticed, which is a major improvement, and I think I may have discovered a long lost relative."

"A relative?"

No need to waste time. He obviously wasn't happy to see her. No surprise there. Maybe she could get the information she wanted and leave him to eat in peace. She placed the envelope containing the pictures of Dr. Mike Flynn on the table. He looked at her questioningly.

"These were taken a couple of weeks ago at a wedding my friend attended in New York."

Her father looked to the heavens as if to ask for strength and pulled the photos out of the envelope. Becca watched as he scanned the picture of the two men and did a double take. When he flipped to the close-up, all the blood drained from his face. He reached for his water glass, took a gulp, and choked on it.

She rose from her seat, and the maître d' made a beeline for the table. Her father wiped his now-sweaty face with his napkin and waved off the advance of the staff and Becca.

Her legs turned leaden as she made her way back to her chair and sat. "Who is this Michael Flynn to you?"

She had never seen such pain in a man's eyes.

"Daddy?"

He moved forward and lowered his voice. "Did you say Flynn?"

"Yes, Dr. Michael Flynn. Who is he?"

"If my suspicions are correct, he's your half brother."

Well, she hadn't seen that coming. A cousin, sure, a branch of the family tree her grandfather had sawed off and refused to allow anyone to acknowledge. But her father's love child? Nope. Before this moment, she'd have said it was impossible. She didn't think her father had the ability to love anyone but himself. The pain evident in her father's eyes could only be caused by heartbreak and loss. It was her turn to gulp water. At least she didn't choke on it. Her mind raced. A brother? A half brother?

Dr. Larsen lifted his hand, and a waiter ran to his aid. "A scotch, neat. Make it a double. Rebecca?"

She couldn't take her eyes off her father. "Sure." He stared at the photographs, and when he looked back at her, he seemed to have aged ten years.

"I guess I owe you an explanation."

Becca had never seen her father look contrite before. Come to think of it, he never seemed to have any feelings. Even when he acted happy, it never seemed genuine. It sure looked genuine now.

He stared at the empty plate in front of him, as if he were watching the story of his life on the china. "You know the story. Your mom and I had known each other since we were children. Our families had always been close, and they planned for us to marry... someday." He shook his head. "I was never serious about Bitsy. I just went along with it because it was easier to ignore it and hope it would all go away."

"Dad—"

He held up a hand to quiet her. "I know I should have put my foot down and refused, but it always seemed so far in the future—it never felt real.

"When I was in New York doing my residency, I met a woman named Colleen Flynn. We dated. Bitsy dated other people too, as far as I knew. But Colleen and I got serious. We fell in love, but I had no idea she could have been pregnant. I never knew."

Becca took a sip of water. Her father was capable of love?

He took a deep breath and wiped his face with his hand. "Colleen and I talked about getting married when I finished my residency. We were so happy together, and I was happy for the first time in my life. I went home for a few days at Easter and had planned to tell my parents and your mother about Colleen and end the sham of an engagement."

Becca's father straightened his silverware and finally met her eyes. "When I told Bitsy that I wanted out, that I was in love with Colleen and wanted to marry her, you can imagine your mother's reaction. She went crazy. My family threatened to disown me. And two days later, both families went behind my back and put the announcement of my engagement to Bitsy in every society page between Philadelphia and Boston."

He shook his head and winced. "When I saw the announcement, I ran back to New York to tell Colleen it was a mistake. By the time I'd gotten there, she was gone."

He took another sip of his water, and his face was devoid of color. "Where the hell is that scotch?" He looked and didn't see the waiter, so he seemed to steel himself and continued. "When I showed up at Colleen's house, her family spit in my face."

Becca reached for his hand before she could stop herself.

He gave her a weak smile. "They told me she'd gone back to Ireland." His voice quivered. "They said she'd married the man they'd approved of—someone who wouldn't cheat on her. They threatened to call the police if I ever darkened their doorstep again."

He patted her hand and sat back, distancing himself like always. "I didn't give up right away. I talked to every one of Colleen's friends trying to find out where she'd gone. No one knew. My family refused to help. They cut off my trust to ensure I wouldn't go off to Ireland to find her. I had no money of my own. As it was, I could barely pay the rent with my meager income."

He took a deep breath and stared at Becca as if he were looking through her into the past. "I was hurt, and although I never loved your mother, I took the easy way out. I was so stupid. I did what everyone wanted me to do. I married Bitsy.

"Becca, your mother was never the woman I loved. Marrying her was unfair to both of us. After all these years, I don't think I ever got over Colleen. And now, to find out she may very well have had our son—"

Becca dropped her head in her hands. Oh God, what have I done?

"I've got to find them. To explain. Christ. Colleen must hate me."

Becca was glad she was sitting down as her head started to spin, thinking of the ramifications of her actions. Her father would offer Mike the world, and the only way

Annabelle would stay with Mike is if he rejected everything that goes along with being a Larsen—the father, the money, the page in the *Social Register*. Everything that Chip was incapable of doing. Her father would find Mike and destroy Annabelle's life again.

"I'd love to say I regret marrying your mother, but how can I? I got you and Chip out of the deal. I know I was never present in either of your lives—at least not in any way that counted. I'd like to change that now, with you, and with Mike. I've already lost one child. I don't want to lose my other children, too. Not when I have a second chance. I'm not going to make the same mistake again."

When the drinks were delivered, he drained half the glass, set it down, and watched Becca do the same.

How was she going to tell Annabelle? Becca didn't think about it before, but she should have told Annabelle she'd taken the pictures and was going to talk to her father. Christ, now it looked like she'd gone and done this behind Annabelle's back. She had, but not intentionally. Becca was so used to her what's-yours-is-mine and what's-mine-is-yours relationship with Annabelle, it never occurred to her to ask permission to take copies of the photos. Now that she had, and then compounded the offense by showing the photos to her father, she'd crossed the line.

Annabelle was going to freak when she found out her lover was Chip's brother, but even worse than that, one of the two people who'd made Annabelle's life miserable the whole time she was with Chip planned to make a place for himself in Mike's life. After all the hell Becca's parents had put Annabelle through when she and Chip were together, Becca couldn't imagine Annabelle would sign up for more of the same.

What would Mike think when he found out his father saw him as the answer to all his prayers. Someone to carry on the family name. A son who followed in his old man's footsteps. Another doctor to carry on his work. Dad planned to right all the wrongs he'd done to both her and Chip, even if most of it was his absence.

Dad wasn't the only one who wanted a second chance. Becca wanted a place in Mike's life, too. It would be nice to have at least one normal family member. Maybe that hollow feeling she'd had since Chip's death, the feeling of being utterly alone in the world, would diminish.

Her father took a sip of his scotch. "We need to order so we don't give them anything to add to the gossip mill."

She was too shocked to argue. "Fine. I'll have a salad, but don't expect me to eat."

She wouldn't be able to eat a thing until she broke the news to Annabelle. Maybe she'd wait until Annabelle called her tomorrow to report on her adventures in dining. Besides, there was only so much a person could go through. Her plan to dine with each of her parents at their respective country clubs within a twenty-four-hour period was over her personal limit. Expecting her to break the devastating news to her best friend was more torture than any human being should be expected to face. No, even Annabelle would understand why Becca waited; that is, if Annabelle ever spoke to Becca again. She took another slug of scotch and waited for the fire to hit her stomach and maybe give her the strength she needed to get through the next day.

Chapter 9

Four days had passed since Annabelle torqued her ankle, and she still wasn't used to the crutches. She rushed through the sanctuary doors. Okay, she pushed one open with her shoulder, and as quickly as possible, got her crutches and the rest of her body through the swinging doors, blessed herself with holy water, and scanned the pews for the family. Her mother always insisted on sitting as far in front as possible and this time had snagged the third pew. Goody. Annabelle tugged at her skirt and pulled her cotton sweater more closely around her before she hobbled down the aisle, ignoring the stares, and the cloying scent of flowers.

There was nothing like walking into church late and on crutches to bring back every nightmare experience she'd ever had within the hallowed halls of St. Joseph's. The memory of Sister John Claire pulling her around by the ear and parading her up and down the aisles in front of the entire school population assaulted her. Every person who attended daily Mass during Lent had witnessed her humiliation. The Friday morning Mass-acre, as she dubbed it, ran on a never-ending loop through her mind like a bad B movie on the late-night cable lineup.

Today only added a new episode to *Annabelle's Life: The Good, The Bad, and The Humiliating*.

The congregation watched as she limped down the aisle like a badly dressed disabled bride. The stabilization boot, obviously designed by a straight man, made her leg look ugly and forced her to wear flats on her uninjured foot. God forbid the designer put a little heel on it, or make it a slingback. Sheesh. No wonder she was depressed. It looked worse than Aunt Rose's orthopedic shoes. Which, when you think about it, went a long way to explaining Aunt Rose's perpetual nasty mood. A mood Annabelle had been suffering from since the day she hurt her stupid ankle.

It didn't help that the morning had not gone as planned. She and Mike had a late night and an even later morning. Okay, so she was easily distracted. Who knew people actually made love in the shower? Although doing it on one leg was a bit of a challenge. Being late for Mother's Day, however, was unforgivable and liable to haunt her for the rest of her days.

Thumping down the aisle late for Mass earned her death glares from both Mama and Aunt Rose. Papa looked as if he was already asleep. He was lucky Mama stared at her instead of elbowing him in the ribs.

Richie gave her one of his annoying knowing looks, which made her want to stick her tongue out at him. God, she was reverting to childhood.

She genuflected—as much as she could, considering the crutch situation—and then hopped on one foot while she tried to figure out what to do with the crutches. You'd think they'd have come up with collapsible crutches by now or at least prettier ones.

After what seemed like an eternity, Rich took pity on her and laid the crutches on the floor in front of the kneeler. He held her elbow as she scooted into the pew. Not ten seconds after she got her butt settled on the bench, the congregation stood to say the Our Father.

Mama elbowed Papa in the ribs to wake him.

Rich gave her a hand getting her butt off the bench. "Nice entrance," he whispered like he had when they were kids.

Mama shushed them just like old times, and the Mass went on and on and on.

When Mass was almost over, Rich retrieved the crutches and walked her out ahead of the crowd, holding the doors open for her as he went. He opened the outer doors, and sunlight spilled in. Annabelle felt as if she could breathe for the first time since she'd arrived. The church wasn't stifling—it was her parents.

She enjoyed going to Mass, but she always went alone. She tried to go Saturday afternoon to avoid her parents. She even begged out of Midnight Mass on Christmas Eve, claiming she was too tired. With the exception of Rosalie's wedding, she hadn't celebrated Mass with her family since before she'd moved to Philadelphia. If Annabelle could have avoided the whole "always the bridesmaid and never the bride" nightmare, she would have skipped that Mass, too.

After moving away from home, she skipped church more often than not. Once Chip got sick, Mass had kept her sane. She prayed constantly he would survive, and when she was sure he wouldn't, she prayed for a pain-free passing. God hadn't granted either.

She hobbled to the bench outside and lowered herself onto the concrete seat. She shaded her eyes from the sun and squinted at Richie, who looked like he wore a halo. Obviously a trick of the sun. As much as she loved him, Richie was no angel. "Where did you get reservations?"

Rich sat beside her and held her crutches upright. "At an old friend's restaurant. He was able to squeeze me in at the last minute."

"Is the food good?"

"Yeah. I haven't been there in years, but it used to be. I'm sure it still is."

"If not, I'm not protecting you from Mama's wrath. You're on your own."

"Gee, thanks."

The rest of the family exited the church after shaking the Father's hand.

Rich rose and hauled her off the bench. "Are you up for walking a few blocks?"

"You don't have your car?"

"Why would I drive? Everything is within a five-block radius."

"Gee, I don't know. Maybe because I fell off a ladder, tore all the tendons in my ankle, and walking on crutches means I'm effectively walking on my hands!" She held her hands out and showed him Band-Aid–covered blisters.

"Want a piggyback ride?"

"No. I want a cab ride."

"Aw, come on, buck up. It's just a block and a half."

"Sure. Okay. No problem." She took her crutch and aimed for Richie's foot, crushing a toe under the rubber-tipped crutch and scarring the Italian brown leather. It felt good to know that she wouldn't be the only one bucking up because she was in pain.

❖ ❖ ❖

Mike loved his mother. He really did. Heck, he even loved Vinny and Mona DiNicola. After all, they were practically family. When you had as few family members as Mike, you appreciated the ones you had. Right now, he was ready to strangle all three of them.

When he'd arrived at the specified time, Mother's Day gift in hand, he'd been stunned to see Rita, Mona's second cousin, sitting with his mother. Rita was beautiful, tall, bleached blonde, twentysomething, and single. Before Nick's engagement, she'd gone after him with a single-minded determination that could only be described as scary. Now she seemed to be targeting Mike. Clue number one was when she muscled her grandmother out of the seat next to Mike. The second and third clues were her leaning into him with both her breasts in his face and whispering in his ear.

Talk about an awkward situation with the potential to turn volatile. The worst part about it was he had no idea how to avoid disaster. Guilt had already invaded his consciousness, and he'd done nothing to deserve it, which made the situation even more egregious, if that was possible. Mike figured that if he was going to feel guilty, he should have at least had the opportunity to do something worthy of guilt. Guilt for something he hadn't done was just wrong.

Rita drew the attention of every man in the room because she wore what had to be a Frederick's of Hollywood skintight dress with a plunging neckline that ended in the vicinity of her navel. Vinny stared at her with a glazed look in his eyes. Most of the men did, but it wasn't the men who mattered. The back dining room was reserved for "family" members, so every woman who saw Mike and Rita together was directly related to someone in "the family" and had known him since he was in high school. In woman-speak, Mike having a date—even the illusion of a date—at a family affair like this meant he was in a serious relationship, which also meant he was seriously fucked.

Annabelle's hair stuck to the back of her neck, her ankle throbbed, and her parents' cold silence covered everyone around them like a cloud of dry ice fog in a bad production of *Macbeth*. She kept her head down and hobbled along behind the family. She didn't pay attention to where they were going, focusing instead on the sidewalk. Annabelle learned from experience that sidewalk bulges from tree-root growth don't mix well with crutches and should have warning signs.

She didn't think Mother's Day could get any worse until she followed the family through thick wooden doors into the bustling restaurant. She raised her head and was greeted by a hostess. "Welcome to DiNicola's."

"DiNicola's?" Annabelle had thought her humiliation was over when she hobbled out of church. But no. "Richie, you never told me you made reservations at DiNicola's."

"Hey, you called and told me I had to make reservations for Mother's Day, remember? Do you have any idea how hard it is to get reservations for brunch on Mother's Day? Let me tell you. It's easier to get tickets to a Springsteen concert at the Garden. With Springsteen at least the scalpers are out. You pay through the nose, but you can get tickets. Nobody scalps reservations. It's a good thing I saw Vinny at Rosalie's wedding."

"Yeah, great."

She had a bad feeling about this. She knew Mike planned to take his mother to brunch, so it wasn't a big stretch to think they'd dine at DiNicola's. After all, the way he talked about Vinny, you'd think they were related. Annabelle would look like a stalker. Worse, she'd look as if she'd arranged this to meet Mike's mother. Something she really didn't want to do—ever. She was oh for two in the impress-the-mother game. Chip's mother had hated her with a bleeding passion, and Johnny's mother had tolerated her only because she'd agreed to marry the two-faced, cheating slimeball.

The thought of meeting Mike's mother had Annabelle's stomach preparing for a future meltdown. All systems were a go for the production of acid because one never knew when one might need to burn a hole or two or three in the lining of one's stomach.

The hostess smiled. "We'll walk through the bar into the back dining room. Please follow me."

Like a lemming, Annabelle took up the rear and made her way into the crowded bar. When the family stopped, she quit paying attention to the inordinate number of chair legs to trip over and looked to see what the holdup was.

Ben was the holdup. Ben decked out in a suit. She'd never seen him in a suit. Ever. "What are you doing here?"

He handed Mama a bouquet of flowers and kissed her powdered cheek. "Thanks for inviting me, Mrs. Ronaldi."

"You invited him?" Mama had the audacity to look proud of herself. She smiled as if expecting a compliment. She should have been worried about how much damage a crutch could do.

"Ben has no family here. Of course, I invited him. When I called for you one day, he answered. I asked if he was going home to spend the holiday with his mother, and he told me both his parents died when he was a little boy. I told him he should come with us."

Annabelle speared Ben with a look that had him taking a step back. Damn him and that devilish smirk.

Richie looked from Ben to her and back again. She gave Rich a shake of the head and received a shrug for her trouble. As if he didn't believe there was nothing between her and Ben. Hell, she couldn't blame him. Even she questioned it.

She waited until the rest of the family moved on before turning on Ben. "Do you mind telling me what the hell is going on here?"

"What do you mean? Your mother called for you and invited me to join your family for Mother's Day."

"Yes, I understand that, but what in the name of God made you accept such a blatant invitation from my mother? You knew she planned to throw us together." She poked him with her pointer finger for emphasis. "My mother has had one thing on her mind since I hit puberty—marrying me off." Poke. "Why would you knowingly submit yourself to my mother's patented form of torture?" Poke. "And why, if you knew you were coming to dinner, didn't you mention it yesterday when we closed the gallery together?" Poke. "You had plenty of opportunity. Heck, you could have told me over lunch."

Ben took her hand before she could poke him again. "Maybe I wanted to spend time with you outside the gallery and didn't want it to have anything to do with work."

"Don't you think this might be something you should consult me about?" She pulled her hand from his.

Ben smiled as if he wasn't speaking to someone who wanted him dead. "No, not especially."

The acid from Annabelle's stomach made its way to the back of her throat. She swallowed in time to keep it from doing more damage than burning the lining of her esophagus. She resisted the urge to smack him. After all, they were in a public place. Had they been at the gallery, she'd have picked up her crutch and popped him one. Then, after he came to, she'd tell him what she thought of him.

"You smug, arrogant—"

Ben put his hand on the small of Annabelle's back and steered her through the bar and into the back dining room.

Annabelle stepped into the room, scanned it for her family, but the first person she noticed was Mike. A woman practically sat on his lap. A strange metallic sound drowned out all others, like a constant gong or a cymbal on steroids. She blinked her eyes and hoped she was seeing things, but even her fertile mind couldn't make up anything like this. She didn't have that good of an imagination for horror. If she did, she'd be the next Stephen King.

She turned to Ben as if she'd never seen Mike and smiled. "Our table is over there." She nodded in the direction and held her head high as Ben, with his hand firmly on her back, led her to the table.

"Richie Ronaldi." She turned in the direction of the rich baritone and saw a rotund balding man with one eyebrow and a big smile pushing his way through the melee of the crowded restaurant. Rich stood next to their table and shook the man's hand. "Vinny, you remember my mother, Maria, my aunt Rose, my little sister, Annabelle, and that's her... friend Ben Walsh, and my father, Paul."

Vinny DiNicola nodded at everyone in turn and gave Annabelle a funny look.

Annabelle smiled her way through the introductions, Ben put his arm around her waist, and she decided to hit him with her crutch just as soon as she could figure out how to make it look like an accident.

The look Mike had given her when she and Ben arrived had nothing in common with the one he gave her when they parted company outside her apartment less than two hours ago. The worst part about it was the guilt written all over Mike's face.

She'd been sweating a minute ago, and now she'd entered a deep freeze. The gong in her head increased in volume, and her scalp got that weird prickly pins and needles feeling. She probably should have eaten something that morning. At least then, she'd have something to throw up when the time came.

She smiled her most pleasant smile as Ben pulled the chair out for her and took her crutches before helping her onto the chair.

Ben leaned over her shoulder and whispered, "That's your doctor friend wearing the blonde, isn't it?"

Annabelle jerked the napkin off the table and wrung it between her hands on her lap, wishing it were Ben's neck. "Yes."

He pushed her chair in. "Don't you think it was rude that he didn't at least say hello?"

His breath washed over her ear as he whispered. She turned her face to him and found herself close enough for a kiss... or bite. The look on her face must have forecasted the latter since he straightened and took a big step back. "My relationship with Mike is none of your business. Now why don't you go and sit with my mother since it's her invitation you accepted."

He nodded and left her sitting with a very clear view of Mike and his *puttana*.

Mike needed to get his temper under control. He was a doctor for crying out loud. He couldn't pummel everyone who touched his girlfriend, especially since he had Rita practically dripping off him. It's hard to act holier than-thou when you don't have a leg to stand on.

There were at least two members of the DiNicola family watching the disaster unfold. Any reaction on his part would be served right along with the antipasti to the entire room.

Mike ignored Rita and caught his mother's eye. He widened his eyes and gave a slight shake of his head while tilting it toward Rita. It's a good thing Rita was known for her bra size, not her intellect.

Mike's mother took the hint. "Excuse me. I'm going to the ladies' room to check my lipstick. Rita, would you mind showing me the way?"

"Sure, I'd be happy to." Rita giggled and squeezed Mike's bicep.

Mike stood and disentangled himself from Rita. After watching them leave, he wove his way through the tables and stopped at Annabelle's side. "May I speak to you in private?" He didn't wait for her response, but simply grabbed her crutches and pulled her chair out before helping her up. He tucked her to his side, turned, and considered taking her to the wine cellar, but if the tension running through her was anger, breakage could be a problem. No need to arm an angry Italian woman, he'd seen enough of them to know when to play it safe.

Mike led her into Vinny's office, closed and locked the door, and offered her a chair in front of the scarred metal desk. He went around to the other side, opened a bottom drawer, and removed a bottle of Jack Daniel's. He held it up. "Can I get you a drink?"

She shook her head even though she looked as if she could use a good belt. Mike grabbed a coffee cup that had been left on the desk, poured the contents into the trash can, and filled it with four fingers of Jack. He raised the glass in silent toast and sent a quick prayer for protection to both his ego and his heart before draining it.

Annabelle wrung the napkin she still held in her hands because Mike hadn't given her time to put it down before he'd practically forced her away from the table. She could only imagine what the family thought. She wasn't sure if upon her return she'd be congratulated or condemned.

Mike swallowed what had to be a hell of an after-burn. She wasn't much of a drinker, as evidenced by the wedding, but she had done shots once. After the first of many shots she remembered feeling as if she could light a cigarette with her breath, and after the last, she didn't remember anything.

Mike rounded the desk and leaned against the front of it, keeping the bottle and mug close at hand.

She had to tilt her head to see his face. "What was it you needed to talk to me about that was so important you felt the need to remove me from my—"

"Date?"

"Not that it's any of your business, but I didn't invite Ben to join the family dinner. I didn't even know he would be here. My mother arranged it."

"Not without Ben's help."

"So?" She let go of everything—she stuck the memory of Mike and the puttana someplace in a lockbox in the back of her mind to deal with at a later date... or not.

"What are we going to do about it?"

"*We?*"

"Yes, you and me."

"Why do *we* have to do anything? We can just go back and pretend we never saw each other." Mike didn't seem to like that idea if the grimace on his face was anything to go by. "Okay, how 'bout you do something. You, being a doctor, can tell my mother I felt ill. She'll have to believe you. I'll grab a cab home, and then you can do whatever you want to do with your own date."

"Oh no, you don't. There's no way I'm going to let you stick me with having to deal with everyone alone."

"Unless I'm mistaken, you were hardly alone, and you seemed to be handling her just fine."

"Her name is Rita. She was after Nick for a long time. Since he got married, it looks as if she's made me her latest target."

"Okay."

"Okay? That's all you have to say? She's a beautiful woman, and she's interested in me…"

Mike was attractive and nice, and any woman in her right mind would be falling all over herself to get to him. It didn't mean she wanted to hear about it. "I know you can get any girl you want."

"Obviously not. Since the only girl I want is you. And for some reason, you're making this whole 'getting' thing not only difficult but frustrating." He moved forward and put his hands on the arms of her chair so that they were practically nose to nose. "What's it gonna be, Annabelle. Me or Ben?"

"Very funny." Her eyes stung, and she could swear that vein in her forehead was popping out. Yeah, it was the only thing she and Julia Roberts had in common—a vein that popped out when they were really mad or about to cry. Right now, she wasn't sure if she was mad or if she was about to cry. Maybe both.

"You think this is a joke?" His voice seemed deeper than usual. He was so close, his heat warmed through her cotton sweater.

"Isn't it? Like I'm the only girl you want. Right. Why don't you leave me alone, and go back to your date?"

"You're serious? That's just great." He stood and stepped away from her. "I'm either totally inept, or you're incredibly difficult. Here I am trying to tell you that I'm hung up on you in a big way, and you're telling me to get lost."

Annabelle pushed her chair back and rose. She couldn't stand being still, and if she was going to fight with him, she was going to do it standing. "What?"

"You're going to make me repeat it, aren't you? You are difficult."

She stepped into his personal space. "Hey, if I'm so difficult, why are you bothering?"

"I think I love you."

Luckily, he didn't give her time to say anything before he kissed her. He'd probably bust something if she told him he thought wrong. She was pretty sure he'd come to his senses eventually and come to that conclusion on his own. After all, he was the smart one. She might as well have been one of Pavlov's dogs. Mike only had to be near her for her mind to shut down and her body to take over. Maybe her hormones were to blame. Whatever it was that caused it, the effect was spontaneous heat. More heat than she'd ever experienced with anyone before. Before she knew it, her mouth opened beneath his, her tongue fought for control of the kiss, her chest heaved, and warmth flooded her abdomen and all parts south. As for all parts north—they felt as if her skin had shrunk like a favorite sweater in a heavy-duty washer on hot. Real hot. Too hot to handle.

She opened her eyes and found Mike had his eyes opened too. Like he was making sure she wouldn't disappear, like he wanted to watch her reaction to him, like he was nervous about it.

The nervousness didn't last long, because when he pulled away, he wore a smug smile. "Maybe Rita did me a favor after all. Now, at least, I know you care about me enough to be jealous—"

She slammed her hands against Mike's chest and pushed him away. "I am not jealous—"

He caught her hands and held them behind her back, which pushed her front against his. "You're arrogant."

"Yeah, and I'm right. You are so easy to read. Whenever you get mad or upset, that vein in your forehead sticks out. I don't want Rita. The only person I thought about when I was stuck sitting with her was you. You're the only one I want, so you can calm down now. Wanna know what I think?"

She pulled her hands from his and crossed her arms between them. She would have tapped her toe if she could. Damn boot. "No, but I'm sure you'll tell me."

"I think we need a united front. We need to tell our families that we're together."

"You have no idea what you're going to unleash if my mother knows we're together. I told Mama we were keeping it light."

"Hey, I don't mind."

"My mother's goal in life is to get me married off, and she'd love to have a doctor in the family. She's a hypochondriac—you'd save her a fortune in medical bills. Believe me when I say you don't want to go there."

He leaned against the desk, crossing his arms and legs in front of him, and stared into her eyes so hard Annabelle wondered if he saw more than she knew. She really wished she'd paid more attention when they were talking about body language on all those news programs.

The whole crossed arms thing wasn't giving her any warm, fuzzy feelings.

"Maybe it's you who doesn't want to go there."

"Mike, I don't know what it is you want—"

"You don't?"

Okay, so she was supposed to do what? Become a mind reader? The only thing she could read right now was he was angry bordering on furious. Did he want to stir up a hornet's nest? Put them under a microscope for all to inspect? "Do you think this is the best time to dissect"— she pointed to him and then herself—"this?"

He set the mug on the desk with a thud. "Maybe you need to take some time and think about what it is you want from…"—he pointed to her and then himself—"this."

"What did I do to make you angry at me? I'm trying to help you out here. I'm trying to warn you about the consequences of your actions. If my mother thinks there's something serious between us, we'll be hounded until you run shrieking into the night about being rail-roaded into marriage."

"Why are you trying to hide the fact that we're together?"

Mike stepped forward. She stepped back. He was well past angry now. They did the two-step until Annabelle backed into the wall. They were nose to nose. He turned red. Her vein throbbed in time with her foot. He licked his lips, and her eyes widened.

She knew she had to explain herself. "You, me, this… thing between us. I thought it was—"

"Sex."

"Hey, don't give me that. I told you I liked you a lot, and I do."

"Yeah, but I just upped the stakes. I love you."

"Hold on. You said you *think* you love me."

"I'm pretty sure I love you."

"You hardly know me. I'm not so great, ya know. You said yourself I'm difficult. And I have bad luck. My first boyfriend died, and my second almost got killed."

"How?"

"I caught him doing the makeup lady next to a dead body. He was lucky there were no sharp instruments around."

"Why are you trying to talk me out of this? Is the thought of me being in love with you so terrible?"

He was too hot, too close, too nice, too dangerous. "No. I just don't know if I'm capable of falling in love with anyone ever again. I don't know if I want to take that chance."

"I'm no expert, but I don't think falling in love is something you choose. I didn't wake up one morning and think, I'm going to fall in love with Annabelle Ronaldi today—it just happened."

"Have you ever been in love before?"

"No."

"Then how do you know? Maybe you just like me a lot. Maybe you're mistaking lust for love. It happens. They even write songs about it."

"Look. I'm not expecting you to feel the same, but I would like you to go back in there with me to tell everyone we're together. Don't worry about your mother. I can handle her."

"Yeah, but I'm not sure I can."

There was a noise outside the office door. A smile transformed Mike's face. "You might not have much choice. It sounds as if we have an audience."

Mike reached over, opened the door, and exposed a strawberry blonde woman with the same gray eyes as his—she had to be his mother, Annabelle's mother, and Vinny with his arm around a bleached blonde woman. If Annabelle had to guess, she'd say it was Vinny's wife, Mona. Fabulous.

Vinny stepped forward. "So, what's the deal wit you two? We came to see if you need help. You got everything under control here, Mikey?"

Mike didn't look as if he believed him, but he didn't look angry either. "Thanks, Vin, we're good. Aren't we, Belle?"

Her stomach started churning again; all she could do was nod.

Mike put his arm around her. "Mum, this is my girlfriend, Annabelle Ronaldi. Belle, this is my mum, Colleen Flynn."

"Annabelle, lovely to meet you."

Annabelle grabbed Mike's coffee cup and drained it. She choked on the after-burn. She should have known better.

Mike smiled and patted her on the back.

"Nice to meet you, too." She croaked.

Mike's mother came forward. "Annabelle, are you feeling all right?"

If her head weren't swimming so badly and her stomach weren't threatening to rid itself of the liquid fire she just swallowed, she'd almost think this was comical. "Thank you, I'm fine."

Mike gave her that diagnostician look, the same one he gave her when she ripped apart her ankle. Sheesh, sometimes hanging with a doctor was annoying. It wasn't helping that she was slowly but surely dying of embarrassment.

"I probably should have eaten something before I left home, but I'm afraid it takes me longer to do everything since I hurt my ankle. I was even late to Mass."

Mike didn't look the least bit repentant.

Richie joined the throng outside the office door. Vinny clapped his hands and then rubbed them together. "I'll just put our tables together, and we can get to know each other. Whada'ya say?"

Everyone must have agreed because he and the woman next to him scurried off. Richie put his arm around Mama—who'd been strangely silent—and smiled at Mike's mom. "Come on, ladies. I'll walk you back to the table. Mike, Annabelle, we'll see you in a minute."

Mike ushered his mother out and passed her off. "Thanks, Rich." He shut the door. "That wasn't so bad. Was it?" He kissed her forehead. "Now, come on. Everyone's waiting for us, and you need to get something to eat. You scared me there for a minute. You're not much of a drinker, are you?"

Chapter 10

WHEN MIKE AND ANNABELLE RETURNED TO THE TABLE, there was no place for them to sit together. He'd be damned if he was going to sit alone, or worse yet, sit with Rita while Annabelle sat with Ben.

"Rita, I want to introduce you to my girlfriend's boss. I'm sure he'd love to hear all about your work. He owns an art gallery."

Rita smiled up at him. "Oh, I'd love to meet him. We'll have so much in common. You know, I'm considered something of an artist myself."

"I can tell. I don't know how you do what you do. It's definitely an art."

Mike helped Rita out of her chair and turned to Annabelle. "Have a seat. This will just take a moment."

Rita made a few adjustments to her dress to show off her assets and nodded at Mike, who was only too happy to dump her on his nemesis. He walked her over to where Ben was seated.

"Ben, I'd like you to meet my friend Rita."

Ben stood and gave Mike a look that was tantamount to conceding the race for Annabelle—today at least. "Nice to meet you, Rita." He took her hand in his to shake, but didn't release it.

"Rita, this is Ben Walsh." Mike pulled out her chair while Ben held her hand as his eyes made the trip from Rita's cleavage to her Care Bear belly button ring.

Mike left Ben to his meal and his consolation prize and went back to Annabelle. She and his mother were chatting. The only thing between them was his empty chair. "There, Ben should be occupied for a while." Mike sat, put his arm around Annabelle, and kissed her temple.

She took a sip of water and gave him a Mona Lisa smile. "Rita is an artist?"

Mike couldn't wipe the grin from his face. "You might say that."

"What exactly does she do?"

He held Annabelle's hand, studying her manicure. "She does women's nails and paints little pictures on them sometimes." Mike watched her try unsuccessfully not to laugh.

"That really is cruel."

"To whom, Ben or Rita?" He figured being stuck with Rita was a lot less painful than the other things he'd contemplated doing to Ben. "Ben doesn't look as if he has a problem with it."

"No. I just hope he doesn't give me a hard time tomorrow at work."

Annabelle's mother whispered to her aunt Rose, all the while keeping one eye on her and Mike—probably making notes for the wedding.

She'd never noticed before how often Mike touched her. It was as if being under Mama's watchful gaze gave every brush of his hand meaning. Every time he spoke to her, played with her hair, or put his arm around her, she felt as if she was being judged.

She wanted to strangle Mike for giving Mama a reason to start the constant questions, the constant advice, and the constant annoyance she received when she so much as went on a date. After this demonstration, Mama would start shopping for a new mother-of-the-bride dress as soon as the stores opened tomorrow. At least Annabelle no longer lived with her parents. She'd have to take a lesson from Becca and screen her calls.

Annabelle tried to pay attention to the dinner conversation buzzing between her parents and Mike's mother. The easy camaraderie between Vinny, Mona, and Richie—she'd have to find out what was up with that. And the curious looks from Aunt Rose.

Mike, to his credit, stood up to his second interrogation—this one by Papa—the smooth yet insistent pressure by Mama, and the gypsy stare by Aunt Rose.

Annabelle tried unsuccessfully to shut out the echo of Mike's words in her mind. "I think I love you." Dear Lord, had he known how badly she didn't want to hear that, he never would have told her.

Why couldn't he keep things simple? He came over, he cooked, they ate, they talked, they had sex, sometimes they slept, sometimes they didn't, and then he left. It was the perfect relationship before he dropped the "L" bomb.

It wasn't as if she didn't feel something for him, because she did. She just did an admirable job avoiding even thinking about it.

She took a sip of her wine and moved the food around her plate. Mike watched and made her feel guilty for not eating. She couldn't possibly eat any more. She felt sick, her ankle throbbed, and she just wanted to curl up in bed with an ice pack and forget today ever happened.

Mike kept checking the time.

"What's wrong?"

"Nothing. I have to get back to the hospital. Someone's covering for me, and I told her I'd be back by three. It's already one thirty, and I want to take you home and help you get settled in."

"Are you sure?" She was really glad he wanted to. Her mother wouldn't get bent out of shape if the news of her leaving early came from Mike.

"Yeah, especially since I don't know when I'll be able to see you again. My work schedule between now and Memorial Day is more insane than usual, since I'm covering for people in exchange for the weekend off."

Annabelle smiled. "I take it you want to leave now?"

"You don't mind leaving a little early?"

"No, not at all."

Mike whispered to his mother, who turned toward Annabelle. "That's fine, Michael. Don't mind me. I've wanted to visit with Vinny, Mona, and the children anyway. I'm sure Annabelle's mother won't mind you seeing her home properly, would you, Maria?"

Mama smiled and made a shooing motion. "Go, go. Of course, you want to spend time together. I remember what it was like when I first fell in love with my Paulie."

Annabelle couldn't believe her ears. Apparently, neither could Rich. They looked at each other and then at their mother. Rich laughed and stopped abruptly, ending in a grunt. Annabelle grinned, thankful she was out of reach.

Mike pushed his chair back and stood. "I'm afraid Annabelle and I have to leave a little early. I want to take her home before I have to get back to the hospital."

Of course, her whole family smiled and nodded, which was good. She didn't think Ben even noticed, which was better. If he had, she'd have hell to pay tomorrow. But Ben didn't seem to have a problem with Rita. He looked as if he was enjoying himself, which was more than Annabelle could say.

She gathered her purse while Mike retrieved her crutches. "Bye, Mama, Papa, Aunt Rose. Richie, will you take care of this, and let me know how much I owe you?"

"Don't worry about it. Take good care of that ankle. I'll call you later."

"Thanks, Rich." Annabelle rose and took her crutches. "Mike, are you ready?"

He pulled out his wallet, and Vinny waved him off.

"Go. Take care of your girlfriend. Come by for dinner sometime, and we'll talk."

She waited for Mike as he kissed his mother good-bye and then made the rounds with her family. Papa shook Mike's hand hard enough to make him wince. Annabelle cringed as he shook Mama's hand. She leaned over and whispered something to Aunt Rose, who, much to Annabelle's mortification, took Mike's face in her hands, kissed him on both cheeks. "You're a good boy. Everything with your job and with Annabelle will work out in time. Have faith… and make sure you got a lot of antacids."

Mike, who obviously wasn't used to dealing with crazy people, seemed so out of his depth he just nodded and smiled. It was a pained smile, since Rose pinched one of his cheeks before she released him.

Annabelle tugged on his suit jacket. "Let's go." She shot Aunt Rose a look that would scare most people. It always worked on Ben.

Aunt Rose only laughed. "Don't look at me with that tone of face. You come talk to your aunt Rose. I'll tell you a thing or two. Not that you'll listen."

Annabelle took her crutches from Mike and did her best to run out of there. They wove their way through the crowded bar, and when they hit the waiting area, Mike stopped her and ran his hand down her back. "That wasn't so bad now, was it? My mum likes you. I knew she would."

She slung her purse at him. "It was a disaster! You heard my mother. And I can't believe what Aunt Rose told you. I swear, sometimes I think the woman is a witch."

"She said I was a good boy, and then something about my job and you... She was weird, but nice. Hardly a witch."

"Yeah, you say that now. You've never seen her give someone the evil eye. Believe me, you don't want to get on her bad side. She says stuff, and the next thing you know, it happens. She scares the crap out of me."

"You think she's psychic?"

"I don't know what to think. Are we going to stand here all day, or are you going to take me home?"

"I'm going to get a cab. Sit here. I'll be right back."

When Mike returned for Annabelle, she practically ran from the restaurant. He helped her into the cab, slid in beside her, and while pulling her close, gave the cabbie the address. He liked the way she fit against him, and he never tired of touching her. He loved the way she felt, the way she smelled, and the way she tasted.

He wanted to soak up as much enjoyment as possible before leaving her. Things at work were getting worse,

but he told himself he'd worry about that after Memorial
Day. Maybe spending a weekend with Annabelle would
help him figure out what direction he wanted to go in on
a career level and a personal level. He was paying big
for a weekend off, and paying in advance. Annabelle
and their relationship were worth it. Now if he could
only get her to believe that.

Tossing his lab coat on the hook in the break room,
Mike opened the back door of the practice and stepped
out into the alley in search of a sandwich, a cup of real
coffee, and a temporary release from the hell the office
had become. He was tired of all work and no life. Tired
of the constant censure he received from the partners.
Tired of the dirty looks, the way all conversation stopped
when he entered the room. The tension in the office ran
higher than the Empire State Building. When he saw
Millie, he wondered if she was doing the same.

Mike was happy to see her. He'd noticed she'd been
preoccupied all morning, and he intended to speak to her
and find out what was bothering her.

"Thank God you left. I need to talk to you, but it has
to be away from here." As she talked, she backed out of
the alley.

He took Millie by the arm, stopping her. "What's
going on? Are you okay?"

"I'm fine, but I'm worried about you." She waved
her hand, urging him to follow. She led him to a hole-in-
the-wall Lebanese place a couple of blocks away. He'd
worked two blocks away for two years, and he'd never
noticed it.

They grabbed a table, and a waiter brought them water. Millie pushed her menu aside. "Get the lamb kabob. It's amazing."

Mike nodded his assent, and Millie, obviously familiar with the menu, ordered for both of them.

After the waiter left, Millie took a long drink before she spoke. "I've never told anyone at work where I go on my lunch hour, because I don't want to see them any more than I have to. You're the only one I've brought here. No one else knows about this place."

"Okay."

"Something happened that you need to know about. When I came in this morning, I took a phone call from a Mr. Tuggle. At first, I thought he was a patient. I asked if I could help him, and he began asking a lot of questions about the practice, and more specifically, about you. When I asked what these questions were in reference to he said he was doing a survey of pulmonary practices, which would make sense, except for the questions that were specifically about you."

"What kind of questions?"

"He asked what kind of doctor you were, whether you were ambitious, easy to work with, knowledgeable, good with patients, that kind of thing. At first, I thought someone was trying to get you into trouble, since the partners aren't happy with your refusal to look the other way when it comes to Dr. Meyer. But he wasn't looking for dirt. I thought you should know someone is looking at you."

Their food was delivered. Mike could see why Millie ate there almost every day. The food was healthy, tasty, and reasonably priced. If that wasn't enough of a reason to love the place, the relaxing atmosphere cinched it. He was sure if he'd been there alone, the lulling music and the trickle of the waterfall on the opposite wall would have put him to sleep. The tranquility of the place, a full stomach, and an average of four hours of sleep a night over the past three weeks had him ordering a double Turkish coffee.

After the jolt of caffeine, he asked Millie to find out if any of the other nurses had anything similar happen to them. It didn't sound like his partners. If they wanted to question the nurses, they'd pull them into their offices and ask. They didn't need to hire a third party and would avoid one at all cost. Digging for dirt on him would risk uncovering something about Dr. Meyer. Still, it made Mike want to look over his shoulder.

He'd make a point to take the business card for the lawyer Nick had recommended to him when he picked up the car. The longer Mike worked toward a partnership that would never be, the more money he lost. Too bad that by getting out of a bad situation, he could be flushing away more than money. He could be flushing away the last two years of his life.

The buzzer rang, waking Annabelle from a delicious dream. Damn, she was just getting to the good part too. Dave barked as she pulled a robe on and half hopped, half stumbled, to the intercom since she'd forgotten her crutches. "What?"

"Is that any way to answer the door? What if I was Mike?"

"Mike has the decency not to come by at ungodly hours unannounced." Though he had been known to phone at ungodly hours, but that never forced her out of bed. She buzzed her mother in and unlocked the front door just in time for Mama to make her grand entrance.

Annabelle discovered Mama scared Dave too, because he went running for the garden. She only wished she could join him.

She made it to the kitchen before the woman in question entered. She needed caffeine, and a lot of it, if she was to survive the ordeal ahead that held all the earmarks of a maternal surprise attack.

She made coffee as Mama placed her purse on the bar separating the kitchen from the dining area and opened the refrigerator, probably in search of milk.

Annabelle tried to remember the last time she'd gone shopping and couldn't. Chances are, whatever milk products were still present in the refrigerator, were not fit for human consumption. From the look on Mama's face after opening the milk, Annabelle was right.

"You'll have to drink it black."

"And this is how you keep your house? There's no food, you haven't vacuumed or dusted, and you have cups and plates lying all over. You're almost as big a slob as your sister."

"Supplies are under the sink if you feel the need to clean. I've been laid up in case you haven't noticed."

The coffee machine made the last gurgle signaling its completion and not a second too soon. Annabelle opened the cabinet where the coffee cups should be only to find it bare. A glance at the sink told the whole sad story. From the look on her mother's face, she noticed the same thing.

"You go get cleaned up, and for God's sake put some clothes on. I'll wash the dishes, and then we can sit down and have a nice talk over breakfast."

"Not unless you have breakfast stuffed in your handbag." She hopped to her room while her mother mumbled in Italian about a mother's curse. What a way to start the day.

Annabelle wasn't interested in hearing her mother's promarriage and children rant. She didn't need to be at work until 11:00 a.m., and it was... geez, not even 8:00 a.m. yet. She threw on shorts and a T-shirt, eager to get through the torturous visit as soon as possible. The next time she saw Mike she was going to kill him for bringing this on her.

She collected her crutches, choosing not to wear her air cast. She left the Ace bandage on and made her way back to the kitchen and the promise of coffee. Unfortunately, coffee had been the only thing she'd had to look forward to lately. She missed Mike. She missed waking in his arms, she missed the food he cooked, she missed the way her apartment always seemed to sparkle when he was around, and she missed talking to him.

"You never return my phone calls. I leave messages, and I never hear from you. I read in the paper how people with broken legs die of blood clots. I almost sent Papa over to make sure you weren't lying dead on the floor, but I decided to come myself. Someone needs to talk sense to you."

And it began. "Mama, I tore some tendons in my ankle. I didn't break my leg. I'm fine."

Mama must have brought food, because there were bagels and cream cheese on a plate on the counter. But then, they could have been in the refrigerator. She never bothered to look in there for food. Maybe Mike had brought them on his last visit.

Mama carried the bagels and coffee to the table, which Annabelle noticed had been set. "So, did you and your doctor have a nice time together on Mother's Day? He's a good man, that one."

Annabelle pulled a chair out, set her crutches against the wall, and sat. She took a bite of a fresh bagel and schmear. She was hungrier than she thought. "He brought me home and then went to work. I haven't seen him since. Maybe you and Aunt Rose scared him off." Lord knew they scared her often enough.

"Nonsense." Mama sipped her coffee and studied her.

She felt like a freaking sideshow.

"Your aunt Rose and I were encouraging. You should take a lesson from us. And you gotta be understanding of his work. He's an important man. He works hard."

Annabelle wiped her mouth on a cloth napkin she'd never seen before and looked at her mother, who sat wearing an apron she was sure Rosalie never wore. Maybe her mother had given it to Rosalie so she'd have something to wear when she stopped by to torture her.

"I am understanding. I understand you're fishing for information, but you're not going to get any out of me. Please, Mama, stay out of my love life. I can screw it up all by myself. I don't need your help."

Mama nibbled on a dry bagel. "Why do you talk crazy like that? You finally have a nice man, with a nice job, and a bright future. You better not break his heart like you did Johnny DePalma's. His mother called me in tears."

"If Mrs. DePalma called you crying, it was no fault of mine."

"Mike is a good man. Your aunt Rose said—"

"Mama, I don't want to know what Aunt Rose said. I want you both to leave Mike and me alone. I'm tired of you running my life. I might be guilty for letting you push me into an engagement with that two-timing snake. But I'm stronger now, and I won't let you do it again. If and when I ever decide to get married, I'll do it on my own without any input from you or anyone else."

She reached for her bagel only to find her plate empty. If she kept eating like this, she'd weigh two hundred pounds before she'd ever be released from ugly-boot hell.

She sipped on her coffee and decided to let her mother have it. "Mama, I'm happy being single. I have a great apartment, a job I love, and good friends. I'm in no rush to get married."

Mama almost spit out her coffee. "What? You been talking to your sister? She learned her lesson and got married. You need to think about your future. You're not getting any younger. I see the way your doctor looks at you. If you want to have children—"

Annabelle set her empty cup on the table harder than she'd intended. "I have plenty of time to decide if I want children."

"Are you insane? Of course you want children."

"Not everyone wants children. Heck, some people shouldn't have kids. Right now, I'm going to concentrate on myself and take everything else as it comes."

She smiled to herself. God it felt good to say it out loud. Mama mumbled Hail Marys under her breath and beat her chest.

Annabelle pushed her chair back to stand. "Mama, if that's all—"

"I'm gonna die before I hold a grandchild in my arms, and you are to blame."

"Hold on. Blame Rosalie and Richie before you start blaming me. I'm the youngest. And for all you know, Rosalie might come home from her honeymoon pregnant. Why don't you pray for that and leave me alone?"

Mama stood and looked as if she'd been slapped. Annabelle had gone too far. She stood, grabbed her crutches, and backpedaled. "Mama, I'm sorry. I didn't mean that. It's just that I need to live my life on my terms, not yours."

"Your terms. Eh? You'll see you're not so different from me. I just pray you see that before you lose something precious."

Damn, was that a curse? Annabelle didn't know what to say. "I have to get ready for work."

"Go, get ready. I'll clean up a little before I go. I wouldn't want your doctor to come over and find a mess like I did."

"Okay, bye, Mama." Annabelle kissed her mother's cheek and did what she was told. Maybe she hadn't gotten that much stronger after all.

Maddòne.

Chapter 11

MIKE KNOCKED ON THE EXAM-ROOM DOOR BEFORE entering. He smiled at Lisa Tandry, who had her nose buried in a book. He checked his watch. He was running on time and was glad for it. Lisa hated being kept waiting. The busy mother of three, who worked full-time out of her home, never stopped—even when she should.

Lisa didn't look thrilled to have to put her book away, but she did.

Mike scanned her chart and smiled. A nurse had written "fat" instead of her weight. "Are you giving the nurses a hard time again, Lisa? It looks as if you refused to get on the scale."

Lisa crossed her arms. "I'm fat. I gained thirty pounds thanks to the prednisone. You want to know how fat I am, you do the math. Besides, it's not like you're going to change the treatment because I look more like an elephant than a gazelle. Are you?"

Mike stepped closer and gave her shoulder a squeeze. "You don't look like an elephant, and I'm sorry about the weight gain."

Lisa shrugged. "It's not your fault, but it sure feels good to blame you. Not only does the prednisone make me want to eat everything that isn't nailed down, it turns me into the bitch from hell. 'Roid rage is alive and well and living in my house. I swear I would have committed murder the other day if I hadn't had my youngest in the car with me. It took some idiot two lights to make a left. I almost got out of the car and pulled him and the little kick-me-dog he had on his lap out through his opened window and beat him senseless. But then he was probably already senseless at the time, hence the rage."

Mike made a note of it in her file. "How are you feeling now? Back to one hundred percent?"

"Almost. I still can't run."

Mike looked over her chart. "Could you before?"

Lisa moved from the chair to the exam table and on the way swatted him on the shoulder. Mike laughed. She was definitely feeling better. The last time he saw her, two weeks ago, they'd fought about IV steroids. He'd wanted Lisa to spend a few hours at the hospital getting a round of IV steroids because she was in pretty bad shape and IV steroids worked better and faster than oral. She told him she couldn't possibly do that. It was her daughter's birthday, and she was expecting twelve little girls at noon the next day, and she hadn't decorated the house or made the cake yet. The fact she couldn't breathe never entered her mind. They'd compromised, and she agreed to two steroid shots, one in each arm. He didn't bother telling her she'd have a hard time hanging decorations because both her arms would be too sore to raise over her head. He figured she'd figure it out for herself.

He listened to her heart and then moved behind her. "Lift up your shirt in the back for me."

"Like you can't do that yourself." She humphed but finally did as he asked. She was still wheezing, and after a half-dozen deep breaths, she went on a coughing jag.

"You sound better than you did two weeks ago, but you're still not up for running. Try pretreating, and let's keep it down to a walk."

He looked in her ear.

"I don't remember asking for advice about laundry." She turned her head so he could look in her other ear.

Mike rolled his eyes. "You know what I'm talking about. I want you to use your inhaler fifteen minutes before exercise and again just before you begin. Open your mouth and say, 'Ah.'"

Lisa did. Her throat looked fine. "I hate those inhalers."

"Dr. Flynn, phone call on line two. Dr. Mike Flynn, phone call line two."

"I know you do. But if you ever want to run again, you'll try it." Mike set Lisa's chart on the counter. "Would you excuse me for a minute?"

"Do I have a choice?" She picked up her book, smiled, and waved him away.

Mike stepped into the hall. Millie stood by the desk and motioned him over.

"What's the deal? You know I don't like to take calls when I'm with patients."

She held the phone. "It's someone from Eastern Heart Specialists calling for you. You need to take it."

He grumbled but took the call anyway. "Hello, this is Dr. Flynn."

"Dr. Flynn, this is Timothy Boyd. I'm the senior vice president in charge of human resources at Eastern Heart Specialists. In case you're not familiar with Eastern Heart Specialists, we are among the top ten cardiology practices in the country."

"Yes, Mr. Boyd. I'm familiar with EHS."

"Very good. We are expanding the practice, and we're looking to hire another pulmonologist, someone board certified in pulmonology as well as critical care. You came highly recommended. I'm hoping we can talk you into an interview."

"Yes, I'm very interested, but unfortunately, I'm not available until…" Mike scrolled through the calendar on his phone looking for a day he could get out until mid-afternoon. "How does the Wednesday after Memorial Day sound?" Millie practically jumped up and down next to him.

"Let's see, that would work. How does the morning look for you?"

"Morning is good. The earlier, the better."

"Nine o'clock all right?"

"Yes." Mike added it to his calendar.

"Good. I'll send you some information on the practice and directions to our office."

"That sounds great, Mr. Boyd. I'll put my nurse on the phone to give you my address and whatever else you need. I'm sorry I have to run, but I have a patient waiting."

"I understand. I look forward to meeting you. Have a nice holiday."

"Thank you. You do the same. I'll see you then on Wednesday, May thirtieth."

Mike handed the phone and his driver's license to Millie. "Could you please give Mr. Boyd my address and whatever else he needs? I have to get back to my patient."

Millie smiled so wide, her face split in two. "Yes, Doctor, it's my pleasure."

When he returned, he checked to make sure Lisa's prescriptions were all up-to-date before he took a seat beside her. "So, how are things?"

"Ah, let's see. What's happened over the last two weeks in my wild and wacky life?" She thought for a moment and then broke out into a full grin. "My son shaved half his eyebrow off and blamed it on his sisters. He said they went into his room and shaved it off while he slept. Do you believe he actually thought I'd fall for that? When I finally got him to admit he lied, he said he did it because he was always getting into trouble and the girls never did."

Mike laughed. "How old is Trevor now?"

"Twelve. And now he's walking around with one-and-a-half eyebrows. I told him the reason he's always in trouble is because he's always doing bad stuff. Fortunately, the girls haven't started with that yet."

Mike sat back. "Just give them time. Jodi is going to be a handful."

Lisa's eyes brightened, "She already is. She spent the whole school year talking about a little girl named Ceekay. I was really concerned about this kid because in one year, she'd broken both her arm and her leg. I was also curious about what kind of name Ceekay was. Jodi said she had red hair, so I figured she wasn't Asian. So there I was at Jodi's school for the year-end picnic, and I asked her teacher which girl Ceekay was. The woman looked at me funny and said there was no Ceekay in the class." Lisa rolled her eyes. "Ceekay turned out to be Jodi's imaginary friend. And to think I fell for it for the whole year. Either she's really good, or I'm really dumb."

Mike busted out laughing. "Jodi's really good."

Mike always booked Lisa's appointments for an extra ten minutes. He'd been seeing her since he first started at the practice. He'd gotten to know her and even her kids really well since sometimes she'd bring them in with her. "What about Sarah?"

Lisa waved her hand. "She's fine. Just dancing her little heart out. I had to take her for shots the other day, and she screamed and carried on. I had her on my lap with one leg crossed over both of hers and my arms wrapped around her so she couldn't move, and the little witch tried to bite my face!"

Sarah's dislike of needles was legendary, but Mike had thought by the time a kid hit the age of seven she'd have gotten over it. Mike tried to keep from laughing; that kid was too much.

Lisa gave Mike a dirty look. "I was in the middle of scolding her, and telling her to apologize to the doctor, when he said it was okay." She shook her head. "Do you believe that? Like hell it's okay! The girl is an animal."

Lisa stood and grabbed her bag. She was definitely one of his challenging patients, but she was also one of his favorites. He walked her to the appointment desk and put her paperwork on the desk for Millie. Before he left, he turned back to Lisa. "You take care, and if I don't see you before, I'll see you in four weeks."

Lisa put her purse on the desk and turned to Millie. "He misses me when I'm healthy."

Millie beamed back at her. "We all do."

Mike went through the rest of the day with a smug smile on his face. He didn't let Dr. Meyer's behavior bother him or the closed-door meeting the partners held.

If this position came through, he'd be able to work like a normal doctor. Sure, a doctor's hours varied, but they weren't supposed to be insane.

He felt as if he'd been living the life of a perpetual resident. If his interview turned into an offer, he might actually have time to spend with Annabelle. A position with EHS would not only solve his social problem, it might also solve his financial difficulties and give him the possibility to change the minds of the partners concerning the Dr. Meyer situation. He'd have more leverage if he had a signed contract with a practice out of the area. The partners would be more apt to do whatever it took to ensure he wouldn't talk behind anyone's back.

In between patients, Mike text messaged Annabelle a dinner invitation. He was with his next patient when his phone vibrated. He couldn't wait until he could get away and check her reply.

Annabelle's phone buzzed, interrupting her work on the plans for the next big show. "Annabelle, you have a visitor."

She checked the clock and wondered where the time had gone. It was as if she'd lost at least an hour. She gave the sketches and plans a once-over and took one last sip of her cold coffee before buzzing her assistant back. "Kerri, could you please send him up?"

She thunked her way over to the mirror, checked her makeup, and as she finished with her lipstick, she turned and caught Mike standing in the doorway, a huge smile on his face. "What happened? Did you win the lottery?"

He kicked the door shut and walked toward her with a lightness about him she'd never seen. "How do you know something happened?"

"I don't know. I just do."

He kissed her, picked her up, and spun her around.

After she stopped screaming and clinging to him, she found her feet back on the floor and kissed him again. "Now tell me the good news."

"I was going to tell you over dinner."

"Why wait?"

"Because I thought we'd get a bottle of wine or champagne."

"We still can, but I want to hear it now."

"Anyone ever tell you you're impatient?"

"Yeah. Come on, spill."

He walked around the desk and checked behind the screens she'd set up to hide the supplies. "I was just offered an interview with one of the top cardiology practices in the country."

"But you're a pulmonologist. What would you be doing in a cardiology practice?"

"Cardiologists and pulmonologists work closely together, especially since I'm board certified in both critical care and pulmonology."

She'd followed and threw her arms around him. "Wow, I didn't know you were board certified. This is great! I'm so happy for you."

"Thanks. The interview isn't for a couple more weeks, but they said I had been highly recommended, and they've already called asking about my performance. Millie, one of the nurses I work with, mentioned it. Thank God they spoke to the one person who still likes me. The head of HR already had references from outside the practice. Since I'm pretty sure I'm not going to get good references from them, it's a stroke of luck."

"Have you told your mother yet?"

"No, I barely had time to call you. I'll tell her tomorrow."

Annabelle stepped out of his arms. "She called me today and said she wants to come by the gallery next week to look around, have lunch, and get to know each other."

"Why do you sound as if you're preparing to be tortured?"

She turned and looked out the window. "I've never had a boyfriend whose parents liked me. They either hated me or barely tolerated me."

He took her in his arms. "I love you, and my mother will love you, too."

"I'd be happy with like. I think love is too much to hope for." She rested her head on his shoulder and enjoyed the feeling of his arms around her. It had been so long since he'd held her. She'd missed him so much that it scared her.

"Annabelle?"

"Yeah?"

"What's up with the screens?"

"Nothing. I was just sick of looking at all the art supplies."

"But you're an artist."

"No, I was an artist. I'm not anymore. Ben put all the supplies up here to bother me, but I took care of that. So, where do you want to celebrate? My place or yours?"

Mike pulled away a little and looked into her eyes in that way he had that made her feel as if he could read her mind. "I thought you'd want to go out."

She loosened his tie and slid open the top two buttons of his shirt while nibbling on his ear. "I think we should pick up a bottle of champagne and takeout on the way home and celebrate in bed. Sound good to you?"

Mike's kiss answered the question.

He kissed her gently, wanting the slow, steady build of desire, but Annabelle wasn't having any of that. It seemed as if it had been ages since he'd held her, touched her, and tasted her. The frantic way her hands slid down the front of his pants, squeezing his erection through the fabric, had him locking his knees to keep from falling down. She touched him as if she couldn't get enough of him, driving him higher because he couldn't get enough of her either. Sometimes you had to go at it hot, hard, and fast—the first time at least. He had all night to make love to her, right now, though, there was nothing gentle about what she wanted, and that was just fine with him.

He'd been hard ever since he walked through the door and saw Annabelle wearing her short-sleeved, double-breasted coatdress made of a noisy material in an iridescent navy blue that matched her eyes. Since that moment, all he could think of was taking it off her. Mike's fingers itched to unhook the wide belt at her waist and unbutton the four buttons holding the dress closed to see what she wore beneath. He'd love to fulfill that fantasy of her showing up in nothing but a trench coat and this was close enough.

Mike had closed the door when he came in, but for what he wanted to do, he needed it locked. Straightening to his full height, he pulled her closer, the imprint of her body hot and soft against his. Slowly, he backed her into the door. With one hand, he engaged the lock, as the other slid up her thigh, raising the hem of the short dress until he hit the soft skin of her bottom. When he slid his hand up her to her hip, he discovered the lace of a thong. He swallowed hard, raised her leg to his hip, and pressed his erection against her. The scent of orange, vanilla, and Annabelle became stronger as her body heated. Breaking the kiss, he moved lower, kissing her neck as he took care of the top two buttons and wide belt. The dress slid down, and she freed her arms so it hung at her hips. A sheer white demi bra offered her breasts to him like a gift. Her dusky nipples showed through the sheer fabric. He opened his mouth over it and sucked her hard nipple deep into his mouth.

Annabelle released his belt, slid open his trousers, and shoved her hand beneath the waistband of his jockeys. A groan ripped from deep in his throat when her hand wrapped around his dick.

"No." He was in grave danger of losing it before he got inside her, and that was out of the question. He extracted her hand from his pants, and she wrapped her arms around his neck and drugged him with a long, hot kiss that almost made him change his mind. Almost.

"Mike, I don't think I can wait any longer. Please. Now."

He turned her around, drew her back to his front, and as he pulled her long hair to the side and feasted on her neck, he took the few steps to the first flat surface he saw. Her desk. Not taking the time to move the mess of papers, he leaned her over, yanked his wallet out of his pants, and removed the condom before sliding her thong down. He freed himself from his briefs, pushing them out of his way, and sheathed himself as his slacks slid down his legs. The belt buckle hit the wood floor with a thunk. She pulled her dress up as he slid his hands over her bottom and around, his fingers brushing over her clitoris, parting her, and teasing the hot, wet folds. She moaned as he parted her legs to accommodate him and arched her back. He slid in and, grasping her hips, held her still. She was tight, wet, hot, and gripping him with her body. The phone rang. "Shit."

"It's Ben. I have to answer it. He knows I'm here."

She looked over her shoulder, and he nodded, took a deep breath, and held it as she picked up the phone. "Yes?"

Mike leaned forward, moving deeper within her, and heard Ben's voice. "Are you leaving now? Or do you want me to lock up?"

"No. I'm in the middle of something. I'm going to be a while, so lock up."

"All work and no play makes Annabelle a dull girl. Why don't you join me?"

"No, thanks. I'm in the middle of something, and I'm waiting for Mike to come. Once he does, we'll take off."

"Do you want me to come and keep you company until he gets here?"

Mike took advantage of the fact she was leaning on her elbows to slip his hands up and snap open the front clasp of her bra. She coughed when he moved the cups aside and palmed her breasts.

"No… um, no thanks. I'm good."

"Is everything okay? You sound funny."

"I'm fine. Just a little… distracted. I'm, um, in the middle of something, like I said."

"Okay. If you're sure you don't need me to come. I can help with whatever you're doing. The two of us can make fast work of it. Then you'll be ready for Mike when he comes. Are you sure you don't want my help?"

Mike whispered in her ear. "Over my dead body."

"Yes, I mean, no, thanks. I've got it under control. See you tomorrow. Bye." She hit the end button, tossed the phone away, and groaned as Mike pulled almost all the way out and sank back in. His arms banded around her, and she pushed back against him.

"More."

Mike's opened mouth slid up the side of her throat to her ear. "This might take a while. I hope you don't expect me to come anytime soon."

"No… no rush. Just don't stop."

There was no chance of that. He kept a leisurely pace, while his hands teased, tempted, and tantalized. He loved this position. It gave his hands the freedom to caress his favorite parts of her body. He kept one hand brushing her clitoris, one hand teasing her breasts, and his mouth on her neck, ear, and shoulder, nibbling, sucking, or just telling her how much he loved making love to her. His hands kept her on the edge without allowing her to go over. She was trapped beneath him, surrounded by him, controlled by him, and pleased by him.

"Mine." A wave of possessiveness so strong exploded in his mind and flew out his mouth before he could stop it, shocking him.

"Yes."

Her assent broke the tight rein of control he held on his more primitive side, a side that, until now, had never reared its head.

"Please. Now." She moaned, her breathing choppy, her movement frantic, until she was straining for release and begging. "Please…"

He lost the battle for control entirely as he thrust hard and fast, holding her, driving her and himself to the brink. His blood pounded through his ears with every beat of his heart, his breathing hot and heavy against her neck. When the first wave of her orgasm pulsed, he bit her bare shoulder as her body drew him in, milking him. She reared up, gasping, changing the angle, increasing the depth, and he thrust in again and again. He plunged hard and deep, pistoning his hips while she screamed his name. His vision grayed as his release was dragged from the pit of his stomach, the pit of his soul. He thrust again and again until she'd milked him dry. He collapsed against her, his legs shaking, unable to move as aftershocks from her orgasm pulsed around him.

As soon as his ears stopped ringing, he took a deep breath in and slowly slid out from within her, kissing his way down her back to her waist where her beautiful dress was bunched. "Are you okay?"

"Hmmm." She sounded half asleep.

He brushed her hair back off her face, struck again by her beauty, her delicacy.

"I don't think he knew."

"That's not what I'm talking about. Did I hurt you?"

"Hurt me? No." She laughed and looked over her shoulder at him. Eyes sparkling from her flushed face.

"I got carried away at the end. I was a little rough. I'm sorry."

She stood the best she could, holding her dress with one hand, turned, and melted against him. He pulled her hair back to see her face. She held him, kissed his neck, and said something.

"What?"

"I like it a little bit rough. I've never done anything like this before, in my office, on my desk, with my boss on the phone. It was so… hot… exciting. I really liked it."

He lifted her to sit on her desk. Her thong hung from around her stabilization boot, her bra hung from the hand holding her dress up, her hair was a mess, and she looked thoroughly ravished. "I'm just glad you didn't invite Ben to come, too. I would have had a real problem with that."

"I'm tellin' you girl. You need a new bathing suit."

Annabelle threw herself on the bed beside the less than half-packed suitcase. Allowing Wayne to "help" her pack for the weekend in the Hamptons proved to be a big mistake. "My ankle feels better, but it's still not up for a shopping spree."

He sat beside her with a smile that reminded her of a shark circling his prey before he strikes. "We'll get you a wheelchair. I'll push you around myself."

"No. I can see you pushing me right down the escalator at Macy's. It's not going to happen."

"Pshaw, where's your sense of adventure? Though I guess you must have one to buy this bathing suit." He held up her little leopard print bikini.

She pushed herself into a sitting position. "What's wrong with that? I've been known to stop traffic in that suit."

He folded his arms, tapped his toe, raised his head, and sniffed. "The point is not to get *everyone's* attention.

The point is to get Mike's attention. Do you really think Mike's going to want every straight man on the beach drooling over his girlfriend?"

"I don't know. I'm not a man."

"Well, I am, and let me tell you, real men don't want every other man undressing their significant other in front of them. That's exactly what will happen if you wear this thing out in public." He threw the bikini back in her drawer. "Mike is not the type to need arm candy to make him feel manly. He's the kind of man who will want to unwrap you like a present. In private. Now let's go get him something delectable to take off you. I promise we can hit all the shops on my list in under two hours. I'm a power shopper. Ask Henry. He absolutely hates to shop."

"Two hours?"

He held up his hand "Scout's honor."

"Don't tell me you were a Boy Scout."

"What did you expect, the Fireside Girls? Even though they were more my speed, I didn't have the right equipment."

By the time Annabelle's two hours of torture were up, Wayne held a scary amount of shopping bags. She had bathing suits for public and bathing suits for private, sexy kicking-around-the-house clothes, and to add to her collection, a few barely there nighties and teddies, which would undoubtedly spend more time on the floor than on her body. Wayne referred to them as gift wrap. She shook her head. He even talked her into buying an incredibly sexy getup that he called "dessert" to wear under a nondescript little black dress. The thought of going out to dinner wearing something so hot under something so not had her squirming in her seat. She couldn't wait. But mostly, she couldn't wait to see Mike.

Becca lifted a box and made her way up the narrow staircase from the brownstone's basement to Annabelle's apartment, Dave trailing in her wake. The dog had shadowed her since she'd arrived. As if he thought she were going to swipe something.

When she'd called to schedule a visit, Annabelle had jumped at the chance for them to spend time together. Mike's work schedule had become insane because of the extra shifts he'd promised to cover in order to get the Memorial Day weekend off, and since Ben was still in town, Annabelle had no problem taking time off.

Becca had spent the past few days preparing to beg forgiveness and somehow break the news of Mike's parentage without losing her best friend or ripping Annabelle and Mike's relationship apart.

Apparently, Annabelle had a different agenda in mind.

Becca set the box in the living room and returned for another with Dave drooling behind. On her way down, she tried with little success to dust off her clothes.

"I really shouldn't complain, because I've been bugging you for two years to go through everything you packed after Chip's death, but if you were going to use me as a pack mule, you could have clued me in. I would have brought work clothes."

Annabelle sat on an ancient stool resting her ankle on the dusty rung and smiled. "Sorry, it didn't occur to me. I was thinking of the emotional support, but I'm really liking the pack mule image."

"I could have given you emotional support two years ago. Instead of dealing with Chip's death, you'd packed up the pain as surely as you packed up all evidence of your life together. You've done everything but deal with the fallout."

"I wasn't ready to deal with it then."

"No, you were too busy letting your mother run your life and pick out a pig of a fiancé for you. I can't really blame her for fixing you up with someone since she never even knew Chip had existed, no less died. But I do blame her for fixing you up with a weasel."

"I don't want to talk about this."

"You better talk about this to someone. You can talk to me or find a good shrink. You spent two years living your life on autopilot. You smiled on cue and acted like everyone expected you to, but I saw the difference. Your spirit was missing."

Annabelle let out an exasperated sound that was a mixture of a groan and a growl. "I thought you were going to help me go through this… stuff. I didn't expect psychoanalysis."

"I don't have to be Sigmund Freud to know you did whatever it took to avoid dealing with Chip's death. Including allowing your parents to make decisions about your future. You were so numb and detached, you didn't care. You condemned yourself to a life without feelings—until the day you woke up with Mike."

Mike had been the only one to reach Annabelle, and now Becca's news may spell the end of that relationship, too. Becca turned her back on Annabelle, pretending to look at something while she pushed aside the guilt. It wouldn't help either of them right now.

She grabbed the top box and dropped it, waiting for Annabelle to look at her. Sure she'd create a streak of dirt worthy of a Hollywood makeup artist. She wiped her brow. Annabelle looked at everything but her. Becca was pushy. She knew it, but damn it, Annabelle needed to get past this.

"Okay, I'll stop the psychoanalysis, not that you don't need it. Just do me a favor. While we're going through this, think about why you've waited two years to do it."

"I was busy with… stuff."

"Stuff… as in a fiasco of a relationship with Johnny DePalma?"

"Stuff like breathing, eating, finding a job, and somehow getting through every day. The relationship with Johnny was—"

"Easier than doing what you should have done. Come on, you packed away your past and refused to acknowledge it ever happened. You didn't begin working through it until Rosalie's wedding."

"Not on purpose. I… I had to. It hurt too much to even think about, much less deal with."

Annabelle's eyes were shiny with unshed tears.

"Honey, that's life. You have to feel the pain before you can feel better. Even if you do it two and a half years after you should have."

"Yeah, and how do you know so much?"

"Therapy. Isn't it nice to know that something good came out of the tens of thousands of dollars my parents spent to find out why I wasn't the daughter they'd always wanted?"

"Maybe I built this up in my mind. I've been dreading this for so long. I never felt strong enough to face it before now."

"Chip would never have wanted this for you." But, he'd have probably found some smug satisfaction in knowing Annabelle had such a hard time getting over him. Of course, it would be much easier for her to move on if the relationship had died a natural death before Chip had. "You feel strong enough to deal with your past now because you're getting on with your life. You're no longer pretending it never happened. Now, if you'd come clean with Mike, you might begin to move forward."

"Why would I do that?"

"Because you have to. He deserves to know. If you want a future with him, hell, even if you don't, you still have to tell him he's a dead ringer for Chip. It's the right thing to do." It would also make breaking the news of her quasi-betrayal easier if Annabelle had already planned to tell him. Maybe.

Annabelle ripped open the box of art books Becca had set in front of her. "I can take these to the gallery."

"Or you can set up a studio in that little den area and start painting again."

"I don't know."

Becca hated the pensive look on Annabelle's face. When they first met, she was anything but pensive. She ate up life in big, overstuffed mouthfuls, reveling in it. Becca pulled out a handful of books and remembered all the hours she'd worked beside Annabelle in their loft. She wiped a clay smudge off one book, knowing full well she'd been the one to leave it there. "When was the last time you tried to paint?"

"After Chip died, before his funeral. I couldn't even hold a brush."

Becca saw a composition book stuck among the art textbooks. "What's this?" She set the other books on top of the box and started paging through it. It was an interesting combination of writing and sketches.

Annabelle plucked it from her hands. "That's my journal." She rubbed the smudged and dog-eared cover. "I used to write every day until Chip got sick. After that, I was too busy." She opened the book to the first page. "I started this before I graduated high school." Digging through the box, she pulled out a half-dozen others just like it. "Look. This one starts right around the time I first met Chip."

Annabelle grabbed the remaining journals and left the box for Becca, who followed the gimp into the apartment and watched as Annabelle took the stack of journals into her bedroom. Becca smiled. Annabelle had some interesting reading ahead of her.

Annabelle rolled over and took another journal from the stack. Reading them was like seeing a movie of her life. The distance gave her a different perspective. She saw things she never expected. The first thing she noticed was how immature she'd been. Not that anyone could have told her that at the time, but she'd seemed like a needy child. Just the type of girl a guy like Chip attracted. In the beginning of their relationship, she'd felt so privileged to be in his presence. Her obvious lack of self-esteem had her running scared and falling all over herself to keep from losing him. Some of the things she'd written were embarrassingly pathetic. Maybe Becca was right. Maybe she needed a good therapist.

Her home life wasn't the best. Her parents' marriage was a disaster, and no matter what she'd done to get attention, she'd always seemed to be in the way. The youngest child syndrome. She and Rosalie were as different as two people could be, one entirely left-brained and the other right-brained. Richie was years older than she was and too busy to be bothered with his baby sister. Annabelle had felt as if she were an only child in a house full of miserable people.

Then when she'd met Chip, for the first time in her life, she'd felt loved and wanted. She'd spent most of their relationship trying to deserve that love and fighting to keep it. Chip had taken all she'd had to give and had made her an unwitting pawn in the chess game with his parents.

Looking back at their relationship, she realized it would have been only a matter of time before one of them outgrew the other. Clearly, the woman she'd become would not have made Chip happy, and Chip would never have filled the bill for her either. The sad thing was that they'd never been given the time to figure that out for themselves. By the time the relationship had progressed to the point where stress fractures were showing, his cancer had returned.

Death has a way of putting compatibility problems on the back burner.

Annabelle got up, wandered to the den, and picked up the sketch pad and pencils Mike had bought and brought them back to bed with her. She lay there wondering if she should try again. Maybe sketch something simple... Her cell beeped. She tossed aside the sketchbook and pencils, grabbed her phone, and slid the bar to unlock it. A text appeared. "Good night, Belle. I miss you."

She typed in an answer. "G'nite, Mike. I miss you more." She turned off the lights and, hugging his pillow to her chest, pictured Mike. She meant every word. She really did miss him more.

When Becca awoke, Annabelle was fully dressed and running for the door. "Where are you going?"

"I almost forgot—Mike's mother called me the other day and asked if I'd show her around the gallery and then go to lunch. You don't mind, do you?"

"No. I'll just go for a walk with Dave and maybe hang out with Henry and Wayne if they're home. Those two are a riot."

"You have no idea."

"So, having lunch with Mike's mom, huh. That's a pretty big deal."

Annabelle rubbed her stomach. "I don't know why I didn't tell her I wasn't working today. I was too dumbfounded to refuse. The woman makes me nervous."

"Oh, come on. She can't be as bad as my mother, and you survived her."

"Only because she didn't have the opportunity to finish me off."

"Maybe Mike's mother will be a sweetheart like her son. Stranger things have happened."

"Not to me. Even Johnny's mother barely tolerated me. I think I have an attraction to men whose mothers hate me."

"Hold on. You were never attracted to Johnny."

Annabelle shrugged. "True enough. I honestly don't know what I was thinking by getting engaged to him."

"You weren't thinking. That was the problem. At least you seem to have rectified that." Becca slid off the couch and stretched. "Is there coffee?"

"On the counter. If I survive, I'll be home before dinner."

Becca swatted Annabelle. "Way to believe in the power of positive thinking. You'll be fine. Just don't babble. Babbling always gets you into trouble."

"Thanks." She blew Becca a kiss and patted Dave's head. "You'd better get dressed. Dave just ate, so you have about fifteen minutes before he needs to go out. The bags are by his leash. It gives new meaning to the phrase doggy bags."

"Aw, man. You did that on purpose."

Annabelle shot her a wicked grin before the door shut behind her.

Annabelle paced her office. She had so much on her mind. Today was not the best day to deal with Mike's mother.

She moved one of the black-and-white shoji screens and couldn't help but think that maybe Becca had been right yesterday. Annabelle had packed away the past so she didn't have to deal with it just like she put up the screens in front of the art supplies. She'd hid everything so well, but just because you didn't see or deal with problems, they didn't just go away.

Last night, everything had changed. Now she saw her life and herself in a very different light. She ran her fingers over the canvases and picked up a paintbrush and stroked her cheek with the soft sable. She waited

for the familiar empty feeling, the crystals of fear, the
memories that haunted her. They didn't come. Yes,
she set down the brush. Maybe things were changing.
Maybe she was ready to try again. But first, Annabelle
had to get through lunch with Mike's mother. She took
a deep breath and let the unease wash over her, but not
because of the memories. Because Annabelle made a
mistake, several mistakes, actually.

When Mike's mother called to invite Annabelle to lunch—
just the two of them—her first mistake had been accepting.
In her limited experience, the only reason the mother of
a man she dated would ever ask her to lunch without her
significant other present was so there would be no witnesses
when she was literally or figuratively fed to the fishes.

Annabelle took the elevator to the gallery. Colleen
had insisted on meeting at the gallery she'd heard so
much about. *Thank you, Mike*. So, not only was she
forced to brace herself for the torment of the inauspicious
encounter, she also had to worry about the appearance of
the gallery. She got off the elevator and looked around.
Even though everything had been dusted, washed, and
rearranged a dozen times that morning to prepare for
Colleen's visit, when Annabelle looked at the gallery
with a critical eye, all she saw were flaws.

"Kerri, could you please put that Hibel back where it
was in the first place? I'm sorry."

She was so nervous she'd chewed her thumbnail down
to the quick, and she had her staff scurrying around like
schoolgirls through Central Park after dark. They kept
moving. But couldn't escape the fear.

She'd have to compensate them with a week of
lunches for putting up with her neurosis. All she had to

look forward to was that by her next day at work, Mike would have already dumped her, and her staff would see her neurosis was well founded. But for now, the sound of her boot hitting the hardwood was enough to make any member of her crew jump.

Annabelle checked her cream-colored dress with splashes of yellow, gray, and blue. It was a simple cap-sleeved, silk sheath—stylish without being trendy, and feminine without being slutty. Well, except for her shoes… or in this case shoe, which wasn't stylish, trendy, feminine, or slutty. She couldn't even claim it matched. The best she could say was it didn't clash.

She turned away from the door, crossed herself, and prayed that the Lord would keep her mouth under control. When she was nervous, her filter tended to become rather… inadequate. She'd pretend Colleen was a rich client, since she had no problem avoiding foot-in-mouth disease when dealing with even her most difficult client and the yappy dog said client wore like an accessory.

She took a deep breath and smiled her most welcoming smile before opening the door for Colleen Flynn. "Welcome to the Ben Walsh Gallery."

"Annabelle, thanks for agreeing to meet with me."

Colleen pulled her into a tight hug. Shocked, she stood like one of the statues she displayed until Colleen's hold relaxed, and she was able to extricate herself without appearing rude. In her rush to avoid further demonstrations of affection, no matter how false, she backed into one of the very statues she'd imitated. Luckily, she was fast on her feet… foot and caught it before it made the ruinous flight to the floor.

There were snickers in the background, which stopped the second Annabelle looked in the direction from which they'd come.

"Um... thanks for inviting me." What was she supposed to say? She'd been looking forward to it? Since Mike never fell for her lies, she didn't think she could pull one over on his mother. Especially since she was so bad at lying in the first place. She kept her mouth shut.

She really wished Mike were there.

Annabelle began the tour of the gallery, going on like a talking head, giving Colleen her canned spiel — a little about each artist, a little about the work itself, comparable artists and works — all the while wondering when Colleen's claws would appear. Expecting the worst, only to have Colleen beam at her. She stopped and looked behind her to see who was the cause. No one was there.

"I certainly see why Michael is so taken with you. You're not only beautiful and sweet but intelligent and talented, too. Tell me something, what can't you do? If I find out you're perfect, I'll really have to hate you."

"You're kidding, right?"

Colleen laughed. "Actually, I'm not. I bet you can even wear red lipstick."

"Yes. Why?"

Colleen ran her hand through her short strawberry blonde hair. "If I wear red lipstick, I end up looking like Bozo the Clown."

Annabelle relaxed marginally. "I'm far from perfect. I can't cook to save my own life, and when I get nervous, I babble. I'm a terrible liar, even when I'm telling a kind, does-this-make-my-butt-look-big lie to a person who has such a big butt it deserves its own zip code. I've totally given up lying. Now I pretty much say what I think."

"I'll remember that." Colleen threaded her arm through Annabelle's and walked toward one of her favorite paintings. They stood in companionable silence while they soaked in the serenity the painting evoked.

Colleen squeezed her arm. "Do you want to tell me why you looked sick when I first got here?"

"Not especially."

"Tell me anyway."

"That's not fair. I just told you I can't lie."

"Then don't."

"Fine. You know how some people are afraid of nuns?"

"Yes. I've heard the horror stories, however exaggerated."

"I know for a fact that some of those are well deserved. Though, I'm sure there are some wonderful nuns who hate the stereotype. Still, there are some people out there who see a habit and break out in a cold sweat."

"Okay."

"I'm afraid of boyfriends' mothers."

"Don't tell me you believe all those awful stories about mother-in-laws. They've replaced the wicked stepmother in modern fairy tales."

"I've never had a mother-in-law. But if I had married either of the two men I've dated seriously, I'd have gotten a mother-in-law who made the psycho woman in *Misery* look like Glenda the Good Witch."

Ben picked that moment to stroll out of the office, saving Annabelle from the awkward silence. An angel of mercy.

"Well, if it isn't the good doctor's mother. I still have a hard time believing it. She's much too young and beautiful to have borne such a bo—"

Annabelle elbowed him in the gut. So much for the angel of mercy ID. The Prince of Darkness was more like it. "Colleen, you remember my boss, Benjamin Walsh."

Ben rubbed his side and smiled politely. "Nice to see you again."

Annabelle slid her arm through Colleen's to move away from Ben. "What do you feel like for lunch? I know a great little Scottish place. All the men wear kilts."

"Really?"

"Would I lie to you?"

By the time Annabelle and Colleen made it to the St. Andrews, they were laughing over the story of Mike and Annabelle's first real date, when he arrived to find her in Ben's arms. In hindsight, the fiasco with her ankle and all of Ben's "help" was funny.

They were still giggling when they entered the St. Andrews and walked through the bar to the dining room. Gareth, the gorgeous bartender Annabelle knew, carried a large tub of ice and winked as he passed them. He was wearing his usual outfit of a tight St. Andrew's T-shirt over highly developed muscles, a kilt, and rugged work boots. The look on Colleen's face had Annabelle biting her cheek to keep from laughing. The woman was ready to swoon, and she hadn't gotten a load of his accent. Gareth was the real thing, the equivalent of a male trifecta—a bad boy with drool-worthy good looks and a Scottish accent. The fact that he wore a skirt just turned up the voltage of all three. Every woman east of the Hudson wanted to find out if he went commando under that kilt. It was nice to see lust didn't discriminate when it came to age.

They were seated at a corner booth. Once the hostess left them with their menus, Colleen leaned toward her. "I've always loved a man in a kilt, which explains Mike's existence."

Annabelle placed the napkin in her lap. "Excuse me?"

"The night Michael was conceived, his father and I went to a masquerade party on Long Island. Christopher was dressed as Rob Roy MacGregor, the Highland Rogue. He was always a very handsome man, but in a kilt, he was irresistible."

"Christopher?"

"I'm sorry. I thought that Mike would have told you about his father, since you two seem so close. Not that I'm saying you're not, you understand. I know it's a sore subject—"

"No, I mean, yes. Mike's told me that he never knew his father. He just never told me his name. I assumed—"

"Flynn is my name. Michael's father and I never married. I found out after Michael was conceived that Christopher was engaged to be married to someone else. That certainly put a damper on my plans." She shook her head.

"Engaged to be married?"

"I was young and gullible. I found out the truth when I saw the engagement announcement in the society pages. I didn't want anything to do with him. Now I wonder if I made a mistake. No matter what happened between

Christopher and me, it was unfair to keep Michael away from his father. The only excuse I have is that I was young and heartsick. I was so ashamed. My parents threw me out, and I ran to Ireland, stayed with my aunt, and had Michael. We didn't come back to the States until Michael was about three years old."

Colleen took a roll from the basket on the table and calmly buttered it, as if she dropped this bombshell every day of the week. Though to anyone other than Annabelle, it wouldn't have been much of a bombshell.

"I thought about telling Christopher when Michael was young, but I never did. I decided not to give him the chance to hurt either of us any more than he already had. Besides, the Larsens were very wealthy. I was afraid they'd take Michael from me.

"Larsen?"

"Yes, Christopher Larsen. The Larsens were one of those very uppity, proper Philadelphia families."

"Christopher Larsen?"

"Yes. Now he's a highly respected cardiologist. Then he was a lowly resident. Michael knows who his father is, but he's never had any interest in contacting him."

Colleen set down her knife and turned her attention to Annabelle. "Are you all right, dear? You look a little pale."

"I'm fine. Just a little warm." This would explain Annabelle's sudden cold sweat. Now if only she could hide the shiver.

Chapter 12

ANNABELLE STOOD IN THE BATHROOM OF THE ST. Andrew's rinsing her mouth and wiping her face with a cool paper towel after throwing up her entire lunch.

She hoped Colleen hadn't noticed her shock. But at this point, it didn't really matter. Her relationship with Mike was doomed. How could God be so cruel? How could he make her fall in love with both Chip and Mike?

Annabelle held on to the sink as another wave of nausea rolled over her. Her head ached, her heart ached, and since she'd stomped around the bathroom muttering curses, her ankle ached, too.

How was she going to tell Becca? Oh God, how was she going to tell Mike?

She dug through her purse, found blusher, and did her best to put some color back into her pasty complexion. She needed to finish her lunch with Colleen without letting on that her relationship with Mike had just been destroyed. She'd always suspected Mike and Chip were distantly related, but she'd assumed it would be in a long, long, long lost cousin kind of way, not in a brothers with different mothers way!

"Annabelle? Are you all right?"

She stuffed her blush back into her bag and smiled at Colleen. "I'm fine."

It didn't look as if Colleen bought that. Damn her inability to lie convincingly. "Okay, you caught me. I feel a little queasy. It's probably from taking a megadose of ibuprofen on an empty stomach. You'd think I'd have learned my lesson after Mother's Day."

For once in her life, she actually got along with a boyfriend's mother, and now she'd have to... How does one tell the man she loves that he's the surviving brother of her first love? Sheesh, the writers of *General Hospital* had nothing on her life.

Colleen didn't buy the ibuprofen bit either, but she was nice enough to let the subject drop. They returned to the table, where Colleen insisted on paying. Annabelle didn't have the strength to argue. She wanted to go home and pretend the day never happened. Becca would insist on a blow by blow. Too bad the girl was going to get the shock of her life. Annabelle knew exactly how it felt and wasn't looking forward to a reenactment.

Becca lazed on the couch with Dave, who, after an afternoon of quality time, snoozed beside his new best friend. Every now and then he'd awaken and give her feet or her face a swipe of his tongue. Becca regretted two things: that Dave was a dog, and that his was the only tongue, human or canine, she'd come in contact with in over a year. No offense to Dave, but she preferred a human male to Dave, who, she had to admit, was the sweetest ox she'd ever known.

The door swung open, and Annabelle stepped in. Becca took one look at Annabelle's red-rimmed eyes and shoved Dave off her lap. "What happened to you?"

Annabelle fell into Becca's arms and let loose a sob that seemed to come right from her soul. Becca had cried on Annabelle's shoulder all through Chip's illness and death, but she'd never seen her shed a tear. It was unnatural the way the girl could hold it together. Annabelle losing it now sent Becca into panic mode.

Dave barked and Henry and Wayne burst through the door like better-groomed versions of the *Ghostbusters*.

"What the hell happened?" Wayne turned on Becca and plucked Annabelle right out of her arms. "What did you do to her?"

"Nothing." She tried to disengage Wayne from Annabelle. "Now damn it! Give her back to me."

Henry pulled Becca under his arm and gave her a sideways hug. "Calm down. Wayne feels protective of Annabelle since her last crying jag."

"She's done this before? I've known her for almost five years, and I've never once seen her cry."

Wayne made shushing noises and hummed something as Henry steered Becca into the kitchen and put the kettle on.

"She mentioned something about that." He pulled a teapot from one of the upper cabinets and opened the small pantry, knowing exactly where to look for tea bags. You'd think he lived there.

"I know you mean well, but I really need to talk to Annabelle about something. Privately."

Henry turned and looked over the top of his glasses at her. "I don't recommend trying to get in between Wayne and Annabelle when he's in full mother hen mode. Believe me, it will be much easier to let him calm her down. I promise to shoo him out as soon as possible. Until then, why don't we give Annabelle a nice big dose of tea and sympathy? You look as if you could use some yourself."

The Fairy Godfathers were both very skilled at "handling" people, though their tactics were diametrically opposed. Wayne tended to wade into the fray and get caught up in all the swirl of emotion, while Henry was the calm and supportive Rock of Gibraltar type. She was certain Henry would be able to walk through a mud pit and still come out clean, pressed, and smelling delicious. Too bad he was gay.

Becca sipped tea and ate cookies that appeared out of nowhere. When Wayne and Henry were sure the waterworks had stopped, they offered to dog-sit and leave the women alone to talk. Annabelle blew her nose and nodded.

They both watched the boys leave. When Becca turned her attention to Annabelle again, she hiccupped, trying to regain her composure.

Annabelle played with the tassels on a pillow she'd made, avoiding Becca's eyes. The pillow reminded Becca of the old Annabelle. Bright colors mixed in a way that one thought would clash, but became something uniquely beautiful.

"I had lunch with Mike's mother and…"

She covered her face with her hands and mumbled.

Becca pulled Annabelle's hands away and held them. "What?"

"Mike's father's name is Christopher Larsen… you are Mike's half sister."

There, Annabelle had said it aloud, and when she got the guts to look Becca in the eye, all she saw was sympathy. Not shock, not horror—if anything she looked relieved.

"I take it this little bombshell isn't news to you?"

Becca only shook her head, guilt dripping off her like water over Niagara Falls.

Annabelle had never felt such rage; she ripped her hands out of Becca's and stood. "You knew and didn't tell me? You're my best friend, and you kept this from me?"

Becca's face turned white. "I came here to tell you. I planned to, but I thought it would be better to tell you after we finished going through your past." She stood and reached for Annabelle.

Annabelle pushed her away. "So you let me find out in the middle of a freaking restaurant? I had to run to the bathroom and throw up. I had to hide it from Mike's mom, all because you didn't want to tell me until after... Hold on. How did you find out?"

Becca seemed to shrink in stature. "I'm so sorry. I didn't think I was doing anything wrong until after I did it. I had no idea..."

"What did you do?"

"I showed the pictures of Mike to my father. I asked him how he was related to us."

"What pictures?"

"The pictures I saw on your computer. Honest to God, Annabelle, I didn't think... I didn't think about how this would affect you. We always shared everything. It never occurred to me to ask your permission. I just printed the pictures and took them home with me."

"And you showed your father?"

"I asked him who Mike Flynn was to us—in the middle of the country club dining room, no less. I thought he was going to have a coronary. Once he heard Mike's last name... well, Mike's mother and he were lovers way back when, and he said she just disappeared. He never knew Mike existed."

"Until you opened your big mouth and told him."

Becca nodded. "I'm so sorry. You can't imagine how sorry I am that I handled this so badly. But, Annabelle, if I didn't tell my father, it would have come out some other way."

Annabelle paced the length of the apartment. Becca just followed behind.

"When did your father find out?" She stopped and turned to Becca. "What's he going to do about it? Oh God, once he finds out that Mike and I—"

"Are in love? You can't let this change anything between you and Mike."

Annabelle threw up her hands. "How could it not change everything? Once your father gets involved with Mike, our relationship is over." She wrapped her arms around herself. "I won't allow your father to treat me the way I was treated when Chip and I were together. Not even for love. It's not worth it. I'm not that same insecure girl I used to be."

Becca took the same pose but made it look stubborn instead of the way Annabelle felt, as if her arms were the only things protecting her from completely falling apart.

"And Mike isn't Chip. No matter how you feel about my father, or how mad you are at me, you need to tell Mike. He needs to hear this from you. You two can work it out. I know you can."

Annabelle shook her head. No way could this end in anything but disaster. If she had learned anything from her past with Chip, it was that she wasn't cut out for a life that included Dr. Larsen. No matter how much she loved either of his sons.

"I'll tell him Memorial Day weekend."

"I'm so sorry, Annabelle. I'm so sorry."

Annabelle walked back to the couch, tossed the pillows to the side, and sat. Becca was right, and she looked as sick as Annabelle felt. Mike would learn the truth eventually. "It's okay. I know you didn't mean it. I probably would have done the same thing if I were you. It's better that this came out now, before I got in even deeper than I already am. I'll be all right."

Eventually, maybe... someday, when her heart stopped breaking.

Annabelle waited for Mike, looking forward to seeing him, and dreading it at the same time.

He'd been working so much, she spent more time texting him and leaving voice mail messages than she spent in his presence. She missed him, even though she tried to put him out of her mind. He'd made such a big space for himself in her life that when he was absent, the yawning hole he left made her feel empty. She tried not to think what life would be like without him. Though, after this weekend, she'd find out. She wasn't looking forward to it.

The Felix the Cat clock on the wall counted down the time, and with every swish of his tail, Mike became later and later. She paced back and forth in her new flats, thankful she didn't have to wear that ugly boot anymore. She straightened the painting she'd hung over the couch—one of her own works she'd painted while going through her Tuscan phase. She'd pulled the colors from the painting and chosen the new drapes she'd hung—a mix of jewel-tone silk sheers she made out of the stash of rich fabrics she'd collected. She'd even had the Fairy Godfathers build her a cornice she'd covered to pull all the colors together. Matching handwoven table runners covered the table and the buffet where she displayed a few pieces of pottery given to her by Becca. She looked around and thought about losing Mike. The only bright side was that she'd made herself a home. It was hers. It looked like her, it felt like her, and for once in her life, she was happy both with her home and herself. She just wished she could change her circumstances.

Her mind spun with a jumble of inexplicable and sometimes diametrically opposed feelings. She never thought she'd find someone who would invade her mind and pop up in her thoughts at the most inopportune times. She'd thought a lot about it since Becca had left. She'd gone and fallen head over heels in love with the one man she'd never be able to have. She'd even sketched Mike—not that she'd meant to. She didn't know she was still capable. But when she cleaned off her desk before leaving for the long weekend, she unearthed her blotter and found a sketch of Mike looking back at her. She must be going stark, raving mad, because she didn't remember drawing it. The sketch—and it was a sketch, not a doodle—was definitely her work, and the subject was definitely Mike.

The phone rang. She checked the caller ID and confirmed her suspicion. Becca. The girl was still pushing her belief that Annabelle's relationship with Mike could survive this bump in the road. What Becca deemed a bump, she saw as a sinkhole the size of New Jersey. There was no way over it, under it, or around it.

"Hello."

"Is he there yet?"

"If he were, would I be talking to you?"

"I guess not. I'm so sorry—"

"I know. Please don't start."

"Okay, I'm sorry."

"There you go again."

"Are you going to tell him?"

"I said I would. I'll tell him when we get back. I promise. I want him to have this weekend before I do. I want what little time we have left to be wonderful."

"How are you going to do that when you have this… thing… hanging over your head?"

"I don't know, but I don't want to spoil our last weekend together. He's worked so hard to get the time off. I want to enjoy it with him. There will be plenty of time when we get back to make both our lives miserable."

"I think that's a mistake. Honey, if you tell him as soon as you get there, you'll have time to work through this together."

"There is nothing to work through. Look, Becca, I've thought about this a lot. Mike is the son your father only dreamed of. He's going to want to give Mike everything. He'll have a new father and you. I don't want him to have to choose between his family and me. I love him enough to let him go. And I won't go back to what I was when I was with Chip. I deserve more."

"Mike might not appreciate you making decisions about his life for him."

"Becca, it's my life. I know what's best for me, and I know Mike. Someday he'll thank me for this."

"Someday, maybe you'll get your head out of your ass long enough to see that you two belong together. I just hope that when you do, it's not too late."

"I've got to go. I think Mike's here."

"Promise me you'll at least think about giving him a chance?"

"Love you, Bec. Bye." She hung up the phone and put the whole situation out of her mind. She was good at it. She'd done the same thing when Chip died, and it worked well for two years. She could do it for another weekend.

Mike parked outside Annabelle's apartment in the Mustang Nick had loaned him. He had his bag packed, the gas tank topped off, a cooler filled with food in the trunk, and an economy-sized box of condoms in the glove compartment.

He also had bags under his eyes so large they could be mistaken for oversize luggage. He'd worked around the clock. Not only did he cover his normal shifts, but also the shifts of those he'd traded to free him for the weekend. Spending Memorial Day weekend with Annabelle was worth every minute—he just hoped he didn't sleep through it.

He couldn't attribute all his sleep deprivation to his long hours at work. He'd also spent time researching Eastern Heart Specialists. He'd prepared for his interview the way he prepared for his board exams. He studied the practice, making lists of specific questions to ask or find answers to. The last thing he wanted was to move from one terrible work environment to another.

It had been years since he'd last looked up the old man, and part of his research was to ensure his father wasn't involved in the practice. As far as Mike could see, his father was still on the board of University of Pennsylvania Hospital, but he'd closed down his practice. Maybe the old guy was slowing down. His father's partial retirement was a happy thought. He didn't want to see the man. Not that he was too worried about it. After all, his father didn't know he even existed.

Mike got out of the 'Stang and straightened his aching body. The sun shone hot against his back. He checked his watch and winced. He was two hours late picking up Annabelle. He'd hardly seen her in the past few weeks, which wasn't helping his peace of mind. The worst part about it was that their lack of time together didn't seem to bother her. The last time he'd seen her, she'd seemed happy to be with him, but unlike every girl he'd dated, she never once complained about his absence. She never called and interrupted him at work, though she left nice messages or texts in answer to his messages or texts. No matter how many times Mike told himself that was a good thing, he had a hard time believing it.

He let himself into the building using the key he'd kept when Annabelle had sprained her ankle. Dick Doyle, Annabelle's doctor, had sent Mike a letter saying pretty much what she'd said after Mike hounded her to go for a follow-up. Her ankle was healing well, and she could stop wearing the stabilization boot unless the pain increased.

Mike knocked. When Annabelle opened the door and smiled at him, it was as if someone had given him a shot of adrenaline. Damn, she looked good. When she wrapped her arms around him and didn't let him go even after Dave nudged his big head in between their bodies, all the tension he'd been holding on to since he'd seen her last evaporated.

He looked around the apartment and was amazed by the transformation. It had seemed like forever since he'd hung the paintings she'd had resting against the walls, but now there were a few more already hung. He smiled when he realized that several of the ones he'd never seen before were signed by her. New drapes, lots of sculpture and pottery. The place looked like a little art gallery, only dustier and hairier. It had been a while since he'd vacuumed, and it didn't look as if Annabelle had.

"I threw together lunch. Well, not personally. I walked Dave down to the deli and picked up salads and sandwiches. I thought that would be safer."

Mike gave her a quick kiss, not wanting to tempt fate. Kissing Annabelle was dangerous business. He didn't want to take the chance they'd end up falling into bed. When they did fall into bed together, he wanted to hear nothing but the surf pounding the shore and heavy breathing—no sirens, no traffic, and no neighbors.

"Can we take it to go? It's late, and I don't want to waste a minute of our long weekend."

"Are you sure you don't want to take a nap? No offense, but you look like you haven't slept in a week."

She wasn't far off. "I'm fine. I stopped at Starbucks and got a couple of ventis for the road, and I got you a raspberry mocha."

"How about I drive, and you sleep? You don't need any more caffeine."

"Do you know how to drive a stick?"

Mike grabbed the sissy bar in the three-tenths of a mile it took Annabelle to turn onto Hamilton Avenue. By the time she merged onto the Brooklyn Queens Expressway, Dave was crying, and Mike was saying Hail Marys.

The woman was a female Mario Andretti on speed. She brought the RPMs up to a racer's whine before shifting, downshifted into turns and accelerated out of them, and passed every car she approached while giving Mike a blow-by-blow of her shopping spree with Wayne. Which, in and of itself, wasn't troubling — what gave him pause was the fact that she talked with her hands. You'd think they were chatting over coffee instead of speeding through rush hour traffic. The estimated time of arrival on the car's GPS dropped at an alarming rate. The way she drove while petting Dave's head and occasionally wiping his mouth with a napkin left Mike amazed.

Mike wasn't used to cars. He grew up in Brooklyn, and he and his mother not only had no need for a car, they had no money for a car. He did get his license when he was in med school, and had even owned a car at one time, but he never felt as if driving was a natural thing for him to do. Annabelle looked as if she'd been born to it and clearly enjoyed driving. The wind whipping through the cracked window teased the curls falling out of the twist held together by a pencil.

He leaned back in his seat, closed his eyes, and let sleep take him. He awoke a few hours later to the crackling sound of tires rolling over a shell driveway.

"Mike, we're here. At least I think we're here. This is the address, right?"

Mike opened his bleary eyes and took a deep breath of salt air. The cedar-shingled house grayed by age rose above them as the roar of the ocean and the scream of seagulls drifted through the windows.

"Yes. This is it."

Annabelle's eyes widened. "Nick owns this place? The whole place?"

"Yeah. He wanted to get a house large enough to sleep the whole family. His mother, grandmother, Vinny, Mona, and the kids."

"He could sleep them and their thirty closest friends."

Mike shrugged. It looked like a typical Westhampton beach house—only bigger. He opened the car door and stretched as he rose. Annabelle followed suit and released the door locks before she reached into the backseat and leashed Dave.

Making his way to the popped trunk, Mike threw his bag over his shoulder and picked up Annabelle's The woman certainly wasn't a light packer. Dave took off with her, his nose to the ground sniffing everything in sight and watering every area of the front yard he could reach to mark his new territory. He wasted no time claiming what was his.

Annabelle turned toward the ocean. "I wish I was allowed to run. I've always loved running by the water. When I lived in Philly we'd take road trips to Ocean City, and I'd run on the beach every morning."

"I never knew you lived in Philadelphia. When was that?"

"A few years ago. I went part-time to art school and waited tables."

There was still so much he didn't know about her. He did know enough to see that something was bothering her. It would be a mystery until she decided to talk to him about it. He just hoped she did. "Give it another month, and once your doctor gives you the okay—"

"Yeah, but in another month, I won't be here. I'll be in Brooklyn."

"Nick usually takes the family out here for a week or two in July. I always get an invite. You and your parents probably will too."

"I don't think so."

"Why not?"

"Can you picture you, me, and my parents trapped on a glorified sandbar? Yup, that's my definition of hell. It would be like a twenty-four-hour marriage channel. All nagging, all the time. You can count me out. There's not a house large enough. Besides… it's against my religion to make plans more than a week in advance."

"Hold on, you spent the last year planning a wedding."

"I'm a recent convert."

Mike dropped the bags and stepped behind Annabelle. His hands went to her waist, and his mouth to her ear. "Wanna hear my short-term plans?"

She inhaled a sharp breath, and when he pulled her against him, she let it out with a whoosh. His hands moved forward and splayed against her stomach just below her breasts.

"Yes."

His lips quirked at the breathless quality of that one word. His dick twitched against her.

"Oh yessssss."

He kissed the side of her neck down to the thin white spaghetti strap holding up her blue and white cotton top. Damn, he knew he should have waited to get inside. "I want to make love to you for seventy-two hours straight."

"I'd like to see you try. But first, I think we need to eat. You're going to need your strength."

For now, the only thing Mike needed was Annabelle, but then, he didn't want her to think the only thing on his mind was sex. They'd have plenty of time to make love… over and over and over again. There was no need to rush it, no matter what his body told him.

He reluctantly let her go and picked up the bags he'd practically thrown on the driveway before. He carried them up the stairs to the deck and unlocked the door.

Dave barged through the threshold and almost knocked Mike over. Then came Annabelle, clinging to the other end of the leash like a skier behind a boat.

By the time Mike caught up with her, she'd gone through the foyer and into the great room, which opened onto the back deck, the pool, and then the ocean. The east side of the house was mostly windows showing off the spectacular view. The sun shone on the water, sailboats with brightly colored spinnakers bobbed in the distance, and the sea grass over the dunes danced in the wind.

"Wow." Annabelle spun around to take in the rest of the place. A large fireplace. Big, comfy white slip-covered couches. A dark wood floor and painted beams gave the house a comfortable feel without it being overly beachy. A figurehead of a hand-carved mermaid hung over the stone fireplace and looked as if it was taken off the bow of a tall ship.

"Amazing." The mermaid called to her, so she approached the fireplace, stepped onto the hearth, and ran her fingers over the weathered wood, trailing over the ridges of the scales chiseled on her tail. "This looks real."

"I'm pretty sure it is. Nick's not into reproductions."

"Oh."

The kitchen on the other side of the room was something out of *Architectural Digest*. Granite counter tops, dark wood cabinets, and industrial-size stainless steel appliances.

Mike disappeared while Annabelle walked around picking up and examining knickknacks. When he returned, he set a cooler in the kitchen. Annabelle opened the cooler and shooed him away. She couldn't really cook, but she was good at putting stuff away. "I'll empty this. Is there anything left in the car?"

"No, I don't think so."

He stared at her so she stared right back. He stuffed his hands in his pockets and rocked on his heels. "I'll bring our bags to the bedroom. Do you want to come up and look around?"

"I'm going to set out lunch for us. I'm hungry. I'll explore with you later. Okay?"

Annabelle was nervous, and she wasn't the only one. Why Mike was nervous, she couldn't imagine. She'd caught him looking at her in that way he had—the way that made her feel as if he could read her mind. God, she hoped he couldn't. If he could, her plans for their first and last weekend together would be destroyed. She didn't want it to end yet. She was going to put it off as long as she possibly could. She loved him enough to give him that. They'd both end up hurting, but at least when he looked back at their time together, he'd have a few happy memories. And so would she.

She emptied the cooler into the refrigerator, dumped the ice, and put the cooler on the porch to dry. She'd come a long way since the day she freaked over Mike telling her that he loved her. The conversation she'd had with Becca came to mind, and she cringed when she realized Becca had known long before she did that this was more than just sex. It had been more since day one. She hadn't realized it until it was almost over.

Annabelle was lost in thought when Mike came up from behind and wrapped his arms around her. "Hey, what's wrong?"

"Nothing. I was going to heat the knishes, but I'm not sure how to turn on that oven."

He'd changed when he was upstairs into a sleeveless T-shirt and a pair of board shorts, and smelled of sunscreen. She stood back and watched as he took over in the kitchen, arranging the knishes on a cookie sheet and placing them in the oven. He took out two plates and began serving the food from the deli containers she'd left out.

Mike moved around the kitchen with the same intensity as he moved around an X-ray machine. Within minutes, he had two plates full of food, napkins, and silverware in his hands.

"Could you grab a few beers? I left some in the fridge last time I was here."

"Sure." She retrieved the beers and followed him out to the deck.

"I closed the gate to the steps so Dave can't take off."

Dave commandeered a lounge chair with a mattress-like cushion and fell asleep with his big head in between his front paws. His back legs twitched as he let out a muffled high-pitched bark. Leave it to Rosalie to have a dog that talked in his sleep. He was probably dreaming of chasing seagulls on the beach.

Mike stared at her like he couldn't believe his luck and guilt slammed into her hard. She smiled and prayed it didn't look as weak as it felt. She had to get her shit together. "I'll go check on the knishes."

Mike watched the emotions bouncing around Annabelle's face like a ping-pong ball with ADD. She must be nervous as hell to choose to do anything in the kitchen. Nervousness could be a sign that a person was moving into unexplored territory. What territory was the question.

He ignored the way she avoided the bedroom. He should be thankful she hadn't joined him, because he had a hard enough time concentrating on unpacking when he was in there alone. He could only imagine what would have happened if she'd gone with him.

He shut down that train of thought, though not quickly enough. Imagining was not helping him to forward his plan. A plan that escaped him as soon as Annabelle stepped out onto the deck. Every time he saw her, his brain went into testosterone overload. It zapped every-thing but his sex drive. She'd donned sunglasses and lost her shoes. Her toenails were painted a fluorescent orange, like some newfangled emergency vehicle. It should have looked ghastly, but it didn't, and then there was that sexy little ankle bracelet.

"I think I turned off the oven, but you better check it later just to be safe." She had a hand stuffed into a lobster oven mitt and held the baking sheet, looking for a place to put it.

Mike was too caught up in staring at her to realize she could use a hand—maybe two. She set the hot tray on a wooden table and tried picking up a knish with her fingers but moved them away quickly. That threw cold water on him. Mike pulled his tongue off the floor.

He took the oven mitt from her and picked up the baking sheet. "I'll just put these on a plate. That way we can set them on the table." God, she was sweet. She turned bright red, and it wasn't from the sun either.

"Sorry. I didn't think about logistics."

Mike gave her a quick kiss. "No problem. Be right back."

He took the burnt knishes back to the kitchen. What had she been doing in here? He got a plate out of the cupboard and using a spatula, proceeded to chisel the knishes off the tray. He stifled a grin. Damn, she really couldn't cook, but the weird thing was, he thought it was cute. How sick in love was he?

When he looked up, he saw her leaning against the doorframe, watching him. "Okay, I burned them. I told you I was bad in the kitchen."

He reached for her hand and, carrying the burnt food in his other hand, took her out to the porch. She nervously fingered the little drawstring on her white skirt. He pulled her over to sit on his lap.

Reaching around her, he moved her plate next to his, and handed her a beer. "I happen to like crispy knishes." He clinked his bottle against hers. "Cheers."

Annabelle shrugged and took a drink. "You really expect me to eat sitting on your lap?"

"Why not?"

"'Cause I'll make a mess."

"I'll chance it. I like being close to you." With one hand wrapped around Annabelle's waist, Mike tried cutting one of the burnt knishes single-handed. When that didn't work, he dipped it in some sour cream, hoping it covered the taste of incinerated potato, and smiled as he took a bite. Chewing it as the crust crumbled in his mouth was a whole new experience.

Annabelle tossed her sandwich on her plate and took the rest of the knish from him. "Don't. Look. I love you for trying, but you'll make yourself sick. I thought maybe we could scrape off the burnt layer."

Mike swallowed and then chased the taste down with some beer. He wouldn't be surprised if he had charred remains of the poor knish stuck in his teeth.

"It wasn't that bad." He lied like a rug and said a silent prayer to whichever saint covered the whole domestic accord area. He'd have to go to his little dictionary of saints and find out. He had a feeling he'd need a lot of help in that particular area, if the look on her face was a clue. "What did I do?"

"Nothing." She squirmed until she sat on his lap facing him and anchored her hands in his hair. The next thing he knew she kissed him like her life depended on it, sucking his tongue into her mouth. He groaned and pulled her against him. She broke the kiss, and when he opened his eyes, she had a sad look on her face.

"I really missed you. More than I ever expected to."

"Aw, Belle, I'm sorry. I missed you too. You do know this was unusual—the way I've been working isn't normal. I won't let us be apart for that long again."

"I know, but it was okay. I'm fine by myself. I'm better with you, but I don't mind being alone."

Mike wondered if she was trying to convince him or herself. "Are you still hungry?"

Annabelle shook her head, and her eyes brightened. "Wanna go for a swim?"

No, he wanted to take her to bed. Right now. But, he'd do anything to put that light back in her eyes. "Sure."

She climbed off his lap and gave him a quick kiss. "I'll get my suit on. Where's our room?"

"Up the stairs, second door on the left."

"Be back in a sec."

Chapter 13

MIKE TOOK A DEEP BREATH. HE SCANNED THE BEACH and was glad to see it deserted. When Annabelle returned, he prayed the water was cold. If anyone else were on the beach, he'd have to cover her with a towel. She wore a black two-piece with a halter top that did amazing things to her chest—not that she had a problem in that department, but the gold trim highlighted her assets. The bottoms—what there were of them—were low with a gold belt. It wasn't the kind of belt to hold things up, either. No, it was the kind of belt to draw your attention with a charm hanging from it that swung from side to side. The damn thing was hypnotizing.

"Hey, Mike. Are you ready?"

"Huh?"

She handed him a towel. "I found these in one of the closets upstairs."

Dave slept on the lounge, so Mike figured they'd leave him to his nap. She walked toward the steps, giving him a rear view that would forever be burned in his memory. He watched her hips sway as she unlatched the gate and then closed it behind her while Mike was frozen in place with his mouth hanging open.

"Last one in the water is a rotten egg!" She took off running down the steps.

Mike shook out of his stupor and checked to make

sure Dave wouldn't run for the gate and bowl him over in the process. Dave awoke when he heard Annabelle yell, but thankfully he only rolled onto his side and stretched out his legs.

Annabelle kept up her full-out run. After a few yards, Mike figured out why. The sand felt like a lumpy frying pan over hot coals. His feet sank into the deep sand. The way she moved like a freaking gazelle over the beach made him feel like a lumbering ox. She ran into the water and dove into the first big wave. He spotted her swimming past the surf just as he hit the water.

She turned around and watched as he swam to her.

"I beat you."

He stood and wiped the water from his eyes. "That wasn't a fair race." He pointed at her bikini. "You came out wearing that... and scrambled my brain like you knew it would. You took off before I even knew what happened."

"You just can't stand losing to a girl, can you? Face it. I'm fast."

"Yeah, you're fast as hell. How does the ankle feel?"

"It's fine. Dr. Dolittle said I was healing, and I didn't need the boot or crutches anymore."

"It's Dr. Doyle, and just because you don't need crutches or the boot doesn't mean you should be running."

"But the sand is hot."

"Tell me about it." He looked at the horizon and saw a huge wave heading their way. "Look out."

She turned and swam out farther.

"We're going to have to dive through it." Mike grabbed her hand. "Ready?"

She nodded. The drag of the water rushed toward the building wave. "Here it comes."

Annabelle dove, and he followed her in. Sand and shell particles brought up from the bottom stung his skin. He popped his head out of the water and searched for her. She wasn't there. He turned and looked toward the empty shore. Mike fought back the panic and scanned the water. "Annabelle!"

She popped up right next to him, laughing.

"You scared the crap out of me!" He reached out and pulled her to him so hard he practically knocked the wind out of her. She grabbed him around the neck like a drowning swimmer, hooked her feet around his waist, and kissed him.

He was tempted to take her right there in the water, but they were on a public beach—presently deserted, but they'd be in full view of whoever walked by. Granted, they were far enough out that someone would need binoculars to see anything, but Mike still had some decorum. Very little, apparently, since he carried her right out of the water, across the beach, and into the house and dumped her on the first couch he hit. Before Annabelle could draw another breath, Mike had her bikini top off and his mouth on her breast. She was his every fantasy come true.

He had his hands full of her. She tasted like salt water and Annabelle, and he'd been starving for her. He pulled down her bottoms and tossed them over his shoulder. He strained against his swim trunks even as she struggled with the drawstring to free him. Mike kissed her and tried to undo the damage she'd done to the drawstring. She deepened their kiss, doing her best to get him so hot he was about to embarrass himself. It had been weeks since they were together in any way other than his dreams, and he was on the edge.

Mike ended up ripping the drawstring off and sliding his wet trunks down. He gazed into eyes as open and direct as he'd ever seen them.

"God, Belle. I love you."

A tear slid from the corner of her eye as she pulled him down to her. "I love you too."

Mike froze, his arms locked, his mind stuttered. He wasn't sure if he'd heard her say she loved him or if it was his imagination. He'd imagined it so many times.

"What's wrong?"

"Nothing?"

"Then why aren't you kissing me?"

"I'm just... did you? I mean, would you please repeat that?"

"Repeat what?"

"That last thing…"

"I love you too."

She gave him a full-body kiss, stealing his air, his heart and soul.

"Mike?"

She expected him to speak? The best he could do was grunt. Before he knew what she was doing, she'd rolled over on top of him. He'd thought she was beautiful before, but man, he'd never seen anything as beautiful as she was now. Her hair wet and wild against her sun-kissed skin, her face flushed, and her eyes dark with excitement all for him. He grabbed her hips, moving her to the rhythm in his head, the rhythm both their bodies screamed for. He was so close. Annabelle chose that moment to slide down, his dick making a path up her body, slipping between her breasts. She nibbled on his stomach and headed south.

Oh God, he was going to die of sensual overload. No doubt about it. His heart hammered his ribs so hard they hurt. His lungs pulled in air and expelled fire. His whole body was one large nerve ending, and everywhere she touched set off sparks of need.

Annabelle nuzzled his dick. She wrapped her hand around the base of it and held it as she rubbed her cheek against it, all the while watching him watch her.

"I still can't get over how soft and hard at the same time."

Mike was mesmerized. It was the most erotic thing he'd ever seen. Annabelle kneeling over him, her cheeks flushed with excitement, her lips shiny and dangerously close to his dick, her wet hair cold against his heated skin, and her ass in the air. When she licked her lips, Mike groaned. Then with a swipe of her tongue, she licked the drop of cum off the head of his dick. He wasn't sure how much of this he could take, but he was willing to die finding out.

Her mouth opened and took him in. Every fiber of his being called for him to first grab hold of all that hair and go deep into the hot, wet recesses of her mouth and throat. Instead, he stayed still, holding on to his rapidly slipping control, and concentrated on not coming. Not yet.

She started sucking in earnest. He couldn't hold out much longer. He had to do something now, or he'd come right there—an appealing thought, but he didn't want to start their weekend by coming in less than two minutes.

"Annabelle, stop."

When she didn't, he reached down, grabbed her under the arms, and pulled her onto his chest—her face just inches from his.

"I know I really suck at that... pardon the pun. I'm sorry."

"Belle, that's not the reason—"

"I wanted to try it again. I've been thinking about it—"

"You've been thinking about what exactly?"

"Making love to you with my mouth. Sucking on you. Pleasing you."

"You have?" Oh, shit, if anything this conversation was making his situation worse.

"I thought about it the whole way here. I've been waiting for hours, just thinking how it would—"

Mike flipped the two of them over. With one hand, he parted her and slid home. She was hotter than he'd ever felt, tighter and wetter, and when she wrapped her legs around his waist and moved, he went deeper than he'd ever been.

"Listen to me."

Her eyes opened wide and stared into his with an expression he couldn't pin down. Fear? He kissed her, holding himself inside her, tasting himself on her lips, and driving himself to the brink. "You are great at that. Too good. I just didn't want it to end so soon. I want you to come, too."

"I think I already did."

"When?"

"Once in the car thinking about it, and once while I was doing it."

There it went, all the control he'd tried to hold on to slipped out of his grasp. The thought of her turning herself on thinking of going down on him was one thing, but getting so hot she came just thinking about it, and again while she doing it…

"I'm sorry, baby." He took her hard and fast, and he could swear he hit her cervix, he was so deep. She came almost instantly, drawing him deeper, blinding him with feeling. He came hard and long with a pleasure so intense it almost hurt. Everything about her was a turn-on, and oh man, when she moved, he lost himself in her. He knew he loved her, but he didn't know a man could feel like this—this insane mixture of lust, love, need, excitement, and fear. He looked into her eyes. It was like looking in a mirror, only her eyes were filled with tears.

It took all his strength not to collapse on top of her, but tears did strange things to men. Giving super-human powers was a new one on him, but that's what it seemed to take to hold his weight up and kiss her. "Hey, what's wrong?"

He started going through a mental checklist. She came, she seemed really into it, and she didn't seem to be in pain… Oh shit. He hadn't worn a condom. No wonder it felt so insanely good. He'd never had sex without protection, not once, but then he'd never been with a woman who could make him forget his own name. "Belle, I'm so sorry, but I swear, I've never done this before, so you're safe."

Annabelle sniffed and wiped her eyes. "What are you talking about?"

"We had unprotected sex. Isn't that why you're crying?"

"No."

"Then what's the matter?"

"Nothing."

"Why are you crying?"

"I have no idea." She hiccupped. "God, this is so embarrassing."

"So you're not upset?"

"About forgetting to take precautions? No. I mean, I'm on the Pill now, and we're both clean and healthy. We're not seeing other people, are we?"

"I'm not. Are you?"

"No!"

"Then why the tears?"

"I don't know. It's like I felt so much. I overflowed, and it leaked out my eyes."

"Happy tears?"

"No. Why would I be happy about smeared mascara and a red, blotchy face?" She started laughing.

"God, I love you." Mike couldn't help himself. He kissed her, and she kissed him back, then wham, things heated up again.

His hand found her breast. Her nipple was already hard, and when it hit his palm, he swore there must be an electric current running straight to his dick. "Come on, we're going upstairs." Just as soon as he could stand. "There's a great big bathtub with our names on it."

So much for the bath. By the time they made the trip from the couch to the bedroom, the last thing on their minds was cleanliness. One minute they were laughing and playing, and the next they were making love. But it was different now—more intense, more satisfying, and more scary.

Annabelle had never experienced so many different
emotions at once. They ran through her mind like bumper
cars careening out of control. She tried to shut them
down, but it was more difficult than she'd expected.
Mike had a way of getting though her every defense.

She lay beside him with her head on his chest, listening
to the beating of his heart. She wasn't sure if he was
awake or asleep, but the poor guy needed to sleep for a
week. The nap he'd taken on the ride out had definitely
done some good, but making love a few times must have
worn him out. She ran her hand lightly down his side and
snuggled closer, throwing her leg over him. Her leg came
in contact with a surprisingly turgid part of his anatomy.
The man could be dying from exhaustion and still be a
veritable Energizer Bunny when it came to sex.

Annabelle moved away, not wanting to start anything.
"I'm going to take a shower. I'll just be a minute." She
slid out of bed and rummaged through her suitcase until
she found a comfy pair of shorts and a T-shirt. She
looked over her shoulder. Mike lay on his stomach with
his arms wrapped around a pillow, watching her without
even pulling the sheet over him. She could look at him
all day. He was beautiful.

"What? You're looking at me funny."

"You make quite a beautiful picture there." One
she'd keep in her mind forever. She tried to memorize
the slightly confused look on his face. "You have a
beautiful body. In this light and against those sheets, in
that pose—"

"I'm not posing."

"I was trying to say you look like you belong on
canvas." The way the setting sun lit the room and the

contrast of his skin to the dark sheets and walls made her itch for a sketch pad, a canvas, and paints.

"The only beautiful body in this room is yours. Besides, men aren't beautiful."

"That's where you're wrong. I find the male form incredibly beautiful. Look at Michelangelo's *David*. I swear it's the most beautiful body, male or female, ever sculpted."

"Oh, so you're talking artistically."

"I guess so." Annabelle laughed. "I better get that shower."

"You sure you don't want company? I can wash your back..."

"Right now, I'm more interested in your culinary skills. I'm hungry. You better make dinner."

Mike rolled over. "I'll take care of it."

"When I get out of the shower, I'll give you a hand."

"You want to help in the kitchen?"

"No, but I thought I should offer."

"How about this? I take care of dinner, and you take care of dessert."

"What do you want for dessert?"

"You."

She bent and kissed him. She was tempted to offer dessert first. Then her stomach rumbled, and they both laughed.

"Okay, I can take a hint. Hurry up with that shower. I want to eat fast."

She walked away, leaving him tenting the sheet.

When Annabelle found Mike in the kitchen, he looked up from whatever he was chopping and smiled. He had on a pair of shorts—or maybe it was a bathing suit—and a T-shirt that was just tight enough to show off his chest. For a guy who didn't spend hours in the gym, he had a really nice chest. She tore her eyes from his chest and met a self-satisfied smirk on his face she chose to ignore.

"You want to eat on the deck?" he asked.

"Sure, what are you making?"

"I thought I'd make barbecue chicken and roasted vegetables."

"Sounds good."

"Yeah. Whenever I'm here, I take advantage of Nick's grill. It's the size of my kitchen at home, and I really appreciate not having to climb through a window to get to my little hibachi on the fire escape."

She had no problem picturing Mike doing just that.

"Hey, we can get a gas grill for the garden behind your place."

"Sure." Annabelle tried injecting enthusiasm into her voice. It was hard to feign excitement about something you knew would never happen. It felt like a lie. Not only was she the world's worst liar, but she didn't want to lie to Mike, or anyone else. She felt guilty enough keeping things from him. When she finally told him the truth, he might not be happy with her decision to spend a perfect weekend together before dropping the bomb.

She hadn't thought of that. Or the fact that not only would their relationship be over, but Mike might come out of it hating her. She didn't think she could stand it if he hated her—not when she loved him so much.

Annabelle slid onto a barstool across from him and watched him chop fresh vegetables faster than the chefs on the cooking shows. He ran the back of his knife across the cutting board and, with his hands, shoveled the perfectly chopped vegetables into a waiting bowl. Then he tossed them in olive oil and spices, added the bowl to a tray stacked with grilling utensils, and topped it with a tray of marinated chicken he took from the fridge. He tossed a towel over his shoulder before hefting the pile and heading toward the deck.

"There's beer in the fridge and red wine breathing on the counter. Why don't you get some while I throw the food on the grill?"

"Sure."

Mike stopped dead in his tracks and looked at her in that disconcerting way of his. "It seems like 'sure' is your word for the day. Is that anything like the word 'fine'?"

"Excuse me?"

"You know, when a woman's angry and the man asks if she's okay, she says she's fine… right before she throws a shoe at his head."

"I'm not angry."

Mike did his X-ray stare again. "No, not angry, but something is bothering you. You look a little sad."

She wasn't sure she could pull this off. "Maybe it's just hormones." Which was partially true. She was completely hormonal, but the only symptom she could blame on it was a fierce craving for chocolate. Now she'd have to add constant horniness to the list, too.

She wasn't sure Mike believed her, but he was a guy, and doctor or not, guys stopped asking questions when a woman mentioned cycles of the female variety. He went on his not-so-merry way to the grill, and she took a wineglass hanging under the cabinet and poured. She took a sip and then checked out the label, because it was really good. It was appropriately called *One Last Kiss*. She gulped another mouthful of the wine and tried not to cry.

Mike watched Annabelle through the wall of windows. The lights were on inside, giving him an unobscured view without her knowledge. He felt like a Peeping Tom when he saw the emotion crossing her face as she stared off into space. She struggled with something, and he was sure it was more than hormonal. He had nothing concrete to go on, just instinct. Unfortunately, his instincts had never failed him. He only wished he knew what to do about it.

Annabelle straightened her shoulders like she had before they left Vinny's office to face their families on Mother's Day. She dreaded having to sit through a family dinner after they announced their relationship, and she was insanely nervous about meeting his mother. He could understand that, but why would she dread seeing him?

She finished her first glass of wine, refilled it, and poured another. Dave let out a whine. He'd been sitting beside Mike waiting for him to drop something.

"I fed you already, you big galoot. You're not getting anything else."

Mike flipped the chicken and decided that maybe he was overreacting. He hadn't spent enough time with Annabelle to know what she was like when she was premenstrual. It would explain the tears earlier. He'd just have to do more to put a smile on her face. A romantic dinner for two was just the beginning. Dave groaned and lay on Mike's feet. Okay, a romantic dinner for three. Then maybe a moonlight stroll along the beach.

Annabelle juggled opening the door while carrying two glasses of wine and the bottle. "Hey, do you need any help?"

She was the one who needed help. Mike rushed over, taking the wineglass she offered him and the bottle before she spilled them all. He closed the door and gave her a quick kiss. "Are you any good at grilling?"

She took another sip of her wine. "No, but I'm good at eating. I can help with that."

"Good. Dinner is almost ready."

Annabelle and Mike spent the rest of the night talking about nothing in particular. They strolled along the deserted beach with Dave running around getting sandy and wet.

It must have been Dave's first beach experience. He barked at the waves and then chased them until one crashed right over him. In the moonlight, the only parts of him visible were his eyes and the white star on his chest. He discovered his inner puppy, and his antics were enough to keep them laughing.

Mike had his arm around Annabelle, and he did his best to protect her from the showers of salt water and sand Dave unleashed when he shook off. But by the time they walked up the boardwalk to the house, Dave had both of them wet, sandy, and smelling like wet dog.

"Come on, Dave. We're hitting the shower." Mike pulled Dave into the outdoor shower beneath the deck to give him a quick bath. Dave wasn't too happy about it. The big dog didn't mind getting his face wet in the ocean, but it was another story when the water came from a hose or a showerhead. Mike was glad there was a lock on the privacy fencing around the shower, otherwise Dave would have escaped. As it was, he butted his big head against the door, trying to rip the lock off.

Once Mike got Dave turned around, he was faced with another problem. "Dave, do you mind? I don't go around sticking my head between your legs." He didn't realize Annabelle was right outside. She was certainly enjoying herself and didn't try to muffle her laughter over his predicament. A couple of towels were tossed over the wooden door.

"Mike, I'm going upstairs to shower."

"Oh, thanks a lot. Desert me in my time of need."

"What are you talking about? I brought down towels for the two of you. Come up after both of you are dried off. I'll just be a minute."

Annabelle took more than a minute… more than fifteen minutes, but hey, it was time well spent if the final result was taken into consideration. She stepped out of the steamy bathroom into the candlelit bedroom.

Mike had candles covering every flat surface above the height of Dave's tail, and a tray of fruit beside him on the bed. He'd not only prepared a healthy dessert, but he'd somehow dried Dave enough to keep the smell of wet dog out of the bedroom. When she stepped into his open arms, she was even more impressed to find he no longer smelled like wet dog either. In fact, he smelled really yummy, and he'd accomplished all of it in less time than it took her to shower, dry her hair, and primp. Damn, did she ever feel inadequate.

From the look on his face, he wasn't complaining. But if they wanted to get any sleep, she should have waited until tomorrow night to wear the nightie that Wayne said would make him consider going straight.

She stepped out of Mike's arms, slid into the robe she'd tossed on the foot of the bed, and tied it around her waist.

"Babe, putting that robe on is like locking the door after the car's been stripped."

Annabelle woke up knowing how lunch meat felt. She was jammed between Mike and Dave, both of whom were sound asleep. Dave gave new meaning to the words "morning breath." His head rested between her breasts, and his doggy breath washed over her with every snore. Mike shared her pillow and had an arm and a leg thrown over her, leaving her no escape. Even worse, she had to pee.

She nudged Dave's head. His eyes shot open, then his tongue shot out and got her right on the mouth. Eww! He seemed happy to snuggle and moved even closer.

"Dave, get down," she whispered.

Dave gave her another kiss. He'd obviously had never learned morning-after etiquette. Mike yawned, stretched, and gave her the third kiss of the morning. Mike had obviously missed the same etiquette class. She'd never been kissed so much.

Mike lingered on the kiss while he gave Dave a shove. Dave grunted, rolled off the high bed onto the floor, and stood staring at them with his big blockhead resting comfortably on the mattress. Mike ran his hand up her naked body, and Dave stuck his nose in a very private place.

Annabelle shot up in bed. "Stop it." She pointed to Dave. "You keep your cold, wet nose to yourself."

Mike laughed.

"What are you laughing about? You're as bad as he is."

He was still laughing. "What? I didn't goose you."

"Not yet." She smacked the hand that slid up her thigh.

"I forgot. You're not much of a morning person."

She grumbled, pulled the sheet off the bed, and stomped into the bathroom.

"Come on, Dave. Let's go brew up some of those magic beans to see if we can change her back into my sweet girlfriend."

"I heard that."

Chapter 14

MIKE PRETENDED TO READ A MEDICAL JOURNAL WHILE surreptitiously watching Annabelle polish her toenails. He'd never seen it done before. Either that or he'd never paid attention, which might be the case. No one had ever captured his attention so completely. She sat with her foot on the coffee table, cotton balls stuck in between each of her toes, and her hair tied in a ponytail on the top of her head so it fell like a fountain of corkscrew curls. She wore his old Columbia sweatshirt with the collar cut out, which slipped enticingly off her bare shoulder, making her look like an '80s *Flashdance* fantasy.

The weather had turned cold and rainy, which gave him an excuse to build a fire and cuddle up with her until she pulled out her smelly nail polish and shoved him away. Until the smell went away or the stuff dried, he had to be content to watch from a distance.

"Would you stop?"

Mike looked over the journal he'd been hiding behind. "Stop what?"

"Not you. Dave."

She put the cap on the bottle of polish and elbowed Dave. "He won't stop breathing on me. He needs his teeth brushed. I saw on a commercial that you're supposed to brush a dog's teeth. It's weird, but it might make his nasty doggy breath smell better."

"I guess. I never had a dog. I wouldn't mind having Dave, though—he's a guy's dog."

"No, he's a girl's dog. He's Rosalie's."

"That's not what I mean. He's not one of those stupid-looking girly dogs women carry around in their pocketbooks, or like an Afghan, who look like they spent their lives being styled. Dave's a no-nonsense, ride-in-the-back-of-your-pick-up-truck type of dog."

"I think he's more of a 'mess-with-me-and-my-dog-will-eat-you' kind of dog. Dave likes riding inside the car."

"I meant that a guy isn't going to want to die of embarrassment when he takes Dave for a walk. You're going to miss him when Nick and Rosalie come back. Are you going to get a dog of your own?"

"Maybe. No offense to Dave here, but I've always wanted a dog to run with. Not only for safety reasons, but for company. It sure would make getting out the door easier if you have to take a dog out anyway. Plus, it just looks cool. Maybe I'll rescue a greyhound."

"I hear they make great pets. Do you want to look into it when we get back home?"

"Sure."

Annabelle got up and walked away from him on her heels so as not to mess up her nails. Dave trailed behind her, whining like he was commiserating for some unknown reason.

Every time Mike mentioned doing anything together in the future, she shut down. Either something was wrong, or the thought of them leaving was as depressing to her as it was to him. This had been the best weekend of his life. They had great food, great laughs, great sex, and plenty of sleep.

He could get used to having her around. Hell, who was he kidding? He had gotten used to having her around. Not that they spent every moment together, but he took her into consideration when he made decisions. He worried about her, missed her when they weren't together, and thought about his future with her in it. Maybe she was worried that if he got the job, he'd leave her.

He hoped if he was offered the position at EHS, Annabelle would want to move to Pennsylvania with him. Move in with him? Man, he wasn't sure how he felt about living together. Sure, he stayed over at her place, but that wasn't the same as living together. The good Catholic boy in him thought Annabelle deserved more—better. Besides, her parents didn't seem like the type to look the other way while their daughter lived in sin.

It was either get two places and be close to one another, or get married.

He'd expected to feel blinding terror at the thought of being tied to one person for the rest of his life, but for some reason all he felt was a sense of rightness.

He and Annabelle were going to have to do some serious talking, but it might be better if he waited until after her hormones and emotions were back to normal, and maybe after he bought her an engagement ring.

The thought of buying a diamond shot a short blast of fear through him, but he attributed it to going further in debt than he already was. He'd get over it. He didn't have much of a choice. The thought of sleeping with Annabelle every night, waking up with her every morning, someday having kids who looked just like her, was too good to pass up. Even if it meant going into hock up to his eyeballs.

Annabelle was a wuss. She should tell him. Every time he mentioned the future, it felt as if he were twisting the knife already rammed through her heart. Part of her wanted to believe Becca. Mike wasn't Chip… but no matter how she looked at it, one blaring fact remained the same, Mike and Chip had the same father, and Christopher Larsen would never change his impression of her. Not only did she refuse to stand between Mike and his family—a family she knew he'd always wanted—but she refused to let anyone treat her that badly ever again. Not even for Mike.

He might say he didn't want anything to do with his dad, but once he learned the truth, he'll change his mind.

Annabelle phoned Becca.

She picked up first ring. "Are you okay? Did you tell him yet?"

"Yes and no."

"What?"

"Yes, I'm okay, and no, I didn't tell him."

"Aw, honey, you sound as if you just lost your best friend."

"I have… or I will."

"Annabelle, you'll never lose me."

"I was talking about Mike."

Becca was silent.

"He keeps talking about the future, buying a gas grill for the apartment, a dog of our own"—tears slid down her cheeks, and she swallowed a sob—"I don't know how to tell him, Bec. What if he hates me?"

"It's impossible to hate you, but you need to tell him and tell him soon. Just make sure you tell him that you love him before you drop the bomb."

"I did… well, I told him once. That's enough, right?"

"No, guys like to be reminded a lot."

"But I just don't go around telling people I love them. It's difficult."

"You tell me."

"Well, yeah, but you're not a man. I love you like a sister, not in a let's run to California before they change the same-sex marriage law way. That makes saying I love you difficult."

"So you're thinking of marrying Mike?"

"WHAT?"

"You said marriage."

"I didn't mean marriage, marriage—"

"You did too. I've seen you through two engagements, and you have the rings to prove it. You love this guy more than you loved the other two put together."

"I never loved Johnny."

"No, but you loved Chip. From what I hear from you, you love Mike differently. It's a mature love. Like a fine wine that's perfectly aged."

The bedroom door squeaked. Annabelle ran the water in the bathroom sink and splashed her face.

Mike pushed the bathroom door open. "Annabelle, are you okay?"

"Yeah, fine." She held up one finger. "Becca, Mike just walked in. I have to go."

"Tell my big brother I said hi, okay?"

"Sure. You're really pushing your luck, Bec."

"Yeah, but you still love me, just not the same way you love my brother. Tell him. Everything will work out. You'll see."

"I'll call you soon. Bye."

Annabelle ended the call. "I needed to check in with Becca."

"You've been crying again."

She wrapped her arms around his waist and buried her face in his neck. "I love you, Mike. Always."

"Babe, I love you too, but you're starting to scare me. Are you sure you're okay?"

"I am as long as you're with me."

He stepped back, raised her chin with his finger, and stared deep into her eyes. "I'm not going anywhere without you. I promise."

She knew he meant it, now. She just wished his promise would last longer than the weekend.

Mike placed the last suitcase in the trunk and went back to the house to hurry Annabelle along. She'd insisted on washing the sheets. He tried to tell her that Nick always had a cleaning service come before he or anyone else visited and after they left, but she wouldn't hear of anyone cleaning up after them.

While he appreciated the thought, he'd already cleaned up. Cleaning was what he did. He was a self-proclaimed neat freak, though he tried to downplay that tendency.

In her attempt to clean, she only succeeded in doing the opposite. He'd spent half the day trailing along behind her and cleaning the messes she made.

It was obvious to him that she didn't want to leave, but they had a three-hour ride home, and he had an interview to prepare for in between work and engagement ring shopping.

Vinny had friends in the diamond district and could probably get Mike a good deal. The only catch was that he'd have to *talk* to Vinny. Oh man, he'd have to go ask Annabelle's dad for permission too, wouldn't he? Did people still do that? Again, Vin would know. Then there was his mother. He'd have to tell her... or maybe he and Annabelle could tell her together—if Annabelle said yes. Man, he hadn't thought about that. What if she didn't want to get married? No, he wasn't going to go there. He didn't have much to offer her now, but after he paid off his student loans, they would be comfortable. He'd probably never be wealthy, but they'd be happy and comfortable.

"Mike, why are you staring into space?"

"What?"

"You're a million miles away." She wrapped her arms around him, her body molded to his as he rested his chin on the top of her head. "You're not thinking about work are you? You had a frown on your face."

"No, I was just thinking that it's time to leave."

Dave stuffed his big blockhead in between their bodies.

"Maybe we can stay one more night and take off early in the morning."

"I have rounds at seven a.m."

"Oh."

He kissed her temple. She smelled so good, he was tempted to pick her up and give the other couch a spin before they left. "I'm sorry, babe. We'd better go. We're going to hit traffic on the way back as it is. I promise we'll come back soon without the family. Just you and me again, okay?"

"Sure." She let go of him and headed for the front door.

He was really starting to hate that word.

Annabelle really didn't want to leave, ever. Their time together was the closest thing to perfect she'd ever had. Except for the time she spent worrying about Mike's reaction. She fell deeper in love with him, and losing him was going to gut her.

Not one prone to melodrama, she knew she'd survive. She imagined telling him a million ways, but every scenario ended with disaster. His reactions ranged from rage to hurt, both of which she expected and yet had no idea how to handle.

When she'd awoken in the middle of the night, slipped out to the deck, and called Becca without a second thought to the hour, Annabelle had begged her to meet them in Brooklyn. Becca refused because she knew Annabelle too well. She explained in that no-nonsense way of hers that Annabelle would try to turn the news into a reunion instead of the end of a relationship. Becca was still under the misconception that Annabelle and Mike could work it out. What Becca didn't understand, and what Annabelle was just beginning to figure out herself, was that she wouldn't allow herself to be mistreated by his father, and she loved Mike too much to allow him to choose her over his family and have him resent her for it five years down the road. No, she wouldn't let that happen.

Nothing was more depressing than the drive home from a vacation, especially when your companion was eerily quiet. Mike tried several times to start a conversation. Planning their next trip to the Hamptons only seemed to make matters worse, and discussing the week ahead met with the same fate. Annabelle set her iPod in the cradle and played a depressing jazz mix as he traversed through holiday traffic on the Sunrise Highway, which he was sure could rival the Long Island Expressway as the world's largest parking lot.

By the time he double-parked in front of Annabelle's brownstone apartment, the tension in the car was almost unbearable. He slid out of the driver's seat, and by the time he finished stretching, Henry and Wayne were waiting beside the car, greeting Dave and Annabelle and carrying her bags in. He'd been counting on privacy to ferret out whatever the heck was bothering her.

"What time will you be finished with work tomorrow?"

She was actually talking to him? "I'm not sure. I have some errands to run. How about a late dinner?"

She turned to Wayne and Henry. "Would you mind taking Dave out to the garden? I'll be right up."

Mike watched them leave as he pulled Annabelle to him. "We need to talk about whatever it is that's bothering you."

Annabelle nodded. "We'll talk tomorrow."

Mike tamped down the ominous feeling he had and chose to figure out how the heck to propose to Annabelle. He walked her into the apartment and, ignoring the domestic duo, gave her a kiss good-bye to remember.

Mike drove right from Annabelle's to DiNicola's, parked in the alley behind the restaurant, and entered through the kitchen door. Vinny took one look at him, passed his orders to his assistant chef, and without a word walked to his office. Mike followed and sat in front of the desk while Vinny poured them both Jack Daniel's.

"Are you gonna tell me what the problem is? Or, are you gonna stare at me until I guess?"

"I need help."

"Shit, I knew that the moment you walked into my kitchen."

"I'm going to ask Annabelle to marry me."

Mike should have let the man swallow before blurting it out. Vin had just taken a sip of Jack, which he spit all over his desk.

Mike reached for a stack of napkins and handed them to Vinny one at a time while he cursed and dried off all the orders he'd soaked in his shock.

"What the fuck is it with those Ronaldi girls? And what's the rush? You take her out for a weekend of hot sex, and you decide you can't live without her? You didn't knock her up, did you?"

"No. I love her. And you're right, I don't want to live without her. I have this interview coming up, and I want to know if I end up moving away, she'll be with me."

"Hold up, where you movin' to? You tell your mother about this yet?"

"Outside of Philadelphia. And Vin, if I do get the job, I'm gonna have to take it. It's one of the best practices on the East Coast. But no matter what happens, I have to get out of the nightmare practice I'm in. If I don't get this job, I'm going to have to find another. I can't stay where I am."

"Okay. You need another job. I get that. But do you have to get engaged before you even have the interview? Why not wait and see how it shakes out?"

"I love her. That's not going to change. Ever."

"Well, at least you're not being a putz like Nick was, but shit. I gotta worry about the timing here. You two been together, what, a month?"

"How long were you and Mona together before you knew she was made for you?"

"Me and Mona are not the subject here."

"No, the subject is how long it took you to propose to her. Oh, and did you have to ask her father for her hand in marriage?"

"Three weeks, and yeah, I did talk to her father, but that was after we… well, you know. Things were different back then. Mona was a nice girl, and unless you put a ring on her finger, there was no… anyway. I talked to her old man, and after meeting Mr. Ronaldi, I'd advise you to do the same. Especially with Annabelle being the baby of the family and all. That's if I can't talk you out of this."

"I love her."

"Yeah, I hear ya, but do you have to marry her now? Maybe we should call Nick. I got his number somewhere…" He started searching through the pile of Jack-splattered papers on his desk.

"I don't need Nick's permission to get married. And I already know what he's going to say, so don't bother."

"He thinks this whole thing is wonky too, doesn't he?"

"Let's just say he mentioned some reservations, but he doesn't know Annabelle and neither do you." Mike took a sip of Jack and stared down Vinny. The man was hard to stare down, but this was important, and even though Mike was on the receiving end of the Brooklyn stare, he had to stand tough. Vin looked away first.

"Okay, so, you're gonna ask her. What do you need from me? I know you didn't come to listen to reason."

"I need you to hook me up with one of your friends in the diamond district. I need to get her a nice ring without going bankrupt in the process."

Vinny flipped through an old-fashioned Rolodex wheel, picked up his phone, and dialed. "Ira, it's Vinny DiNicola. How you doin'?"

Mike sat back and listened to Vinny set up an appointment. Ira would meet Mike in Vinny's office at lunchtime the next day with a sample of his wares.

Vinny and Ira talked for a while, and when Vinny dropped the phone onto the cradle, Mike knew there was another lecture coming.

"Now, Mikey, just because you get a ring on her finger doesn't mean you need to marry the girl right away. You two should plan a nice long engagement—like a year or two. Get to know each other better. Make sure this isn't just your Johnson talkin', if you know what I mean."

"Vinny, I love her, man."

"I know that's what your thinkin' now with all the great sex your havin'. But once the great sex cools down, and believe me, my friend, it will, you gotta like livin' with the chick. You hear what I'm sayin'? You gotta love her even when you don't feel like it. Love is a decision, not a feelin', because believe me, you won't be feelin' the love a whole lot of the time."

"I hear you."

"Now, you know Mona's gonna be here sniffin' out those rocks tomorrow, so you better talk to your mother about this before Mona does. You don't want her to hear that you're engaged from Mona. That'll hurt her feelings, you know?"

"Okay. I'll talk to Mum."

"Ira's gonna want to deal in cash. I'll make sure I got enough in the safe tomorrow. You can pay me back after you get that new high-falut'n job. And if this thing with you and Annabelle don't work out, get the damn ring back. You don't need to be padding no chick's jewelry box. You get what I'm sayin'?"

"It's going to work out, Vin. I—"

"I know, I know. You love her."

"I do."

"And there's no way I can talk you into waitin' on this?"

"No."

"Okay, I hope you know what this is gonna cost me."

"I'll pay you back."

"It's not the money. Nick is gonna fuckin' kill me."

"Nick needs to mind his own business."

"Now don't be givin' Nick shit. He's worried about you. We all are."

Vin stood and raised his glass. "Well, I wish you all the luck in the world. You're gonna need it."

Mike drained the last of his drink and set the glass on the desk before he stood. "Thanks. I appreciate it."

Vin grabbed Mike into a tight hug and slapped his back. "Now, get your ass over to your mother's place before it gets too late. I'll see you tomorrow."

Mike followed Vinny through the kitchen. "Nino, pack up a few cannoli to go. Mikey here is going to see his mama."

Nino made up a to-go package and handed it to Mike. "You say hello to your mama for me, eh?"

"Sure, Nino. Vin, thanks again."

Vinny smiled at him. "Now get the hell outa here. I got work to do."

Vinny was right. He needed to tell his mother. It didn't mean he looked forward to it.

All his life, it had only been him and Mum. She liked Annabelle. She certainly raved about her enough after their lunch together. But she'd only met Annabelle twice.

He hoped she wouldn't have the same reaction to the news that Vinny had. Even more than that, he hoped she wouldn't cry.

Mike could handle any emergency you could throw at him, but he couldn't handle his mother's tears. Happy, sad, made no difference. His mother crying just wigged him out.

Mike used his key and let himself into his mother's apartment. "Mum, I'm home." He set the cannoli on the dining room table and went into the kitchen to get plates.

"Michael, what are you doing here? I thought you'd be with Annabelle on the last night of your vacation."

She kissed him and then wiped the lipstick off his cheek. He wasn't even sure she actually had lipstick on, but she rubbed his cheek whether it needed it or not.

"Did you have a good time? Is everything okay?"

"Yeah, it was fine. We had a great time. That's why I stopped by. You want some tea? Vinny sent over some cannoli."

His mother filled the kettle while he pulled out the cups.

"You had a nice time, but instead of staying with Annabelle, you went to Vinny's and then came here?"

"Mum, I'm going to ask Annabelle to marry me." Oh man, he knew it. She teared up. "Please don't cry. You know I can't stand it when you cry."

She turned her back to him and fussed with the teapot. "I'm not crying. I think it's wonderful. Sudden, but not unexpected."

If she was crying, at least she had the decency to pretend she wasn't. It still bothered him, but not as much as when she was out-and-out crying.

"So, this is okay with you?"

"Michael, you're in love with the girl. I think it's wonderful. You were always one to make a quick decision. I'm not surprised. I wish you and Annabelle every happiness."

"Thanks, but I haven't asked her yet. I'm not sure she even wants to get married."

"She's in love with you. You're a wonderful man. Why wouldn't she want to marry you?"

"I don't know. This weekend was incredible, and we had a great time, but I think something was bothering her. I'd catch her looking at me, and she seemed... I don't know... sad, I guess."

"So talk to her. Find out what's wrong."

"We're having dinner together tomorrow night. I went to Vinny's to see if he could hook me up with one of his friends in the diamond district."

"There's no need for that. I have a ring I've been saving for you. It was your grandmother's. It's beautiful. I have it in the safety deposit box at the bank. I'll get it for you and take it to have it cleaned on my lunch hour tomorrow."

"You never told me you had Grandmother's ring."

"It was from your father. He'd given it to me as a promise ring... I hadn't thought to mention it. You were never serious with anyone before. I put it away years ago. I guess it slipped my mind. It's a beautiful ring, though. Annabelle will love it."

"Are you sure about this? You know you can have it reset."

"I'm not the diamond type. You know that. If I'd wanted to have it reset, I would have done it ages ago."

Mike hugged her, and she waved him off. "You go call Vinny and tell him to cancel that appointment. And make sure you thank him, too."

"I will."

Mike never knew his mother had a ring given to her by his father. It made him feel a little weird, but it would save him a fortune. So who was he to question it?

He and his mum had tea and cannoli and made plans to meet the next afternoon.

Chapter 15

MIKE MET HIS MOTHER THE NEXT DAY AT THE JEWELER'S where she'd had the ring cleaned. When she opened the box, the size of the stone astonished him. It was as big as, if not bigger than, the rock Nick had bought Annabelle's sister, and Nick had money to burn. Mike didn't know anything about diamonds, but this one was brilliant. He couldn't imagine how much it was worth. To think all the times his mother had struggled to put food on the table and pay the bills, she'd never sold it. Amazing.

"I told you it's perfect for Annabelle. She can carry it off. I always felt as if it wore me rather than the other way around."

"You wore it?"

"Yes, for a time, when I was pregnant with you. I wore it and a wedding band."

"Oh."

He put the ring on the tip of his finger and watched how it caught the light. She was right. Annabelle would love it. It was unusual, big, bold yet delicate, just like her.

"It's amazing. Thank you."

"Why are you thanking me? It's rightfully yours. It's all you have of your family heritage."

"It's not much of a family, but it's a great ring."

"I suggest you get it appraised for insurance purposes. But you can have that done when you have it sized for Annabelle."

"Right." Mike nodded. He was nervous as hell.

He checked his watch. "I have to go. I'm meeting Mr. Ronaldi at two."

She kissed his cheek and then rubbed off the lipstick. "You'll be fine, Michael. Just remember one thing."

"What's that?"

"She's lucky to have you, just as you're lucky to have her. This isn't a one-sided relationship."

Mike hoped not. "Love you, Mum. Thanks again… and I'll call you… you know, later."

"I'd be surprised to hear from you before tomorrow. Have a wonderful night tonight. Make it one that neither of you will ever forget."

"Okay…"

"And Michael, remember this is something she's going to tell your children and grandchildren about. Don't propose in a way that would force her to lie every time your daughter asks how you proposed. Make it special."

"Right… special." Shit, this was more complicated than he thought it would be.

Mike parked Nick's car in front of the Ronaldi's house. The front door flew open before he hit the first step. Mrs. Ronaldi waited, smiling, holding the door.

"Michael, so nice of you to come. Here. Come in, come in."

He followed her inside. "Thanks, Mrs. Ronaldi. I'm supposed to meet your husband. Is he home yet?"

"He's changing. Sit, sit. Can I get you a coffee? Espresso?"

"No thank you, I'm good." Mike had absolutely no idea what he was supposed to say to Annabelle's mother. His mind was a total blank.

She motioned for him to sit on the couch in the living room. When he did, the air escaped from the plastic that encased it.

Mrs. Ronaldi sat in the chair beside the couch. "Did you have a nice holiday?"

He wiped his damp palms on his pants. "Yes... I took Annabelle out to the Hamptons for the long weekend. We stayed at Nick's place. It was really relaxing."

"I hope she took good care of you. Both my girls are wonderful cooks."

"Actually, I usually do the cooking. It's a hobby of mine. I don't think I've given Annabelle much of a chance to um... show off."

"You cook?"

"Yes, I learned when I worked at DiNicola's. I don't get to cook nearly enough. Annabelle doesn't seem to mind my taking over the kitchen, though."

"Oh, well. I guess if it's your hobby, eh? It's a good thing then."

"Yeah, it's all good."

Mr. Ronaldi thankfully came down. "Maria, get the man a drink."

Mike stood to greet Mr. Ronaldi. He had the same good looks Annabelle's brother, Richie, had with a bit more meat on his tall frame—and a lot more muscle. Mike wouldn't want to meet him in a dark alley. "Mrs. Ronaldi already offered. I'm fine." Mike shook his hand. "Thanks for meeting me, Mr. Ronaldi."

"I'm having a beer. You wanna change your mind?"

Mike cleared his throat. "Fine. A beer would be nice. Thanks."

Mr. Ronaldi turned to his wife. "Well, you heard him. Go get us our drinks."

Mrs. Ronaldi scurried away, embarrassed. Mike couldn't help but feel sorry for her. He couldn't believe the way Mr. Ronaldi spoke to his wife, but ignored the urge to tell Mr. Ronaldi where to get off. It probably wasn't a good time, especially considering the question Mike came to ask.

"Mr. Ronaldi—"

"Paul. You call me Paul."

"Fine, Paul. I came over today because… I love Annabelle, and I want to marry her. I came to ask for your blessing."

Something crashed in the kitchen. Mike jerked his head toward the noise. It was probably a couple of beers.

"You didn't knock her up, did you?"

"No, sir. I love her, and I want to marry her. If she'll have me."

Mrs. Ronaldi ran out with the beer, shoving Paul's at him. "Of course she will have you. A nice doctor like you, so well mannered and handsome, why wouldn't she have you? You're Catholic?"

"Yes, ma'am, I'm Catholic."

"Good, then there's no problem."

"I hope you're right." He turned to Mr. Ronaldi. "Do I have your permission to marry your daughter?"

Mr. Ronaldi looked him up and down. "Yeah. You can marry her. You better take good care of her, though."

"Yes, sir. I will."

Mr. Ronaldi raised his glass. "*Salute*, and good luck."

Mike sipped of the cold beer. He could really use it. The luck that is. He hoped proposing to Annabelle would be less nerve-racking than asking her father for his permission had been. Somehow, he doubted it.

Mike did his best to come up with a romantic way to propose to Annabelle. Unfortunately, romance wasn't his forte. The best he could do on short notice was a nice romantic dinner.

He went shopping and bought a few filets mignons, mushrooms, a good Marsala wine to use in a mushroom and wine reduction, and everything else he'd need. Lord knew, he couldn't count on Annabelle to have anything on hand in her kitchen. He bought candles and prayed that Rosalie had left candlesticks. There weren't any in the market, and he didn't have any at his place either.

Mike hurried to Annabelle's and let himself in. If he wanted to have everything ready before she got home from work, he needed to move fast.

After taking Dave out for a quick walk, Mike got down to work. He set up his little hibachi in the garden, started the coals, and locked Dave in the apartment to make sure he didn't go sniffing around the fire.

Once the coals were heating, he searched for candlesticks. He checked every cabinet in the kitchen to no avail before moving to the den, which was now filled with boxes he'd never seen. There was an armoire hidden behind a pile of boxes. He hoped it contained a set of candlesticks because he really didn't have time to run to another store. A large three-foot-by-five-foot canvas rested against the armoire, its back facing out. He looked for a better place to rest it, but the room was so cluttered, he found none. Heck, maybe he should hang the damn thing because there was no floor space left to speak of. Beside the canvas were the remains of the crate it must have been shipped in, as well as a pink and purple polka dot toolbox with Wayne's name stenciled on the side.

He opened the toolbox, took out the hammer, a picture hook, and a nail, and after finding a stud in the middle of the wall, he drove the nail in. The canvas already had a metal wire and had obviously been hung before. Maybe it was something Annabelle brought home from the gallery. She probably didn't want it hanging in the den, but she wasn't there for consultation. If she wanted him to move it later, he would. But for right now, it was better to get it up off the floor before it was damaged.

Mike lifted it over the stacked boxes, turning it carefully so as not to knock any of her things over, and was surprised to see it was a painting of a naked guy. He couldn't help but notice it was a naked guy with a little dick. Not that he usually checked out guys' dicks, but it was literally right in front of his eyes.

He cursed as he tried to get the wire on the damn picture hook. Finally it caught. Mike straightened the canvas a little and stepped back to see the whole picture so to speak.

Mike couldn't believe his eyes. It was a painting of him... but not. Christ, whoever painted this needed to have his eyes examined. The nose looked just like his nose before he'd broken it, the mouth was all wrong, and damn, he certainly didn't have a little dick. Even the eye color was wrong. It wasn't him. He looked for some clue as to who it was, and all he saw was Annabelle's signature and the year it was painted.

She'd painted it four years before they'd met. It couldn't be him. It was a relief to know she didn't think his dick was that small. But shit, who was this guy? And why did he look so much like him? And what was she doing with a naked guy who looked like he could be his twin?

That bad feeling Mike had since he and Annabelle left the Hamptons was so strong it threatened to crush him. The front door opened and closed. Annabelle greeted Dave and called Mike's name, but he couldn't take his eyes off the painting.

He didn't turn to face the open doorway; he knew she'd found him when he heard the sharp intake of breath. Any hope that this was some kind of joke dissolved with her slow exhale. He turned. Annabelle stood holding on to the doorframe like she needed the support. He could really use some too; support that is. The shock and horror on her face gave him the feeling that the bottom had just dropped out of his plan for the night and for the rest of his life. Christ, he was nervous before—now he felt sick to his stomach. Annabelle looked pale, but worse, she looked guilty as hell. "Who is this painting of?"

Annabelle grabbed the doorjamb tighter; the tone of his voice was so cold, as cold as the look in his gray eyes. In every nightmare she'd had about his reaction to the moment he found out the truth, his eyes were never like that. She'd never felt such distance between them. When she moved toward him, he held his hand up to stop her.

"Just answer the damn question."

"Please don't look at me like that." The vein in her forehead pulsed double time. She tried to blink away the tears welling in her eyes. Mike never blinked. This was it. This was the end. Oh God, it hurt. It was all she could do to stay standing. She wanted to curl into a ball to protect herself from the cold pain in his eyes. Instead, she covered her mouth with a trembling hand, either to cover a sob or to keep herself from blurting out the truth.

She nodded and took a deep breath. "I was going to tell you today. I would have told you as soon as I found out, but I didn't want to ruin the weekend you'd worked so hard for." She looked away; she couldn't watch him, and she couldn't bear to see the hate in his eyes. "Michael, I never lied to you, not about anything. I want you to know that."

Mike let out what sounded like a growl. "Yeah. Okay. Sure. Would you please just say what you need to say?"

"I love you." She wiped the tears running down her face. She had a hard time breathing. She wrapped her arms around herself and kept going. "Becca came to visit. I thought she came to help me unpack everything I've had in storage." She gestured to the boxes everywhere. "I left to meet your mother for lunch. Remember?"

Mike remained silent, and Annabelle didn't have the guts to look at him. "I found out that Christopher Larsen is your father. I didn't know before then. I swear. I ran home to Becca to tell her. She knows. The painting is of Chip. He posed for me. It was done a few months before we found out the cancer had come back. Chip and Becca are twins. Becca's your sister."

"You called me Chip that night at the wedding."

Annabelle nodded. "I thought I saw a ghost."

"That's why you went home with me. Because I looked like him?"

"I don't know, maybe at first. But Mike, that's not why I kept seeing you."

"And you expect me to believe that? Especially since you've been so honest with me about everything else."

She nodded and looked at her feet. This hurt so much more than she could ever have imagined. "It's the truth." Oh God, part of her wanted to run to him and beg him to stay. She envisioned throwing herself at him and hanging on as he tried to escape. No, she wouldn't beg a man to stay with her again. She'd begged Chip every day as she watched him wither away, refusing to fight for their relationship or his life. "I'm sorry. I really am."

Mike nodded. "Yeah, me too."

Dave stood beside her, Mike's underwear hanging from his mouth, looking from Mike to her. He whined and butted his head against her thigh, almost knocking her over.

"I lit a charcoal grill in the garden. You might want to douse it before you let Dave out there."

"Okay."

He was telling her about a grill in the garden. Like she really cared about a grill. He'd just taken a wrecking ball to her life. Her heart shattered. She'd known this was coming, but she'd never expected it to feel like this. She wasn't sure how much longer she'd be able to hold it together and couldn't bear to watch him leave.

Annabelle hugged herself to keep from reaching for him as he passed. She leaned against the wall and

staggered into her bedroom. The front door slammed
as she dropped onto the bed. She pulled a pillow to her
face and cried.

Chapter 16

ANNABELLE CRIED WITH A PILLOW OVER HER FACE. THE last thing she needed was the Fairy Godfathers trying to cheer her up. She hurt, and after what she'd done to Mike, she deserved it.

She knew that letting him go was the right thing to do. He'd never have left if she explained how she felt about Chip, the differences in their relationship. He would have forgiven her, and after meeting his dad, he would have stayed with her, supported her. She was even sure he'd have told his dad where to go. But the only loser in the situation would be him. She wasn't sure when, but someday he'd look back and see how much being together had cost him, and whether he admitted it to himself or not, he would resent her for it.

No, this was the best thing for both of them. It just felt as if she was dying inside, and eventually, she'd learn to live with the pain and learn to live without Mike. Eventually. She hoped.

Right now, she wasn't sure giving Becca's way of dealing with excruciating pain a try was the right thing to do. Feeling the pain when she should. Another sob escaped, and she didn't recognize the sound. She cried so hard she could barely breathe. It hurt everywhere. Her body was racked with sobs, her throat was raw, her eyes burned, and she was exhausted, physically and mentally. Dave circled the bed whining before he finally jumped up and lay beside her. Letting Mike go was the best thing she could do for him in the end. When she made the decision, she had no idea she'd feel like this. She had no idea she'd hurt him as much as she had, no idea how to live without him, and no idea how to live with the guilt.

Mike walked out and wanted to punch something. What was wrong with him that he couldn't attract a woman of his own? He finally found the one woman he would love forever, and she didn't love him—she loved his dead brother. She was just like all the rest, only worse. He knew the others had been getting over Nick. With them, there was no pretense. Annabelle had blindsided him. He'd had no idea she'd been with his double—and the man was almost an exact double—which explained her shock when she'd awakened with Mike the morning after the wedding.

And to think, he was about to make a complete ass out of himself by proposing. At least she'd saved him that humiliation.

Mike had just found out he had a sister and a dead brother, and he could care less. He only saw an empty life without Annabelle in it. He only felt pain and anger—he could barely breathe, and he'd be damned if he knew what the hell to do.

She lied to him, she led him on, and she played him like a fucking fool. How could he be so dumb? How could he still be so in love with her?

He got into Nick's car, drove, and somehow he ended up in front of DiNicola's. Mike walked in the front door of the restaurant, right past Mona, sat at the bar, and started drinking. By the end of the night, Rita was hanging around his neck. He'd drunk most of a bottle of Jack and was seeing double.

Mona and Vinny poured him into their car and took him to their house to sleep it off. But Mike couldn't sleep. He wasn't sure if it was because he was lying in a tiny white bed in a pink room, or because the room was full of stuffed animals that, in the light from the street, looked as if they were watching him. Or because every time he closed his eyes, he'd see Annabelle's face, tears streaming down her cheeks. He'd felt as if she'd stabbed him in the heart; then he'd see that fucking picture. Not only had he lost his girlfriend, he'd lost a brother he never knew existed. Now he had a sister he had no idea what to do with and the father he'd never wanted. Fuck.

Becca was worried sick. Maybe she'd made a mistake. Maybe she should have gone to Brooklyn after all. What if Annabelle needed her? She didn't think Mike would be a jerk about it, but what the heck did she know? All she knew about her brother was what Annabelle had told her. And Becca knew as well as anyone, Annabelle didn't have the best taste in men.

It was after eleven o'clock, and Annabelle still hadn't called. She'd promised she would tell Mike the truth today. She promised she'd call Becca after she did.

Becca made another lap around her apartment. She climbed into the swing she'd hung from the open ceiling of her loft. When swinging didn't help calm her nerves, she tried her old standby. She curled up on the window seat and used her stuffed Snoopy as a pillow. Most of Snoopy's fur had been worn off. The poor guy. She rubbed the sleeve of her sweatshirt between her thumb and pointer finger—a nervous habit. Over the years, she rubbed holes in the cuffs of all her jeans and sweatshirts, which is why Annabelle hated when Becca borrowed her clothes.

Not able to stand the torture of not knowing what had happened one more minute, Becca grabbed her phone, hit the speed dial, and prayed Annabelle would pick up.

When the ringing stopped, Becca heard a long hiccup, like when someone was crying and had to stop to breathe. Oh God. "Annabelle?"

A sob came over the line. "Oh, Becca..."

Becca stood and resumed pacing. "Are you okay?" She was crying too hard to talk. "Okay, you need to calm down. You're going to hyperventilate and pass out."

"I... I can't. Oh God, Bec, he's gone."

What an asshole. "Oh, honey, I'm sorry. You're going to be okay. Maybe when he calms down, you two can talk."

"He... he saw the painting of Chip. He hates me, Bec. Oh God. He hates me, and it's all my fault. I hurt him."

"Stop it. You didn't know."

"But I suspected... I should have told him in the beginning. He said I lied to him. He doesn't even believe I love him."

"Look, he's in shock. If he's half the guy you say he is, he'll calm down and talk to you. He loves you remember?"

"I don't know. But it doesn't matter. It's over. It's better this way."

"Better for whom?"

"You sound like your mother."

"I do not. Just because I refuse to butcher the English language by ending a sentence in a preposition does not mean I sound like Mother. Now answer the question. Because I for one don't see how either of you could possibly be better off apart."

"Mike will be fine without me. He's going to have you, your father, not to mention everything he's ever wanted. A family, a future, both of which he won't have if he stays with me. Becca we talked about this. I can't live like I did with Chip. I can't stand for your father's blatant contempt, and I won't make Mike choose between me and the life he's always wanted."

"No, you'll choose for him. That's real nice of you. How do you know what's best for him? He's a grown man. He has the right to make his own decisions and his own mistakes. Who are you to take that away from him?"

"It doesn't matter what he decides. I'm not changing my mind. I'm doing what's best for me."

"That's why you're what, lying on the bed with the dog, crying hysterically because what you're doing is the right thing for you?"

"How did you know I was in bed with Dave crying?"

"I know you better than you know yourself. I'm telling you, you're making a big mistake. I just hope you realize it before it's not only too late for you, but for Mike, too."

"I love him, Becca. I'm doing this for him as much as for myself."

"I know that's what you think. Do you want to know what I think?"

"What's it matter? Nothing I say is going to stop you from telling me."

"True. I think this is an easy way of protecting yourself."

"Excuse me? How could this possibly be protecting myself? I'm dying here? I never thought it would hurt so much, and the way he looked at me, Bec. I'll never forget the coldness I saw in his eyes. How is that protecting myself?"

"Because you aren't giving him the choice of whether to work it out or not. You're feeling all high-and-mighty, doing the right thing for him. Ha, you just don't think he loves you enough to fight for you. You're afraid he's a weakling like Chip. Chip swore he wouldn't treat the cancer if it came back. He said he'd rather die than go through that kind of hell again. It had nothing to do with you. Don't you get it? Chip was weak. He was too weak to stand up against our parents for you, and he was too weak to fight for his own life. You're afraid that Mike is the same way, willing to toss you aside to please his new daddy."

"You're wrong. I won't allow myself to be treated badly by your father, or anyone else for that matter. Not for Mike, not for anyone, ever again. If I'm protecting myself, so be it. I won't put myself between a man I love and his family ever again."

Becca shook her head. Annabelle was so stubborn. She was incapable of lying, so she actually believed the bullshit she spouted. Well, fine. Let her believe it. There were two ways to deal with this, and Annabelle had no idea what Becca was capable of. She was not going to know what hit her.

"Do you want me to come up and stay with you?"

"So you can lecture me? No thanks."

"I promise I won't lecture." Becca crossed her fingers behind her back.

"I'm doing what you told me to do. I'm feeling the pain so I can feel better… someday. I don't need help to feel like shit. I'm doing that pretty well all by myself, thanks."

"I love you."

"I know. Would you do me a favor?"

"Anything."

"Call Mike and make sure he's okay?" Her voice cracked, and she hiccupped again into the phone before noisily blowing her nose. "I'm so worried about him. I don't know where he went, or what he's doing. I just need to know he's okay. Please?"

"You want me to call my brother? That's going to go over well."

"I don't know who else to ask. I don't think he'd talk to me, and I'm afraid to call his mom. It's late. I don't want to upset her."

"Fine, I guess I'm going to have to introduce myself eventually. What's his number?"

Annabelle gave her his home number, his cell, and his pager.

"Okay, I'll call you back."

"Thanks, Becca."

"Yeah… well. Don't thank me yet. I haven't done anything."

She hung up the phone and looked at the numbers. Her brother. She was actually going to talk to her brother. But what the hell could she say to him?

❖❖❖

Mike lay in a little white bed with pink sheets and comforter with one foot on the floor. The room spun like a top, and he couldn't remember a time he felt so sick. Then his cell phone rang and gave new meaning to the word pain.

He answered to stop the ringing and the flashing pain shooting through his skull. "Flynn here."

"You know, I thought you were different. But you're just the same as all the rest."

"Who is this?"

"Becca. Your sister and your ex-girlfriend's best friend. I gotta tell you, Mike. I'm not too thrilled to have a brother who's such an asshole."

He sat up, and the spinning increased. He took a deep breath through his nose and did his best to avoid both spilling his guts and the contents of his stomach.

"I'm an asshole?" God, he slurred his speech. He had to do better than that. He'd speak more slowly and enunciate. "I went to propose to her, and instead of finding a candlestick holder thing… I find a life-size painting of my goddamn double."

"You proposed?"

"No. I said I was gonna propose. I didn't, thank God. I don't want to marry someone who doesn't love me. She loves some dead guy who looks like me. Fuck. Pardon me. I meant to say shit."

"How much have you had to drink?"

"Obviously not enough."

"You're not driving, are you?"

"I might be dumb enough to fall for her, but I'm not stupid. Christ, give me some credit, would you?"

"Where are you?"

"In bed."

"I know you're not in your bed. Whose bed are you in?"

"What business is it of yours?"

"Listen to me, bud. I don't give a shit if you are my brother. If I find out you picked up some barfly just to get your rocks off, I will come over there and kick your ass."

"What? Look, the last thing I need is another woman. Annabelle did enough damage for a lifetime, thanks. My friends took me home. I'm sleeping in their little girl's bed alone if you must know. Not that I'm sleeping... I'm talking to you."

"Mike. I know how this looks, but you got it all wrong, buddy. You need to talk to Annabelle. She loves you, not Chip. Until I found out how you treated her, I thought you were better for her than Chip ever was."

"How I treated her? She lied to me. You know she told me she was incapable of lying, and I bought it. I should have known. I've seen it often enough before."

"Yeah, the only thing you've seen is the bottom of too many shot glasses. Do me a favor, will ya? Sober up, get over to her place, and talk to her."

"What day is it?"

"Why?"

"Dammit, just tell me what the fuckin' date is?"

"It's the thirtieth, as of about ten minutes ago."

"Oh, shit."

"Why? What's the big deal?"

"I have an interview today... in nine hours."

"Well, good luck with that. I recommend coffee, aspirin, lots of water, and Listerine. Maybe you should go make yourself sick and try to get some of the alcohol out of your system the hard way."

"Yeah, Sis. Thanks for the advice."

"I'll call you tomorrow in case you don't remember talking to me."

"Not likely."

"Good luck with the interview. And when you're done with that, you better get your ass back to Annabelle and talk to her. Give her a chance to explain."

Yeah, over his dead body. Which would be a definite improvement. He would have said so, but all he heard was dead air.

As soon as Becca hung up on Mike, she called Annabelle and wondered why God saw fit to give her two brothers who could be real assholes when they set their minds to it. Then, the apple doesn't fall far from the tree, does it? This, since she was her father's progeny too, might explain the fact that she hadn't had a date in close to two years.

Every now and then, she reminded herself that it wasn't as if she hadn't been asked. She just hadn't been asked by anyone she would consider letting into her apartment, much less her body.

Annabelle answered on the first ring.

"He's fine. Drunk, but fine."

"Mike is drunk? He never drinks much."

"Well, he did tonight. He's hurtin'. I guess friends with kids took him home, and Mike is sleeping it off in some little girl's pink bedroom. Oh, and he remembered he has a big interview in nine hours. He's gonna be one unhappy camper in the morning. I guarantee it.

"Oh God, I forgot about that. He was so excited about the interview. I'd never seen him so happy. If he doesn't do well, that'll be one more thing he can hate me for."

"It isn't as if you sat on him and poured alcohol down his throat. He did that all by himself. He's a big boy. He'll be okay."

"How did he sound?"

"Other than drunk?"

"Yeah."

"He sounded like he just lost the love of his life. He sounded like shit."

"Well, thanks for calling him for me. At least I know he's safe."

"Yeah. Physically, he's fine. Mentally, I'm not so sure. But then I don't think he's in any worse shape than you are. You're both stubborn and miserable. You deserve each other."

"Becca, you're going to love him. Don't let this affect your relationship. Please. He's your brother."

"I know. But it's not like we grew up together. We're two people that happen to have some of the same DNA."

"And the same smile. You share a lot more than a little DNA. Why do you think I love you both so much?"

"If you love him, you need to fight for him. He thinks you're in love with Chip. He thinks whatever you felt for Chip is automatically transferred to him because they look alike. He said you're like all the rest. Tell me, does he make a habit of dating all of Chip's exes?"

"No. I have no idea what he means, but he's drunk. He's not supposed to make sense."

"Either that, or he makes perfect sense, and you just don't understand. In any case, it doesn't matter.

He sounds as if he's been hurt before by other people's lies."

"I didn't lie to him."

"You withheld information. To him, it's the same thing. Sorry, tootsie pop."

"Whose side are you on, anyway?"

"Mine. I want to see my best friend and my new brother happy together. Now, try to get some sleep. I'll talk to you in the morning."

"Okay, thanks for checking on Mike."

"No problem. And Annabelle, he's hurt, he's angry, but he still loves you. Keep that in mind."

"Night, Bec."

"Night."

Becca hung up the phone and thought about calling Annabelle back to tell her Mike had planned to propose. No, maybe they'd work things out. If not, she could always use the information later. Neither of them was going to get over this love of theirs any time soon. They were going to be miserable apart for a good long time.

Becca crawled into her big, empty bed and thought about how nice it would be to have someone to curl up with, but after watching Mike and Annabelle's disaster unfold, Becca couldn't help but think that her battery-operated boyfriend might not be such a bad substitute.

"Wake up, Mikey."

Mike saw Annabelle's mouth moving, but the voice that came out was Vinny's, which was enough to scare the crap of him. Or in his case, wake him out of an alcohol-induced sleep. He opened his eyes to find Vinny standing over him.

"What?"

"Eh? Don't you got that big interview today? I thought I should, you know, wake you in case it's early. It's gonna take you a few hours to get your ass down there, and you still got to go home and change."

"What time is it?"

"Four thirty."

"Oh, Christ, you're right. Thanks. I have to leave by six to get down there by nine during rush hour."

"Put your pants on, and I'll drive you to your car."

Mike sat up, and his head felt as if he'd had massive brain injury compliments of Jack Daniel's.

What had he been thinking getting shit-faced the night before the biggest interview of his career? Oh right, he thought that his life was over. The memory of what happened blindsided him again, and the pain of it just about knocked the wind out of him.

"You wanna tell me what happened now that you're relatively sober?"

"No."

"I take it the proposal didn't go well?"

"There was no proposal. It's over."

"Hold on there, Mikey. One minute you're all, 'I love her, Vin. I'm gonna marry her.' And now you're sayin' 'it's over' and you're not gonna tell me what the fuck happened?"

"Why? So you and Nick can say I told you so? I don't think so. I've had my fill of humiliation for one lifetime."

Mike gave up searching for his socks—it hurt too much.

He found his shoes, slipped them on, and turned to Vinny. The guy acted as if Mike had just cold-cocked him.

"I don't make a habit of kickin' guys when they're down. I'm sorry it didn't work out. If you, ya know, change your mind and wanna talk about it, I ain't gonna be the one sayin' I told ya so. I will tell you a man don't fall out of love over a bottle of Jack, though. I know that for a fact. And, if you love her as much as you said you did, you won't let nothin' stop you from gettin' her back."

"This isn't nothing. This is something so big, I don't see a way around it." His eyes burned, either because he was about to cry or they were too bloodshot. Either way, he needed to change the subject. "I'm sorry. I can't talk about this now. I have to get down to that interview and see if I can move the hell away from New York. Being a hundred miles away from her won't be far enough, but it beats Coney Island."

Vinny grabbed him and pulled him into a guy hug. That did it. He lost the battle against tears. Shit. Vinny let him go and was nice enough to pretend not to notice he was crying like an idiot.

They drove to the restaurant in silence. Vinny gave him back the keys to Nick's car and didn't mention Annabelle again. Not that the lack of conversation kept him from thinking of her; remembering how she drove, how she smelled, how she tasted, and finally how she looked while she shattered his heart. Damn, he still worried about her, then he reminded himself that she wasn't in love with him. She was in love with a dead guy who looked like him. Unfortunately, it didn't make him love her any less. He didn't even know who he could call to check on her without her finding out. God, he was a dumb shit. A dumb shit who was still in love with his dead brother's girl.

Mike drove back to his sorry excuse for an apartment and realized he hadn't been there much in the last month. When he hadn't spent the night at Annabelle's, he'd slept at the hospital, or not at all. His place smelled stuffy, which didn't help his stomach any. He opened the windows, grabbed a fresh towel, and jumped into a cold shower—and it wasn't cold by choice. He really needed to get the hell out of his old apartment, his old neighborhood, and his old life.

Chapter 17

MIKE MADE THE TWO-HOUR DRIVE FROM CONEY ISLAND to Bryn Mawr, Pennsylvania, at the crack of dawn with only his iPod and two venti Starbucks to keep him company. The coffee worked its magic, and the Visine he bought at the convenience store where he stopped to fill up the gas tank did its job. Now all he had to do was get some food in his stomach. Luckily, he arrived early enough and hunted down a diner along the main drag. He hadn't eaten in… damn, since lunch the day before when he'd grabbed a couple of street vendor hot dogs that he'd been burping up ever since. Everything ingested after that had been liquid. He parked, got out of the car, and stretched. His head ached, his body ached, but most of all his heart ached. God, he'd never thought he could hurt so badly.

He'd driven past Eastern Heart Specialists three blocks down. The four-story building was impressive. The only question in his mind was the proximity to his biological father. If Becca knew he existed, it wouldn't be long until his father knew, and the last thing Mike wanted was to be rubbing shoulders with the old man.

After getting a copy of the *Philadelphia Inquirer* out of a machine outside the diner, Mike took a seat at the counter and checked out the local real estate listings while he ate. He wouldn't be able to afford a house for a few years. Main Line prices were outrageous. But, it wasn't as if he had to worry about having a wife and family any time in the next century. He had a feeling it would be at least that long before he could get Annabelle out of his mind.

After breakfast, Mike went to his interview. In the parking lot, he straightened his tie in the car's reflection, donned his suit jacket, and grabbed his briefcase. He didn't look like he spent his evening getting his heart stomped on and then shit-faced, he just felt as if he had.

He entered the office and introduced himself to the receptionist. She stared at him openmouthed.

"Is there something the matter?"

She quickly shut her mouth and shook her head. "No. Nothing, Doctor… "

"Flynn. Mike Flynn. I have an appointment with Dr. Connor."

"Yes. If you'll just have a seat. I'll tell her you're here."

"Thank you." Mike took a seat and checked his cell phone to make sure it was on vibrate. The last thing he wanted was to get a call in the middle of an interview. A woman who walked with an air of authority stepped out of the elevator. "Dr. Flynn?"

Mike stood. "Yes."

"Hello." She shook his hand. "I'm Shirley Payne, Dr. Connor's assistant. I'll take you up. If you'll come with me?"

"Certainly." Mike grabbed his briefcase and followed her into a waiting elevator. She slid her key card through the reader, and the elevator took them to the fourth floor.

Shirley led him to what looked like the boardroom, offered him coffee, and left him alone to await Dr. Connor.

He'd done his research. Dr. Connor was one of the managing partners, in her early fifties. She'd made her name in the area of geriatric care and was voted the number one geriatric cardiologist on the East Coast by other cardiologists.

When Dr. Connor entered, he stood and shook the hand of a surprisingly petite woman. She couldn't have been any taller than five feet, but her bearing in no way equaled her diminutive stature.

"Dr. Flynn, thank you for agreeing to come down for an interview."

"I'm flattered to receive an invitation."

She motioned him to sit, placed a file on the conference table, and then fixed herself coffee from the thermal carafe on the bar.

"We've recently merged with another practice and gained a new managing partner. He brought with him a full patient list, leaving us in desperate need of another pulmonologist. He strongly suggested we interview you. We've heard great things about you."

"That's quite a compliment."

She turned to him and smiled. "I'm told it's well deserved."

What did one say to that? "I like to think so."

"I've looked through your file. I know you've done quite a lot of research. You held either the number one or number two position in your class all through medical school." She sipped her coffee and checked the notes in her file. "It says here, you received one of the most sought-after fellowships in your field and obtained glowing reports from all you've studied under." She closed the file and pushed it aside. "We didn't look into your present situation for fear we'd raise suspicions, in case you weren't interested in making a move."

He let out a breath of relief. "Thank you. I appreciate that. I was told that a Mr. Tuggle spoke to one of my nurses regarding my work habits. When she asked what it was in reference to, she was told it was a survey of pulmonology practices."

Dr. Connor shrugged. "We wanted to make sure you were easy to work with. We're a close-knit group and are very particular when it comes to the partners we invite in. We look for team players and want to make sure you'd be a good fit. Your nurses raved about you. Though you don't have patients in the area, your youth and background make up for that."

She handed Mike a presentation folder. "Here's what we'd be able to offer you. I'll give you a few minutes to look it over, and then another managing partner will be in to speak with you. There are four managing partners at present, but unfortunately, due to the holiday, we're the only two available to meet with you. We do have the authority to make you an offer today if all goes well. He'll be in to see you in a few moments."

She closed the file, left it on the conference table, and rose. Mike stood and shook her hand. "Thank you. It's been a pleasure meeting you."

She covered his hand with both of hers. "I hope it all works out. I think I'd enjoy working with you. I'll see you before you leave." She left the room, closing the door behind her.

Mike opened the offer and was glad he was sitting down. Maybe he would be able to buy a house after all, though, what would be the point? He'd be living alone in a big house. The practice didn't require a buy-in, had a more than generous salary, profit sharing, partnership in two years, and with the benefits, the position, if offered, would be impossible to turn down. Especially when he took into account the distance it would give him from Annabelle.

The door opened, and Mike stood. He held on to the table to keep upright. Dr. Christopher Larsen was obviously the new managing partner Dr. Connor spoke of. Christ. Mike had seen his pictures, even imagined meeting him in the flesh, but was totally unprepared for the reality.

"I see by the look on your face you know who I am."

"Yes. I've known who you were since before I can remember. It's not news."

"I find myself at a disadvantage. I only found out about you a few weeks ago."

"If you hadn't been cheating on my mother with your fiancée, you would have found out much sooner."

"I never wanted to marry Bitsy. My family forced the engagement, and I just went along."

"Sure you did. People get engaged every day and don't mean it." Heck, his own father had been engaged to two women at once, and Mike couldn't even manage one.

"It was never real, at least not in my mind. It always felt so far away, and then I met your mother. I was in love with her, and I knew I had to come clean."

"You didn't come clean with my mother. She didn't know until she saw the announcement of your engagement in the *Times*."

Larsen blanched at that and took a deep breath. "No, I told Bitsy I was in love with Colleen and wanted out.

Everyone was in an uproar. My family cut off my trust fund, and a couple of days later, Bitsy said our parents announced our engagement behind our back. I had nothing to do with it. I found out years later that it was all Bitsy's idea. She said she'd put them up to it. That's when I divorced her."

Mike reached for his briefcase. "I have nothing more to say to you." He slapped the offer down on the conference table and stepped away.

"Now wait just a minute." Larsen stood in front of the double doors, blocking the only exit. "Let me explain." Christopher raised his hands. "I ran back to New York to tell your mother that the announcement was a mistake, but she'd already left. Your grandparents spit in my face."

"You deserved it."

Christopher hung his head. "I did. I should never have let my parents force me into a relationship I never wanted. I'm not perfect. I was young, and they held the purse strings. It was easier to go along to get along.

"Colleen's parents told me she'd gone back to Ireland and had already married someone they approved of. They threatened to call the police if I ever showed my face again. I wanted to go over there to find her, but she was already married. I was too late."

"Well, that's a lie."

Larsen looked stricken, "Michael, I'm not proud of myself. Believe me, I've paid for that mistake every day of my life. I'm not lying. Unfortunately, I did what was expected and eventually married Bitsy."

"Mum was never married. That was a lie. You left my mother pregnant, alone, and brokenhearted. She was thrown out of her home and disowned by her family all

thanks to you. She went back to Ireland to stay with
the only person who would have her—her aunt. That's
where I was born."

Mike's father pulled a chair out and sat. "She didn't
get married?"

Mike shook his head.

"Oh Christ. They said she was married. If I thought
there was a chance... I loved your mother. I loved her,
damn it. I loved her."

If his father was lying, he was the best actor Mike had
ever seen. Shit, the man was on the verge of tears. Mike
didn't know what to think. He sat and watched the man
who fathered him try to pull himself together. He looked
at Mike through glassy, pleading eyes.

"Is she okay? Colleen?"

"Yes, she's... we're fine."

"I need to talk to her, to explain. I... I... Jesus Christ,
I would never have married Bitsy if I thought there was
a chance for us."

"Bitsy? You're kidding me, right? There are actually
people named Bitsy?"

"Yes, there are. We're divorced now."

"So you did marry Bitsy."

"Yes, I did, a couple of years after your mother left. I
married her and had children—twins. Is your mother...
is she married?"

"No. Never. How did you find me?"

"Your sister found you, actually. You have a striking
resemblance to your late brother, Chip. She saw a picture
of you at a wedding." Larsen raked his hands through
his short, graying hair. "Becca brought me your picture
demanding to know if you were somehow related to us.

She told me your name. I knew you were my son." His eyes were glassy and distant. "I still can't believe your mother never told me…" Larsen stood, pushing his chair back. "I'm sorry. I shouldn't have dumped all this on you so suddenly. Can I get you a water?"

"No, thank you. I spoke to Becca last night. She called me after… well, after I found out about her and Chip. I found a painting of Chip at my girlfriend's apartment. You can imagine my shock."

"You do have an amazing resemblance."

"Annabelle never told me."

"Annabelle Ronaldi? What does she have to do with any of this?"

Mike had never seen such hatred on anyone's face. "I dated her seriously for the last month or so."

"Shit, she's got her hooks into you, too. She lost her meal ticket when Chip died. I guess when she found you, she worked the same scam."

Mike stood. "Hold on, I don't care who the hell you are. I won't let you or anyone talk about Annabelle like that."

Larsen held up his hands in surrender. "I don't know what the girl's got, but whatever it is seems to appeal to the Larsen men."

"I'm a Flynn." All the anger he'd tapped down last night returned and threatened to overflow.

Larsen smiled. "Damn, you've got your mother's temper, don't you? You must feel as if you've been run through the ringer. I've known about you over a week, and I still have a hard time, but then I look at you…" He shook his head and then stared at the floor. "I'll be right back. Please just give me a minute. I have something to show you."

Mike nodded. He wasn't sure what he was riled about. It wasn't as if Annabelle cared for him. She only saw him as Chip's replacement. He backed into a leather chair and sat.

Larsen returned a moment later with a file. "I had my assistant pull this for me." He opened it. "Here's my divorce decree. You'll find my marriage date listed there."

Mike looked at Larsen and then took the paper he offered. At the moment, he could really care less when Larsen married. The date highlighted was less than a month before Mike's second birthday. At least the old man hadn't lied about that.

"I know you don't owe me anything, but I think working here, at the practice, would be a good move for you. I'm aware of the problems you're having in your present position."

Mike picked up the proposal folder and ripped it in two. He calmly set it back on the table and slid it to Larsen without a word.

"Now, calm down. I merely asked a few friends in the area if they'd heard about you and what they thought. I'm told there's a rumor going around that you're causing problems over an incompetent partner. Lucky for you, you're not the only one who has noticed his incompetence."

Mike nodded. It was the truth.

"Come here and work. I won't say anything about our relationship if you'd rather I didn't."

Mike let out an incredulous laugh. "That seems kind of senseless doesn't it? When I walked in the building, the receptionist was stunned speechless. I don't know what Becca looks like, but it seems I look as much like you as Chip did. I'd be surprised if news of your bastard son hasn't hit the society page of the *Philadelphia Inquirer* by now. You can bet you'll be the topic of conversation at the country club."

Larsen winced and shook his head. "I'm not concerned with what the *Inquirer* says, or anyone else for that matter. The only people I care about in this whole world are you, your mother, and your sister, Becca. And as for you, you can bet your life you would have been born a Larsen had I known about you. What your mother and I had... well, it should have lasted forever."

"Yes, well it didn't, and my mother and I have done quite well on our own."

"I'm glad. I'm so proud of you both. It couldn't have been easy. Believe me, if I could turn back time... But I can't. What I have done though is make sure you're given your birthright."

"Excuse me?"

"You are my son. That makes you and your sister the beneficiaries of half the Larsen estate. The house automatically gets passed on from first son to first son. I'm still living in it. I thought I'd give it to Becca once she married. But since I've found you —"

Mike sat. "I don't want your estate or your money."

"I'm sorry, but it's not mine. It's yours. I've only been a steward of the estate. It's been held in trust for years. It was never mine. I only control it. I'll need a copy of your birth certificate for the lawyers."

"Inheritance? Are you serious?"

"Yes, I am. You have a rather large inheritance. I can get you an exact figure if you like."

Mike gripped the arms of his chair. "No, a ballpark estimate will be sufficient."

"I'd say somewhere in the neighborhood of seven million dollars. That's not including the value of the estate."

"You've got to be kidding."

"No, son, I'm not." Larsen sat beside Mike. "I know this is all a shock, and it's going to take some getting used to."

Mike laughed. "A shock was seeing you walk through that door. But this... well, seven million bucks in the bank is a hell of a lot more than a shock."

"Look, why don't you follow me to the house. I can show you around, we can have lunch, and you can take some time to decide what you want. We're pretty hard up for a pulmonologist, but we can give you a few weeks to make a decision."

Mike stood and looked at the man who fathered him. He was the same height, a bit heavier, but Mike attributed that to age and diet. He probably ate three meals a day. His hair was graying but looked as if it had been the same color as Mike's when he was younger. He looked good for his age. "I could use some time. I... I don't know what to do about the money. I don't feel as if it's mine. I'm sure Becca..."

"Becca never cared much about the money. Your brother, well, he lived on it, but Becca never has. She lives in a loft apartment in South Philly. I worry about that girl, but she stopped listening to her mother years ago. I don't think she ever listened to me. She's a bit of a free spirit."

"After our conversation, I'm not surprised."

"Well, what do you say? Care to join me for lunch?"

"As long as you understand that my joining you means nothing more than that."

"Okay. I suppose it's a start." Larsen stood and held out his hand.

Mike pushed out of his seat and took his father's hand in a firm handshake. "I guess it is."

"Rebecca Elizabeth Larsen, I insist you return my call."

Becca had ignored the last five voice mails her mother left and was likely to ignore this one too.

"I just received a phone call from Janice Hopkins. She said there's word at your father's practice that his love child is being given a position at EHS. This is very serious. Return. My. Call."

Oh, so Mommy Dearest heard the news. My, my, my, doesn't good news travel fast?

Becca hit her speed dial. "Hello, Mother, you rang… repeatedly?"

"You don't care that you're losing seventeen million dollars and change?"

"Not especially, no." Becca had more than enough money to live comfortably for the rest of her life without her inheritance. She had invested wisely. Her parents forced her to go to college. After learning from mistakes other debs who had lost their inheritances to social climbing men more interested in their trusts than in them or to crooked accountants, she majored in finance and minored in art. Who knew she was both left- and right- brained. As far as her mother was concerned, she was neither.

"I have it on good authority that your father's lawyer is taking more than half your inheritance and giving it to this bastard child who popped up out of nowhere."

"Stop it, Mother. That's my brother you're talking about."

"Your brother is dead."

"Yes, but Mike is alive and well, and taking his rightful place in the family."

"Have you seen proof of paternity?"

"Mother, there is no need for a DNA test. The proof, as they say, is in the pudding. He and Chip could have been twins if Chip looked a bit more like Daddy."

"You're going to allow him to waltz in and take what's rightfully yours?"

"He's taking what's rightfully his, and as for the estate and the inheritance, he's more than welcome to it."

"You're not going protest this travesty? You're going to let this bastard from Brooklyn move in and take all I've worked so hard to build for you?"

"Mother, the only thing you've ever worked hard on was getting your own way and making Daddy miserable. You screwed up, and you lost. Stop this, or you'll lose more than just your marriage and your home. You'll lose me, too."

"How dare you talk to me that way? I'm only looking out for your best interests."

"Ha. You've never looked out for anyone but yourself. If you're worried about my money, it's because you have plans for it. What are you going to do, Mother? Embezzle a few million?"

Becca moved the phone away from her ear before her mother started screaming. She didn't need to hear it. She'd heard it all before. "Good-bye, Mother. I have to go." She hung up the phone. The way she looked at it, if she said good-bye, she wasn't hanging up on her mother, she was just ending a conversation before her mother was ready to. Her problem, not Becca's. But then all the problems between her and both her parents were theirs and not hers. It's a wonder the two didn't get on better.

"Rebecca, it's your father. Please return my call. It's important."

"Oh God, not the other one too." Why couldn't she come from a single-parent family? Becca wasn't in the mood to deal with either of her parents today.

"Okay, listen. In case you're screening your calls, I wanted to tell you that your brother Michael and I are on our way to the house. I've called ahead and asked Madge to prepare lunch. I hope you'll join us. I'd like you to meet Mike... in person."

He knew she'd spoken to him on the phone? Becca looked at her watch, it would take forty-five minutes to get there, and she needed to change. What did one wear to meet her long lost brother?

Becca threw riding tights, boots, a T-shirt, and a hard hat into a duffel bag. It had been a long time since she'd been home; she wasn't going to miss an opportunity to ride Big Red. Maybe after a swim in the pool, she'd ride down to the pond and see how everyone was doing.

She chose her clothes wisely—a bikini, matching shorts, and a top. Of course, the top wasn't quite long enough to cover the tat or the belly-button ring. Daddy would likely have a coronary, but not in front of the new heir. Hmm. That might actually be fun.

Mike followed Larsen west on the main drag, which ran parallel to the train tracks, hence the name, the Main Line. They turned onto a side street and drove through horse country. Houses the likes of which he'd only seen in the Hamptons dotted the countryside. Old stone mansions with matching stone barns that were bigger than his apartment building.

He'd entered an alternate universe. Mike left Coney Island and his home with its perpetual scent of kraut and sausage, and came here to a land where people were actually named Biff and Bitsy. Where men wear Lilly Pulitzer pants and paid big bucks to look like one of the kids in *The Sound of Music*, running around in clothes made of old curtains—and not for the laughs either. This alone was proof positive that money wasn't indicative of brains or taste.

Larsen signaled a turn, drove through the opening in a stone fence, past what looked like an old-fashioned gatehouse. Mike wondered where Larsen's house was. Right now, all he saw was a big stone barn, which was even larger than the others he'd seen along the way. He followed Larsen's BMW closely through the gate, looking for a street sign. There was none.

About a mile down the road, they passed several houses, greenhouses, and a lake. Up ahead looked like a country club. It was a massive old mansion, beautifully kept. Mike pulled in to the circular drive and parked behind Larsen's car. When his father jumped out, Mike followed suit. "I thought we were going to your house."

Larsen turned and gestured to the mansion. "This is the house. The estate is on three hundred eighty-seven acres. There are seven cottages, three stables, three industrial-size greenhouses, a pool, tennis courts, a stocked pond, and a live trout stream. I can give you a tour later if you'd like."

"This"—Mike pointed to the four-story mansion—"is your house?"

"Yes."

"I've always known where you lived, and Mum said you were from a wealthy family, but I never imagined anything like this."

"Your mother told you about me?"

"She wanted me to know where you were in case I ever needed or wanted to contact you." Mike shrugged and dropped that subject.

"Well." Larsen cleared his throat. "Shall we go in?"

Mike nodded and walked beside Larsen up the steps to the front door. It was a massive hand-carved door with a huge knocker, and it opened before Larsen even reached for the doorknob.

A woman of indeterminate age welcomed them. She smiled as they stepped into the cool foyer, and after getting a look at Mike, she paled.

Larsen took her arm to steady her. "Elaine, this is Dr. Michael Flynn, my son."

"Mike, Elaine Rogers runs the household. She's in charge of everyone and everything on the estate, including me."

Elaine gathered her bearings quickly. "It's wonderful to meet you."

"Nice to meet you, too." Mike shook her hand and tried to get a handle on the fact that he'd been introduced as Larsen's son. He wasn't sure how he felt about that, but from the look on the woman's face—the same look he remembered Annabelle wearing the first time they'd met—he figured it was unavoidable.

She looked from Mike to Larsen. "Madge has lunch waiting for you in the family dining room."

"Thank you." Larsen put his hand on Mike's shoulder. "I called and invited Rebecca to join us. I thought you'd enjoy meeting her. The girl never answers her phone so I don't know if she got the message or not."

Mike took in the huge foyer. The rose-colored marble covered the floor and a grand, curved staircase. Still digesting it all, he looked at his watch. "I'm going to have to leave in a couple of hours. I'm on call tonight." He was really looking forward to working. At least there, he'd be so busy, he wouldn't have time to think about Larsen, Becca, or Annabelle and Chip.

A topless, candy-apple red BMW Roadster squealed to a stop before they closed the front door. Mike looked from the driver, with her wind-whipped blonde hair, wide smile, and challenging raised eyebrow to Larsen, who looked as if he'd been out in the sun too long.

Tension anyone?

At that point, introductions were unnecessary. Mike recognized his sister from a picture Annabelle kept on her dresser of Becca and her together.

Becca grabbed a hold of the top of the windscreen, stood, and jumped from the car. She certainly knew how to make an entrance. No wonder Annabelle loved her so much. Mike tried to smile as the pain slammed into him again. He'd caught himself reaching for the phone a hundred times since he'd walked out her door. Sharing things with Annabelle had become second nature, along with sleeping with her, thinking about her, worrying about her, and loving her. He wanted to ask Becca if she'd heard from Annabelle, but they hadn't even been introduced yet.

"Mike," Larsen said. "This is Becca, my daughter."

What do you do when you meet your sister for the first time? Shake hands? "Hello."

Becca stood in front of him, wearing board shorts low on her hips, a tank top, the hem of which missed the waistband of her shorts by about four inches, and flip-flops. She was tall, lanky, and beautiful. She stared at him with green eyes shot with gold, a bit of copper, and a whole lot of curiosity. She had some amazing eyes, and right now, they were taking his measure.

"I'm not sure whether to say welcome to the family or tell you to run like hell."

"Rebecca, that's enough."

"I get the feeling that both are equally heartfelt."

"Annabelle said I'd like you. So, how are you feeling today?"

He couldn't help but stare. He'd seen almost the same eyes on Chip's painting, but Mike remembered that Chip had one eye that was half green and half brown.

"I'll survive. Have you talked to Annabelle?"

Larsen's face turned even redder. Mike wondered if he had blood pressure problems.

The old man swallowed hard. "I thought you were no longer seeing that…"

"Watch yourself, Daddy. You wouldn't want Mike here to know how badly you treated the woman he loves."

"I'm just worried about her. I need to know she's all right."

"What do you think she's going to do, Mike? Jump

off the Brooklyn Bridge? If that's all you're worried about, don't bother. She's been through tougher things than having her heart broken by you. This is a walk in the park compared to watching the only other man she ever loved die."

Larsen butted in. "She was after Chip's money. Just like she's after Mike's."

Mike laughed. "I don't have any money."

"Yes, you do... or you will. Which is exactly why she got her hooks into you early."

"That's ridiculous. She never mentioned a word about Chip—at least not unless she was drugged."

"So, she has a drug problem, too? It's not surprising."

Mike was beginning to really dislike Larsen. "She hurt her ankle and was on prescription painkillers. What is it with you? The only thing Annabelle is guilty of is loving Chip and not me. It's a textbook case of transference. She probably doesn't even know she's doing it."

Becca laughed. "I thought you were a pulmonologist. I guess you're a shrink now, too? You spend a week's rotation in the psych ward during med school, and all of a sudden you're Dr. Freud? You wouldn't know transference if it bit you in the ass."

"Yeah, and how the hell do you know?"

"Rebecca, Chip, that's enough. Both of you."

The old man looked from Becca to Mike. Becca paled and so did Larsen and Elaine. Mike couldn't believe this was happening again. "I... I have to go."

"Mike. I'm sorry. It was a slip of the tongue."

"No, I'm sorry. I can't do this right now. I've had a hard couple of days, and I have to get back to work anyway. I need some time."

Becca grabbed his arm. "Mike, wait."

"No. I need to go."

"Not while you're upset."

"Becca, I've been upset since yesterday. I'm fine. I'm a doctor, for God's sake. I can handle it."

Becca looked at her father pleadingly.

Larsen deflated like a balloon a week after the party. "I'm sorry, Mike. But seeing you and Rebecca fighting... just like she and Chip always did... well. I'm sorry."

"Yeah, so am I." Mike turned to leave.

Larsen touched his shoulder, and he stopped. "Michael, drive safely."

He nodded, opened the heavy door, and walked out into the sunshine. Becca followed close behind.

"So, you're running away again."

Mike had had it. He was pissed, and she just pushed the wrong button. "I don't need you or anyone telling me how to run my life. I've done fine without you and your father for thirty-two years. I'll do fine without you now."

Becca smiled, walked right up to him, wrapped her arms around his waist, and hugged him. "I'm still glad I found you. Or that Annabelle found you. Whether you want to admit it or not, you're my brother, and I love you. Daddy does too, probably more than you could even imagine. After all, you're the product of the love of his life. You might as well get used to our family. Take your time. I'm not going anywhere, and you know what? Neither is Annabelle. Once you get over your bad self and your wounded ego, you'll see she loves you, too."

Mike's eyes stung. He wanted to throw her off him, but he couldn't. Nor could he ignore what she said.

He stepped back, and Becca let him go. Larsen and Becca watched him from the steps. He gave them a nod, got in, and drove around the circle going out the same way he'd come in. He raced toward the entrance of the estate, toward freedom. He drove down the driveway, past the gatehouse, through the opening in the stone fence, and off the property, but he didn't feel any less trapped.

Chapter 18

"WHAT TRUCK RAN OVER YOU?"

Annabelle looked up from the sketch pad she scribbled on and saw Ben's eyes scrunched up and his lips pressed together. He made himself at home and sat on her desk.

"I thought you went to the Hamptons with Dr. Mike for the weekend?"

"I did."

"Are you sick?"

"No."

"Am I going to get more than a two-word answer?"

"Mike and I broke up. Are you happy?"

"Not if you aren't. I'm sorry."

She felt the tears coming again. "I can't talk about this." Shit. She reached for a tissue and tried desperately to stop embarrassing herself.

"You're really hung up on him, aren't you?"

"Gee, whatever gave you that idea?"

"You're drawing him. I figured it must be love to get you to sketch anything but plans for a show."

"Oh God! You're right. I didn't realize... I was just making dots... and then—"

"What are you going to do?"

"About what?"

"About Mike."

"Nothing. What's there to do? Some things aren't meant to be. Mike and I are a perfect example."

"You sound sure of that."

"I am."

"There's nothing he could say to get you back?"

"He wouldn't want me back. Even if he did, I can't see it ever working out. I can't be what he needs.

"He might just need you."

"No. He doesn't. He has everything he needs now. I talked to Becca. She told me that his father offered him a job at this great practice—he has money, a family, a fabulous career—everything he's ever wanted."

Ben picked up a paperweight and tossed it from hand to hand. "He doesn't have everything he ever wanted. From what I saw, he wanted you."

"He doesn't want me now. Besides, even if he did, I would come between him and his family, and I'm not going there. I never want to put myself in that position again."

"You're sure of that?"

"Positive."

"Okay, then. Marry me."

Annabelle burst out laughing. By the time she realized Ben wasn't laughing, she had tears running down her cheeks. "You're kidding, right? Ben, tell me you're kidding."

His usual smiling face and twinkling eyes were gone. He shook his head. His folded arms and posture didn't shout levity.

"You're serious?"

Ben didn't smile, he didn't frown, he just looked grim.

Annabelle held up her hand. "Hold on, don't tell me Mike was right, that you've been secretly lusting after me. I mean, I know I don't have such a great track record

with men, but I think I would have noticed if you ever
looked at me like —"

"Mike? Like I want to undress you with my eyes?"

"Well, I wouldn't have put it that way, but yeah."

"Would you accept my proposal if I told you I find
you attractive?"

"Whoa. You find me attractive? Since when?"

"Annabelle. You're a beautiful woman. You know
that. I've never thought about you in that way. Not seriously, at least."

"Then why in the world do you want to marry me?"

"I don't. I *need* to get married. I have one year to
settle down and marry, or I'll lose the only thing in the
world I want that I don't have."

"Huh?"

"My grandfather owns the ranch I grew up on.
He wants me to put an end to my single days, settle
down, and have children, or he'll sell the ranch to a
ski resort developer."

"Why don't you just buy it yourself? You have
money. How hard could it be?"

"He's getting old. His health is failing. He says he
wants to see me married in his lifetime. If I don't get
married, I don't get the ranch. It's the only thing that I
have left of my parents. It wouldn't be a real marriage,
just a marriage in name until I can get the ranch. Once
he signs it over, we can get an annulment or a divorce,
and I promise we'll have a prenup that will leave you
very comfortable."

"Ben, I can't marry you."

"Why not? You said yourself you and Mike are over.
Your mother would be happy."

"Yeah, until the divorce, but—"

"Look, just think about it. You don't have to give me an answer right away. I wouldn't ask you, but I don't know anyone else I can trust not to get the wrong idea. I don't want to get married. And I know you don't want to marry me. It'll be great—you can move into my place. There's plenty of room, you'll have your studio here, and your commute will be a ride on the elevator. I'll pay for everything. Just think about it."

"I can't."

"Yes, you can. What do you have to lose?"

She shook her head.

"Nothing, that's what. You have nothing to lose and everything to gain. Hell, take the gallery if you want. I'll give it to you. Just help me get my home back. Please?"

He looked so disheartened, so desperate. The guy who could have anything he wanted couldn't get the only thing he seemed to need. "Fine, I'll think about it. But I'm not promising anything."

Ben tapped her desk and kissed her cheek. "Thanks. I'll have my lawyer draw up a prenup, and you can take a look at it."

"I didn't say I'd do it."

"No, but you said you'd think about it. Seeing the prenup might push you to the altar. Besides, wouldn't you want to own your own gallery?"

"If I do this, I'd do it for you, not for the gallery."

"Okay, but you treat the gallery as if it's yours anyway. We might as well make it official."

She shrugged. "I'll think about it. Now, get out of here. I have work to do."

"Thanks."

"Don't thank me yet. I haven't agreed to anything. I said I'd think about it."

"Fine. I'll get my lawyer on it right away. I'll have something for you to look at in the next couple of days."

"No rush."

"I have eleven months to find a bride. I have no other option than to rush."

Mike drove home, and for the first time, he drove on autopilot. He became one with the car, he thought of nothing, felt nothing, and in no time, he drove over the Verrazano-Narrows Bridge. He didn't know how he got there. One moment he was trying to remember how to get back to Lancaster Avenue in Paoli, and the next he heard the familiar sounds of home.

It made no difference who his father was, or how many millions he had in the bank, Brooklyn was home. He drove to Coney Island since he wasn't on call until seven o'clock. He just prayed for a busy night. Anything was better than dealing with the disaster his life had become in the last twenty-four hours. God, had it only been yesterday that he'd planned to spend the rest of his life with Annabelle? Yesterday when he was blissfully unaware and looking forward to the future? Now the only thing he looked forward to was the day he wouldn't think of her every minute of every hour. The day he wouldn't see the look on her face, the tears streaming down her cheeks as she took a sledgehammer to his life. The day he wouldn't feel the pain.

❖ ❖ ❖

Becca sat beside her father in the Benz. She'd wanted to drive because he was upset, but her father wouldn't hear of it. She counted herself lucky he'd allowed her to come at all. Of course, she would have followed him if he hadn't.

She never took no for an answer, and she wasn't about to start now. Not when things were really getting interesting. If Becca read her father right, the man was afraid. For the first time in her life, she saw her father as human with real feelings.

Her mother tortured people who showed any emotion. Her father never showed any—probably for self-preservation. Becca grew up thinking he had no feelings, never knowing he'd kept them hidden all this time.

Today something snapped and made it impossible for him to disguise his feelings. Maybe he finally saw all he'd lost. She wasn't sure, but whatever caused his display of emotion made her want to help him for the first time since she was a little girl. Her parents had deserted her and Chip when they needed them most. Maybe not physically or monetarily, but emotionally they'd left them alone to deal with all life threw at them, and life threw a hell of a curve ball.

"Daddy, you're speeding."

He stared straight ahead, the stress evident on his face. "Do you have the address?"

"Yes. I programmed it in the GPS. Remember?"

"I know, but she probably lives in an apartment. I need the apartment number."

"What you need to do is call. Showing up unannounced

isn't a good idea. It'll be a shock. Besides, how do you know she'll even be home?"

"Becca, either way it's going to be a shock. If Mike hasn't spoken to her yet, then maybe she'll listen to me. If he's already spoken to her, chances are… I don't know. I haven't set eyes on her in thirty-three years. I used to know what she was thinking. I used to know what she was going to say before she said it. Now, I don't know anything. All I know is I need to see her, and I need to make sure Mike is okay. If she's not there, I'll wait outside her door for as long as it takes."

"He probably went to the hospital. From what Annabelle said, he practically lives there."

"Her again?"

"Yes, Daddy. Annabelle is my best friend. She never did anything to deserve the way you and mother treated her. Why can't you see that? Mother was so afraid of losing her Queen of the Castle status, she tried to drive Annabelle and every other woman Chip dated away. Not that any woman in her right mind would want to share a residence with Mother, there is no estate large enough if you ask me."

"She was living with him on his dime."

"If she was after the money, why didn't Annabelle marry Chip when he'd asked her? Chip knew he was dying, he had nothing more to lose, and she would eventually get the money. He offered to marry her. She refused not because she didn't love him, but because she didn't want to prove you and Mother right. She didn't want a cent from either of you or the estate."

Well, that got him thinking. "Annabelle worked. That money in their joint account you and Mother took was money she earned and had saved for school. Chip was cheap as hell. He paid half the bills. She took care of everything else. You left her penniless. I had to give her train fare back to Brooklyn. Why did you think it was a year before I spoke to you again? I only did that because I had to."

He took his eyes from the road and stared at her. She'd hit the target she never knew existed. She never thought he'd even noticed she'd disappeared from his life for a year. He reached over and squeezed her hand.

"You know Mother. People like her believe everyone is as vengeful as they are. She expected Annabelle to behave as she did when she was in the same situation. How long were you married before she made life so miserable for Uncle Aaron, Aunt Carol, and their kids that they left the family estate?"

No need to answer, because his expression told the story. Shame. Pain. Embarrassment.

It was past time she told him what she thought and cleared the air. She was an adult, and she no longer needed her parents. She hadn't in years. "All Annabelle ever did to Chip was love and care for him. Believe me, Daddy, Chip was not an easy person to love. He was brought up to think the sun and moon revolved around him. He was spoiled, and thanks to you and Mom, he had a warped view of love." Becca drew her sweater around her, either the air conditioner or her father froze her out. "It took Annabelle a long time to get over Chip. She loves Mike now, and whether or not he admits it, Mike loves her. He wanted to marry her. If you make him choose between you and Annabelle, you better believe he's going to choose her." If he ever gets his

head out of his ass. "This is the second time someone
in my family broke Annabelle's heart. She should have
told Mike about Chip, but who could blame her for not
wanting to see history repeat itself."

"If we were so off base, why didn't Chip say anything?
Why didn't she?"

"Chip was more concerned about losing his trust than
he was about her. Annabelle was eighteen. She was a
child when she allowed you and Mother to treat her so
badly. She's a grown woman now, and she's strong.
She'd rather let the man she loves go and keep her
dignity and self-respect. She'll never again allow anyone
to treat her as if she were a second-class citizen. That's
why she's not fighting for Mike. She doesn't want to
come between him and this so-called family."

Becca crossed her arms, pulled her leg under her,
and turned her back to the door so she faced her father.
"Mother was always a monster, and you allowed her
to treat Annabelle like that. That makes you as guilty
as she is."

"I never… I guess I didn't realize."

"No, Daddy. Be honest. It was easier to allow Mother
to destroy Annabelle than it would have been to go
against your wife and put yourself in the line of fire.
There was nothing in it for you. You two led separate
lives, and as long as Mother left you alone, you didn't
concern yourself with the people she targeted… until
you found out that she was behind the whole marriage
announcement, and you and Mike's mom were her first
victims. That's when you divorced her. That was the
only thing she'd done to anyone you cared enough about
to retaliate."

"When did you get so smart?"

She laughed in relief. "Brains were never lacking in our gene pool, just humanity."

"Not with you it wasn't."

"Ha. I just learned a lesson early on, and all the years of therapy you and Mother insisted I needed helped, too."

He shot her a cocky grin, making him look much younger than his sixty years. It made him look surprisingly like Mike.

"Hey, after a few years of messing with my therapists' heads, I decided to turn my punishment into a gift. I got my head on straight."

He grinned again.

"Okay, as straight as it can be, considering."

"I've always admired your spunk, Rebecca. You've grown up to be quite a ballbuster. I really like that about you."

"Except when I use it against you."

"Even then. Yesterday, you purposely showed off your piercing and your tattoo when you knew I couldn't say a word about it. That was the plan, wasn't it?"

Busted. "Of course. Pushing your buttons is something of a hobby of mine. It's nice to get a reaction from you."

"I'm sorry you feel the need to resort to shock to get my attention."

Is that what she'd done? Damn, maybe she wasn't so smart after all.

Lost in thought, she considered what her father said and what she wanted from him. She'd all but given up on both of her parents, but today, for the first time in years, she saw a glimmer of hope. Maybe a seminormal relationship with her father was possible after all.

"This neighborhood sure has changed. When I lived down here, it was like a war zone."

She was surprised to see they were already in Brooklyn. "Why did you live here then?"

"It was all I could afford at the time. I wasn't old enough to get my trust fund, and your grandparents didn't think any son of theirs should go into medicine. That's why they started the grandfather trust. They threatened me with it, and I told them to go to hell. Sometimes you remind me of myself when I was still young and idealistic. I was going to save the world."

"What happened?"

"I lost Colleen. I honestly didn't think I could go on. After two years I gave up. That was the worst night of my life. After a night of drinking myself into a stupor, I awoke with your mother—"

"She got pregnant, and you did the right thing."

"That's when I learned that sometimes good things come from bad decisions. I got you and Chip. I can't regret that. But I'm not sure I did the right thing by marrying your mother. I don't think I did you and Chip any favors. I'm sorry."

He parked the car on a side street. It was almost six in the evening, and he slid out of the car and looked around.

"I used to live in that building over there." He pointed to a four-story brownstone.

"It's beautiful."

"It wasn't then. It had been broken up into studio apartments. The pipes rattled, there was no hot water, and more often than not, no heat, but I can't remember a time I was ever happier. I think Colleen's place is just up the block."

Becca followed her father into a simple brick apartment building. He took a deep breath as he read the list of residents. A woman with two children in a stroller left the building. Her dad held the door for the woman and walked in without announcing himself. "Come on."

"Dad, I really think we should ring her apartment."

"So she could tell me to go to hell over a speaker? I don't think so. It's much harder to reject someone standing in front of you, and I'll take any advantage I can get. I'm going up. You can wait out in the car if you'd like. I'd actually prefer it."

"Not on your life."

"I knew you'd say that."

Chapter 19

CHRISTOPHER LARSEN ENTERED COLLEEN'S BUILDING with Becca following fast on his heels. He hit the button for the elevator, and when that took too long, he took the stairs two at a time to the third floor. He scoped out the apartment and knocked. When no one answered, he knocked again.

"Coming."

The locks tumbled; the deadbolt rolled. "Michael, did you forget your key?" The door swung open, and then there was dead silence.

Becca felt as if she were watching a play. Her father stood tall, his hands in his pockets, something she'd never seen him do. He was fastidious about his clothes. Standing with your hands in your pockets stretched out the material, and maybe hid one's nervousness.

Colleen Flynn was beautiful. Reddish blonde hair, petite, with gorgeous gray eyes wide with surprise. Mike had his mother's eyes.

"Colleen."

She held the door like a lifeline, swallowed, and pasted on a smile that was more nervous than sincere. "Christopher."

The two of them stared at each other for what seemed like hours. Becca could only guess the silent conversation going on between them. And there was definitely one going on. Becca coughed, breaking the connection. She waited for her father to introduce her, but he didn't. She smiled and held out her hand. "Hi, I'm Rebecca Larsen."

Colleen shook Becca's hand without once taking her eyes off Christopher.

"Oh, I'm sorry, please come in. I was just in the kitchen. I have a roast in the oven. My son called and wanted some comfort food. He's upset."

Christopher took a step toward her. "He told you?"

Becca had never heard his voice sound like that. Deep, full of uncertainty and something else she really didn't care to think about.

"No. I didn't ask while he was working. Michael tells me things in his own time. He's a grown man, after all. Now, isn't he?"

Becca's dad nodded. "He's a fine man."

"And how would you know?"

"I spent much of the day with him."

"Did you, now? I suppose it was your practice where Michael interviewed."

"Colleen."

She held up her hand. "Why don't you come in so we're not airing the dirty laundry out in the hallway?"

Becca's temper started to boil. "There is no dirty laundry."

Colleen looked from Becca to Christopher. "I see your daughter has your temper."

Christopher nodded. "And our son has yours."

"Touché."

The woman had a lovely, soft Irish accent. She looked a little pale, but if Becca hadn't seen the color leave her face, she'd never guess Colleen had just had the shock of her life.

Colleen closed the door and showed them into her apartment. It was nice—normal. Nothing like the monstrosity where Becca grew up and her father still lived. Colleen's home was comfortable and warm. The scent of pot roast and homemade bread filled the small apartment, and Becca found herself relaxing.

"I'll fix a pot of tea, and you can tell me why my son is upset."

She pointed them to the dining room table, large enough for four, nothing like the table that sat thirty in the main dining room or the one that sat fourteen in the family dining room. Becca sat at the highly polished table and imagined Colleen doing normal things like cleaning her own home and polishing the furniture.

Her father didn't sit at the table, but followed Colleen to the kitchen. She began to wonder what in the world she was doing there as she watched him stop right behind Colleen, place his hands on her shoulders, and speak so softly Becca wasn't sure if she heard him correctly. She'd never heard him sound afraid.

"You must hate me."

Colleen wrapped her arms around herself and shook her head. "How could I hate you when you've given me the one person I love most in this world? I've never hated you."

"I'm sorry for the misunderstanding."

"Misunderstanding? Is that what you call it now?" She had fire in her eyes. "You were engaged, Christopher. You cheated, and you call that a misunderstanding?" What started out as an Irish lilt became more pronounced.

He shook his head. "My family wanted me to marry Bitsy. I never wanted that. I should have stood up for myself and said no earlier. I let them think what they wanted. I never cheated on you. Not once. Don't you understand?"

"No, you cheated *with* me. You turned my love for you into something ugly."

"I wasn't engaged. Not really. That was just something our parents cooked up. I went home that week to end it. I refused to let it go any further. I wasn't anything but madly in love with you."

"But I saw that engagement announcement in the society pages. My mother saw it."

"I'm so sorry. Bitsy and our parents ran it after I ended the sham of an engagement. I had nothing to do with it."

Colleen shook her head. "But why would anyone ever do such a thing?"

Becca knew the answer to that. "Because she saw her meal ticket getting away. Unfortunately, stunts like that are typical of my mother."

"I loved you. In my heart I was engaged to you and only you. When I saw the announcement, I came back to find you gone. I was frantic. Your parents said you'd gone back to Ireland and were married. That you'd married someone they approved of. I didn't marry Bitsy until 1980, and I only did that because—"

Becca interrupted. "Mother got him drunk, took advantage of him, and got pregnant with Chip and me. Dad did the right thing."

"There are two of you?"

He nodded. "Bitsy had the twins. We divorced a few years ago after my son died."

"Oh, Christopher."

Somehow, he and Colleen ended up in each other's arms. Becca wasn't sure when that happened, but the two fell into it so naturally, she felt like a voyeur who needed to give them some space. "Dad, I'm going to go and get something I left in the car. I'll be back in a while." Neither heard her. They were so wrapped up in each other. She figured she didn't have much of a chance to get the keys to the car, so she decided to take a walk, and while she did, she'd call Annabelle to find out how miserable she was.

She pulled her cell out of her purse and speed-dialed Annabelle.

"It's about time you called. I've been leaving messages for you all day."

"Honey, your day can't be as eventful as mine. Wait till you hear what happened."

"Wanna bet? Ben just proposed to me."

"Proposed what?"

"Marriage."

"Okay, you got me beat. You told him no, right?" There was silence on the line. "Annabelle, tell me you said no." Silence again. Shit. "What the hell is wrong with you?"

"I didn't say yes… I said I'd think about it."

"You'd think about it? What are you nuts? You're in love with my brother, you nitwit! What is it with you and getting engaged to men you don't actually want to marry? You don't love Ben. Why in the hell would you even consider marrying a man you don't love—again? Wasn't once enough?"

"It would only be temporary, and Ben needs me. It's

a long story, but he's got less than a year to get married, and well, he wants to marry someone he can trust not to fall in love with him and confuse the situation."

"The only person confused in this situation is you. If you accept Ben's proposal, Mike is going to freak. He's already on edge. Daddy handed over the trust and the keys to the castle right before he mistakenly called him Chip."

"Oh God. He didn't."

"Yes, he did, which is why I'm standing about ten blocks from your place. I drove up with Dad because he was so upset. He came up unannounced to talk to Mike's mom, whom he hasn't seen in thirty-three years."

"You're kidding."

"Hell no, I'm not. Let me tell you, there is some strong mojo zinging back and forth between them. I haven't seen chemistry like that since the day I burned magnesium and accidentally set my lab partner on fire. Daddy's still got it. He showed up on her doorstep, and when I left the apartment, neither of them noticed."

"That's great. I'm so happy for all of you. Maybe things will work out, and you'll be like a richer version of the Brady Bunch or something."

"You're kidding, right?"

"You and Mike can finally have the family the both of you always wanted. I'm really happy for you."

"Which is why you sound so miserable."

"I'm fine… or I will be eventually. At least I was right. The important thing is that you and Mike are happy."

"We are, huh? Mike is the most miserable happy person I've ever seen, and it had nothing to do with his hangover either. It had everything to do with you. And if you end up getting engaged to Ben, I swear you'll regret it."

"No matter what happens between Ben and me, you have to know there's no way Mike and I could possibly be together. I mean think about it. Your father and Mike's mother can pick up where they left off. I know Colleen loved him. Things can work out."

Just not for Annabelle. No matter how she professed being stronger and making her own decisions, the scared little girl was still inside afraid she wasn't worth fighting for. If Chip weren't already dead, Becca swore she'd kill him for hurting Annabelle the way he had.

The gods were against Mike today. He hadn't had one call. There was no full moon, no holiday weekend, and no flu epidemic to give him what he needed—a night of solid, nonstop work. Instead, he was left with no valid excuse not to go to his mother's for dinner. He had no valid excuse to avoid telling her what happened just before he planned to propose to the woman he loved. He had no valid excuse not to tell his mother the woman he loved was in love with a brother he never knew he had, much less lost. Unfortunately, telling her those difficult things were going to be a whole lot easier than telling her he'd met his father and his sister.

The only thing he wanted to do involved a large bottle of Jack Daniel's and a glass, although it didn't seem to help the night before. If he weren't on call, he'd be willing to give drowning his sorrows another try. Unfortunately, the Irish in him gave him a huge tolerance for alcohol, not that he tested it often, and the fact remained he was on call.

Mike hooked his pager and his cell onto his belt and took off for his mother's. She expected him for dinner, and she'd promised to make his favorite—pot roast—not that he had much of an appetite. Dealing with what he'd experienced today while hungover was a real test of his fortitude, and it would get worse before it got better.

The whole way to his mother's apartment, every person he saw seemed part of a couple. His friends had even paired off, leaving him the odd man out. The story of his life. Just when he thought he'd had it made, his life fell to shit. Worse than that, he had no clue how to get past it, or how long it would take to recover. He only knew that living like this sucked, and there was no end in sight.

Mike let himself in, tossed his messenger bag on the hall table, and heard voices. Maybe she had the news on. "Mum, I'm home."

The voices stopped and his spidey sense went on alert. Turning the corner, his worst fear was realized. His mother and Larsen were on the couch, and Becca was curled up in his favorite chair.

"What the hell are they doing here?"

The look on Mum's face made him back up a step. She stood, smoothed her skirt, and walked toward him. "Michael Christopher Flynn. I'll thank you not to use profanity in my home. Is that any way to treat our guests?"

Larsen stood and moved toward her. "It's all right, Colleen. Mike's had a rough time of it, and I'm afraid I haven't helped matters."

"Damn straight you haven't helped matters. Now answer the question."

"I was worried about you." Larsen gestured toward

Becca, who hadn't moved. "We both were. We came to make sure you were all right. I see you are, and in no mood to deal with us, so we'll go now and let you have your dinner. I'm sorry about what I said earlier. I hope you'll consider the offer… both offers." He turned to Colleen. "Becca and I will get a couple of rooms for the night. You have my cell, if there's anything you need. You can reach me anytime."

What the fuck was going on here?

Colleen nodded and walked Larsen to the door. Becca took her time getting out of Mike's chair and smirked at him as she passed. "Good going, Ace. Way to clear a room."

At the door, Colleen spoke so softly to Larsen that with the blood rushing through Mike's ears he couldn't hear what she said. Whatever it was brought a smile to Larsen's face and his hand to her shoulder. Colleen leaned forward, kissed Larsen's cheek, and wiped away the lipstick. Jealousy shot through Mike, surprising him more than Larsen's and Becca's appearance had.

Colleen hugged Becca before she turned to Larsen and smiled. It wasn't a polite smile. He'd seen her smile to acquaintances before. Mike had never seen this smile—a smile he wished like hell she hadn't aimed at anyone. Especially not Larsen. Fuck.

Mike squeezed his eyes shut and waited until he heard the familiar sound of the locks being engaged. He was going to have hell to pay, but his only consolation was that he no longer had to tell his mother what happened, well, at least not everything that happened. It was obvious she'd already heard about the disaster that took place in Pennsylvania.

❖ ❖ ❖

Mike's mother walked right past him to the kitchen. Not
knowing what else to do, he followed.

"You best set the table while I finish getting dinner
ready."

Nodding, he took a couple of plates, silverware,
and glasses out of the cupboard before retreating to the
dining room.

Okay, so he was a coward. He'd never walked into his
mother's house and not received a kiss. He'd never seen
her kiss another man. He'd never seen her wipe lipstick off
anyone else's cheek. And he'd never once been unsure of
her reaction to anything. When he was a kid and got into
trouble, he knew exactly what to expect. He'd have more
chores, no television, and no social life for the foreseeable
future. But he was no longer a kid, and he'd never before
seen such disappointment on his mother's face.

She brought the roast surrounded by vegetables and
the bread to the table, poured herself a glass of wine, and
passed the bottle to Mike before she sat and pulled her
napkin over her lap.

He went to the kitchen and filled his glass with water.
He was on call, and for once, he wished for an urgent
page. He really didn't want to deal with anything more
right now, not even his mother.

"You might as well come out with it." She sliced the
bread. "Do you want the heel?"

He sat and took a drink of his water. "No thanks."

"No thanks, you don't want the heel, or no thanks,
you don't want to talk about it?"

Both, but he couldn't say that. "I don't want the heel."

"Then you do want to tell me what happened between you and your Annabelle?"

"She's not my Annabelle, she's not my anything... she never was."

"Oh saints preserve us, you've gone and had your ego dented."

"Mum, she was in love with Chip, not me. I found a painting of my brother she'd painted four years ago. He looked just like me... well, except for the eyes, the lips, and a few other things, but basically, we could have been twins."

"Yes, but she fell in love with you. I know what love looks like. I also know what pain looks like. I saw both in Annabelle. I told her who your father was. I saw the shock. She had no idea."

"Okay, maybe she didn't know for sure, but she suspected. She never said anything. She'd never have gone out with me if I hadn't looked like Chip."

"That's nonsense. If two people are meant to be, then fate will push them together. If you hadn't met at the wedding, you would have met some other time."

"And she would have thought I was a ghost then, too."

"Did you propose to the girl?"

"No. Thank God."

"I see no reason to thank God for that. You'd planned to propose."

"I did. But then I saw the painting—"

"And got mad you weren't the first man in her life?"

"No."

"Oh, I see what it is, she could have had other men in her life, but they had to be someone you didn't know or was in no way related to you. Then it's okay."

"Well… yeah. I mean, she doesn't love me. She loves him. It's obvious."

"Is it now? Did she talk about him?"

"No. She only talked about him when she was drugged. She never meant to. She kept him from me."

"She didn't tell you about him?"

"Yeah, she did, but she never said we looked exactly alike."

"So the problem was she didn't say you look like her old boyfriend. Did you tell her she wasn't the only brunette you dated?"

"No, but it's not the same."

"No, it's not. But it's not unforgivable. She didn't cheat on you. She didn't lie to you. All she did was fall in love with two men who happened to be related. It wasn't as if she'd planned it."

"Larsen thinks she did."

"Christopher is not the subject here. We've all made mistakes in our lifetimes. My mistake was not giving Christopher a chance to explain himself. Unfortunately, that mistake cost your father and me thirty-three years of unhappiness. Learn from my mistake, Michael. Don't repeat it."

"Mum, this thing with Larsen—"

"Is not up for discussion. You need time to process the changes in your life, as do I. But the one thing that has nothing to do with Larsen, your brother, your sister, or even me, is your love for Annabelle. Don't be foolish and throw something that precious away. You might spend a lifetime looking and never find it again."

His mother took her fork and knife and tossed them

on her plate along with her untouched dinner. She stood and reached over to take Mike's plate.

"Hey, I'm not done. I haven't even eaten yet."

She took the plate right out from in front of him. "That's okay, you weren't hungry anyway. You have a lot to think about and a lot to do. You can't be doing that here. Go home now, Michael."

He followed his mother to the door.

She handed him his messenger bag. "You go on and think about what I said and the reasons you're so angry with Annabelle, and see if they still hold water when you think about them logically. Good luck, honey." She kissed his cheek and wiped away the imaginary lipstick. "I'll talk to you in a few days."

She gave him a shove, and Mike found himself standing in the hall with the door closed firmly behind him.

When Annabelle got home, she wasn't surprised to see Becca and Dave snuggled up on the couch together. "I assume you're staying over?"

Becca muted the TV and stretched. "Yeah, Dad was going to put me up at a hotel with him, but I told him I'd rather stay with you. Besides, I wouldn't be surprised if he and Colleen end up sneaking around together, and I so don't want to see that."

"You're kidding. Colleen doesn't seem the type."

"You didn't see the look in her eyes when they said good-bye or the way he acted and looked when he was with her. The two of them never got over each other—that much was obvious. All this time Daddy was a normal guy, he just hid it well. Really, really well."

Annabelle had a hard time seeing Christopher Larsen as anything other than an uptight snob, and well, a total unfeeling prick too. "So you think he acted like he has because he was miserable with an unhappy marriage and a broken heart? What? He liked to spread the pain around?"

Becca pushed Dave off her lap, followed Annabelle into her room, and plopped on the unmade bed while Annabelle changed out of her work clothes. "No, I think he acted like a prick so my mother would leave him alone. If he did anything to go against her, she made his life more miserable than it already was. He didn't stand up to her until he found out he and Colleen were Mother's first victims. Then he raised hell. I guess he went along to get along, not that it makes it right or anything, but having been on the receiving end of my mother's rage, I can almost understand it."

Annabelle hung the light jacket to her suit in the closet and turned around for Becca to help her with the zipper. Annabelle would rather die than admit she understood it, too. Chip and Becca's mother was scary as hell. "So, has Colleen heard about... Well, you know, has she seen Mike?"

Becca got up and unzipped Annabelle's dress. "He showed up for dinner and was less than happy to find me and Daddy there. He looks like hell. Between you and my dad, you really did a job on him."

She stepped out of the dress and tossed it on the treadmill. "I never meant for him to find out the way he did. I was going to tell him."

Becca lay back and pulled a pillow under her as she rolled over like Mike always did. How weird was that?

"Yeah, and you were going to dump him. Either way, Mike was going to get hurt."

Annabelle threw up her arms. "It's not as if he's the only one hurt here. You didn't see the look on his face. He hates me." She walked around the bed, pulled a pair of running shorts and a T-shirt from her dresser, and put them on.

"He can't hate you. He loves you."

Annabelle stuck her head through the T-shirt just before she lost the war with her tears. What was it with her? Every since she cried on Wayne's shoulder, she'd been a freaking watering pot. "You didn't see him. He said I was just like the rest."

"I know he did. But can't you see that was a knee-jerk reaction? You need to get over this whole thing with Dad. Dad might see you in a different light, and even if he doesn't, the hell with him. Mike loves you. You're worth more to him than any trust fund."

Annabelle rummaged through her drawers looking for a clean pair of athletic socks. "Easy for you to say, you've never lived like Mike and his mom did. They struggled. Heck, Mike's still struggling to pay his student loans. It wasn't as if he had Daddy Warbucks paying for college and medical school." She sat on the bed with her back to Becca and pulled on the last pair of clean socks she could find.

"Yeah, well, he's not going to be struggling much longer. He has it all. The estate, the trust fund, everything but you. He'd give it all up in a heartbeat if he knew that was the only thing standing between the two of you."

Annabelle dropped to her knees and searched for

the running shoes she hadn't seen in ages. "It's not the money, and you know it."

"Yeah, the money is easy to deal with, so is my father. The biggest obstacle Mike has to face is you and your insecurity. He knows you're worth it. I know you're worth it. You're the only person who doesn't."

Annabelle reached all the way under the bed and grabbed her running shoes, coughed up the dust that followed them out, and shoved her feet in. She looked up at Becca as she tied the laces. "You have no idea what you're talking about." She rose and grabbed her ankle to stretch her quads. "Now leave me alone. I'm going for a run. I can't take any more of your loving support."

"Are you supposed to be running so soon?"

Ignoring Becca as she warmed up on the front stoop, she wished there was somewhere to run so she wouldn't have to spend the rest of the night listening to Becca's psychobabble. It was going to get worse. Becca hadn't even started in on Ben's marriage proposal.

After a good long run, ignoring the increasing pain in her ankle, Annabelle finally limped back home. When she entered the apartment, Becca wasn't alone. Rosalie was waiting, too. Annabelle wasn't looking forward to dealing with her perfect sister.

Becca smiled her you-are-so-busted smile, and Annabelle felt like smacking her. Obviously, the jig was up.

Rosalie walked right up to Annabelle and wrapped her arms around her. "I understand why you didn't tell Mama and Pop, but you could have told me and Richie. I'm so sorry you didn't feel you could talk to me. Oh God, what you must have gone through."

Annabelle looked over Rosalie's shoulder at Becca's satisfied smile. Right now, she wanted to kill her. "Ro, I'm fine." Becca's fake cough did nothing to help the believability value of Annabelle's assertion, nor did it do anything to help her escape from forced familial affection.

"Becca showed me the painting of Chip. I can't believe the resemblance." Rosalie pulled away a little, giving Annabelle a small margin of breathing room. Rosalie held her shoulders and looked at her with wide eyes. "Mike isn't built *exactly* like Chip was, is he?"

What is it with people? "Mike has a much bigger dick, if that's what you're asking."

Becca stuffed her fingers in her ears. "I so don't want to hear this." She began singing to herself and driving Annabelle closer to the edge. Rosalie just looked relieved.

"Maybe you should go home and be with Nick. I'm sure I'm not his favorite person now, and I don't want to cause marital problems."

Rosalie finally let her go. "Nonsense. Nick just knows Mike is hurting. He doesn't know the whole story."

"And you do?"

Rosalie nodded. "Becca filled me in."

She didn't know whether to kill Becca or thank her, since she wasn't sure how much more explaining she was capable of. She couldn't even control her tears.

Becca watched Rosalie comfort her sister and couldn't help but feel a little jealous. Still, it was good for Annabelle, and as soon as Rosalie told her husband about everything, it would be good for Mike. At least she hoped it would. She'd been racking her brain for the last twenty-four hours trying to come up with a way to get the two most stubborn people in the world back together. It wasn't until she talked to the Fairy Godfathers and remembered hearing how close Mike and Annabelle's brother-in-law, Nick, were that the plan came together. All it took was a call to Rosalie, and everything fell right into place.

Poor Annabelle didn't know what she was up against. Rosalie was a master.

"You need to take some time and think about what you want. Call that boss of yours, and tell him you're going to take some more time off. Tell him you're considering your options."

"I don't know, Ro. Then I'll just have more time to think. Thinking hurts."

Becca stepped closer. "You need to pull out your paints again. Painting always made you feel better."

Rosalie lit up. "Yeah, that's a great idea. Why don't you go back to the beach house? Just take a week, paint, think, and enjoy the beach. The last thing you need is to be stuck at work with Ben, or worse, get a visit from Mama."

Annabelle groaned. It was clear she'd do just about anything to avoid her mother.

Within an hour, Annabelle was packed, stuffed in Rosalie's VW Beetle, and on her way to the Hamptons.

Damn, Rosalie was good. She called Nick to pick her and Dave up and left Becca alone at Annabelle's with the promise to keep in touch. After seeing Rosalie at work, she had no doubt about Rosalie's ability to somehow get Mike back to the beach house and together with Annabelle in record time. Now all Becca had to do was deal with her father.

Chapter 20

THE LAST PLACE ANNABELLE WANTED TO GO WAS THE beach house, but she didn't feel like explaining that to Becca and Rosalie. She never actually told them she'd go. She just smiled, nodded, and left. There was only one place Annabelle could go where Mike had never been. She took the Manhattan Bridge over to Ben's apartment above the gallery. Ben was out of town, and he'd given her an open invitation to use his guest room in case she wanted to crash there instead of taking the subway home late at night. Since she couldn't stay home with Becca, the amateur psychoanalyst, and she wasn't up to driving all the way to the beach house, where she'd be haunted by memories of Mike, Ben's place was her only hope to escape thinking about him. Unfortunately, she wasn't sure she'd be successful. He'd taken up residence in her head.

She let herself into Ben's apartment, tossed her suitcase in the guest room, grabbed a water out of the refrigerator, and studied the selection of frozen dinner entrees. Ben always cooked for himself but stocked her favorite Lean Cuisines in case she couldn't get out for lunch or dinner and there were no good leftovers in his fridge to microwave. Nothing looked good to her. She closed the freezer door and decided microwaving was just too much trouble.

Eating real food made by Mike had spoiled her. Still, going back to two-minute meals wasn't nearly as depressing as the thought of going without sex for the rest of her life. And after what she'd been through with Mike, she didn't think she'd ever have it in her to start dating again.

Annabelle was antsy and couldn't stand the perfection of Ben's apartment. Everything he did, he did perfectly. Dressed, decorated, cleaned, cooked—he annoyed the hell out of her. She couldn't imagine living here with him, even platonically. She unpacked and found Becca had included the sketch pad and pencils Mike had given her. She took them to her office.

Since she couldn't beat the memories of Mike, she decided to embrace them. She curled up on the couch and fingered the metal coil at the top of the pad, took a deep breath, flipped open the cover, and, holding a pencil, closed her eyes and pictured Mike lying in bed on his stomach, a pillow pulled under his arms while he watched her.

An hour later, she had a half-dozen sketches of Mike on the beach, in the kitchen chopping vegetables, in bed, in the water, but the one picture she wanted, she didn't have.

Sliding off the couch, Annabelle pulled one of the prepared canvases out of a bin, set it on the easel, and, with charcoal, did a quick sketch before uncapping the oils for the first time in years. She looked down at her clothes and ran back to Ben's to raid his ragbag. He threw his dress shirts in there the second they showed the slightest bit of pilling from his beard, or God forbid, weren't as white as he deemed acceptable. Annabelle slid her arms into the sleeves, rolled up the cuffs, and returned to her office. She twisted her hair into a topknot and stuck the end of a paintbrush through her makeshift bun. Once she turned up the music, she dove right in.

For the first time in years, she felt grounded. It wasn't as if she didn't hurt—she hurt like hell—but she wasn't swimming in it. She worked through the pain instead of running from it or ignoring it. Maybe Becca and Rosalie were right after all.

Annabelle worked the way she once had before Chip's death—with total concentration—and was thrilled with the image that appeared on the canvas. At first, the brushes felt foreign to her hands, and the smell of the oils seemed somehow stronger than she'd remembered, but after a few hours, it was as if she'd never stopped painting. Her brushstrokes had the same intensity, the colors she mixed were just as true, and night slid into day without her noticing.

Mike finally got a call in the middle of the night and spent the rest of the night at the hospital. The next morning, he answered a cryptic page from Nick asking him to meet at the coffee shop across the street from the hospital. He cleaned up, left his lab coat on, and ran across the street. He spotted Nick and sat across from him in the booth.

Nick looked over the rim of his coffee cup. "You look like shit."

Mike turned over his coffee cup. "I feel like shit." Like clockwork, a waitress appeared out of nowhere with a full pot of coffee.

"I hear congratulations are in order."

"For what?"

"I'm told you're a very rich man now that you have your father's money."

Mike shrugged. "For a guy who supposedly has everything, Larsen seems pretty miserable."

"So your sister said."

"You've been talking to Becca?"

"No, but Lee has. She heard some scary stories about your 'family.' Becca's mother makes Mrs. Ronaldi sound like the freakin' mother of the year or something. No kidding." Nick stretched his long arms along the back of the booth. "What are you going to do about the old man? Go to work for him and join a country club or something? Hey, maybe you can take up golf, meet some high society broad, and be just as miserable as your old man."

"At least I'd be a hundred miles from Annabelle."

"So you two are done? Over? Kaput?"

"Yeah. She doesn't love me, man. Annabelle was just looking for a replacement for my dead brother, and I looked the part. It makes me wonder if Larsen is doing the same thing. He even called me Chip."

"That sucks about you and Annabelle. You really loved her, huh?"

Mike nodded and nearly lost it right there in the diner.

"Yeah, been there, done that. The time Lee and I were on the skids was the worst month of my life. Which is why I called you. I found out something I think you ought to know. My wife is probably gonna kill me for tellin' you, but sometimes us men have to stick together."

Mike didn't need any more bad news. "What is it now?"

"Did you sleep at all last night?"

Mike shook his head. "No, why?"

"I'm wondering how bad you're going to freak when you find out, that's all."

"Nick, I'm done. Nothing you can say will even surprise me, no less cause me to lose it."

"You sure about that?"

Mike rolled his eyes. He would give his eyeteeth just to be left the hell alone. Though really, he was alone. There was no one else who gave a shit. Even his mother threw him out. "I'm sure."

Nick pulled his wallet out of his pants pocket, took out a twenty, and threw it on the table.

"What's that for?"

"The bill. Just in case I have to chase you out of here."

Mike took a sip of his coffee and stared at Nick. That's when he started to worry.

"Annabelle's boss proposed to her."

Mike slammed his cup on the table and broke it. Hot coffee burned his hand, and he was out the door of the diner before it stopped dripping. He didn't bother saying anything. Nick ran after him. Mike crossed the sidewalk, put his coffee-soaked fingers to his lips, and whistled for a cab. He had the door opened before the cab stopped.

Nick practically jumped over the trunk to get in the other side and slammed the door as the cab sped off. "What are you going to do?"

Mike relaxed his grip on the seat back in front of him and spared Nick a glance. "You mean besides kill Ben Walsh?"

"Yeah, besides that."

"I don't know."

Nick rearranged his feet the best he could with almost no legroom. "It's not like Annabelle said yes… yet."

After that crack, Mike considered killing the messenger, too.

"Mike, you gotta take a minute, man. Think about this. What's Annabelle gonna think if you go walking into the artsy-fartsy gallery and mess up her boss? Does that say 'I love you' to you?"

Okay, maybe Nick had a point. But Mike didn't want to say I love you to Annabelle. He wanted her to love him. His love was never in question. He sat back. Pushing the front seat forward was not making them move any faster, it was just making the cab driver nervous.

"After the way you left things with her, you got some major ass kissing to do to get back into her good graces. Beating the shit out of her boss will make you feel better, but it's not going to do a whole hell of a lot for your relationship. What's more important, that you kill him or that you keep him from marrying your girl?"

Mike sank into the seat and stared out the window. "What's it matter? She doesn't love me."

"Yeah, right. Lee said Annabelle was willing to give you up so you could have some kind of storybook family with your father, mother, sister, and trust fund. She didn't want to come between you and your long lost dad."

"What?" He turned his attention back to Nick. "That's not why we're not together. I found out she loved my brother, not me."

"Come on. Lee told me that Becca even said that trust-fund baby brother of yours was kind of a schmuck and didn't treat Annabelle right. As a matter of fact, Becca said that if he hadn't been dying, he and Annabelle would have never stayed together. She was just a kid. Once he got sick, she couldn't dump his ass, could she?"

"She could, but she wouldn't." Mike scrubbed his face with his hands. Not Annabelle. She was loyal to the end, heck even after the end, which was the problem.

"She stayed, and she grew up a whole lot. She went through hell and back. I got to hand it to you." Nick tapped him on the shoulder. "You were right about her. She's special. Lee found out that Annabelle took care of your brother until he died, all while his parents treated her like shit. She knew your dad would never accept her with you either, so she bowed out. Who could blame her?"

Mike sat up a little straighter. "I'd never let anyone mistreat her."

"I know that, and you know that. But it sounds as if that's exactly what your brother did. Becca told Lee that Annabelle came home traumatized. That's why she let her mother stick her with that putz Johnny DePalma. I was wrong about her. So are you."

When the cab pulled up in front of the Benjamin Walsh Gallery, Mike still wanted to kill Ben, and then he wanted to talk to Belle. If Nick was right… shit, if Nick was right, Mike had really screwed the pooch.

He got out of the cab. Nick told the cabbie to wait and followed Mike out.

"If you know what's good for you, you'll talk to her before you go near Ben. If it doesn't work out, I'll hold this Ben dude down while you beat him, okay?"

Mike took a deep breath and let it out, his temper firmly under control. "I'm good."

"Are you sure? I'll have hell to pay if I have to bail your ass out of jail."

Mike nodded and got a slap on the back from Nick.

"Oh, I almost forgot." Nick pulled something out of his pocket. He handed Mike the ring box and the keys to the Mustang. "Vinny caught Little Mia wearing this ring. She found it after you left for the interview. He thought you might need it once you screwed your head on straight. Oh, and the Mustang is parked around the corner."

"Thanks, man." Mike shoved the keys in his back pocket, took the ring out of the box, and stuck it in his front pocket before tossing the box back to Nick. "Hold the box for me, okay?"

"Sure. Now go get the girl. I'm going to try talking my wife into playing hooky."

Mike had no choice but to walk toward the car and make believe he was going straight to the Hamptons to see Annabelle. He figured once he knocked Ben into next week, he'd have plenty of time to drive to the beach house and beg forgiveness before Ben came to.

After he was sure Nick's cab pulled away, he snuck back to the gallery to take care of Ben.

Tossing the brush into a jar of turpentine, Annabelle stretched her aching back and stepped away from the canvas. She was happy with what she saw. She wanted exactly what this painting portrayed. "If only it could be like that."

The intercom on her phone beeped, disrupting her thoughts. "Um… Annabelle. Could you please come down here?" Her assistant, shit. She checked her clock and noticed the time. Great, she should have been down there a half hour ago. Kerri wouldn't have buzzed her if there wasn't a problem.

Annabelle reached over the desk and buzzed Kerri back. "I'm on my way." She wiped her hands on her smock and couldn't imagine how she looked. She was wearing a pair of plain black yoga pants, a black T-shirt under the smock covered with paint, and she hadn't brushed her teeth, but she didn't have time to do anything about it. She popped a few Altoids in her mouth and ran her tongue over her teeth on the way down in the elevator. The door opened, and she understood the problem.

Mike.

He waited in the middle of the gallery, and he was royally pissed about something. He stared at her chest, and when she looked down to see why, she noticed Ben's monogram on the shirt. Shit.

"I need to speak with you. Alone."

Oh God. She really was in no shape to deal with him. She hadn't slept in days, she hadn't showered or even had coffee, and as much as she hated it, all she wanted was to crawl into his arms. She was a total weakling. "This is really not a good time."

"Too bad. You either invite me up to your office, or I'll make a scene."

"You will not. Besides Kerri is here—"

"And she thinks I'm really romantic. Are you going to invite me up?"

"No, and I'm not going anywhere."

"I wouldn't bet on that."

Before her muddled, caffeine-starved brain registered what he was doing Mike had picked her up and thrown her over his shoulder. She screamed and pounded on his backside, but it didn't seem to faze him.

"You have one more chance to change your mind."

"Put me down!"

"Are you going to invite me up?"

She reached beneath the waistband of his jeans and yanked on his underwear.

"I'll take that as a no. Well, it's your choice."

He stomped to the elevator and pressed the Call button. Annabelle strained to see her assistant, who looked as if she were watching Rock Hudson and Doris Day in *Pillow Talk*. "Call my brother, and tell him I'm being kidnapped!"

Kerri smiled and waved—a co-conspirator. Fabulous. All the blood flowing to Annabelle's head made it pound with every beat of her heart, and with Mike's arm wrapped around her thighs, she couldn't even kick him. He stepped into the elevator, turned, and from the reflection in the mirrored walls, she saw him wave to Kerri, the traitor. She also noticed the hand prints of paint all over her smock-covered butt. She just hoped there was sufficient paint on her front to ruin his shirt.

"You're kidnapping me."

"No. I'm keeping a promise."

"What promise?"

"I promised I wasn't going anywhere without you. And right now, I'm going to your office, so you're going with me."

"I can't believe you're doing this."

"Babe, you're not giving me a choice here. I'm not going to give up on you, and I'm not going to give up on us—ever."

"You walked out on me three days ago. Now you're not giving up on me? Lucky me. Now put me down and leave. I'm not interested."

The elevator door opened, and ignoring her, he walked right toward her office. She squirmed more. Anything to keep him out of her office. She hadn't covered the painting, and the last thing she wanted was him to see it. God, she was mortified. "Don't go in there."

"Why?"

"Have you ever heard of privacy?"

"Is he in there?"

"He who?"

"Ben. You know, the guy who proposed to you?"

God, she wanted to kill Becca. "Is that what this is about? You came out here because you're jealous of Ben?" She was tempted to tell him she'd already said yes to Ben's proposal, but she couldn't lie even though, in the end, it would probably be less painful for both of them. He walked into her office, and she cringed as he stopped dead in his tracks with her still hanging over his shoulder like a freaking rag doll.

"That's me. You're painting me?"

"Wow, it's so nice to hear I haven't lost my touch. Now would you please put me down?"

He set her on her feet but didn't let go of her as he stared at the painting. "It's beautiful. I've never seen anything like it."

She guessed it was too late to cover the canvas. She pulled away, wiped her hands on a rag, and took a drink of water that had gone warm. Her throat was dry, and she didn't know what the heck to do. He looked awful and wonderful at the same time. Kind of like she felt. Well, except for feeling totally exposed. Mike stared at her painting like he sometimes stared at her, as if he could see within her.

"I never noticed how much Becca and I look alike. It's weird seeing us together like that."

Annabelle nodded. She'd painted Mike and Becca with their arms around each other and their heads together. They had smiles on their faces as if they were posing for a camera and sharing a joke.

She hadn't started on the background, and the clothes were rough, but she had their faces down, and he was right, they did look an awful lot alike. They also looked happy, something she really wished for both of them.

Annabelle knew he was right behind her. Still, when he put his hands on her shoulders she jumped.

"I've missed you."

She couldn't take the touching. She was too close to either falling apart or falling all over him. She stepped away, faced him, and wrapped her arms around herself. "You got me here. What do you want?"

Mike stepped closer. "I came here to talk to you. To apologize."

She needed to get away from him. But she needed to end this even if it killed her. "For manhandling me?"

"No. For jumping to conclusions. For not talking to you and hearing you out. For not believing in you and in us."

She shrugged and stepped around her desk, trying to put some space between them. "There is no us." Her chest ached, her head ached, that damn vein in her forehead throbbed—she hurt everywhere. "I'm sorry I didn't handle it better. But it really doesn't matter now. No amount of talking is going to change things." No matter how badly she wished it would.

Mike followed her. "How can you say that?"

"Because it's the truth."

"I love you."

She shook her head and bit her lip to keep from blurting out that she loved him, too. She dared to look at him in the eyes and saw her pain reflected there. Still, it had to be done. It was best for him. "Yeah, but I know better than most that sometimes love just isn't enough."

"So you're going to give up on us and marry your boss? You don't love him."

"Ben has nothing to do with this."

"I came out here to ask you to marry me. I want you in my life, in my home, in my bed. I want a family with you. I want to spend the rest of my life loving you and only you."

Annabelle shook her head. God, if only everything were as easy as that. She loved him. She wanted a life with him and kids. It was a perfect dream, but she knew the reality. She felt as if she had a steel band wrapped around her chest, making it hard to breathe and think. She was sure something was going to burst. "I can't." Her voice cracked. That damn vein in her head throbbed, and her eyes stung from unshed tears. No amount of blinking could stop them.

"This is about Larsen, isn't it?"

She slid past him toward the door. "No. This is about me. I can't do this again."

"Do what?"

"I don't fit in with your family—" Her back was to him. She could barely see through the blur of tears.

"That's bullshit. You fit in just fine. My mother loves you. Becca is your best friend—"

"Your father hates me. And I don't care what you say. In time, you'll resent me for coming between you and your dad."

Mike had moved and now stood planted against the door. There was no way she'd be able to leave until he let her go. The way he stood with his feet spread and his hands fisted on his hips made it abundantly clear that wasn't going to happen any time soon.

He reached out and pulled her toward him. "You're not coming between me and anyone. I'm not Chip. Damn it! If Larsen has a problem with you, he can go pound rock salt. I spent thirty-two years of my life without a father. I don't need one now."

"I know you're not Chip. You're nothing like him. But that's not the point. There's the estate, the trust fund, the job." She pulled away from him and wiped the tears from her face.

He stepped closer, crowding her. "Nothing is worth losing you."

"I don't want you to give anything up because of me." As she stepped back again and backed right into the wall, he sandwiched her in and held her close. She had no choice but to face him. He looked at her in such a way, her feeling of being exposed increased tenfold.

"You don't trust me."

"What?"

"You don't trust me. You think I'm going to throw you under the bus at the first sign of trouble."

"No. It's not you. It's me. I just can't do this again. I won't stand between you and your family."

"What do you think you're doing right now?" He tugged her closer and kissed her while he gently pulled her arms around him. "Don't you see? You're the only family I want or need. You're the family I've been looking for my whole life. Not Larsen, not Becca, not even my mum. Just you."

Mike felt so good, and the way he talked made it sound almost possible. But it was just talk. She'd been down this road before. She knew how it felt when ultimatums were given, and she was tossed aside.

He rested her head against his shoulder, his hand pushing her hair off her face while the other arm encircled her waist, holding her tight against him. "Let's fly to Vegas. We'll get married and then decide what to do from there."

He was so warm, and his voice rumbled in his chest and mixed with the sound of his steady heartbeat. "No." She tried to get away, but he held her gently but firmly.

"No to Vegas or no to getting married?" He didn't sound particularly hurt, but then he was so close she really couldn't see his face.

"Both."

"You mean you're not going to make an honest man of me? Your mother and father aren't going to be too happy about that. After all, they've already given us their blessing."

"What?" She pulled away enough to look him in the eye. He looked so damn pleased with himself.

"I asked them for your hand in marriage. I'm a responsible adult, not some kid. Your family is important to you, so that makes them important to me. It was the right thing to do."

"When was this?"

"Tuesday."

"I can't believe you did that." God, part of her wanted to hug him. Asking for her hand was so sweet and old-fashioned, not to mention difficult. Especially with her parents. Then there was the part of her that wanted to kill him, too. Now, she not only had to deal with Mike, she had to explain to her mother why she wouldn't marry him.

Mike let her go, reached for the silenced cell phone on her desk, and slid his finger across the screen to unlock it. "There are forty-seven voice mail messages. I'll bet most of them are from your mother. The others are probably from your sister, my sister, or my mum. She threw me out, you know."

"She did not." Annabelle took her phone from him. He didn't need to see several of those calls were from Ben.

"She certainly did. It seems Mum thinks she made the mistake of a lifetime when she left the States before talking to Larsen. She told me not to make the same mistake. Then she said I wasn't hungry, took away my dinner, and told me I had things to do. Namely figuring out a way to get you back. She was right you know. I don't want to grow old alone and miserable like Larsen. He sold out. He lost my mother because he didn't care enough to get her back. He went home with his tail between his legs and for what? For money and that big-ass estate. He's been miserable ever since. It took me a while to figure it out, but now that I have, I'm not going to give up. I want you back. I need you." He reached out and tucked a strand of hair behind her ear. "And you're not making this easy."

Annabelle closed her eyes and shook her head. "You're the one who isn't making this easy." She was a mess, she hurt, and she was being manipulated. As if it wasn't bad enough that she was dying inside, she was mad.

"What are you afraid of? Talk to me. Don't run away like you did before."

"I didn't run away. I was thrown away. You want to know what I'm afraid of. Fine. I'm afraid of losing myself again. I'm afraid of failing again. I loved Chip, and there was nothing I could do to make him love me. And when he left me…"

"He didn't leave you. He died."

"He left me by refusing treatment. He never even tried. He gave up on me and on our life because it wasn't worth fighting for. I wasn't worth fighting for." Spent, she sat on the couch and, with her elbows on her knees, held her head in her hands.

The cushion beside her dipped, and Mike's arm wrapped around her, pulling her to his side. He kissed her temple and held her for a moment. "Babe, I'm nothing like Chip. Maybe he didn't have the courage to try. No matter how much you love someone, if they don't have that kind of courage, you can't give it to them."

Mike took a deep breath. "I promised you I wouldn't go anywhere without you. I broke that promise, and you can't imagine how sorry I am I let you down. But babe, I'm back now, and I won't make the same mistake twice."

"Mike—" She turned to face him, pulling her leg up under the other.

"No, let me finish. I'm not afraid to fight for you, for us, but I can't do it alone. I guess you were right. Sometimes love isn't enough. You have to be willing to risk everything for that love. Chip wasn't, but I am. Are you? Or are you going to run away from what you really want?"

Exhausted, she had no tears left to cry. She was empty. "You say that now, and I really think you believe it, but when your father finds out about us, he's going to threaten to take it all away."

"There are other jobs."

God she loved him; everything was so black-and-white. He didn't understand. "He used to threaten to cut Chip off without a cent. You don't know what he's like."

"I could care less about his money. Money is great, but I'm not going to sell my soul for it. That's what I'd have to do in order to take the money over you. I'm not going to sell out like my father. I'm not like Chip. I don't need money to make me happy. I just need you." Mike lifted her onto his lap and held her tight.

Her face was pressed against his neck, his pulse thrummed against her cheek, and her arms tightened around him. "I'm scared. Losing Chip almost killed me, and I didn't feel for him what I feel for you. If anything happened..."

Mike lowered her onto her back and, resting on his forearms over her, kissed her so tenderly before his eyes met hers. "Babe, I can't promise I'll never leave you, but I can promise I'll never leave you by choice. We can have a life together. We can build it to suit us, you and me. Are you going to let fear of losing keep you from that? Heck, if you do, we both lose. I don't know about you, but I can't imagine my life without you in it."

Annabelle had no problem imagining her life without Mike. A life filled with pain and loneliness. It would be an infinite number of days like the last few days had been—seemingly endless. He was close, he was real, and he loved her enough to try. He loved her enough to make her want to try. Maybe you can give someone else courage after all. "I don't have to imagine it. I've spent the last three days living it."

"God, I hope they sucked." Mike smiled down at her.

She was laughing and crying at the same time. "Really, really bad."

"So are you going to marry me and let me put you out of your misery?"

Her heart pounded, but she wasn't sure if it was because she was scared to death, or if it was because Mike was lying above her so close, giving her that look that always made her mouth dry and her panties wet. She figured it was both. They were about to jump off a cliff together, and all she could do was trust in him and in them, if not herself.

Chapter 21

"Damn." Mike forgot all about the ring. He had to stand up to get it out of his pocket. When he did, Annabelle sat up.

"What's wrong?"

Mike knelt down in front of her. "I'm sorry. I didn't do this very well. I guess that's why they put rings in funny-shaped boxes, so you don't have to go searching your pants pockets for them."

"You got me a ring?"

"Of course. It was my grandmother's. If you don't like it, we can get you another one... eventually. After I get another job." Mike slid the ring on her finger, surprised to find it fit.

Annabelle stared at the ring with wide eyes. "It's... it's beautiful. I love it."

That was a relief because if she didn't, he'd have a heck of a time getting her another one. Especially since he was most likely out of a job and out of money. They might be poor, but they were happy. "Does that mean you're going to marry me?" His heart was beating double-time, and he could swear he was beginning to sweat. She just stared at the ring like she was wondering if it was real—both the diamond and the proposal. Heck, he couldn't blame her, if he hadn't spoken to the jeweler, he'd wonder if it was a fake. The proposal, even though he totally botched it, was straight from the heart. The wait seemed an eternity.

A slow smile covered her face, and she lunged at him, almost knocking him on the floor. "Yes." She wrapped her arms around his neck so tight she practically strangled him as she kissed him. God, he'd missed her, and he wanted her, but not here, not now, and not with her wearing some other guy's shirt.

He gently disengaged himself and put some distance between them. "Good. Now come on, let's go celebrate."

She looked confused. "Mike, it's the middle of the day."

"So? I have off, and I'm sure if you tell Kerri we just got engaged, she won't give you a hard time about leaving."

"Okay, fine. But let me at least shower and change."

"Sure. We can go back to your place—"

"No need. I stayed here last night… Well, I was up all night painting, but I was going to crash at Ben's. I brought a change of clothes."

Mike swallowed the first remark that came to mind, the second, and the third ones, too. "Why were you staying at Ben's?"

Annabelle tossed a sheet over the painting and moved the easel out of the center of the room. "Becca was at my place, and Rosalie and she ganged up on me. They wanted me to go to the beach house, but I couldn't so I came here."

"To stay with Ben."

"Not with Ben, just at his place. He's out of town. Why, what's wrong with that?"

"What's wrong with you staying at a guy's apartment who recently proposed to you?"

"Mike, Ben and I are just friends."

"Right, that's why he wants to marry you."

"He wanted to marry me because he needs a wife... temporarily. It's a long story. He just needs to marry someone who isn't going to go after his money or get confused about their... relationship. It's nothing personal."

"Nothing personal?" My ass. "So he picked you? After all you've been through?"

"Well, yeah. It's not like I had anything better to do. You dumped me, remember?"

"No, you dumped me."

"Are we going to fight, or are we going to celebrate?"

"Celebrate. But why don't you just get your stuff out of Ben's apartment, and we can put it back where it belongs."

She rolled her eyes. "If it'll make you feel better, I'll get my stuff, and we can go to my place."

"It will." Actually what would make him feel better would be to knock some sense into Ben's thick skull, preferably with his fist. Ben took advantage of Annabelle by asking her to marry him so shortly after Mike and she had broken up. He couldn't believe she actually bought that line about needing to get married. Ben was a man, and he'd had his eye and sometimes hands on Annabelle since Mike had met her. He wasn't fooled by Ben's we're-just-friends act.

Annabelle took off for Ben's apartment, and Mike waited in her office. When he heard footsteps, he stood expecting to see Annabelle.

"Annabelle, I have that prenup from my lawyer for you to look at."

Mike took one look at Ben's smug face and slammed his fist into it. Damn that hurt.

Ben fell back into the wall and gave his head a shake. "I was wondering how long it would take you to come to your senses. I guess I deserved the punch, but did you have to go for the face?" He wiped the blood from his lip.

"Ben? Is that you?"

Ben put the documents in the breast pocket of his suit jacket. "Yeah, I was just talking to Mike here."

"Oh, I didn't expect you back until tomorrow."

Annabelle strode in and walked right to Mike. He put his arm around her shoulder and held her close, hoping his hand wouldn't swell up too much.

Ben pointed to her ring and smiled a kind of lopsided grin since his lip was beginning to swell. "I hear congratulations are in order."

"Mike told you?"

"Yes, he did. I wish you both the best of luck."

"Thanks for understanding, Ben."

"Not a problem.

Annabelle looked at Ben and then tilted her head. "Are you okay? You don't look so good."

"I'm fine. I assume you're going to take the rest of the weekend off."

"Yeah. I was hoping to." Annabelle threw her duffel bag over her shoulder before Mike took it from her. She shot him a smile and ran around her desk to get her purse. "I'll see you on Monday, okay?"

Ben nodded and turned for the door. "That's fine. Have a good weekend."

Annabelle took Mike's hand and whispered, "Ben didn't look so good. What did you say to him?"

Mike shrugged. "Nothing. You know, the usual guy stuff." He tried not to wince when she squeezed his hand. "Come on, let's go celebrate."

❖❖❖

Mike pulled up to the apartment and couldn't keep the smile off his face. Unfortunately, Annabelle didn't have that problem. She was sound asleep. He got out of the car and opened her door. "Come on, sleepyhead." She opened her eyes and let out a huge yawn.

"I'm tired. I'm so sorry. I was painting all last night… and well, I haven't slept much since—"

"Yeah, me either." Mike helped her out of the car and smiled. "What do you say we go inside, curl up together, and take a nap?"

Annabelle stifled another yawn. "But what about our celebration?"

"We have the rest of our lives for that. Right now, you need some shut-eye."

They went into the apartment, and Annabelle kicked off her shoes as soon as the door was closed. "It's so weird coming home without Dave here." She pulled off her top as she walked toward the bedroom. Mike followed carrying her shoes. He caught her top as she dropped it. "I miss him."

"We'll get a dog, just like we talked about."

She looked over her shoulder and gave him a sleepy smile. "Yeah, that'll be nice." Reaching behind her, she unhooked her bra and tossed it on the dresser, before shimmying out of her pants and crawling into bed. "Are you coming?"

He tossed her clothes in the laundry hamper and pulled the blinds down. "I'll just be a minute. I have to make a phone call."

She murmured something as she tugged a pillow under her head.

Mike left the bedroom, closing the door behind him. He removed his tie, pulled his cell phone off his belt, and dialed Nick.

"Mike, you better have a really good reason for calling me."

Damn, it sounded like he had interrupted something. But right now, Mike didn't care. It was time to call in a favor. "Nick, I need you to do something for me… "

Mike awoke slowly. Annabelle's leg was thrown over his, her head cradled on his shoulder and her hand over his heart. He rolled her onto her back and smiled as she grumbled in her sleep. God, she was beautiful, and she was his.

Running his fingers lightly over each breast, he was struck by the fact that even in her sleep she responded to him. Her reaction mesmerized him. Her breathing sped up, her nipples tightened, and when he brought his mouth to her breast and suckled, her heart pounded against his lips.

While his mouth made love to each breast in turn, his hand took the slow, tantalizing trip over her rib cage, past her stomach, and down to the triangle of dark curls covering her sex. He teased her with a light brush of his fingers, and her legs spread instinctively. He pressed his hand down, covering her mound, and she ground against it, her hips moving, searching. He parted her and slid a finger down between her folds and deep within her sheath. She was wet, ready, and still asleep.

"Annabelle?"

She sighed and rocked her hips, taking his finger in deeper, pressing down on his hand in frustration. He rolled over her, covering her with his body. Her legs spread as he moved down, his mouth joining his fingers. He figured she'd wake up eventually. He slid another finger in as he sucked on her. Her muscles grabbed and held his fingers pulling them deeper.

Annabelle's eyes shot open, her breath hitched, her hips rocked, and she was on the verge of an orgasm. She awoke from the most delicious dream only to find it wasn't a dream at all. Mike was on her, in her, making love to her. Every nerve ending in her body seemed to be somehow attached to the bundle of nerves he currently had between his teeth. When her eyes met his, an orgasm ripped through her. Mike gripped her hips and, in a heartbeat, slid into her, stretching her, filling her, and intensifying an already mind-bending orgasm. With every thrust, he took her higher, and when his mouth came down on hers in a hot, wet, soul-stealing kiss, he groaned as his body tensed and ground against her, holding her tight as he exploded within her setting off another wave of ecstasy.

Mike lay on top of her, his weight solid and comforting against her, pressing her into the mattress. He moved to roll off, but she tightened the hold her legs had around his waist. "Not yet. Please."

Mike rested his forearms on either side of her to take his weight off her and kissed her so gently, so tenderly, it brought tears to her eyes, "I love you."

Annabelle took a shuddering breath, wrapped her arms around his neck, and kissed him, pouring all the feelings bombarding her into the kiss.

Mike pulled away, brushed the hair from over her eye, and smiled. "You're crying…"

Annabelle nodded and hiccupped. "Sorry… it was so intense, so overwhelming…"

He kissed away her tears, which only served to make her cry harder, and held her close. "God, what is wrong with me?"

Mike slid out of her and rolled over so she rested on him. "Nothing. It's been a big day. We've been on an emotional roller coaster. You're allowed happy tears." He kissed her forehead and held her close.

Annabelle curled up against him and was more relaxed than she could remember. Mike startled her, shaking her out of her daze.

"Oh, shit."

"What?"

"Come on." He pulled her out of bed. "We have to get showered and dressed. We're going to be late."

Annabelle allowed him to drag her to the bathroom. "Late for what?"

Mike started the shower and kissed her. "It's a surprise." He took her hand and stepped into the tub.

She followed him in and groaned as the hot water soaked her hair. "I hate surprises." She wrapped her arms around Mike's neck as he pushed her hair off her forehead and gathered it behind her as the water massaged her scalp. He turned them around so she could shampoo her hair.

"You don't hate surprises. You just hate not knowing what they are. There's a difference." He kissed her and took over washing her hair, massaging her scalp and then her neck, her back, her bottom…

Annabelle pushed him away. He stepped back, but

only to make room for his hands between them. "I thought we were late."

Mike sighed and nibbled on her shoulder while his hands teased her breasts. "We can make love in the shower and be ready to go in forty-five minutes. Can't we?"

"No!"

When Mike said they were going to celebrate, Annabelle never expected him to take her to a bed and breakfast, especially not the Bed and Breakfast on the Park. Talk about romantic. He pulled up in front of the B&B, and she knew he'd really outdone himself. This was the nicest B&B in all of Brooklyn. She'd walked past the beautiful old brownstone a thousand times and heard it was magnificent. They stepped into the foyer, and she got a good look at the interior. The praise wasn't exaggerated. The place was spectacular.

A woman came into the foyer and greeted them. "Dr. Flynn? Your party is expecting you. They're in the parlor."

People had parlors? "I didn't know we were meeting anyone."

Mike smiled and wrapped his arm around her. "I made a few calls before our nap."

"To whom?"

The woman opened a set of large carved-wood doors, Mike led her through, and within seconds, her parents, Aunt Rose, Mike's mom, Becca, Rosalie and Nick, Vinny and Mona, Richie, and even Dr. Larsen surrounded them.

"Surprised?"

Surprised? More like shocked, and not in a good way, either. So much for her dream of making love on an antique bed the size of a football field. Everyone shook hands, checked out her ring, hugged, and kissed. Dr. Larsen stayed to the side, which worked for her. She did her best to ignore the fact he was there. That worked too, until Mike pulled her around to the last man on earth she ever wanted to see.

"Belle, you remember Christopher Larsen."

She nodded but didn't look at him. Why was Mike doing this to her?

"Annabelle, Mike. Congratulations."

Mike shook his father's hand. "Thank you."

She waited for the public humiliation, and when it didn't come, she got the nerve to raise her eyes toward Dr. Larsen. He looked different than she remembered. Strange, uncomfortable—almost as if he was unsure of himself. He looked almost human. She'd never seen the man not take charge of a situation. Not that she spent much time in his presence, but she'd seen him in action enough to know he wasn't acting like himself.

Her mother joined them. "Annabelle, we were just getting acquainted with your friend Becca and Dr. Larsen. He said you were a great help to his family."

"He did?"

Dr. Larsen nodded. "Yes. I don't believe I ever told you how much I appreciated your... kindness. Thank you."

"I was glad to have helped."

With another nod of his head, he stepped back, walked past a table laden with Italian cookies, coffee, wine, and champagne, to the window on the other side of the room. With his back to everyone, he stared out. Annabelle watched him before searching the room for Becca.

She spotted Becca and Richie with their heads together. Close together. Richie stood in Becca's personal space, and Annabelle wondered how long it would take Bec to shut him down. She gave Rich ten minutes max. Instead of watching her brother take the hit, she interrupted them. Becca dismissed Richie, stepped away, and pulled Annabelle into a hug. Richie was gob-smacked. Annabelle doubted he'd ever been dismissed before.

"I'm soooo happy for you. Just think. We're going to be sisters!"

"What's up with your dad? Is he okay?" *Possessed* was the word she meant, but she didn't want to hurt Becca's feelings.

"He's trying. It's not easy for him. Thanks for being so wonderful."

"He didn't say anything to my parents, did he?" All they needed to hear was that she'd lived in sin with his other son. She might as well have a big "P" for *puttana* tattooed on her chest.

"About Chip? No. I threatened him. Not that I needed to. He's trying to impress Colleen." Becca looked over at her father and Mike's mother. "It seems to be working."

Annabelle followed Becca's gaze. Dr. Larsen stood close to Colleen, talking quietly, and smiling. Annabelle had never seen the man smile before. It was amazing how much Mike looked like Dr. Larsen just then.

"He's probably just waiting for the crowd to thin. Less witnesses if it gets messy."

"Way to have a positive attitude."

Annabelle shrugged. So, the old man didn't come out swinging. That didn't mean he'd turned into the reincarnation of Mr. Rogers. This kinder, gentler version of Dr. Evil did nothing to ease her nerves. If anything, it just strung them even tighter. Her stomach churned like Mt. Vesuvius on a bad day.

Mike brought her a glass of wine, and just as she took it, a beefy arm wrapped around her waist and pulled her into a hug. "Welcome to the family." Vinny kissed each cheek as Mona kissed Mike. Then they switched.

"Thanks."

Vinny gave Mike a guy-hug, kissed both cheeks, stepped back, and took a handkerchief out of his pocket to wipe his damp eyes. "God bless. Mona and me, we're so happy you got everything straightened out." He put his arm around his wife and looked back and forth between Annabelle and Mike. "Everything is straight, right?"

Mike tuned to her as if he needed confirmation. She nodded. "Yes, everything is fine."

Mike, Vinny, and Mona let out a collective sigh of relief when she answered. She only wished she could do the same.

Annabelle took a sip of her wine and remembered her churning stomach and the fact she hadn't eaten since lunch yesterday. She looked for a place to put her wine and contemplated maybe eating a cookie or two, not sure if it would help or do the opposite. Settling on an S cookie—bland, not overly sweet, good for teething babies or for dunking—she poured a cup of coffee, and had just stuck the end of a dunked cookie in her mouth, when her parents and Aunt Rose surrounded her. Luckily, Mike was still talking to Mona and Vinny.

Mama tsked and handed her a napkin. "You eat like an animal."

"Animals don't dunk."

Aunt Rose gave Annabelle a funny look, the kind that reminded her of Endora on *Bewitched* just before she put a spell on Darrin. "Raccoons always dunk their food before they eat it. You got the same circles under your eyes as a raccoon. You need to take better care of yourself. Think of your health."

Her mother crossed herself. "She's marrying a doctor."

Annabelle forced herself to swallow. "I'm fine."

Mama stepped closer. "I knew Rosalie's marriage to Nick would help get you settled. Mike's father said he has a prominent position waiting for him in Philadelphia, and when I asked where you would live, he said Mike has an estate. Who knew you were marrying a wealthy man?" Then she looked a little confused. "You've been friends with his sister for years. How come you only met her brother at Rosalie's wedding?"

Annabelle really didn't want to get into this now, for all she knew her mother would say something embarrassing about Mike's parents and would give Dr. Larsen yet another reason to hate her. "It's a long story, Mama."

"Have you set the date yet?"

Aunt Rose gave Annabelle that look again. "You better make it soon."

Mama glared at Aunt Rose. "Of course it'll be soon. They're going to move to their estate near Philadelphia so Michael can start his new job. Maybe we can talk to Father and see if we could rush things along. After all, Annabelle was baptized there, and he's known her all her life. And it's not as if she hasn't already gone through Pre-Cana Marriage Preparation Classes with Johnny. Has Mike?"

"No, I'm his first fiancée."

"Oh, that's a shame."

Mike put his arm around Annabelle, and she really wished he would leave so her family wouldn't embarrass her around him. He kissed her temple and pulled her in front of him before turning to the whole room. "I have an announcement to make. I've decided not to take the job in Philadelphia."

"What?" Dr. Larsen stepped forward, and Becca took his arm as if she was trying to stop him. The man looked shocked, and why wouldn't he be? No one had ever turned him down… well, except Becca. He speared Annabelle with his gaze. Mike must have seen the look and quickly changed positions with her.

Mike had said he didn't want to take the job, but she never expected him to actually say it. Not in front of everyone. Part of her was proud of him, and the other part felt as if she just tied herself to the knife-thrower's wheel as Mike gave it a spin and handed out Ginsus. No wonder she felt sick. She tried to pull her hand from Mike's, but he wouldn't let go.

"I've decided not to take your job offer. Annabelle and I have our lives here. We have our families are here. Dad, Becca, I'm glad we've found each other. You both are important to us, but this is our home. I've had my family here in Brooklyn for years before I ever met you. I don't want to leave them."

Mike's grip on her hand tightened, and he shuffled his

feet and looked over at her. She nodded, not sure what else she could do. Speaking was out of the question. Mike shocked her speechless and made her so proud. The determination in his voice gave her all the security she never knew she lacked.

"Vinny and Mona adopted my mum and me when I was just a kid. He's been a cross between a big brother and an uncle to me. He gave me a job, taught me to cook, got me drunk the first time, and even taught me a thing or two about women. He's the one I've always turned to for advice. He's helped make me the man I am."

Vinny took his hankie out and dabbed his eyes again while Mona rubbed his back. Annabelle's eyes burned. He not only stood up for her, but for everyone he loved.

Mike turned his attention to Nick and Rosalie. "Nick is like a brother to me, he and the whole DiNicola-Romeo clan—Nick's mom and Nana, Vinny, Mona, their kids—they've always treated me and Mum as if we were a part of their family. We've spent every holiday with them. And now, with the addition of the Ronaldi's, Annabelle and I have even more of a reason to stay."

He faced her and took both her hands in his. "I don't want you to worry. I'll find another job. We'll be okay."

Annabelle could only nod as he enfolded her in his arms.

"Dad, I've gotten through my whole life without your help, and though I appreciate the offer, Belle and I want to do it on our own. That means without the trust and without the estate."

Dr. Larsen radiated pride, which overshadowed his disappointment.

Mama gasped, pounded her chest, and prayed to the Virgin Mother in Italian—after she stopped cursing. She obviously didn't realize that most of the people in the room were fluent.

Aunt Rose whispered something to Mama who crossed herself and looked up as if she were thanking God for something, Annabelle couldn't imagine what.

Becca, with tears in her eyes, hugged Mike, then Annabelle. She laughed. "I'm so glad you gave him a chance. I told you he'd come through. Oh, and you know all that money he just said he didn't want? He's going to be pretty disappointed when he finds out it's his, free and clear."

"Huh? But your dad always threatened Chip with taking away his trust."

Becca shrugged. "He had limited control of the trust until we turned twenty-five. Then all control reverted to us. It's ours to do with what we please. Mike might want to start his own practice, maybe buy a house. I don't know. I guess you can donate it to charity or something if you really don't want it. Dad has a life interest in the estate, which means Mike can't sell the place until after Dad's death. Then, I guess, he can do whatever he wants with it."

"Your dad doesn't own at least part of the estate?"

"Nope. Nada. His parents got mad at him for going into medicine instead of the family business. They put everything in a grandfather's trust for us. He's always had a portion of the interest to live on. Even the estate is owned by the trust, and now, by Mike."

Annabelle studied her future father-in-law and wondered what was different about him. He'd aged a little, and maybe losing Chip and finding Colleen again had changed him for the better, she didn't know for sure. Then it occurred to her that the difference wasn't Dr. Larsen, it was her. She was no longer the scared little girl who cowered before him. She was all grown up, and she didn't see the monster she once imagined him to be. The only thing that had changed was her perception of him.

Vinny, who finally got his emotions under control, poured champagne while Mona served.

Mike's arm tightened around Annabelle. "You look happy."

"I am. I've never been happier. I love you."

Vinny raised his glass and interrupted their kiss. "To Annabelle and Mike. *Per cent'anni* — for a hundred years. *Salute*."

Everyone held up their glasses. Aunt Rose handed Annabelle a glass and leaned in close. "Just take a sip," she whispered. "Alcohol, it's a no good for the baby."

The End

Acknowledgments

WRITING A BOOK IS A REAL TEAM SPORT. HERE ARE THE major players to whom I owe so much:

My husband, Stephen, who is always there for me in that quiet, supportive way he has that still makes me melt after almost twenty years.

My children—Tony, Anna, and Isabelle for putting up with all my deadlines and always being so supportive. You're my pride and joy.

My parents—Richard Williams, Ann Feiler, and George Feiler.

My sisters—Suzanne Smith and Nadine Feiler.

Dr. Michael Tolino, my go-to guy for all things medical and one of the absolute best doctors I know.

My critique partners—Robin Linear, Laura Graham-Booth, Carla Faker, and The Goddesses—Gail Reinhart, Peggy Parsons, and Kay Parker.

The incredible women who make up the Valley Forge Romance Writers.

My agent—Kevan Lyon, for all you do.

My Sourcebooks Casablanca team: Dominique Raccah, my publisher; Danielle Jackson, my publicist; my editor and friend, Deb Werksman; and all the Casablanca authors I've grown to know and love.

And finally to my friends at the Carlisle Crossing Starbucks who keep me laughing and fueled up while I work.

About the Author

Robin Kaye was born in Brooklyn, New York, and grew up in the shadow of the Brooklyn Bridge next door to her Sicilian grandparents. Living with an extended family that's a cross between *Gilligan's Island* and *The Sopranos*, minus the desert isle and illegal activities, explains both her comedic timing and the cast of quirky characters in her books.

She's lived in half a dozen states, from Idaho to Florida, but the romance of Brooklyn has never left her heart. She currently resides in Maryland with her husband, three children, two dogs, and a three-legged cat with an attitude.

Robin would love to hear from you. Visit her website at www.robinkayewrites.com or email her at robin@robinkayewrites.com.